THE
LONG WAY
HOME

THE LONG WAY HOME

A · N · O · V · E · L · BY

ALAN EBERT
WITH
Janice Rotchstein

CROWN PUBLISHERS, INC.
New York

Grateful acknowledgment is made to the *Denver Post* for
permission to reprint excerpts from
"For Some Veterans, Viet War Goes On"
by Dana Parsons,
copyright © March 15, 1979, by the *Denver Post*.

Published by Crown Publishers, Inc.,
One Park Avenue, New York, New York 10016, and
simultaneously in Canada by General Publishing Company Limited
Manufactured in the United States of America

Library of Congress Cataloging in Publication Data
Ebert, Alan.
The long way home.

1. Vietnamese Conflict, 1961–1975—Fiction.
I. Rotchstein, Janice. II. Title.
PS3555.B49L6   1984   813'.54   83-26289
ISBN 0-517-55365-1

10 9 8 7 6 5 4 3 2 1
First Edition

For those who seek
For those who find . . .
The long way Home

PROLOGUE

NEW YORK CITY —ASSOCIATED PRESS —MAY 31, 1972
URGENT
CANDIDATE JOHN OLLSON ASSASSINATED
DAUGHTER MARTI TIERNAN NEAR DEATH

JOHN OLLSON, CONGRESSIONAL CANDIDATE AND PU-litzer Prize author, was assassinated today; and his daughter, actress turned activist Martha "Marti" Tiernan, was gravely injured during a campaign rally near Lincoln Center.

Wife, Carolyn Tiernan, suffered minor injuries when sister, Margaret, shoved her out of the path of the assassin's bullets. The two internationally known actresses were rushed to Roosevelt Hospital and treated for shock and superficial bruises.

Within seconds of the shooting, police arrested Brandon Copague Bettylwin, 24, an unemployed Vietnam veteran. Police believe Bettylwin was "acting alone," although they are investigating the "possibility" of an accomplice or accomplices.

Ollson, 59, was an outspoken opponent of the Vietnam War as was his daughter, Ms. Tiernan, 34. Police speculate this was the motive for the assassination.

The Vietnam War has played a significant role in the Tiernan/ Ollson family. Eldest son, Captain Thomas Ollson, USAF, 34, winner of numerous medals and citations as a squadron leader of the Triple Nickel, is currently a POW in North Vietnam, where he was shot down in December 1969. Youngest son, John Ollson, Jr., deserted the U.S. Army shortly after completing basic training at Fort Dix in April 1970. Ollson, Jr., is living in exile in Canada and faces imprisonment should he return to the United States.

Friends and family, including Ms. Tiernan's children, eleven-year-old twins Alison and Mark, are maintaining a vigil at Roosevelt Hospital where the Oscar-winning actress is undergoing surgery. A hospital spokesperson revealed should Ms. Tiernan survive the "delicate operation" to repair the shattered carotid artery in her neck, she could be "irreparably physically and mentally incapacitated."

BOOK ONE
1 · 9 · 7 · 3
DEPARTURES

1

MARTI LAY QUITE STILL ON THE EXAMINING TABLE. The wires placed on her head led into an amplifier and were recording the normal electricity that the brain emits. Marti knew if there was damage to a section of the brain, the pattern would slow down; if there was little to no damage, the wave pattern would be normal. Marti also knew that, since her speech had been affected, the doctors would be concerned with the middle of the left side of her brain.

It was a year this week. April showers bring May flowers and the anniversary of her "incident," as she politely referred to it. For a moment, Marti wanted to yank the wires from her head. She hated the hospital and the tests she endured there every few months. Hospitals were for the sick and dying. She had been taken to one when she was both. She had been comatose and then, when she wasn't, she wished that she were. Even death seemed kinder and certainly easier those first few days. The pain was little in comparison to the fear, and the fear was secondary to the horror.

"You can dress now, Miss Tiernan," said the doctor.

Marti smiled at the truth of his statement. She could dress now. By herself. She no longer needed others' hands for buttons and zippers. Her own functioned again, often without hesitation. She could also walk on her own, call her own taxi—which she

3

would do the moment she left the hospital. Things that just a year ago had been so hopelessly complicated were now simple. Not that there still weren't moments, days when she fell up or down a step, but they were infrequent.

"You're doing quite well, Miss Tiernan," said Dr. Gerard Charles when he reentered the room. "I'm pleased with both your physical-therapy assessment and the EEG. Actually, considering all you've been through," said the internist as he sat on the edge of the examining table, "you're very fit. In fact, we can wait six months, rather than the usual three, for your next checkup."

She stared at him grateful but concerned. Wasn't he being premature?

"It's all behind you," said Charles seriously. "My advice is to leave it there and not carry it like excess baggage. Which reminds me. A few rules. No overexertion and no crazy diets. Avoid fatigue states and alcohol because your brain is vulnerable to stress and stress can cause seizures. In other words, do as I tell all my patients: eat well, get proper rest, and avoid getting hit by a truck."

Charles waited for the usual laugh but instead received a question. "Are there any other restrictions?"

"Only those you'll unnecessarily place on yourself," Charles replied. "You're a free woman, Marti Tiernan. And a young and a lucky one at that. My advice is to go out and live."

Later, as she stood before the hospital on Fifth Avenue across from Central Park, Marti considered the doctor's words. Free, lucky, and young, he had said. Obviously this is one doctor who knows more about medicine than the mind, decided Marti as her eyes searched for a taxi. Young she would never be again even if she were less than her thirty-six years. Her youth had died the day she didn't. On a pielike island across from Lincoln Center. Campaign buttons, banners, and streamers. John Ollson for the U.S. Congress. Her father . . . dead. Truly dead where she was only giving an imitation of the lifeless state. She would not think about it. She never thought about it. Never visualized her own near death, the blood or the bullets. She wouldn't now. Marti squeezed her closed eyes, but the pictures that pierced her brain would not disintegrate. He was there again. *He* was always there. Brandon Copague Bettylwin. A blond, blue-eyed Iowan, winner of numerous 4H Club awards as a child, he was, according to his neighbors who expressed shock, a "good boy." But with a closet filled with Nazi memorabilia and handguns, one of which he had used to kill her father and shatter the carotid artery in her neck, causing paralysis and a loss of speech. *He* was dead now. Physically. But his presence was everywhere and in everyone. She could feel it. He ruled her life or what passed as a life.

A man had tried to kill her. Some say he had acted alone; others wondered and worried. None any more than she.

She was lucky the doctor had said. Yes, considering the depth of her wounds, she was indeed lucky. He had also said she was free. A foolish notion. Time had healed the physical wounds, but the emotional remained raw, sometimes bloody and sometimes not. Go out and live, the good doctor had urged. How easy it is for others to give advice when it isn't their lives that are on the line.

It is all behind you. Those words, spoken so casually, meant so well by a doctor who had seen her through the crisis, continued to echo. Because it wasn't all behind her. It remained a constant dream, a recurring nightmare that erased sleep and appetite as it created the stress the doctor had told her to avoid.

"Hey, lady, ain't you Marti Tiernan?" asked the cab driver as he pulled up to the curb.

"Mea culpa," Marti replied.

"Jees, but the wife and I used to love your movies. Whatever happened to you?"

She looked at him in disbelief. Didn't he read the newspapers?

"I don't know, my friend, but I've got someone working on the case. When I find out, I'll let you know."

⁎   ⁎   ⁎

He was alone, unable to move as the hideous metallic cacophony split the silence. The terror mounted as the sounds became louder, more piercing . . . closer. Frantically he sought someplace to hide. There was none. The door was flung open and he screamed into the blackness.

His heart racing, his body cold despite the sweat that covered it, Thomas Ollson lay still against the gray cotton sheets, unable

5

to move until reassured he was in his home in Rancho Santa Fe, the woman next to him was his wife of fourteen years, and that, despite the nightmare, nothing more threatening awaited this October day than his uncompleted manuscript.

The abdominal spasms, once again familiar, pulled him from the safety of the bed to the cold of the tiled bathroom. He had thought his colitis had ended last March when he stepped from the C-141 at Travers Air Force Base and into civilian life. As he brushed his teeth and then his once blond but now prematurely white hair, the mirror reflected the results of a dream he did not understand and a night of frequent tossings. It had been past one when he had come to bed and it was after two when he felt Reese slip out and down the stairs; her insomnia having resumed concurrent with his stomach problems, and with it, her nighttime drinking. He had wanted to follow and confront her but was stopped when he imagined her face accusing him of slights real and imagined.

As he zipped into his khakis, Thomas watched Reese as she slept, her mouth open as she breathed heavily. Her face was pale and puffy and looked tired, worn, even in sleep. But not accusing. Reese hated his book. To her, it represented time, time she insisted she had earned, taken away once again. And for what? The war had been fought and concluded in Vietnam. Why was he continuing it day after day into night in their den? What did he owe others that he didn't owe her and his family? She had been without for six years, the last two, when he was a prisoner of war, the worst as she wondered if she would be without forever. She felt she was owed, which Thomas found ironic as owed was exactly how he felt. Only Reese knew from whom she wanted recompense, where he did not.

The book had become his obsession. If he could win this battle, perhaps he could change the outcome of the war.

"Why can't it wait six months?" Reese had demanded.

"Because it is stuck in my throat now and I can't breathe," he had tried to explain. She did not understand but his publisher, delighted to have the Ollson name and the potential sales that name produced, did. They wanted the book yesterday, last week, a month ago. Immediacy was the name of their game. He did not object. He could not think of himself as discharged until this duty had been performed. Someone who had been there had to make clear the price that would one day be paid for the war's lack of support *before* the national need to sweep Vietnam under a coast-to-coast carpet was met completely.

And so he was writing a book despite the fact he had never written anything more ambitious than a term paper for his undergraduate studies at M.I.T. He and Reese had met there. She had been a student at Wellesley. Her friends thought them an odd mixture of fire and ice. She of the high spirits, spontaneous and purposefully silly; and he, often rigid, usually structured, and always serious in his approach to life. He gave her order. She made him laugh. She saw through to the real person and was not intimidated by the exterior.

For years he had been perceived as cold and unfeeling. It was not an altogether untrue perception. Yet his cool demeanor was mainly protective coating, worn through a troubled childhood and adolescence. It had made him officer material for the Air Force as it distinguished him from the more emotional others. It rewarded even as it penalized him. Until Reese, he had been alone. Once they had found each other, she became his ballast, his sole source of support. For the first time he felt understood. He wanted that support and understanding now as he fought his book and a pervasive feeling he could not identify, as Thomas Ollson had never experienced unnamed fear before.

It awakened him each day before dawn. After the nightmare and before the morning, it sat on his chest and stomped through his gut. There was no need for him to be at work with the sun. Force of habit he told himself. In the camps, there was no sleep past dawn. There, you awakened before your captors to secure yourself, to batten down hatches they would pry open if they knew there was a crack. Work . . . the book. It alleviated the fear. It battened down the hatch. It gave him someplace to go and something to do.

As he stood in the hallway, Thomas looked for signs of life in the form of light under the three doors behind which his children slept. Seeing none, Thomas, shrouded in a sadness he felt whenever he thought about Reese, descended the stairs to the hallway

7

that divided the living room from the dining room. The light was on in his wood-paneled den, evidence that Reese in her midnight meanderings had participated in his book. The manuscript, however, hadn't been touched but lay there waiting on his desk along with the pages of suggested revisions from Ross Ramsey, his editor. Thomas had fired the first draft of the book in four months. Now, Ramsey was trying to rekindle that fire. Not that Thomas didn't want to finish the book. He just couldn't.

As he sat at his desk, Ramsey's question raised in red ink screamed across the page.

"How do you feel about this???"

He had written of that time between night and morning when his captors had marched him from the "Hanoi Hilton" to the "Heartbreak Hotel" courtyard at Hoala Prison. There, before men who looked to him for leadership, a captain who would soon be a major, they had read his parents' quote from one of the thousands of newspapers in which it had appeared.

"The John Ollsons have two sons, one in service, one not. They are equally proud of both."

His captors had asked in loud, mocking voices, just as Ramsey was now asking in his soft but insistent fashion, how he felt about this. He hadn't felt, having taught himself not to. Wars were fought and won by actions, not feelings. Survival depended on action. Particularly in the camps. There, to live, one died a little, turned off that part that felt, as any emotion shown was a tool for the enemy to use. Thomas Ollson had never once given the enemy an extra tool with which to dig his grave, not even when he was stuck, figuratively and literally, in "Calcutta," that six-by-two-foot black hole, for days, or was it weeks?, in broiling sun and drenching rains.

Once again, Thomas thumbed through the manuscript noting Ramsey's remarks. It was not the facts his editor questioned but the feelings, that personal data that would make the book a personal experience for the reader. Ramsey's demands were similar to those placed upon him during his teenage years when with his twin sister, Marti, and their cousin, Vinnie, he had starred for four TV seasons in the detective series, "Tiernan & Company."

Then it was magazine editors who felt their readers had a right

8

to know more than he was willing to reveal. He was never in the Tiernan tradition that way; never like his mother and aunt, the famous Tiernan Sisters, legends of Broadway and Hollywood. Never like Marti or Vinnie. And least of all like JJ.

JJ . . . he would not think about him, although his book was a constant reminder. But he no longer hated his brother, just what he did.

The front door opening and closing brought the nightmare back into focus. In the dream, he did not know who was at his door, but at daybreak, at precisely six-thirty every morning, he knew Karl would be off and running, wrapped in a gray hooded sweatsuit, his gait showing no signs of the accident suffered when he was four. He was responsible for that. He had urged, pushed, prodded Karl into exercising the leg that had been shattered. Even from Thailand, before his capture, he had sent home tapes weekly in which he reminded Karl to walk straight, stand tall, be the man of the house. All before the boy was eight years old.

The sound of water from the upstairs bathroom signaled Kristan was awake. Like Karl, she was exact in her schedule. Consistently she used the hour before breakfast and then school to review her homework and the day's lessons. The nuns at Our Lady of Peace said she was a perfect student, although somewhat serious for a twelve-year-old. Kristan was like her year-older brother in that respect too. She was a responsible little adult.

Of all the children, thought Thomas, a smile creeping across his face, only Kelly was irresponsible and irrepressible and happy to be both. Her grades at St. James Academy proved she was no student. With a transistor radio seemingly growing out of her ear, Kelly marched to a different drummer or bassist or guitarist or whoever was Top Forty that week. Her sole aim in life was to dance on "American Bandstand." At ten, Kelly was the Reese he once knew. Of boundless good cheer and high spirits. Exams and house rules might rumple her face for a bit, but never for long.

He was surprised by the sense of impending doom that fluttered over him whenever he thought about his children. Why now and not when he was in the camps? For six years he had been a father in absentia. Now he was home, although Reese insisted in body only. Just as his own father had been when he returned from the war shell-shocked and battle scarred in 1946. His father was never a father again. Except later . . . when JJ was born.

His mother had just recently pleaded anew that he make peace with JJ. He couldn't. The crime was too grave. Murder cannot be easily forgiven.

The front door's opening and closing and the thud of feet as they bounded up the stairs announced Karl's return from his hour-long run. Thomas knew in exactly fifteen minutes Karl and Kristan would emerge from their respective bedrooms. As one tended to breakfast, the other would tend to awakening and dressing Kelly, a task more difficult than the preparation of any breakfast, no matter how elaborate. All this while Reese slept. Reese frequently slept, even when she was awake, drifting from day to day. Nothing ventured, nothing gained.

Like his work at the typewriter. Another morning had passed without another word being written. How did he feel about this? Lousy. His stomach knotted and threatened to untie itself before he could reach the bathroom. He *would* finish the book. He would! He had to. Otherwise, what had it all meant?

*   *   *

The bed was warm but JJ felt chilled. He sought the fire be-neath him but it was too late as his own had died out. Rolling off and away, JJ lay separate and apart from the young woman who said nothing as she sought her own solace. Shivering, JJ flung himself out of bed, into a new day, once more determined to work, fear or no fear.

The morning was as bleak as his mood. The sky promised more snow, which was not unusual for November in Canada. Shoes in hand, JJ walked from the sleeping area to the huge ex-panse beyond it in which he lived, aware the young woman, her blond hair fanned on the pillow, was studying him. Sitting on the long gray suede sofa that divided the bedroom from the living area, JJ, as he pulled on heavy wool socks, could feel the young woman's intensity although she said nothing. As if he were alone, he slipped into his jeans, a rumpled sweatshirt, and midcalf boots. The house keys were on the kitchen counter.

The studio, one flight down in his three-story home in the

Toronto suburb of Rosedale, housed all the equipment to make and process film and tape. Soundproof, the studio was JJ's inner sanctum until recently. Now it was a constant source of harassment. The tape machine was waiting . . . again. Each morning when he entered the studio, JJ hoped something would be different. He left each night knowing nothing had changed.

Since last May, he had been wrestling with his *Face of an Assassin*. Yet his investigation into the lives of those who killed with forethought still lacked definition and cohesion. He was seeking the connective tissue between the men: the psychological and the political. He had hoped to root out the man from his environment, trace the Face from womb to moment of murder, and by doing so had hoped to discover that thread that wove together such men as Sirhan Sirhan, James Earl Ray, Lee Harvey Oswald, and Brandon Copague Bettylwin. Faces All. To date, despite his numerous re-edits, he had nothing that showed any connective tissue between the Faces other than the destructive act itself. They were all killers and perhaps all were mad. That is what the jury who tried his father's murderer had decided. They condemned him to a mental facility where someone else who could not distinguish between right and wrong slipped into Bettylwin's life to end it with a knife before he slipped into anonymity.

Prior to Bettylwin's death, JJ had sought evidence to prove a double-gun theory, but he could not find any. But neither could he prove to his own satisfaction that Bettylwin had acted alone. He was still left with possibilities and nagging doubts, among them: were there other Vietnam veterans who, like Bettylwin, were potential time bombs about to explode? Would they in time assassinate those they considered to be detrimental to the welfare of themselves and their country? It was the kernel of an idea, but it was something that might bring understanding to the incomprehensible. JJ had been looking for that understanding for the past eighteen months. If he could find it, perhaps *he*, like his father, could also rest in peace.

Never did it cross JJ's mind that April morning in 1970 when he deserted the army and his country that he would never see his father again. The pain when he learned of his father's murder, of Marti, was unlike anything he had ever known before or since.

The funeral had been salt in an open wound. He could not attend. He would have been arrested the moment he crossed the border. He had considered risking it when he learned Marti was near death, but his Aunt Margaret had convinced him to remain in Canada and not add further to his mother's trauma and tragedy. He had complied, but in doing so had felt as though encased in a box, separate, apart, and alone. He was feeling that aloneness this morning, Thanksgiving Day in America, and the day of Vinnie's marriage to Este Hollis in Miami. The entire family would be there. Even Thomas. Thomas . . . if for no other reason, he was reason enough to finish the documentary, to prove his point. Murder is murder no matter who pulls the trigger, even if it is your brother.

Brother . . . his mother's words . . . Thanksgiving . . . call. Be grateful you are both alive, she had said. Make love, not war, she had urged, reminding him of the slogan that had been his anthem. It was impossible to love Thomas. He had been eight when Thomas had left for college. He hardly knew him then; he didn't wish to know him now.

Kay's words emerged over the sound of running water as soon as he reentered the apartment, his work of the morning discarded. "The turkey should be in the oven at three hundred and fifty degrees." As JJ adjusted the oven's temperature, he looked at the bird, big enough to feed twice the number of expected guests. He had hoped Marti would fly to Toronto with Ali and Mark directly after Vinnie's wedding. But Marti wasn't traveling much these days. Actually, Marti wasn't doing much of anything these days, thought JJ with annoyance. Although she had made a near full recovery—an almost imperceptible limp and an occasional difficulty with speech were the only evidence of her bout with death —she was "vegging out," as Ali said of her mother's inertia. To JJ it seemed the sister with whom he had written, produced, and filmed *Soldiers: A War of Their Own* had retired from the screen, writing, activism, and life itself.

Bitterly JJ thought how fortunate for both Thomas and Marti to be so certain of what they were doing, even if it was in Marti's case nothing. He felt no such certainty about anything. His life felt much like his documentary—on hold, waiting for something to inject meaning and substance into it.

1 2

"I think we should talk, JJ."

He looked at the woman standing before him and thought how talk was the last thing he wanted to do, particularly with Nelson due momentarily. "There's nothing to say, Kay," he began. "It's not about you. It's me and I'm sorry," said JJ as he ran his hands through the thick black hair that fell to his neck. "I've just got a lot on my mind."

"And none of it is me or us. If just a portion of what concerned you was us, I'd be content. But the truth is, I'm a convenience. You don't think of us as a relationship. You have no commitment to me . . . to us. I'm just a nice girl, a bright girl who saves you from the discomfort of having to look for someone to get you through the night."

"Kay, that's not fair. If that's all I needed, I could go to Grossman's most any night and pick up one of the groupies that follow the exiles around. But that's not me."

"What is you, JJ? Do you know?" asked Kay bitterly. The confused and then pained expression on his face softened her anger and her approach. "Perhaps I should tell you what I see." When JJ didn't protest, Kay continued. "I see a man who is letting the past rule him. Not just his own past but his father's, his sister's, his country's, and some boy named Bettylwin. That's a heavy load to carry, JJ. No wonder you're buckling underneath it.

"JJ . . . do the documentary. It's important work. But let go of the dream. You can't bring your father back. You can't change one damn thing except perhaps your anger, your bitterness, even your hatred. And, JJ, so much of what you feel isn't about your father's assassination but your own."

She looked at his face. Was he hearing her? The set of his jaw said he was, but it also said he didn't like what he was hearing. "JJ, with all my heart I believe you did what any responsible, thinking, caring American should have done: said no to the war, to the injustice of it. You made the right decision. Live with it."

She could see by the flicker of his eye, a nervous spasm that fluttered his cheek, that he was listening.

"It's hard some days," he said softly. "Sometimes I get lost in the rhetoric with which I was raised, and that's when the guilt sets in. Perhaps I might have served my position better, and thus the country, had I not deserted, but gone to prison."

1 3

"What would that have solved?" asked Kay wearily, having had similar conversations with other exiles. "What would have happened to the work you've done here? Who, other than you could have, would have turned the first floor of his own home into a dormitory for exiles until they could find lodgings of their own? And what would have happened to Nelson if you hadn't taken him in the day I called from the exile center saying I needed a bed for an illegal entry? Although it put you in jeopardy with the Canadian government, you did it. You saved an eighteen-year-old boy and in the process gained a friend, a son, a brother, or all three. If the documentaries and various interviews you've done have changed a half dozen people's minds about the war, you have contributed far more than you could have in a prison, JJ . . . in your heart you know you made the right decision. Your mind should know it, too."

He nodded in agreement.

"I know you, JJ. Given who you are as a person, you did the only thing possible—did what makes you, you: a man I respect, admire, and care about. Which is why I wish you would turn yourself around; turn from the past to the present. Bettylwin killed your father. Don't let him make a dead man of you at twenty-six."

He cringed, thinking the "dead man" was a reference to his impotence of the morning and of other nights and days when he had failed her.

"You know," said Kay as she removed the bath towel from her head and shook free her hair, "it's a pity we're just friends and that you're not in love with me. That at least would be present tense. More important perhaps, you'd be committed to something in the present. As you are, you're neither fish nor fowl."

"I don't understand," said JJ.

"I know, and it's so simple, JJ. Look at me. What do you see? An American who picked up her roots in protest against American foreign policy and planted them firmly in Canadian soil. I'm twenty-five and growing. Do you realize in eighteen months, I'll have my veterinarian degree? Now look at you, an American who has picked up his roots and placed them in a jar of water as he waits to decide where and when he wants to put them down. You're not Canadian, JJ, and yet you're not quite American either.

You're between the two. Make up your mind, my friend. What do you want to be when you grow up?"

JJ looked at Kay Andersohn with surprise. "I want to go home and home is America."

"Yes, I thought so," said Kay, her voice sad, almost defeated. "And what will you do there? How will you live? JJ, do you really think all will be forgiven and forgotten and you or any of the others will be just another American citizen someday?"

"But that's what amnesty is all about," said JJ. "That's what we're working toward."

"Then I say we are all fools if any of us believe for one minute that forgetting and forgiving is possible," replied Kay. "What do you think, JJ? Tell me, do you really believe it is possible?"

JJ stood there trembling. In the space of minutes Kay had asked all the questions he had been asking himself and he had no better answers for her than he had for himself. Which is why he felt lost. Which is why he faced each day with just a little more fear that had no discernible definition but that was nonetheless there. After a long silence, JJ asked almost hesitantly, "Will you still stay for dinner?"

Kay smiled, although she felt she would choke on the sadness that was lumped in her throat. "Well, where else would I go if not to my family on Thanksgiving."

*   *   *

Marti loved B. Altman's. Even when it wasn't wrapped in holiday trimmings as it now was, she found the department store, despite its immensity, snug and warm. Perhaps it was its tradition and the sense of permanence its age gave one, or perhaps it was its proximity to the house in Chelsea—whatever, Altman's made Marti feel safe.

Bundled in a windbreaker, a wool hat with a pom-pom bouncing about its top, Marti looked more the average Christmas-shopping housewife than she did the celebrity. That was her intent. These days, when Marti did summon the courage to leave the house, she sought anonymity. Behind tinted aviator glasses, she saw out but few saw in.

She had arrived at Altman's shortly after two-thirty when she knew most of the lunchtime officeworkers would be back at their desks. Other than the nagging anxiety, Marti felt good. Dinner was prepared and the dining table was set, ready for her mother's birthday party that evening. Fifty-eight. It was hardly possible.

The store was even more crowded than it had been yesterday when she had shopped for the twins, finding for Mark the exact Shetland sweater he wanted and for Ali, the simple gold chain she knew her daughter, a recent teenage convert to femininity, would love. Today's mission was presents for her mother and Margaret. Shopping for her aunt was simple but not enjoyable. Marti now liked to "make an afternoon" of Altman's, selecting her gifts with inordinate amounts of care and time. As though her life depended on it. She did the same at the Barnes & Noble bookstore on lower Fifth Avenue. Marti hated to find what she was seeking immediately. It left too much time to do other things . . . if one had other things to do. She didn't. It didn't matter. The restlessness of her youth was long gone. She had lots of time now. With luck. And care.

There were just so many things one could buy for Margaret. Despite having been clothed by Hollywood's great designers over the years, and despite having a body women half her age of fifty-seven envied, Margaret refused the fashion for slacks—she never called them jeans—and sweaters. Her only ornamentation was the wedding band now worn on her right hand since James's death, and the Mickey Mouse watch given to her by Vinnie on her last birthday to commemorate, he said, their "Mickey Mouse relationship." Margaret treasured both the gift and the appropriate sentiment.

A set of designer scarfs caught Marti's eye. Elegant yet functional, they would attractively hide the one place where Margaret's age showed—her neck. Taking money from her shoulderbag, Marti, as she purchased and then had the gift wrapped, pondered the possibilities for her mother. Which was fun—since unlike Margaret, her mother liked everything. Unfortunately, unlike Margaret, she could not wear everything. Always top heavy, her mother was now "bottoming out," as Margaret so indelicately referred to her mother's spreading. Even the doctor had urged that she cut back on her cholesterol and weight. Yet, she was still lovely. Her hair was more black than gray, and her skin still had a faint flush that made its alabaster tone all the more striking. The Tiernan trademarks. All the women shared them. Marti was her mother all over again, except at five feet six she was two inches taller. Alison would be taller still.

Marti was seeking something beautiful yet functional, something her mother could take with her to California when the sisters began shooting *Cataclysm*, an all-star disaster epic, in late January. Marti didn't like to think about the upcoming prolonged separation. It made her nervous. There would be still more time to fill; other safe places like Altman's and Barnes & Noble to find.

Although she was still bundled in her windbreaker, Marti began to tremble as she held aloft and opened a combination makeup and music box to the light. Her hands were shaking as she lowered the box to the glass of the counter. "Please," she said to the salesgirl as she thrust two one-hundred dollar bills at her, "wrap this quickly. I'm in a terrible hurry."

She had seen the face in the music box mirror. Just behind her. Staring. It reminded her of the face from yesterday. It might even be the same. Don't turn. Don't look. Don't panic, she commanded herself.

She could feel him now but inches away, examining the makeup boxes. Or was he examining her.

When the salesgirl returned, Marti snatched her mother's present, her change, and the receipt and walked quickly toward the Fifth Avenue exit. Without looking, she could feel him following. She increased her pace, praying as she did that a taxi would miraculously appear through the holiday traffic from the moment she stepped outside.

"Miss . . ."

The voice was low . . . urgent. She ignored it as she began to run.

"Miss Tiernan!"

Hearing her name called made her gasp. He knew her! She was almost crying when she burst through the store's front doors and found a taxi just depositing a fare. As she flagged him, she heard the voice demand: "Miss Tiernan, stop!"

She waited for the sound, the claplike thunder, the burning, the searing of flesh, as she wrested open the taxi's back door. An arm, *his* arm, stopped her.

"Miss Tiernan, you left your purchase."

She looked dumbly at the extended hand holding the gift-wrapped package. Margaret's scarfs. Unable to speak, she took the package, smiled, and raised her hand in what she hoped was a gesture that would convey what speech could not. He smiled back and closed the door behind her as she settled into the cab.

When the driver asked her destination, words wouldn't come and when they did, Marti could see from the man's expression that they were unintelligible. She tried to calm herself, knowing the sooner she did, the quicker the aphasia would pass. Even with her eyes closed Marti knew the driver was studying her, wondering what kind of a New York crazy he had for a fare this time. Finally, Marti spoke again and was relieved to see from the driver's face that she had given clearly the address of the brownstone on West 22nd Street. As the cab began its slow descent down Fifth through the holiday and commercial traffic, Marti, curled in a corner, kept her eyes and emotions closed. She would not go to pieces. Within minutes she would be home. Then, there would be only one more ordeal to face. And that made her cringe anew, huddle even deeper into the safety of the back seat's corner. But in the late afternoon, the twins would be home from school and in the early evening her mother and aunt would arrive for dinner. The family would be together and she would be as safe and as snug as she had thought herself to be in Altman's.

Tomorrow she would cut her hair, she decided. She should have done it sooner. It was too identifiable. Everyone knew her with long hair. Better something short. Besides, it would be simple to care for. And different. Far different from the Marti Tiernan who had appeared with the entire family on the cover of *Newsweek* two weeks back. That had been the mistake. A terrible mistake. One that she must immediately rectify. She wasn't that Marti Tiernan anymore. In fact, in a month, she would no longer be Marti Tiernan but Martha Ollson, the name with which she was born. It was a simple legal matter, her lawyer had advised. Tiernan had been her professional name, but she was no longer that professional. Just your average person . . . mother.

The article had suited the family's purpose but not hers. But had she refused, the magazine would have refused the story. Theirs was simple but effective blackmail. Till then, she had rejected all offers for interviews and even the million-plus advance a publisher had offered for her memoirs. She did not have any, she had lied. No memoirs. No memories. She was looking ahead, not back.

If only that were true. The past was ever present. There was no way to obliterate those terrifying sounds, the ones that came from *her* mouth when she first tried to speak after she had gained consciousness in the hospital. And the paralysis, the total helplessness—that, too, could not be forgotten. The fear . . . all kinds of fear . . . that she might die and then the fear followed by the depression when she knew she wouldn't. And the guilt. She had lived and her father had not and she was glad that if one had to survive it had been her. Then the anger. The incredible, overwhelming anger that made her slowly relearn how to speak and walk. Pain. Humiliation. Fear. Rage. Depression. Of these Marti had no wish to write. *Newsweek* had reported there were "no telltale scars" and that "she could return to the screen tomorrow and no one would ever guess from appearances the hell she has endured."

But she was not returning to the screen, to writing or public life of any kind. A major part of her had died next to her father on the pavement near Lincoln Center, and there were no transplants available for what she had lost. And so she vegetated. It was the easiest and safest thing to do. Which made JJ think she was copping out. From what, other than some madman's attack? Hadn't he or Thomas learned that nobody gives a damn? The war is over except for the casualties. Number me among the wounded and the missing in action.

As the cab turned west on 23rd Street, Marti wished herself into her safe, unchanging bedroom. Soon she would light the fire in its fireplace and curl up on the couch in the bed- and sitting room. Such a pretty room, thought Marti, with its parquet floor and scatter rugs of Oriental design. It was a wonderful place to drift and doze, to forget everything. Which was work. Full-time work demanding total concentration. It only took one slip, like cooperating with a *Newsweek*, to shake that concentration and wreck everything one had so carefully built after one had realized the fear—*her* fear—was ever present. Now she had no one but herself to blame for it. Dumb. It had been dumb. And dangerous.

The interview had taken place the day after Vinnie's wedding. They had all been relaxed and warmed by the occasion and the Florida sun. Before she could think through her impulsive decision to cooperate, they were being interviewed, en masse, and Vinnie was speaking of his work at New Hope House and how the drug rehabilitation center was in danger of folding if public funding wasn't made available. His plug had been accomplished. Then Thomas spoke of his book and how he now expected to finish it by Christmas, well in time for May publication. Another plug for another project close to heart and home. Her mother and Margaret had used the magazine to explain how their one-million-plus-eight-percent-of-the-gross salary on *Cataclysm* would enable them to continue their work at the financially troubled Tiernan Repertory Company. Thus, everyone's special interest had been served. Except hers. And wasn't it strange how she, who had nothing to promote and nothing to say, was the one about whom they had written the most.

Marti almost laughed as she recalled being likened to the Jacqueline Kennedy of 1963. A national heroine admired for her courage and integrity. Now *that* was funny. What courage? Equally amusing was the magazine's treatment of her three former marriages. Once grist for the gossip columnists and a source of embarrassment to her, now, according to *Newsweek*, her marriages were part of a "growth process that led to political activism." A book, *How to Be Your Own Man*, which their reviewer had hated when it was published, was now declared "the young feminist's handbook." It seemed, if she could believe the article, every error of her ways had been forgiven. But not by all. Within three days of the article's publication, the first of the letters arrived at the house. Two days later, another came. And then another.

Her mother had insisted the letters be given to the FBI and their analysis showed no correlation between them and the ones her father had received throughout his political life. They need not be taken seriously, said the FBI, who knew too well how celeb-

2 0

rities are often the brunt of crank mail. Her mother agreed. There were many disturbed people who wrote many disturbing letters. Ignore them.

But Marti couldn't. They weren't meant to be ignored. She had suspected she would hear from *him* eventually, that *he* above all others would make himself heard . . . somehow. That was the fear she had lived with ever since her wounds had healed but her mind became sick with worry. Exactly for whom had the bullets been intended? Just her father or her, too?

The cab stopped before the ivy-covered brownstone. As Marti paid the driver she could feel the fear tighten each muscle in her already tight body. The one more ordeal was at hand. The mailbox on the inside of the front door. Would there be another letter? Would this one, too, not just threaten but promise her death?

The letters would stop. She would make them stop, vowed Marti as she walked slowly up the stairs to her front door. She knew how. If she stopped, they would. If she did nothing but shop at Altman's, browse at Barnes & Noble, give birthday parties for her family, if she reerected that wall between her world and the one in which she had once lived, no one would care about her. And she would be safe. Or so she believed. Sometimes.

*   *   *

Settling uncomfortably into a stiff-backed wing chair, Thomas got down to the task at hand. With effort, he rearranged his face into what he hoped was a pleasant expression. It was the last day of his ten-city publicity tour and he was tired and somewhat disgusted with both others and himself. The tour had been his publisher's idea, believing it to be the most effective way to sell the book. Basically, Thomas quickly learned, it was selling himself, often to people who weren't buying. Interviews frequently became debates with interviewers more hostile than open to what he had to say about the Vietnam War. Equally often, they degenerated into a kind of gossip-column invasion into his and "The Tiernans" privacy. He may have sold his book, but in doing so Thomas frequently felt he had sold out.

Reynolds Trahey was busily buttering one of the sweet rolls

on the breakfast tray that sat before him and Thomas on the coffee table. His mouth was watering and only his innate good taste prevented his lips from smacking. But not from gluttony. At least not the kind that results in calorie intake. Reynolds Trahey was about to score a journalistic coup. The previous week, he was one of a handful of reporters invited to Toronto by the PBS publicity department to view the final version of John Ollson, Jr.'s, *Face of an Assassin*. He was one of an even smaller group permitted to interview the documentary's creator/producer. Now, he sat in Washington, opposite John Ollson, Jr.'s, brother, about to do what no other reporter would: interview both Ollson men within the same week. As the Ollson's were news in anyone's lexicon, Trahey knew his syndicated article would reap great professional and financial profits throughout the world.

As Thomas waited for Trahey to begin his round of questions, his eyes went to the window where the dome of the Capitol Building was gleaming in the bright May morning sun. That night, thank God, he would be flying home. And then would come the wait to see how America reacted to what was more for him than just a book.

"Tell me, Mr. Ollson," began Trahey as he brushed crumbs from the corner of his mouth with an index finger, "how is it, considering the sentiments expressed in your book, that you opted to be a civilian rather than remain in the military?"

"Because I am not a military man in the sense that you mean. I served because it was my duty as an American, a duty I felt both to my country and myself. Once the war was over—at least over in its physical sense—I felt my duty was to my family, to be a father and a husband," added Thomas, wondering how Reese would react to his words if she were not sleeping behind the closed door leading to the suite's bedroom.

"Another question I'd like to dispose of at the top," said Trahey as he thumbed through his notes. "My research shows that a year ago, shortly after your discharge, Governor Reagan appointed you to his Extraordinary Committee on Vietnam. What happened to that appointment and the committee?"

"Nothing," said Thomas. "Absolutely nothing. Not with the appointment or the committee. It never got off the ground. But then, if this country could not mobilize itself or its forces, couldn't take a firmer position to win a war it was fighting, how can we expect it to launch a committee?"

"Bitter, Mr. Ollson?" asked Trahey.

"More angry and alarmed," replied Thomas as he poured yet another cup of coffee from the sterling silver pot on the center of the tray between the men. "But then there is much to be angry and alarmed about."

"Your book makes that quite clear. By the by, don't you think your title, *No Honor/No Peace*, is a bit ambiguous?"

"It says exactly what I mean it to: that a man, like a country, can have no peace, no *internal* peace, without honor. Many of us who served in Vietnam feel stripped of our honor and thus are without the peace of mind we need to live with ourselves and within our country. We would like to recoup our losses."

"How, Mr. Ollson?" asked Trahey, secure now that the interview was exactly where he wanted it to be.

"Honor us. Give us our due. The American people must understand that we, *their* men, were not murderers . . . hired hit men. Those of us who were officers were highly intelligent, well-educated men. None of us lived in a vacuum. None of us thought our country was perfect, but to a man we believed it to be the best this world has to offer. We knew what we were fighting for and we believed in it."

"Elaborate if you will, sir," asked Trahey in his clipped British accent.

"But I said it all in the book. In every chapter I made it clear we were Americans, soldiers fighting international communism. We were not just fighting the North Vietnamese but to maintain the freedom of all Southeast Asia."

As Trahey took down Thomas's words in his speedwriting technique, not trusting his tape recorder to do the job alone, he thought of John Ollson, Jr., and the thought he had expressed but a week ago in a rambling barn of a café called Grossman's.

"We had no right to be in Vietnam," the younger Ollson had said passionately. "We were there to protect our business interests and not the Vietnamese or the world from the threat of communism. That's pure imperialistic and militaristic bullshit. Further-

2 3

more, the war should have belonged to the Vietnamese people and not to those with foreign interests."

Trahey recalled the look on JJ Ollson's face. It was intense as he spoke. "Let me remind your readers that the creation of North and South Vietnam by the Geneva Convention in 1954 was only supposed to last until the country held national elections. Or until the Vietnamese could decide *for themselves* what type of government they wanted. Now this, Mr. Trahey, is fact not fiction: When our government realized if elections were held the country would probably go communistic, we backed a man who not only canceled the elections but who set up his own regime. Justify that if you or anyone can, Mr. Trahey."

He had been surprised. Trahey had not expected the younger Ollson to go on the offensive but to be defensive, particularly in light of his deserter status. Quite the opposite had occurred even under the glare of his continued questioning.

"Tell me, why is it you didn't declare your conscientious objector status the day you were drafted?"

"Because I was dumb or naïve. Perhaps both," the Ollson boy had replied. "I never thought in terms of killing or being killed. That wasn't real to me."

"When did it become so?" Trahey had asked, noting immediately the cloud of remembrance as it passed over JJ's eyes.

"At Fort Dix. During my basic training. They called it 'war games.' I was given a pugile stick and was told to hit and knock down my adversary before my adversary could do the same to me. I couldn't do it. Repeatedly I was knocked to the ground, battered about the face and body. I kept getting up, waiting for the anger the military counted on to surface, anger that would make me retaliate, fight and kill, but it never did. I couldn't hit a fellow man. I somehow lacked the killer instinct. So since I couldn't kill and didn't want to be killed, I deserted."

"So it wasn't in opposition to the Vietnam War but to killing itself," Trahey had asked, his trap baited.

"I don't know that I can separate the two," Ollson, Jr., had said. "Most of those who fled the country, refused to serve it, did so because we thought both killing *and* our national policies were immoral. And let me correct a popular misconception here: By and large, we were not radicals or communists. Nor were we hippies or drugged-out freaks, as the government would have many believe. Statistics prove that between 1965 and 1970, the majority who deserted or resisted were middle-class, fairly well-educated whites. All of us feel we made a great commitment—to our *country* as well as ourselves—by taking the position we did. And that commitment carried a great personal cost."

"You know," said Thomas Ollson, interrupting Trahey's recollections of the previous week, "a lot of our country's best men died in Vietnam. Not in vain. Not for them. Because they considered their principles more valuable than life."

"Oh, come now, Mr. Ollson," said Trahey somewhat impatiently, "you can't really expect people to believe or accept that in this day and age."

"I damn well do," said Thomas, his annoyance rising. "I saw it daily in the camps. Had some of those men denied their principles, given in to the North Vietnamese, they would have lived. Instead they chose death. There was honor in that. There would have been no honor in living had they given in to the enemy's demands."

"And honor is more important than life . . . than the actual act of staying alive?" asked Trahey incredulously.

"Don't you understand, there is no life without honor. And if there is, what kind of life is it? I realize, Mr. Trahey, that it is difficult for many to understand that, and that it is equally difficult for some to understand that there remains among many Americans a sense of duty to their country. I know patriotism is a dirty word these days, even one that's often ridiculed—but let me tell you, Mr. Trahey, that's just too damn bad. Too damn bad that people don't believe as they once did in their country, their president, and the intrinsic values of this country. And it's a damn shame that you're looking at me as if I were some nut case. But why not? Lots of others do. Which is why I'm so damned confused. There are thousands of us veterans who don't understand yours and their country's reaction to the war and the men who voluntarily and wholeheartedly fought it and for the right of it. Sometimes it does seem we got left holding the shit's end of the stick. And *I* don't like it."

2 5

Trahey looked at the weathered but handsome face of the man opposite him. He wondered if the North Vietnamese had seen that very same intense and determined expression. Ollson's eyes were a steely blue. Cold and yet volatile. Muscular and trim, Thomas Ollson was an impressive man, almost intimidating when he rose to his full height of six feet. Strange, thought Trahey, although their coloring was not alike, there was a great physical similarity between the Ollson brothers. Both didn't just command but demanded attention. Again Trahey allowed himself to dwell on the interview that had passed and his impressions of the younger Ollson.

"Had you considered jail as an option or only desertion?" he had asked. Ollson, Jr., had fired back an almost hostile response. "Jail is for wrongdoers. Since I viewed my country as the wrong-doer, I felt it, not me, should be incarcerated. I had to leave. I had no options. Not when bumpers stickers everywhere were telling me: 'America: Love it or leave it.' That's pretty scary shit. It's also as anti-American as you can get. The Bill of Rights and the Constitution guarantee us dissent, but Americans seem to have forgotten this. Or not thought about it. Of course in the military, you're not encouraged to think. A thinking soldier is a dangerous soldier is what my commanding officer in basic training used to say. He was right. If we set about thinking, more and more soldiers would have wondered what they were doing in the middle of some God-forsaken place serving. . . . Serving what, Mr. Trahey? Can you tell me? Was it their country or some monied interests?"

"About your brother," said Trahey, suddenly turning his attention to Thomas and moving in for the kill.

"I don't discuss my brother," said Thomas coldly, outraged by Trahey's impertinence.

"You do in your book," argued Trahey.

"I discuss desertion and how under the guise of patriotism some men not only mask their cowardice but commit murder."

"Murder?" asked Trahey, trying to temper his excitement, knowing he was now getting exactly what he wanted. "You hadn't written of murder."

"When you do not support or defend your country, when you draw energy, money, passion, away from your country's fight, you are committing murder. Many lives were lost in Vietnam, some needlessly. It might have been a different war with far fewer lives lost if the country had waged an all-out battle—if people, like deserters, hadn't dissipated the nation's energies. Because of the antiwar factions, men, soldiers, representing this country, were without the support they deserved. That's a form of murder."

"Then your sister . . . your father, too, were murderers," coaxed Trahey.

"In a sense, that's true. I hated their politics. But I respected the avenues they took to express them. They didn't run; didn't hide. If you can follow this, although I feel they basically expressed anti-American sentiment, they did it in the American way. Although the American way can sometimes be very mystifying. That men who desert can be thought of as heroes . . ."

"Like your brother?" interjected Trahey.

". . . And others, like me, as hawks, as birds of prey, almost defies reason. So to go back to one of your previous questions, how can there be peace where there is no honor for so many of us, when inequities can only be termed gross? All around me I saw men fight and die in a war for their country. Yet others who didn't fight, who fled, found comfort in Canada. And in my brother's case, not just comfort but support. Where is the sense of it? That any man could make antiwar, which were basically anti-American, documentaries and have them not only shown on public- and government-funded American television but have them be the recipients of honors ranging from Emmys to Peabodys is not only senseless but a reflection of the sickness in our society."

"So you object to men like your brother getting off, living scot free?" pursued Trahey.

"I wouldn't call being exiled from one's country being scot free. In the eyes of his government and many of his countrymen, the deserter is a criminal. And he will be treated like one. He cannot enter this country without being arrested. That to me is not living scot free."

Trahey stretched. He reached for the pot of coffee to borrow time. He was remembering Ollson, Jr.'s, response to the same question.

"I do not live scot free, as you put it, but I suspect I live a lot freer and with a much clearer conscience than many who served in Vietnam. I don't have blood on my hands or on my mind. I have not killed anyone."

Trahey had not hesitated but plunged into the heart of what had become *his* matter. "Then you see your brother as a murderer."

"I see anyone who takes up arms against another when his own life is not in danger as a murderer. And that a country not only condones but rewards murder horrifies me. My horror is twofold. One: that a soldier can justify murder under the guise of duty. That is convenient! Such 'patriotism' obliterates any moral responsibility for taking the lives of others, be they innocent victims, like civilians, or men who fought under a foreign flag. Often I wonder not how the country will make peace with me but how I will ever make peace with it. Where do you begin talking to men and a country who receive and accept what the other gives— medals for murder?"

"Are you aware," Trahey had asked, "that there are those equally enraged, that there are many within the United States who would give you a medal?"

"Yes," JJ had said naturally. "To some I'm a hero of sorts, although I'm not. I'm just a man who said no to a wrongdoing. I'm no more a hero than I am a traitor or a criminal. It's strange that some would think that. I mean, when Nureyev defected, deserted, from Russia, no one thought of him as a traitor or a coward but as some kind of hero. In just about any film you see that is about one man's defection to America, that man is always the subject of reverence. Isn't it strange that when someone defects from America he is viewed negatively. Talk about your double standards."

Thomas Ollson had risen and was standing at the window looking out on the city that housed American government. "You know, Mr. Trahey, the entire time I was imprisoned, the North Vietnamese tried to convince me and the others that we were dupes of our government, that our cause was unjust, and that the American people were not behind us. The last was rough because they had the newsreels and newspapers to prove it. But we always knew the demonstrators were the minority. We never believed the bullshit—not the enemy's or the demonstrators'. Funny, but now we veterans seem to be in the position of convincing our fellow Americans that we were not dupes, that our cause was just, and that we were simply soldiers fighting for our country; soldiers who now need their country to fight for them.

"God, if people could only know, only understand, what the Vietnam veteran has lost, has missed, has given up in order to serve his country," continued Thomas as he turned back to face Trahey. "Youth, for one. It's irreplacable. You lose it in a war. You can't imagine how seeing death ages one. Being responsible for it changes you forever. Many of our troops went over as boys and returned as men. Maybe I'm wrong but it seems to me nobody should have to be a man at nineteen or twenty or even twenty-two or -three. But that's the price we sometimes must pay."

Trahey had asked Ollson, Jr., about the price. It had been the only time the young man's composure seemed shaky.

"You can't calculate the cost because the price is still being paid, and will be paid, for years to come. My God . . . to leave a life you're just beginning. And just when you're in the process of trying to find yourself, who you are and where you fit in. It's devastating. Suddenly, you're without roots, without family. Perhaps forever. So many of the men here no longer have family. They've been disowned. So . . . you just can't add up our losses . . . family, friends, familiarity, and a personal history. We're like persons who have lost everything in a fire and find we must begin all over again. And so many of us who were kids, forced into making adult choices, will never be young again. No matter how young we are chronologically."

Reynolds Trahey looked at the man who was once again sitting opposite him. Thomas Ollson looked both thoughtful and troubled. "I'm just about done," Trahey said almost apologetically. "I would like to close asking you this: Do you think the war was justified and could this war have been won?"

"The answer to both questions is yes. War sometimes, ugly as it is, is the only answer . . . the humane answer. Do I shock you?" asked Thomas, noting the look that crossed quickly over Trahey's face. "Then let me remind you that a 'master race' of murderers would be ruling Europe today, and perhaps all of the world, if

America had not gone to war in 'forty-one. Yes, war kills innocent people, but was it not the innocent people Hitler was killing throughout Europe that made war the only answer? And . . . was the enemy any different in Vietnam? At the heart of the matter, didn't they, and don't they still, want world dominion? And yes, we could have won the war against these communist forces in Vietnam if we had marshaled our forces and put our strength into an all-out effort. Then the war might have taken months rather than years and this country would not have experienced the anguish and dismay it so obviously has. We would not be a polarized nation today had the right path been pursued."

"So the position you take in your book is the position you continue to maintain," said Trahey.

"And will continue to," said Thomas emphatically.

"Tell me, Mr. Ollson," said Trahey as he began to pack up his tape recorder. "Now that your book is published, what do you intend to do next?"

It was the question all interviewers eventually asked. Each time they did, the familiar fingers tightened in Thomas's gut. Only on this tour had he realized why it had been so difficult to finish his book. A year had passed since his discharge and not once had the phone rung with the offer of a job.

"I haven't thought much about the future," replied Thomas. "Once the book is launched, I intend to give all my time to my family. They need me. We have not had the time together that families need. I've promised myself to rectify this."

As Reynolds Trahey closed his stenopad, he was reminded again of John Ollson, Jr. He, too, had been evasive and uncertain about his future after *Face of an Assassin*. It had been clear then in Toronto, at Grossman's, just as it was clear now in Washington, at the Captiol Hill Quality Inn, that neither man had the vaguest idea what he would do with the next five minutes, let alone the rest of his life.

*   *   *

They were partly moans, partly whimpers. Awful sobbing sounds of pain. Not long ago, they used to frighten Karl. Now, he was immune to them, although he hated the fact that his father, sleeping next to his mother, did nothing to stop her nightmares when she always awakened to help him through his.

"Ma? Mother, wake up!" he heard Kristan command gently as he eased himself down the steps to the main floor below. "Ma. You're dreaming. Wake up, Ma."

As he opened the front door, Karl heard his mother say weakly: "What is it? Is there news? Is he dead?"

Kristan heard the downstairs door close as she was soothing her mother back to sleep. "It was just a dream, Mom. Dad is fine. Just a dream."

Reese's nightmares had begun shortly after Thomas had been taken prisoner in Vietnam. Like Karl, Kristan had become used to their occurrence if not to the effect they had on her. As she applied a cold washcloth to her mother's forehead, she felt Reese's hand cover hers in gratitude. She felt its faint squeeze as she smoothed her mother's damp blond hair off her face. The trembling was beginning to subside on both their parts. As Kristan tucked the covers about her mother, she kissed her as she repeated: "It was just a dream, Ma. Just a dream."

From her bed, Reese could hear as Kristan opened the door in the hallway nearest the master bedroom. She was checking on Kelly to see if, as usual, she had slept through the disturbance. Reese smiled as she imagined what Kristan would see: Kelly, atop a pile of pink sheets and blankets, her arms tightly wrapped about her pillow. The bed, like the rest of the room, would look like the aftermath of an earthquake. Amidst the rubble of jeans and junk held dear by an eleven-year-old, the Osmond Brothers added a soothing touch. Their poster, slapped somewhat off center above the bed, gave the room its smile.

When the door to Kristan's room closed, Reese remained as still as she could command her body to be. As she lay on her back with her head pressed against her pillow, trickles of sweat ran down and under her chin and slid into the creases of her neck. Her feet were numb to the point of nonfeeling.

"There is nothing to be afraid of," Reese told herself just as she did each morning when she awakened in this state. Suddenly, as she held her body against the trembling that often undermined her resolve to be brave, Reese remembered that this particular morning there was something to be afraid of. Remembering made her bladder burn. Quickly, she left the bed and Thomas for the bathroom. Her urine came slowly until she felt herself relaxing. This was the day she and Thomas would drive to Los Angeles to appear together on "Dinah." She had hated the idea when Thomas's publishers had presented it when they were in Washington. Hadn't she done enough for the book? Hadn't she been "a good little soldier" through the luncheon with the Republican club, the tea with the wives of the Veterans of Foreign Wars and the American Legion? So what if she had had to fortify herself with *a* drink, maybe two, prior to attending the functions, and another or two while at them. She had performed. She had served her husband and her country well. Had she not always "served," Reese would never have agreed to any of these public appearances. But she knew it was important to Thomas that they all do their jobs. She had been doing hers for seven years now. Time for a sabbatical from holding on and holding tight and holding together. When Thomas was in the Air Force and then the POW camps, she had been the glue that held the family together. Now the glue was coming unstuck. She was letting go and it frightened her.

Reese had been certain that if and once Thomas was returned to her, all would be well. She would then lean, be held and supported. But that had not been the case. The past year, as Thomas did his book, she had been alone, unable to be of support to anyone. Although she tried. God knows I've tried, Reese told herself at bleak moments. But Karl runs from me. Karl runs from everybody. Karl runs. Period. Only I don't know toward what or if it is just away from. And Kelly had Kristan and Karl and a thousand little girlfriends. Thank God for Kristan who was there, always there.

She would do her job once more, decided Reese. Only God knows how, she thought as she examined her face in the bathroom mirror. The lack of sleep showed mainly in her eyes. Visine would help their redness and cold tea bags, pressed against her lids, might reduce their puffiness. But nothing could help her hair, except, Reese hoped, the hairdresser provided by the show. Perhaps between him and the makeup man miracles could be performed. Too bad they don't have a ventriloquist. If they did, she could sit on his lap and let him do all the talking.

But it will be different this time, she heard herself thinking. Thomas will be there. He'll support me.

There were no tears. Just dry, hacking sobs. Quickly, Reese turned on the water faucets full blast, hoping the noise of the rushing water would drown out her distress. Her husband had been home fourteen months, the first of which she felt safe in her house and bed again. Then came the book. Thomas's involvement had been total, even obsessive. She saw him only at dinner and then later in bed . . . sleeping. Again she felt alone, only this time Thomas was there—which in some way made her aloneness even worse. She could reach out and touch him but she could never quite feel him. She had tried. She had begged him to talk with her or to just be with her. He couldn't. He could only be with his book. She tried to go about her daily business but suddenly no longer understood what that business was. Nobody needed her. Not really. Everyone in the household was quite self-sufficient. Except her.

Once again, her father, when she sought his advice, prescribed Librium, and once again Reese took it. "A difficult adjustment period" had been the doctor's diagnosis. "Lots of wives experience it after their husbands' return from the war," Morgan Tomlinson had insisted in the letter that accompanied the Librium through its parcel-post journey. Reese had accepted the diagnosis and the pills because without one, she couldn't have the other.

But she could always have Kristan. Kristan was her strength, her comfort, and her support. The days that her nerves and migraines were so bad that the noise of the vacuum and the blender and the washer and the disposal was so unbearable, Kristan cleaned, Kristan cooked, Kristan disposed of everything. She was now the glue that held it all together.

Kristan, Librium, and a drink every now and then. Not that she was an alcoholic. Reese scoffed at the notion. Alcoholics drink, whereas she only needed to know vodka was in the house, if needed, for her to get through the day. Sometimes she didn't take more than *a* drink for several days. Except before bed. That was a nightly necessity and strictly medicinal. My God, but she didn't want to get hooked on sleeping pills, did she? And liquor was quicker and safer. Having liquor in the house, she once told herself, was like having a fire extinguisher in the hallway. You used it only in emergencies but took comfort knowing it was there. Just in case.

It was necessary and there this morning. Normally, Reese avoided drinking before sunset or at the very least before lunch. Except when there were extenuating circumstances. And today was one of them. She had not been born in the limelight as Thomas had. What's more, she hated its glare. Often she yearned for a return to the quiet life she knew as a child growing up in a big white Colonial house with green shutters and a screened-in porch on an elm-lined street in Bridgeport, Connecticut. Some-place where she and the family could just be without the world observing and judging.

Thomas was still asleep in the king-size bed when she left the bathroom. The clock on the night table read seven-fifteen. After slipping into her robe, Reese closed the bedroom door softly be-hind her as she stepped into the hallway. Then, taking the utmost care with every step, she slowly, ever so slowly to avoid any pos-sible creak, crept down the carpeted stairs to the wet bar in the living room below. As she poured vodka into a tumbler of orange juice, Reese wondered if Dinah was nervous on the day of her show and if so, did she, too, take a drink to steady her nerves. As she considered the possibility, Reese envisioned Dinah Shore's face and figure. Immediately, Reese knew she was drinking alone that morning.

*   *   *

The TV studio's Green Room was filled with the frayed nerves of the show's five guests. Thomas and Reese were sitting side by side on one of the tweedy couches. Reese was sipping from a Styrofoam cup, watching the monitor as Dinah warmed her audi-ence with southern comfort and charm. The Ollsons were sched-uled to appear after the actress and the comic but before the rock group and the psychologist. Thomas was napping, using the time to relax from the strain of the past two weeks. He had hoped Reese would drive from Rancho Santa Fe to Los Angeles but she had been too nervous. Her ashen face and cold hands were witness to that fact. In the car, Thomas had carefully rehearsed her re-sponses, trying to anticipate the questions Dinah would ask, based on the phone interview Reese had had with a talent coordinator. At the studio, that same coordinator, after introducing herself, assured them: "Dinah is easy. You'll enjoy her." Both Thomas and Reese bought the first but doubted the second.

Strangely, it was at these moments just before he would be required to perform in some way that Thomas was at his most lucid. That had been particularly true in the camps. When he had known his captors were coming to interrogate him, his responses and course of action were always consistent and well defined. Thomas was not one to panic or lose control. Only recently did he have the feeling some mornings that he would like to crawl up and into Reese and stay there until whatever was bothering him had passed. On tour, people had conceived and nurtured all kinds of rumors about his future. In Washington, the *Post* intimated he would be offered a position with the Defense Department. Although Thomas had denied the rumor, Reese had panicked. She could not be a Washington wife; could not compete on that level, she had all but cried. Reese had been even more shaken when the *Los Angeles Times* announced, erroneously, that Thomas was a candidate for the California state senate.

As he rested, Thomas thought of the woman sitting next to him. Suddenly, he wished the show was over. Thomas was worried about what Reese would say and how she would say it. She had no skill at subterfuge. She never had. It was one of the many things that had initially drawn him to her. There was just no bullshit about her. She had never lied or played games. Particularly in bed. She had been a virgin the first time they had slept together but she admitted, more than he could, to numerous wants and needs. She was the best person Thomas had ever known.

It frightened Thomas when he realized he was thinking about someone from his past. Often Reese seemed unresponsive to life and to him, although she never denied him when he asked for the kind of comfort they had once so much enjoyed. Thomas tried to remember when he had last heard Reese laugh or make an attempt at humor. Or when she had last been, as described by her college yearbook, "pert and perky." As he drifted between the then and now of their relationship, a stab of pain brought Thomas to his feet.

"The bathroom?" he asked of the talent coordinator.

As he was directed, he was warned: "You have about six minutes." Thomas's face must have revealed his momentary panic when he realized Reese was missing. As if reading his mind, the talent coordinator whispered: "The ladies' room. She's making last-minute repairs." When another spasm ripped through him, Thomas ran toward the designated area.

In the ladies' room, Reese was retching. Unable to bring up anything other than phlegm, she sat on the toilet seat and lowered her head between her legs. She wasn't going to make it. She would be best off telling that nice girl, the talent coordinator, now so she could tell Dinah or whoever. She simply couldn't do it and it had been foolish to think that she could. Look at her. Awful. The navy suit instead of a basic black or beige dress had not slenderized as she had hoped. The jacket actually made her look even shorter and stockier. A middle-aged matron of thirty-five. I won't do it. Not even for him, thought Reese petulantly.

The door to the ladies' room opened: "Are you all right, Mrs. Ollson? You're on in two minutes."

"Out in a mo'," said Reese as she stood and lowered her skirt. After buttoning her suit jacket, she reached into her purse and pulled out the cologne bottle. She stared at it for a second, surprised that it was near empty when it had been full when she had left the house that morning. Carefully, so as not to spill a drop, she removed its top and in one gulp, drained it, feeling the warmth of the vodka immediately line her body. She was now as ready as she would ever be.

Thomas was waiting for her, and he clasped her hand as they listened to Dinah read their introduction from the cue cards. As the studio's applause sign flashed its command to the audience, the Ollsons entered. Reese fixed on her hostess's face. It was friendly. Warm and friendly. Pretty, too. But Dinah's attention was focused on Thomas and it remained there through the first commercial break. It was somewhere during the next segment that Reese heard: "And what was it like for you, Reese, when your husband was missing?"

As if from a great far-off place Reese heard herself reply: "Awful."

"You mean lonely?" assisted Dinah.

"Yes. No. Loneliness you can live with or you learn to live with. This was different. Beyond loneliness. Worse. Because you lost hope. And faith. Yes, that too. Your faith. You just couldn't understand why this was happening. Not just to your husband but to you and to your children. The waiting . . . oh, God, that awful waiting . . . for a word. Any kind of word. Is he alive? Is he dead? Something . . . anything, to let you know where he is so you can know where you are. And you imagine such awful things," said Reese beginning to tremble at her own recollections. The audience was stirring, uncomfortable, no longer feeling comforted or charmed but harassed.

"Every time the phone rang," continued Reese, talking more to herself than her hostess, who was about to change the mood with a question, "you thought it was them. *Them*, telling you your husband was dead. There were times when you almost wished for that because it was easier than imagining what kind of hell he might be living through."

People in the audience gasped. Thomas stared at Reese too shocked to interrupt.

"You stop watching the news. Soon, you stop leaving your house because people know your husband is missing and they're safe and secure in their safe little worlds. You resent them for that. Yes, you do. And I resented that because some felt it was all right for my husband to be behind enemy lines, alive or dead, because he believed in a war for our country that they did not.

"And your children hear that," whispered Reese. "And they wonder why their father is called a hawk and what that means exactly. And what is this camp he is in. Camp is where kids go to play each summer. Is Daddy playing? Will Daddy be back like the other kids in time for school in September?"

It was time for a commercial break but Dinah was ignoring her cues; her eyes remained riveted on her guest.

"The waiting is the worst. No one really knows about waiting," said Reese. "People think they do. Oh, they wait for planes and buses or a furniture delivery—but that's not waiting. Oh, no. Real waiting is when there is no scheduled departure, arrival, or delivery date. It's just something that goes on and on and on. Like life.

Life goes on. With or without you. People tell you to keep busy. I did. I was a wife and mother. But I lost me being busy. I did get a job in a card shop. But the sympathy and anniversary cards . . . I just couldn't read them . . . couldn't help people make a selection. And yet I loved every one of them. I would imagine sending them to myself.

"You know," said Reese as tears fell softly down her face, "my children are very beautiful. They look so much like doves that it amazes me some people could even think they were hawks."

At that second, Thomas realized Reese was drunk. "My wife," he interrupted, "we were apart for many years and it was in some ways harder for her than me. I always knew where she was and that she was alive. Someone long ago said it best: 'They also serve who stand and wait.' "

"And the waiting doesn't end with the war or when your husband returns," interrupted Reese, her voice now beginning to slur. "Nooo. The waiting goes on and on until you're all safe again in the lives you once led and you are all the people you once were. But it takes so long. It takes so very, very long."

In the Green Room, the talent coordinator who had interviewed Reese clutched a handkerchief to her mouth, trying to smother the sounds of her sobs. All of her ached to rush past the rock group and the waiting psychologist and wrap Reese in her arms. As she watched the monitor, she saw from the look on Dinah Shore's face that she had the exact same inclination.

2

THE HOUSE WAS STILL, TOO STILL FOR A FRIDAY night. As Ali closed the front door behind her, she felt apprehensive about what awaited upstairs where normally a light shone in the hallway. Ali wished Mark was with her since she did not want to climb the stairs and face whatever was, or wasn't, there alone.

The door to her mother's room on the second floor was open. The only light came from the embers in the fireplace; the sole sound from the hum of the air conditioner. Her mother was the only person Ali knew who built a fire no matter what the season because it soothed her. As Ali entered the shadowy room, she saw Marti lying on the sofa, facing the fireplace, her eyes open but not seeing.

"You watched it, didn't you?" said Ali. When there was no response, she yelled: "I don't understand. Why?"

"Because I had to," said Marti, her voice thin and tired.

"But Uncle John warned you. He, himself, said he didn't believe in the two-gun theory and that it was just a remote possibility."

"It's not so remote," said Marti, her voice still listless.

"Mom, don't you think if someone was out there he would have tried something by now," said Ali, using the same logic Thomas had used when she and Mark had confided their fears to him during his visit to New York. "You're not a total recluse. And

3 9

people do get shot in supermarkets. I don't know why you have to make yourself crazy."

"Because there is a crazy man threatening me with crazy letters and he just might be the crazy person your Uncle John suggests as the second gunman," said Marti as Ali switched on the floor lamp that arced over the sofa and into the living area of Marti's bedroom. Ali saw her mother's face was tearstained and drawn.

"Mom, Uncle John told you that the evidence is inconclusive. He even said there *could have been*, not that there was, someone besides Bettylwin who fired a gun," said Ali as she walked to the small pantry with its mini-sized refrigerator that held Marti's "fixes-for-frenzies."

"What's it to be? A Tab or some Heavenly Hash?" From the look on Marti's face Ali knew it was a Hash night and probably topped with Cool Whip at that. "How was the rest of the documentary?" asked Ali as she scooped ice cream from a half-gallon container into a bowl.

"Confused," said Marti. "It was bits and pieces of ideology and theories, of which the two-gun theory was one and the Vietnam-vet-as-a-potential-bomb-about-to-explode-in-society was another. Mixed in were the assassins and," added Marti in a small voice, "the people they killed."

"C'mon, kid, if you shove over a little, I can lie next to you," said Ali as she handed Marti her ice cream, "just like I did when I was a little girl frightened by a bad dream."

"And now I'm the little girl frightened by a bad dream," said Marti as she moved her body as far as the sofa's back cushions would allow. "Oh, Ali, it was awful," Marti cried as she buried her face in Ali's shoulder. "It was like having an out-of-body experience while perfectly aware you are rooted within your own. I was watching me get shot, fall down, and lie helpless in a pool of blood. I saw the thread . . . that thin precious thread between life and death."

"Mom, I don't want to hear this," said Ali, her voice shrill. "No more. Never again. I saw it. I still see it almost every night when I close my eyes and try to sleep. And just when I think I can't see it anymore, I see you cowering through life, hiding as if you're constantly thinking a bullet is going to come through our front door and kill you. I hate it, Mom. I just hate it."

Ali was sobbing. "And Mark hates it, too. We all do. We don't want to hear it anymore."

"Oh, my God. My dear God," said Marti as she rocked Ali in her arms. "I'm so sorry, Ali. I never realized it must be as awful for you as it is for me. You never talk about it. No one ever talks about it. Everyone pretends that it never happened."

"Ma, no one pretends. No one can pretend. We were all there. We just want to forget it. But you won't let us."

"Ali, it's not me who won't forget but him, the man who sends me letters."

"Mom, it's got to be easier to die than to live the way you do," said Ali. "If it were me I'd rather be dead than deal day after day with the fear of dying. Mom, the FBI told us that people who send threatening letters rarely act on them. Why can't you believe them?"

"Because it's not a certainty. Damn it, Ali. You're like my mother and JJ. Get on with it. Put it behind you, they say. It is so easy to judge or mouth platitudes when you're not the one involved."

"Oh, we're involved," said Ali bitterly. "We have to be. We have no choice because you have no life of your own. You go nowhere. You do nothing . . ."

"I have you and Mark," interrupted Marti defensively. "And that's quite a lot."

"You're smothering us and we hate it. It was so much better when you were doing your thing and allowed us to do ours," said Ali angrily, as she bounded up from the couch and began to pace, her Tab sloshing over the edge of her glass.

"Children do not have a 'thing,' " said Marti nastily.

"Yours do and you know it. Mark has his composing and, Mom, he's really good. And he's got this great girl. You don't even know about her, do you? Why? Because Mark won't bring her home."

"He's too young to have a girl," said Marti, her voice flat.

"You're not listening, Mom. He's got a girl but he won't bring her home because his mother's a drag. It's like me with Andreas.

He's a fan of yours. He grew up on your movies. He thinks you're neat. In fact, the only reason he wants to photograph me, I'm sure, is because of you. But, Mom, I don't want him around the house either. I have fun wearing those silly clothes and doing silly things for him in front of his camera. And it would be even more fun if I didn't have to worry about you all the time."

"You've got that wrong, missy," said Marti angrily. "I spend half my life worrying about you."

"Then find something else to do, because it's not really me you're worrying about but you," cried Ali. "Yes, you! So stop pretending otherwise. When you're on my case or Mark's back, wanting to know where we are and with whom, it's not out of concern for us but for you. Our curfew is for you. You're less anxious knowing where we are at all times and when we'll be home. For you. It makes you feel safe knowing that at eleven o'clock we'll come walking through the door. It makes you feel protected knowing if you need us, you can phone the number you insist we leave. It's all for you, Mom. Face it, 'cause we have."

Marti lay on the sofa, shocked less by the words than by the truth of them. Tears began to fall slowly down her cheeks, prompting another outburst from Ali. "No. Don't do that. It's a trick. A trap. It catches me. I don't want to be your mother anymore, Mom. I want to be a kid again. You're supposed to take care of me; not me, you. I need someone to go to when *I'm* afraid and I have *my* bad dreams."

"What's Mark's girl's name?" asked Marti softly.

"Karma."

"Is she nice?" continued Marti.

"Yeah, she's nice. Weirded out but nice. Like Mark. They hum Mahler to each other on the telephone. She's also a music major."

"Is she pretty?" asked Marti.

Ali snorted. "I don't mean to be mean but . . . she looks like Lawrence Welk in drag. In fact, each time she speaks I expect her to begin with: 'And-uh-one-and-uh-two-and-uh . . .' "

Marti was laughing. "That bad, eh?"

"But she's really very nice. Her father plays violin with the New York Philharmonic."

"Ali, why are you afraid?"

Ali's back was to Marti as she faced the fireplace. "Mom, I've thought a lot about that and I don't mean to lay a guilt trip on you, but I think it's because you make me afraid. You make us all afraid with your fear. Mom, sometimes when I'm invited out with the kids, I'm afraid to go because you have me convinced someone may come in the house and kill you. And my dreams are about that. And sometimes," said Ali as her shoulders began to heave, "sometimes I find myself wishing it would happen already. Get it over with so I wouldn't have to be so afraid anymore. And I hate myself for that," said Ali as she burst into tears.

Marti was instantly beside Ali, holding her, caressing and kissing her face and her hair. "It will be all right, baby. It will be all right," she crooned. "I understand, and things will be different."

"Mom, what are you going to do?" asked Ali in a near whisper.

"I don't know, baby. But something will come along."

*   *   *

Having suffered enough, Carolyn Tiernan was impatient to go to her final reward which in her mind was New York City. Since seven-thirty that morning—six hours ago—Carolyn had been waiting to die. The six hours now seemed more like six days, and still the crew on *Cataclysm* was wrestling to complete her living room built in a tank. The delay was but one of the many that had plagued the film since it began shooting at the end of January. Now, with a little luck and some hitherto mainly lacking professionalism, the film would end this day that June had begun, and Carolyn would be sadder but wiser and, according to Margaret's overtime calculations: "a helluva lot richer."

Cranky and strangely out of sorts, Carolyn decided her headache was caused by the noise on the set as workmen tested the chutes that would bring the flood waters, caused by the tidal wave, which was caused by the earthquake, which was caused by the massive underground government testing of a new nuclear weapon, into her living room. This day, Michigan or Montana—one of those states beginning with an *M*—would be gone and she, with it. Only the Dakotas would be standing by the day's end. The Dakotas and Margaret Tiernan, who as mayor of a small town would find herself next in line to succeed the very dead president, of which there had been seventy-eight since the cataclysm had begun. The film, insisted the producers, one, a short, fat man given to wearing caftans even on the set, was making an important statement. Carolyn agreed; about the statement but not the content. The film used a trendy idea to sell garbage.

Her first film in Hollywood Carolyn remembered—and was it really forty years ago?—had also been garbage. It was titled *Waifs in the Wind* and that is what they had been. My God, had she and Margaret ever really been that naïve and young? But not stupid. Oh, no. She had been one waif who had allowed that wind to blow her back to New York and the stage where she had belonged. And she had the awards to prove it. She had never liked Hollywood or filmmaking. They were both fake. Still, Margaret had made them work for her.

For a moment, Carolyn measured her successes against her sister's, something she rarely permitted herself to do. She had been a great star of the stage, radio, and then television. Yet, she thought with annoyance, she was not Margaret, but then who was? Like a Hepburn or a Davis, Margaret was an original.

Her headache had worsened and Carolyn knew her dwelling in the past wasn't helping. Soon she would be thinking about John and how they had met in Hollywood. John was dead and so was the life she had lived with him. Leave it be. Don't bring that pain to the set. You have enough pain today without it, she cautioned herself.

As she sipped her tea, Carolyn felt her eyes grow heavy and her body sag. The sleep that had escaped her the previous night was now available. Only she wasn't. Carolyn knew food would help but she had been without appetite. Only hot tea with honey calmed her queasiness. It was not worry that was bothering Carolyn, although she always worried about her children. JJ would have to find his own way as would Marti. Long ago, Carolyn had learned to let go and let God, although she was certainly willing to give Himself a boost when needed. Which is why she had offered to babysit at Rancho Santa Fe when Thomas and Reese had gone on tour. Something within her sensed the children needed a grandmother and not a stranger in the house. It had not been easy for Carolyn. On those few days when she was working, it took nearly two hours to drive to the studio in L.A. and two hours back. The trip, the work, and the children had exhausted her.

Carolyn had not been upset by JJ's documentary. She was not naïve. Who could be naïve, she wondered, after the Kennedys. Nor was she upset by Marti's reclusiveness. Not everybody had a Greek bearing gifts to whisk her off to an island of security. Marti would have to make her own island and her own security, and Carolyn was sure she would. She was less sure of Reese, however. She ached for her daughter-in-law at the same time she ached for her son. Often she had the strangest wish to introduce them to each other, as if an introduction was all that was needed to cure the estrangement both so obviously felt from each other and their society. But Carolyn did what most mothers-in-law are accused of not doing: she minded her business. But not without misgivings. There was always that. With all her children.

"We're ready for you on the set, Miss Tiernan."

Slowly, Carolyn walked to the center of the living room now built into the tank that would eventually hold four feet of water. Once again she listened as the director carefully explained what was about to happen. She would be sitting at a desk, balancing her checkbook, when she would hear a deafening roar meant to symbolize onrushing flood waters. As she would rise in panic, water would be released from the top of the set, slide down a chute, gathering momentum until it broke through a window and then a wall to flood the living room. Carolyn would immediately be pulled under. The camera would photograph her flailing about the waters, trying to grasp any piece of floating furniture before it either broke or the rushing waters took it from her reach. Her job, explained the director, was simply to flail and show panic. On cue, she would go under the raging waters for a brief second or two and then bob to the surface before being swept down and away as the rest of the living room came tumbling down about her.

The miracle of filmmaking, thought Carolyn as she stepped to the desk. Off to the set's side she saw the pumps that would bring in the floodwaters and then remove them once the valve below her was opened.

"Ready, Carolyn?" asked the director. When she signified she was, Carolyn heard the familiar phrases: "Quiet on the set, everybody. This is a take. Lights. Camera. Action."

The noise, as promised by the special-effects designer, was deafening. Carolyn rose, fear contorting her face. As the waters came rushing down upon her, she was seized with panic. A very real panic. Swept up by the raging flood, she felt she would vomit. Desperately, Carolyn fought the waters that were dragging her down, her arms flailing about until they became too heavy to move. And then the pain, not scripted and all too real, became unbearable. She cried out before she went under, but those on the set thought it was the actress, not the woman, who was in trouble. Water filled her mouth and lungs. The pain threatened to sever the upper part of her body from the lower. Once again Carolyn tried to force her way to the water's top. The effort was too much for her. As the walls of the living room collapsed around her, Carolyn felt herself sucked under, out of the unreal world of moviemaking and into the real world of death.

"Cut!" called the director. "Perfect. Print it!"

As the valve was opened and pumps removed what had just been raging floodwaters, a dozen hands reached in to assist the star from the tank. At first, her dead man's float was thought to be one of her occasional jokes. But quickly, screams reverberated throughout the closed set. A doctor, on hand for just such an emergency, pushed his way through to Carolyn, where a rapid check of her vital signs proved she was alive—but barely. As they waited for an ambulance, he told her not to move, and Carolyn, as she drifted far away into the onrushing blackness, thought that was the funniest and yet the most solid direction she had yet received on what was now definitely a disaster movie.

⁂　　⁂　　⁂

The doors parted. Reese entered and was immediately sucked into the noise and confusion of the airline terminal. As people flurried on by, often jostling her with their carry-on bags or packages, Reese stood rooted before the United ticket counter. Although her eyes were on the Arrivals and Departures computerized board, her mind was on the cologne bottle tucked away in the recesses of the glove compartment. Just out the door. In the parking lot. In her car.

4 6

Thomas's flight from New York was on time. Quickly, before she could think about what she would soon be facing and what she was leaving behind in the parked station wagon, Reese walked to the moving sidewalk that would take her to the United landing gate. Keeping as close to the wall as possible, her head turned away from others, Reese hoped to avoid the recognition that had followed her since her appearance on "Dinah." Frequently since then, people had approached and said something to her but she never knew what as she never heard.

As the sidewalk moved slowly toward the lounge area, Reese raged against Thomas. Silently, of course, since she never raged in front of him. No, that she saved for herself, nurturing her anger as it nourished her. But this time she should have said something, should have protested that he take a flight into the much closer and thus much more convenient San Diego airport. Why should it be her problem that none of the travel arrangements into San Diego had convenienced him? What of her convenience? Nobody cared about that. What had she to do that was important anyway? So what if it were getting more and more difficult for her to leave the house? Nobody cared because nobody noticed.

Once, not so many years ago, Reese remembered, she used to love meeting Thomas anyplace and at any time. She used to love how his handsomeness turned peoples' heads in their direction. Then, she was proud of the attention that indirectly focused on her after it was through focusing on him. Now, she hated meeting Thomas. She hated the recognition he obtained. It seemed apart from her, as though he belonged more to them than to her. And when he drew attention, like it or not, so did she. The wife of the war hero, of the best-selling author, of Thomas Ollson. It caused her to wear a face that didn't fit. Often Reese wondered if people saw the same thing she did when they looked at her: nothing.

The tension between his shoulder blades grew tighter as the 747 began its descent into the Los Angeles area. As the jet slowly sank into the smog, Thomas sank into reality.

Reese would be waiting. She would have to understand.

"Would you like anything else before we land, Mr. Ollson?"

the stewardess was asking, her face as open as the invitation. The landing gear had already been lowered and the seatbacks raised, so Thomas knew it was not another drink the pretty young girl was offering.

"I'm fine, thank you," Thomas said. The smile remained fixed on the girl's face as she backed off. As Thomas watched her walk down the aisle, her skirt molded perfectly to her perfectly molded buttocks, he saw she was a replica of Ann Turner, his editor at the paperback house. Her actions toward him were proprietary, as if the house had bought more than his book. She, too, had wanted to know if there was anything else she could do for him before he embarked for California. He had declined, but it bothered him that he had not only noticed but had entertained the thought but not the possibility.

Thomas thought of other planes and another woman. Not long ago. Honolulu and his month-long leave between extensions of duty in the Air Force. He and Reese, flying together, in the air and in bed. She had always been the most willing partner. He hoped she would be that now, hoped she would understand that it was business. A wonderful business. Something to do and somebody to be.

As Reese stepped off the moving sidewalk and into the United lounge, the clock read two-thirty-five. Twenty minutes before Thomas's plane was scheduled to arrive. Anxiously, Reese searched for a seat off by itself but, seeing none, selected instead a position at the huge glass windows overlooking runways and hangars. A group of women passed, vacationers all wearing polyester pastels. Reese stared and saw herself. Again, she thought of the cologne bottle waiting.

Reese had been cautious about her drinking ever since "Dinah." Not that anyone had mentioned her "performance." Had they, Reese would have felt less mortified. But that no one, not Thomas, not her children, and not her parents ever alluded to it, only increased Reese's feelings of guilt which in turn increased her feelings of alienation.

She was not looking forward to seeing Thomas, which was strange as they would finally be alone. At last their lives would belong solely to them. They would have time to renew and explore. Like dating. It was all that was needed, Reese reassured herself, all *she* needed to set herself right again.

The past eight weeks had been a terrible strain. They had hurt when they should not have. After her mother-in-law had survived her massive heart attack, she had barely seen Thomas as he all but lived by his mother's side at the UCLA Medical Center. She couldn't fault him for that and yet she did. She faulted him even more during the five weeks her mother-in-law had convalesced in their home, five weeks in which she watched as Thomas gave to his mother all the things that she, as his wife, so much wanted him to give to her. She had been frustrated and resentful but still, as always, she had been his good little soldier. And just as always, she had hated it. And she hated her hating it. She couldn't forgive her niggardliness. And when she looked in the mirror mornings or saw herself reflected as she did now in the glass of the airline terminal, Reese hated herself for everything but mainly for the nonentity she saw herself as being.

"Ladies and gentlemen, we would like to welcome you to Los Angeles where the time is two-forty-six and the temperature at L.A. International Airport is one hundred and eight degrees. The captain has requested for your safety that you remain seated until . . ."

As the stewardess droned on, her voice lost on those passengers who reacted to the predictable August heat wave, Thomas wondered how the house would feel now that his mother was gone and the children were away. Empty, he suspected. Empty with just him and Reese there all day . . . alone. A finger grabbed at his stomach. It could be good, he told himself. The finger became a hand clenching and unclenching. But Kristan would be home in the evenings. They would not be totally alone after all. The fingers loosened. By five-thirty, Kris would leave the job she so loved at the nearby animal shelter. At her own request, Kristan was working, learning the value of work and the money one is paid for doing it. Thomas approved of her decision, deeming it character building. Which is exactly why he had sent Karl and Kelly to camp.

He had tried to call Karl at his Boy Scout camp before leaving

New York but again had been unsuccessful. Either he was truly missing Karl each time he phoned or the boy, in anger at having been sent away for the summer, was refusing to speak with him. Despite the unspoken tension that existed between him and Karl, Thomas did not regret his decision. Boy Scout camp did indeed build character and solid young men. It prepared them for life. Not that Karl was a problem. The boy was actually a model of behavior. Except he lacked friends, which Thomas interpreted as a lack of leadership qualities. In the Scouts, Thomas reasoned, Karl's natural athletic prowess would earn him the position Thomas desired for him. And Kelly, his delightful but undisciplined youngest, perhaps would learn order and modes of behavior acceptable to society. Like Karl, her respect for herself and then of others would blossom and grow in a controlled environment where one learned the disciplines necessary for good citizenship.

I have good kids, thought Thomas as the plane taxied to its landing gate. I'm proud of them, he told himself, something he somehow never thought to tell them. Then and there he decided the family, as a whole, would visit New York at Christmastime at Marti's invitation. There, they could be a true family.

Reese hated the utter aloneness she was experiencing in the crowded lounge. She wished Kristan was with her and when she allowed to surface the reason she was not, her anger flared anew. He had taken Kristan away. He had taken all the children away. He didn't think she was competent. Not that he had said that, but why else camp and a job? Her children didn't need to be taught responsibility. Any more than she had as a child and she, too, was always being sent somewhere, anywhere others could mold her into something they deemed of excellence. Suddenly she remembered the arguments and her mother's final words.

"It's for your own good."

As if he were still hugging her, Thomas could smell the perfume his mother had been wearing when they said their good-byes that morning at Marti's. Her hug had surprising strength, considering how frail she now was. But that, Thomas decided as he waited to deplane, was his mother: a woman of surprising strength. As a child he had thought her weak, spineless even. Now he perceived her butterfly wings were made of iron and steel. He saw that same quality in Marti and was surprised to realize she was unaware of it. When she left her cocoon Thomas was certain she would see it. Better still, she would feel it.

His mind went to the Intensive Care Unit at UCLA. His mother's first thoughts upon regaining consciousness were not for herself but for Margaret. She had whispered to Thomas, "Watch over her if I die." In those few frightening weeks when his mother's death was a distinct possibility, Thomas observed the relationship between his mother and aunt. They were the flip side of each other, with each feeling useless without the other's support. At home in Rancho Santa Fe, Margaret had been a constant visitor, driving in from her hotel near San Diego daily. She had only accepted the European film offer when Carolyn was clearly out of danger and had agreed to live with Marti until the doctors were certain she could again live on her own. It had been Margaret who had answered the phone the first time JJ had called from Toronto. But it was he who had answered the following day.

"Hello?"

"Thomas, this is JJ."

The silence had seemed endless with each expecting or hoping that the other would say something. Neither did.

"Hold on. I'll get Mother for you. There's an extension by her bed."

Later, she had been so pleased. Before drifting off to sleep, she had asked but really said: "You spoke wth JJ," and he, seeing no reason to say anything but yes, agreed that he had. Her smile had been his reward.

"Your briefcase, Mr. Ollson," said his overly friendly stewardess as he prepared to deplane. "You wouldn't want to leave that, would you?"

Actually, a part of him would, which is probably why he had, thought Thomas. In it was the business at hand. An outline for a movie, one based on his book, his life. Filming would begin as soon as there was a completed script. The hope was for the film to air when the paperback was published either next spring or early fall. A completed script. Three little words. But filled with both excitement and yet terror. A script, as it was explained by the producers, could only be completed when the writers had "lived with" him and Reese. Which they were coming to do the following week.

Reese would understand. She would have to. She would.

The clock read two-forty-nine. Eleven minutes before Thomas was due. Panic again tightened its grip about Reese. Unable to loosen it, she walked quickly but not so quickly that she drew attention, to the bar just off the restroom. Thank God it was cool. And calm. Oh, so very calm, thought Reese. As she ordered her vodka on the rocks, Reese prayed the look she had come to know so well on Thomas's face would not be there when he stepped off the plane.

Through the smoked-glass window of the bar, Thomas watched Reese, saw the look on her face as she took long sips of her iced drink, and was so very glad that she, in turn, could not see the look on his. With his briefcase firmly clenched under his arm, he opened the plate-glass door of the bar and walked toward Reese, who dropped her glass on the floor when her eyes met his.

*   *   *

No one had ever accused Jessamyn Giroux of being shy. Nor was anyone ever likely to. Jessamyn was not ashamed of her ambition, particularly since she knew she had the talent and the intellect to accompany it. The day the new president of the United States, Gerald Ford, announced his intention to grant limited amnesty to some fifty thousand Vietnam War draft evaders and deserters, Jessamyn, a recent graduate of Columbia University's School of Journalism, conceived her plan for her successful career. One month later, on September 16, the day Ford offered conditional amnesty to those who agreed to work up to two years in public-service jobs, Jessamyn put her plan into action. Using the phone number she had obtained through her New York contacts, she placed a call to Thomas Ollson, claiming she was a reporter for the *Toronto Daily Star*. As if he had been waiting for just such a phone call, Thomas had instantly denounced the entire concept of amnesty, insisting it would have an adverse impact on national security.

"If every young man eligible for service decided to evade or desert, this country would be in dire straits," he said. "The nation's security demands subjugating the individual's wishes to the needs of the country."

Perhaps a minute passed between the time Jessamyn spoke with Thomas Ollson and the phone call she then placed to John Ollson, Jr. This time, posing as a reporter from the Associated Press, Jessamyn, after reading Thomas's statement to JJ, asked for his own. From her blatant actions, it was obvious to JJ that Jessamyn Giroux had learned her lesson well from Reynolds Trahey.

In JJ's hesitation to answer, Jessamyn smelled disaster. "Look. I can be at your place within the hour, with a tape recorder, if it will make you feel more comfortable."

Within the half hour, Jessamyn Giroux was standing before the news editor at the *Toronto Daily Star* offering what she would soon have from the Ollsons in exchange for a job. She left no room for doubt that if the *Star* refused her, their competitors at the *Globe and Mail* would not. Which is how Jessamyn Giroux became a staff reporter for the *Daily Star*. It is also how her very first assignment happened to gain national syndication in the United States. It never occurred to Jessamyn to send a note of thanks to Reynolds Trahey, from whom she had "borrowed" the concept, but then it would never have occurred to Reynolds Trahey that she would.

Pierre Giroux used to tell friends that his twenty-two-year-old Jessamyn was the son he never had. All of Giroux's hopes for immortality were squarely placed on his daughter's rather small but sturdy shoulders. Where some would say Jessamyn as a child had been spoiled, Giroux would maintain she had merely been indulged. As one of Toronto's successful small businessmen, Giroux had been able to give his daughter everything. In return, all he had asked was that Jessamyn one day bring greater bearing to his name in a city he loved.

Jessamyn's interview with JJ had been brief but to the point.

Amnesty, JJ had maintained, was not a new concept but a tradition in America. She had been surprised to learn that amnesty had been granted as far back as the time of George Washington when the then president bestowed it upon those who had participated in the Whiskey Rebellion and that Andrew Jackson had granted it to deserters of the Mexican War and that no Confederate soldier had ever been tried for treason after the Civil War. She also had not known that after World War I, amnesty had been granted on an individual basis to draft resisters.

She had been impressed by the rhetoric, but what were his own feelings on the subject? Ford's plan was an outrage, a perversion, one that must be boycotted, JJ had insisted. "If Richard Nixon, who is a true criminal, can be pardoned by his fellow Republican and given a one-hundred-ten-thousand-dollar yearly allowance, then how dare Ford demand exiles take a loyalty oath and be asked to do alternate service for two years! That is harsh and unwarranted punishment. We do not see ourselves guilty of a crime, whereas the world agrees Richard Nixon is guilty of indefensible crimes.

"Furthermore," JJ had continued angrily, "Ford is going to make us wallow in shit as well as carry it in bedpans in hospitals and prisons. The alternate-service work the man proposes will be the most menial and degrading work imaginable. And at the end of this supposed rainbow awaits a clemency discharge. Who knows what kind of stigma will be the ribbon attached to this discharge paper? Frankly, I think big business will not accept it. I think there will be mass discrimination."

John Ollson, Jr., had impressed Jessamyn. At the end of her allotted thirty minutes, Jessamyn had decided JJ not only had a fine mind but a beautiful face and quite possibly the most expressive hands she had ever seen. As she was leaving his studio, Jessamyn allowed herself to wonder what those hands, with their long fingers, would feel like on her body. Excited, she carelessly bumped into a young man on the ground floor who, after introducing himself as Nelson Naismith, asked if he could ride with her into downtown Toronto. Which is how Jessamyn came to know Nelson. Within minutes of their conversation, she realized the young man was a potential source of valuable information. Thus, when he suggested coffee at Grossman's, she accepted.

Although Jessamyn, like most who lived in Toronto, knew of the exile community living in the "Annex Area," Grossman's was her official introduction to it. A large, multiroom wooden structure, Grossman's was a landmark, a meeting place for artistic and political types, and a dump. Not by anyone's standard was it so much of a restaurant as it was a place that rocked to the rhythms of various rock and country bands on weekends and political discussions daily.

Jessamyn's coffee date with Nelson soon emerged into periodic dinners, all "dutch" of course, as Nelson was self-described as "a rung above destitute." Although it occurred to Jessamyn that Nelson might be interested in something more than just friendship, she decided that was his problem and therefore not one with which she needed to be concerned. Instead, she busied herself with meeting the leaders of the various factions within the exile community. She was impressed that they were united against Ford's clemency program and that they frowned upon those who were seriously considering it.

It was through Nelson that Jessamyn learned of JJ's idea for a new documentary that would follow those who accepted Ford's terms and returned to America as well as those who flatly refused. It was also through Nelson that Jessamyn later learned that Marti Tiernan Ollson had refused to cowrite and codirect the project, leaving JJ without someone to head his American unit. Instantly, Jessamyn knew this was a job she had to do, mainly because of what the job could do for her. That she had less than two months working experience and none whatsoever in television was not a deterrent. Jessamyn Giroux had always believed that what she didn't know, others did, and from them she would learn.

JJ could not remember a Jessamyn Giroux when she called, leaning heavily on her friendship with Nelson. With so many reporters coming in and out of his life, in JJ's mind they all blended into two groups: those who printed the facts and those who distorted them. That he did not remember Jessamyn was in her favor. It meant she belonged in the first group and was probably trustworthy. That she also was "close" to Nelson convinced JJ to see Jessamyn, although he hadn't the vaguest idea of her intent.

Jessamyn could not have picked a better time to enter JJ's life. Not that she could have known he was feeling extremely vulnerable and needy. Having nearly lost his mother to a heart attack and now feeling he had lost the sister he had once so admired and loved, JJ needed female support. A part of him yearned to take part in Ford's program, to see his mother and reestablish family ties, but he could not, as he explained to his mother when she asked, compromise himself or his beliefs.

JJ had been interviewing Canadian documentary makers when Jessamyn phoned. He was still interviewing, with no success, the morning he opened his studio door to find Jessamyn Giroux standing there with snow falling off her pea jacket. JJ was surprised when she removed her coat, surprised that he had met her before but had not remembered the tall, slender, but full-breasted young woman. With her large, almond-shaped black eyes and hair that matched her eye color and gleamed every bit as brightly, she was not a woman who blended into backgrounds.

"I haven't been checked out like that since I was last in Maxwell's Plum in New York," said Jessamyn as she swept into the room. "You needn't stop. I rather like it. But it's only fair to tell you I'm here about a job."

She had taken the offensive and had successfully rattled him. "None of the men at the *Daily Star* take notice of me in that way anymore. Although they do take notice. Above my desk they've hung a sign reading SHARK WARNING."

"Are you a shark?" asked JJ, somewhat amused.

"More a barracuda, as I'm sure you've noticed," she replied. "And you are still staring."

"I'm sorry," said JJ awkwardly. "It's just that I hadn't remembered you."

"Very flattering. You sure know how to charm a girl."

"Do you get many jobs coming on like this?" asked JJ as he now purposely stared at the girl whose eyes refused to waver as they met his.

"I tend to come on strong when I'm nervous," Jessamyn said. "Even us barracudas have defense mechanisms."

"And what are you nervous about, Miss Giroux?" asked JJ as he waved Jessamyn to a seat on the sofa.

"Call me Jess. Everyone does. At the moment, to answer your question, I'm nervous about becoming your assistant or coworker or whatever you want to call it, on your documentary. I'm good. I haven't any experience but I'm good. I'll be even better once you teach me what I need to know. I've been well trained at Columbia. I've got keen sensibilities. I'm a damn good writer and a terrific researcher. I'm resourceful. I don't discourage easily. Perhaps most important: I know the exile community here in Toronto."

"To be perfectly honest, I'm looking for a man," said JJ, now conscious it was she who was staring at him. "The sex here is important, since only a man can understand how an exile feels. It has much to do with one's sense of maleness."

"Oh, bullshit! If that were true, you wouldn't have been hot after your sister to collaborate," Jessamyn responded.

"Nelson?" JJ asked.

"I don't reveal my sources, Mr. Ollson. Not ever," said Jessamyn firmly and yet with a lilt in her voice.

JJ had the distinct impression Jessamyn Giroux was playing with him. His reactions were confusing. On one hand he found her exasperating and on the other . . . exciting.

"My sister once did a documentary with me on men who had gone AWOL. I found she was able to think like a man," JJ replied.

"What a sexist remark! And by the way, it's exactly what was wrong with that documentary," said Jessamyn, playing what she hoped would be her ace. "It 'thought' like a man. It negated the woman viewer as it failed to ask any of the questions a woman might. It also ignored the women in those men's lives and how they reacted or were acted upon. I can give you what your sister did not. I can ask questions a woman would. I can obtain that loathsome thing known as the woman's point of view. You simply don't ask questions a mother or a wife or a girlfriend would.

"For example," continued Jessamyn as she began to hammer home her point, "of the men who will return, had you planned on speaking to any of the women they were leaving behind? Had you planned to speak to those they had already left once and were now hopeful of returning to? Don't you think this would be of interest to the viewer and add a needed dimension to your documentary? And regarding the issues: that you can teach me. Remember: I'm hungry. I want this job and I can do it."

Jessamyn Giroux's energy created energy. As he considered

all she had said, JJ was feeling an all too unfamiliar stirring as he continued to stare at the girl who continued to stare at him. She had a wonderful nose, he decided. A proud, upturned nose from which he expected any moment to see fire when her nostrils flared.

"I was just about to have some coffee. Would you like some?" JJ asked.

Jessamyn Giroux relaxed. "You bet I would, particularly if you've got some cognac to go in it."

3

As she looked about her living room with its groupings of family, Marti felt as if the torch had been successfully passed. Until this year, Christmas had always been spent at her mother's but that had changed, as had so many other things in her mother's life, with her heart attack. Surrounded by the noise of competing conversations, Marti, adrift in her bentwood rocker, felt peaceful and happy. With the exception of JJ, the family was together. In spirit as well as body.

JJ . . . she missed him, thought Marti as she rocked contentedly. If she had not felt there was still a risk involved, she would have visited him between Christmas and New Year's. But chances were not to be taken. Not now that the letters had stopped. As she had stopped. To travel to Toronto was to risk being seen, photographed, written about. Not that she felt she was being watched; she just was uncertain that she wasn't. But speaking with JJ and making him realize she was no longer the person he wanted her to be was a present in itself. He had understood. She sensed that this very afternoon when he had called to wish everyone a Merry Christmas. Well almost everyone, thought Marti, remembering how everyone but Thomas had lined up to speak to JJ. Marti wondered what Karl, Kristan, and Kelly felt when they saw Ali and Mark rush to speak to a man who was also their uncle. But then Marti wondered what Thomas's children felt about so many things as they were seen but not heard. Except for Kelly, whose voice even now carried from the kitchen where the girls were doing the dishes while the boys put away folding chairs.

Drifting and dreaming as she contentedly rocked, Marti, her face illuminated by the lights of the Christmas tree and the fire that crackled in the fireplace, smiled as she watched Margaret snatch a maraschino cherry from her mother's hand. Marti missed not having her mother with her, but she no longer blamed Margaret for that fact.

Margaret . . . thought Marti. She had arrived the morning after Thanksgiving in a limousine. After she ordered it to wait, she ordered Carolyn from the house and back to her own life in her own apartment. Her mother, as if waiting for just such a command, was packed and out of the house within the hour. Within the week, she announced she would return in January to her director's post at the Tiernan Repertory Company, and to the schedule of classes she had once taught. Marti recalled how Margaret had stood at the curb as her mother slid comfortably into the back seat of the car and then turned to Marti and yelled, "One of these days, kiddo, I'm coming back for you, and you better damn well be as ready as the ole lady here."

Margaret didn't change,thought Marti as she caught her aunt catching her mother with that same maraschino cherry in her mouth. She had enraged the producers of *Cataclysm* by refusing to promote the film, which had just opened for the Christmas holidays, until they reminded her attorneys that her contract specifically stated she would. Margaret, being Margaret, had honored her commitment by telling Barbara Walters on "Today," "If it's disaster movies America wants then they shouldn't miss *Cataclysm* because if ever a movie was a disaster, this one is." The producers then threatened to sue if she *did* promote the film.

From across the room, with her aunt's face bathed in firelight, Marti felt Margaret's joy. She remembered exactly how her aunt had looked when Vinnie, after all the gifts had been opened, announced he and Este had one more to give but that they would all have to wait six more months for it to arrive. Margaret had looked confused and then, when Vinnie had taken her hand, had burst into tears. When she was finally composed, she ordered Este "to keep that kid in the closet until he's twenty-eight. I'm not about to take on Dietrich for the title of the world's most glamorous grandmother."

It had been a day of extraordinary happiness, thought Marti as she gazed at the presents under the tree, looking somewhat naked now without their wrappings. In the darkest corner, by the farthest wall, Marti saw Reese sitting on the floor, her knees to her chest and her hands wrapped about a brandy snifter. There was something in Reese's manner that made Marti leave her rocker for a place by her sister-in-law's side. Although Reese had been active in the kitchen preparing the dessert, she had also been quiet. During dinner, she had sat between Thomas and Kristan and there had been a moment when Marti felt she was watching a well-worn book being supported by two bookends.

For several minutes, the two women sat under the tree with neither speaking. Although Marti had a very strong feeling for Reese, she felt helpless since Reese had always kept her a stranger. Awkwardly, Marti tried conversation.

"Your coconut cream pie was delicious. Kristan tells me it's your specialty."

Reese's response was as flat and as devoid of feeling as the tone in which it was spoken.

"I don't have a specialty. I'm not like you or Thomas or JJ. I do a lot of things but nothing is a specialty or even particularly special, for that matter."

Without measuring or thinking about her actions, Marti took Reese's hand in hers. As she did, Reese turned toward Marti.

"Do you know what my mother gave me for Christmas?" asked Reese as tears slid down her face. Marti knew Thomas had taken his family to see Reese's parents in Bridgeport the night before, but she had no idea what had transpired. "My mother," said Reese, her words coming like her breath, in short, staccato tones, "bought me a copy of Marabel Morgan's *The Total Woman*. It's a very big best seller I'm told. It's for all us Christian ladies who have forgotten what our specialties are . . . *if* we ever had any. It's a how-to book. A how-to be a better wife, a better helpmeet, a better mother, a better woman. In short: how to be something, anything, other than what you are."

"Reese," began Marti softly as she stroked her sister-in-law's hand, "I'm sure your mother meant nothing by it. You, yourself, said it's a big best seller."

"So is *More Joy: A Lovemaking Companion to the Joy of Sex*. Why didn't she buy me that? God knows I could use it," said Reese bitterly as she drained the remaining Courvoisier from the snifter.

Aching for Reese, Marti tightened her grip on her hand. "Look. I have a terrific idea. Our kids are going to be gone most of the week seeing the city. Thomas says he has meetings with his paperback publisher and the TV network. Why don't we do a day or two together. We can get all gussied up, beginning at Elizabeth Arden, and take in a matinee or two."

Marti could feel the change in Reese as she sat next to her. "I've always wanted to see Georgette Klinger's, have a facial, and then just drop in at Elizabeth Arden. Maybe we could have lunch at . . . where is that place all those proper ladies with their little hats and white gloves meet? Patricia Murphy's! We could lunch there. Or the Russian Tea Room. First thing tomorrow when the stores open, I'll buy a hat and gloves so I'll fit in."

For the first time that day, Reese's face looked hopeful. As she used a finger to wipe away Reese's tears Marti said: "You need never worry about that, Reese. You fit in fine just as you are."

From across the room where he was sitting on the sofa with Vinnie and Este, Thomas, even as he spoke, was watching as his wife and sister hugged under the Christmas tree. Reese's tears had not gone unnoticed, but in the midst of a discussion, they had gone untended. "Remember. We are not discussing JJ here," said Thomas, "so let's keep our personal feelings separate and stick to the issue. Amnesty is immoral."

"How can you say that?" said Vinnie impatiently. "Amnesty is forgiveness and forgiveness can never be immoral."

"It is immoral," continued Thomas, "when it rejects the feelings of those who fought in a war in which this country was involved. It also rejects the feelings of those who fought in the war on demand and not like me out of a sense of duty. How do you explain amnesty to those who fought while hating every single second of the fight? How do you rationalize or explain it to those who lost husbands, fathers, and sons in the war?"

"It seems to me you simply explain that there are two sides to an issue and that dissent is a guaranteed American right," said Vinnie.

"Wonderful. A great example to future generations," said Thomas sarcastically. "By granting amnesty to deserters and resisters we are telling future generations that rules can be broken if one wishes and that pardons will be forthcoming no matter what the infraction. I don't subscribe to that."

"Thomas, you can't be that rigid," said Vinnie.

"But I can! We must, Vinnie. Look what is happening in our permissive society. Our nation has run amuck. We have crime in government and crime in the streets. People no longer know right from wrong. They live without rules and regulations. They create their own to suit themselves. A society cannot function in this manner."

"Thomas, half the kids I treat at New Hope House come from backgrounds where one or both parents were totally rigid in their rules. Wait!" cautioned Vinnie as he saw Thomas was about to interrupt. "The other half come from households that were too permissive—to the point where the kids felt they could do anything because there was nobody there to stop them or to care. All I am saying is that a meeting ground must be found. You can't always legislate right and wrong."

"That's not true," said Thomas thoughtfully. "My children have been brought up with regulations. They respect the rights of others. They know right from wrong. They have learned that well."

"But at what price?" asked Vinnie.

Without having intended to, Vinnie saw from the look on Thomas's face that his rhetorical question had cut deep. "Thomas," he began, "more and more I'm getting the impression that you're itching to run for office. At least you'd be the exception: the honest politician."

"Actually, I don't know what I'm going to do," said Thomas, suddenly sullen. "For so many months now, I've had so many

schedules prepared for me by publicists and publishers and producers that I haven't yet made one of my own." As Thomas continued to speak, Vinnie saw that his cousin's eyes were on Reese.
"I've thought about politics, but I'm not certain my running for
office would be such a good thing for the family. Your life becomes
an open book when you run. The press doesn't feel you're the only
one they're entitled to own. I'm not sure I want to put her through
that."

Vinnie didn't have to ask. He knew who *her* was.

"She isn't like us, Vinnie," continued Thomas. "She wasn't
born into the spotlight. It frightens her. She wants a normal life
and hasn't had one for many years. Me? I started out wanting to
write a book that might change things. That mattered to me. It
still does, damn it," added Thomas, upset.

"I admire you for that, Thomas. There aren't many people
who stick their necks out, who stand up and be counted, as they
say," said Vinnie.

"Yeah . . . well . . . as some stand up, others fall down," said
Thomas wearily. "While still others run. As though their lives
depended on it."

"As if whose life depended on what, Daddy?"

Thomas was startled by Kelly's sudden appearance and question. Gently he replied: "Honey, haven't I told you not to interrupt
when others are talking?"

Sighing, Kelly patiently explained as she insinuated herself
into her father's lap, "We're all done in the kitchen and you promised to take us to see the tree at Rockefeller Center."

"Well, a promise is a promise," said Thomas, "so if you guys
are ready, get yourself in gear and I'll get your mother. Tell the
others to take their things because we'll go back to the hotel from
there. You still coming, Vin, or should I just send Ali and Mark
back in a taxi?"

"No. I'll go," said Vinnie, yawning as he rose. "But I don't
think Este will make it."

"You're right," said Este. "I'm going to hang out here with
'the girls.' See you when you get back."

It was like a sudden storm. Suddenly there were hoofbeats on
the stairs as the kids ran up and down to the bathrooms and to
closets to take the extra sweaters Marti insisted they carry. The

noise of four teenagers and one preteen as they prepared to descend on Fifth Avenue was akin to that of the cavalry arriving in a Western movie. When they left, Marti collapsed on the floor at the foot of the sofa where Este was lying.

"If anybody wants anything, they'll have to get it themselves," said Marti, as she gave into her pleasant exhaustion.

"I want nothing more than to lie here until the baby comes," said Este. "Marti, I don't suppose you'd wait on me hand and foot for the next six months."

"Don't tempt her, miss. In case you hadn't noticed, she does that sort of thing rather well," said Margaret dryly.

"Oh, but it would be lovely not to move, not to cook or clean but to live off the fat of the land," continued Este.

"By 'fat of the land,' she means my son," said Margaret as she pulled her chair closer to the sofa. "I always knew you were a gold-digger. I bet you planned this pregnancy. I bet it's just another one of your tricks to get my little boy to marry you."

As Este flashed her wedding ring in Margaret's face, she said lazily: "I've been working since I'm eighteen and it's time to relax."

"Not with my grandchild, you don't!" cautioned Margaret. "Relax, indeed. I always knew you were a bimbo."

"Margaret," said Este ever so sweetly as she raised her head but slightly so she could look directly at her mother-in-law, "fuck off!"

"My dear. If 'fuck off!' is how you speak to me on Christmas, then spare me a card on Mother's Day. I fear the sentiment you might express."

"Believe me, old lady, it wouldn't be anything you haven't heard before in several languages and many times over," said Este caustically.

Marti laughed, enjoying the camaraderie between the two women who so obviously adored each other.

"I really could get into doing nothing for a while," said Este. "I've earned the right. First all those years in the chorus, dancing in tights. Then all those years getting tight as part of my job in public relations. And finally, ugh! Rescuing the Tiernan Sisters from *Mothers & Other Relics of the Dark Ages*."

"Now watch it, sister," said Margaret. "Those were two of the best nights we ever spent on Broadway. And we might have gotten a third, who knows, maybe even a fourth, if our blond bimbo publicist hadn't been doing her best public relating after the show with its director. My son!"

"Oh, you're just jealous, Margaret, because I still can and you can't," said Este teasingly.

"Would you listen to that mouth! Really, my dear, as the expression goes: Just because there's snow on the roof doesn't mean there isn't a fire in the furnace. Isn't that right, Carolyn?"

Marti was laughing.

"Take that smile off your face, Marti, or I'll knock it off," said Margaret menacingly.

"Come on, Marg. Don't tell me you still think about men," said Marti, still amused.

"You're damn right I do, and if you hadn't been so self-involved the past year, you'd know it," replied Margaret huffily. "What do you think all these damn laugh lines are from? Not Carol Burnett alone, I assure you. I smile a lot, my dear, and you know why? Because I have a man who makes me laugh in bed. My, but how the priorities do change as one gets older. If any man in my younger days had made me laugh in bed, I'd have kicked him out. But now, it is lovely to laugh and giggle and talk and then sometimes remember there was something else you set out to do, were actually doing it, until you got sidetracked. Well, he may not be Superman in bed but, let's face it, I ain't exactly Wonderwoman anymore either."

"You're seeing somebody?" asked Marti, stunned and not attempting to hide it.

"Oh, yeah! Right on and all that shit, Margaret," said Este, beaming.

"Damn straight I'm seeing somebody and have been ever since bringing your mother home from California. We walked into this DC 10—God, how I hate to fly one of those things—and I yelled out to the crew: 'You better fly this thing goddamn carefully unless you all want to go down in history as having killed the Tiernan sisters.' Well, it didn't get a laugh from the crew, but it sure did from the man sitting alongside us. His name is Alden Richards. He's a lawyer . . . a widower."

"How old?" asked Este.

"Forty-eight," answered Margaret.

"But he's younger than you," said Marti, almost as a protest.

"Christ! At my age, name twelve men who aren't. Besides," added Margaret, "he's toilet trained."

"Are you thinking of marrying him?" asked Marti, still somewhat dazed.

"God, Carolyn, but what decade is your daughter living in? I tell her I'm seeing some man and she equates that with marriage. How quaint! No, my dear, I'm not thinking of marrying Alden Richards or anyone else. Maybe ten or twenty years ago, but not today. I prefer my freedom. I also prefer seeing a man when I choose to and not when I must. I also like the anticipation of dating, of wondering what I should wear and whether he will like it enough to want me to take it off. It's all very exciting and romantic. Something more binding, however, does not interest me. It would your mother though. Right, Carolyn? In fact, just last week, on the church bulletin board, she hung a sign reading, 'Available: One Slightly Used Virgin. All reasonable and *legitimate* offers will be considered.' "

Carolyn laughed. "I attend one church function and look at the abuse I take. Will religious persecution never end?"

When Carolyn saw that Marti was staring at her with considerable surprise, she shrugged as she said, "Well, a person does have to get out once in a while. As you'll see after the baby comes, Este. You may think now that you'd like nothing better than to take off the rest of your life, but take it from one who nearly did, you'll change your mind. You need things to do, people to be with."

"Mom, would you marry again?" asked Marti.

"I honestly don't know," said Carolyn thoughtfully. "I don't see how you can know until someone comes along who interests you . . ."

"And proposes," added Margaret interrupting. "That's very important. Without the proposal . . ."

"Oh, shut up, Margaret," said Carolyn. "As I was saying, I don't think living alone is all that wonderful. Nor do I think living for oneself alone is too terrific. I like doing for another. But what about you, Marti. Would you marry again?"

6 7

The question startled Marti. "I haven't thought about it," she stammered.

"For crissake, Lynnie, ask her something more pertinent. Like: when was the last time she got laid," said Margaret.

"Probably for all your talk, the same as you: sometime during the War of 1812," snapped Marti angrily.

"Oh, come now, Marti. Don't get all huffy on me," said Margaret as she left her chair to sit on the floor by Marti. "And Carolyn, just because my back is to you, doesn't mean you can pig out on that candy! What I was trying to say, Marti, clumsily I'm sure, is that a woman with your capabilities should be acting on them in some way, not hiding from life."

"It's what I was alluding to before," said Carolyn as she sat herself down on an edge of the sofa near Marti. "When I was convalescing here I thought I enjoyed lying around, being treated like a queen. I thought it was the life. For some, I suppose, it would be. Well, it may be a life but it isn't living. Your aunt of the big mouth here made me realize I would rather die doing something than live doing nothing."

"But I *am* doing something," protested Marti, near tears. "I'm being a mother to my children. And wait! Hear me out," she said as she saw the arguments about to come at her. "Yes, there were times in the past when I took care of them because it was the safe thing to do. I was hiding. But not now. I'm here today because I love it. Truly love it."

Marti's face darkened as she reached back into the years to make her point. "When my children were babies, I was away at the studio all day. I was busy, active, involved. When I think back, I cannot remember which of my children took the first step or spoke the first word. I can't even tell you what their first words were. Nor do I remember their first day of school or my daughter's first party dress. Do you know what that feels like?"

From the expressions on her mother's and aunt's faces, she knew they did. Her history had been theirs. "I love caring for my children," said Marti softly. "I love caring for others. Mom, taking care of you when you were ill was one of the most wonderful times of my life. I was finally giving back just a small part of all you have given me. And today I felt that. Today, taking care of everybody in my home was wonderful. Sometimes I think if I could do any-thing with my life, have any wish, it would be to have children. Children upon children. Because it all goes by so quickly. One day you have a little girl and the next you have a daughter who is soon to be a woman. If I could just stop the clock—just be a mother forever."

"That's not an unattainable wish," said Margaret as she put her arm about Marti's shoulder.

"Just what are you telling my daughter?" asked Carolyn, too involved with her own reactions to Marti's words to have fully grasped their meaning.

"I'm not telling her anything, Lynnie," said Margaret softly. "It's Marti who is telling us, and I hope she heard it as clearly as we did."

*   *   *

Propped on his elbow, JJ was watching Jessamyn as she slept, thinking how rare it was to see her absolutely still. Whatever doubts JJ had experienced about Jessamyn's ability to assist him had vanished. She compensated for her lack of experience by being a voracious learner, a person who pounced on problems and then wrestled them into submission. Certainly she had done this with him and he had loved it.

As his index finger lazily traced the bridge of Jessamyn's nose and then the curve of her chin, JJ's other hand held the press release Jessamyn had obtained months ago from the White House. Although it was several months old, its words continually affected JJ deeply. Often with shock; always with disgust. It had become a ritual: to read it each morning as though it, and not a good break-fast, a cold shower, would energize his day.

> . . . a program of clemency. . . . Only those who were delinquent with respect to required military service . . . *Draft evaders* will acknowledge their allegiance . . . agreeing with the United States Attorney to perform alternate service . . . 24 months. . . . Upon satisfactory completion . . . a certificate . . . to dismiss the indictment. . . . If the draft evader fails to perform . . . the United States Attorney will be free to resume prosecution of the case. . . . *Military absentees . . . deserters* . . . will be required to

execute a reaffirmation of allegiance and pledge to perform a
period of alternate civilian service . . . 24 months. . . .
Participants . . . will be separated with an undesirable discharge . . . not be eligible for any benefits provided by the
Veterans Administration. . . . Upon certification that . . . work
has been satisfactorily completed . . . the Service will then issue a
special new type of discharge—a Clemency Discharge . . .
substituted for the previously awarded undesirable discharge . . .
the Clemency Discharge shall not bestow entitlement to benefits
administered by the Veterans Administration.

The White House proclamation served to motivate both JJ
and Jessamyn. Early in January, after weeks of preparation, with
JJ's guidelines, Jessamyn had followed one young deserter across
the Canadian border to Spokane, Washington. The boy had been
nervous, fearful that jail awaited despite governmental assurances
that he would be treated fairly. Both he and the government had
been wrong. When Jessamyn's subject reported to the U.S. Attorney, he was advised for reasons unknown that his case had been
dropped twenty months ago. Only someone . . . *everyone* had neglected to tell him. The outrage and grief the young boy had felt
when he realized he had been needlessly living an exiled life had
been captured harrowingly and hauntingly by Jessamyn on film.

Back in Toronto, searching for yet another deserter to follow
through the reentry program, JJ found a rather reluctant subject
living on the fringe of the exile community. Initially the man had
been hostile to the idea of a camera following his return to America, but suddenly one day that hostility inexplicably turned to total
cooperation. Neither JJ nor Jessamyn thought to question why. In
late January, with camera and crew, Jessamyn witnessed the man
receiving his undesirable-discharge papers at Fort Benjamin Harrison. She was prepared for that but totally unprepared for what
followed. Through his lawyers, the former exile had found a loop-
hole in the program. He was refusing to perform the alternate
service. He was a free man, suffering nothing more than "bad
discharge papers," which seemingly did not bother him. For the
camera, and for the rest of his life, the man gave a big smile and
then a big finger to the clemency discharge and the United States.

Jessamyn had returned to Toronto annoyed and more than

7 0

somewhat surprised that JJ had been pleased with what she had on film. Patience was not Jessamyn's long suit and she had no concept of something JJ had learned years ago—that it often took months of striving to obtain that one success. Yet she did comprehend that she had captured an interesting background for the man or men they hoped to bring to the foreground. But when? That was the question neither Jessamyn nor JJ could answer. For weeks they had visited Grossman's hoping to hear of someone who was partaking of Ford's program. There seemed to be very few, as the exile community was united in its boycott. Words like *unjust* and *criminal* were constantly hurled at the plan.

In the past month, JJ estimated he and Jessamyn had talked with hundreds of men, all of whom were firm in their resolve not to add further complications to their already complicated lives by putting their faces on camera. Both he and Jessamyn heaved a sigh of relief when Ford extended the end of the program from January 31 to March 31. Jessamyn redoubled her efforts, deciding there had to be among the three thousand draft evaders and fifteen hundred deserters the government estimated to be living in Canada, one—just one—and with a little bit of God's help, two men who would be willing to "serve," as Jessamyn put it. She was spending the bulk of her days and much of her nights finding these men.

Among the exiles, she was called Hurricane Jessie, and, for JJ, being with Jessamyn was akin to being caught in the eye of a storm. To date, she showed no signs of blowing herself out. JJ relished that. Not since his student days at Columbia had he felt so involved and vital. He wasn't just walking through his life any longer but seemed to be living it at a breakneck pace. Jessamyn's energy bred energy. Her obvious excitement generated his own. Both were wildly and totally in love, he with her and she with the job at hand.

Gently, JJ smoothed Jessamyn's face with the hands that so excited her. Bending, he kissed her, whispering her name as his lips traveled her face. She responded by turning toward him, reaching for him instinctively as she did. Sex had not been on his mind when awakening Jessamyn but soon, as her hand massaged his groin, it was all JJ could feel and smell. She was already moaning as she arched toward him, not needing the foreplay she usually enjoyed for protracted periods of time. Within seconds they were molded together, blending into one person. The rhythm was slow and sensuous until Jessamyn took over. It then became chaotic, frantic in her urgency. She was atop him and then under, alongside and then over. She was aggressive and demanding. Only after both had achieved a release from the spectacular tension that had been created did Jessamyn open her eyes. Beyond JJ's shoulder, she saw the clock.

"Oh, my God, it's eleven A.M.," she shrieked as she jumped from the bed and ran toward the kitchen. "They'll be here for lunch in an hour."

As he lay back in bed, JJ watched as Jessamyn, working at full speed, chopped onion, garlic, green pepppers, carrots, and stringbeans. Along with four chicken breasts, she threw the vegetables into a pot of boiling water. After she pulled three or four condiments from the kitchen cabinet, she said as she sprinkled them into the pot, "In ten minutes, stir in two cups of rice. And lower the light to a simmer," she added as she ran toward the bathroom. The door slammed. Then it opened. "And don't just lie there, you chauvinist. Wash and spin the salad." The door slammed and he heard the shower as she opened the faucets full blast.

Slipping into his jeans, JJ, barefoot, walked lazily to the kitchen where he took the salad fixings from the vegetable bin. On the second shelf of the refrigerator, the cake with its HAPPY BIRTHDAY NELSON written in chocolate perched invitingly. It seemed right to JJ that Nelson should share George Washington's birthday. Nelson, too, could not tell a lie. It was part of his charm and his undoing. He had come to Toronto because he could not lie, could not pretend an acceptance of American policy in Vietnam when he was so opposed to his government's actions. He had been vocal about his dislike and his distrust of "American imperialism," words guaranteed to shake the foundation of his school and the small-town mentality of Middleville, Michigan. Soon, according to school officials, he was a known "rabble-rouser." Because of his political leanings, they made life difficult for him but they could not expel him, although they would have had he not dropped out after a near physical confrontation with his political science teacher.

Ironically, Nelson's low lottery number for the draft did what the town could not: drafted him for Vietnam. Middleville looked upon Nelson's "Greetings" as sweet revenge, but that revenge, much to its frustration, was never realized when Nelson deserted both the town and what it considered to be his duty.

"Did you put the rice in?" yelled Jessamyn from the bathroom."

"Yes," replied JJ as he quickly measured two cups of brown rice into the bubbling waters of the pot. "Anything else?"

"For chrissake, yes! Make the bed. It looks like London after the blitz. And set the table. Is the wine iced?"

JJ smiled at the thought of Jessamyn orchestrating a birthday party even as she scrubbed down. Entertaining was not one of her specialties. Nor was cooking. But certainly eating was. The only person JJ knew who rivaled Jessamyn's enormous appetite was Nelson. He attributed it to the fact they were both twenty-two and still growing.

JJ had never known as he had never asked what the extent of Nelson and Jessamyn's relationship had been prior to his and Jess's meetings. He doubted that it had been anything other than platonic but he nonetheless had the feeling that Nelson did not trust Jessamyn. Suddenly, JJ realized how Noel Coward-ish the afternoon was going to be. He and Jess and Nelson and Kay. An odd foursome of twosomes, past and present. Not that he felt awkward with Kay. Actually, he felt more comfortable with her now than ever. Each had seemingly realized there was genuine feeling between them that transcended their aborted affair.

Although they had met at Grossman's several times, Jess had never asked about Kay. She seemed to accept that Kay was more Nelson's friend than his. Whatever Kay felt about Jessamyn remained a mystery as Kay was not one to wear her feelings on her sleeve or her face.

Kay was a remarkable woman, thought JJ as he stripped off his jeans, preparing to shower now that he could hear Jessamyn was through with hers. She had been a friend to most in the exile community, but particularly to Nelson. Once the Canadian government had issued a formal amnesty to illegal immigrants, she had secured a job for Nelson at the kennels where she now worked part time as a fledgling veterinarian. For Nelson it was not much of a job, cleaning cages and feeding the puppies, but it was steady, paid minimum wage, and he was treated like a person. A radical change from life as an illegal entry living underground.

As JJ pushed his way past Jessamyn into the gray-and-black tiled bathroom, he remembered Nelson as he was when he first entered Canada and his life four years ago. He was a lanky, skinny kid of all arms and legs. His large black eyes dominated a face of cheekbones and chin. His hair then had been a black mess of unruliness. He was just eighteen, alone and frightened. He had arrived in Toronto with the clothes on his back and forty-five dollars. He had no other financial resources, no diplomas, no letters of reference, and no job awaiting him. Thus, he had been unable to secure a Landed Immigration Card which meant that if he remained in Canada he would be an illegal immigrant, wanted by the Canadian government for deportation and by the U.S. government for prosecution. He had been sleeping in hallways, hustling dimes and quarters from strangers, when he met Kay at Swedish Hall, the exile halfway house. Until Kay had sent Nelson to him, JJ had no idea how impoverished and terrifying life was underground.

Nelson had been a frightened child then, thought JJ as he washed his hair. Happily, there had been Kay and then him to help Nelson through his fears. Suddenly, JJ began to smile. He was happy, happy that they would all be together this day to celebrate Nelson's birthday.

Nelson sat quietly before the cake, the candles illuminating his face. He could not, as he was being urged, blow them out. Nor could he make a speech. He could only cry and, as he did, first Kay, then JJ came to his side. They waited, the expressions on their faces speaking of their concern, until Nelson could talk.

"I'm going back," he said slowly. JJ stared uncomprehendingly. "I'm going home. I've thought it through and I must go. There's no life for me here. I can't clean out cages forever. If I don't go back, I'll have nothing, be nothing, the rest of my life. I want to be somebody, not a nobody. I want to finish school . . . have a future. I don't want to be wallowing in shit or taking shit or shoveling shit the rest of my life."

As Nelson began to cry again, JJ was sitting on his haunches by his side. "Nels, it's just a matter of a little more time. If we all hold out, don't give in to Ford's program, the government soon has to give us unconditional amnesty. It's what is deserved. Nels, I'm telling you. It's just around the corner."

"I can't wait, JJ, I just can't live like this anymore. I need something and someone of my own. I can't be anything here. I need a future."

"Nelson, you won't have one there," said JJ. "Not this way. Not yet. No employer will hire you. It will be too tough on you," pleaded JJ.

"How much tougher can it be than it is here?" asked Nelson as he watched the candles melt into the cake.

Through it all, as JJ was pleading with Nelson and Kay was fighting her own emotions, Jessamyn stood to the side, observing it as one would if one was holding a camera. In her mind, Jessamyn was already at work on the documentary she now viewed as much hers as JJ's. It would follow this twenty-two-year-old boy to the country he had fled as a child. She and her camera would be there as the boy made his peace with his country and his family. Together, they would observe President Gerald Ford's clemency program in action. It would be Nelson's experience, but the world would see it through Jessamyn Giroux's eyes.

4

Aᴍ ɪ ɢᴏɪɴɢ ᴛᴏ ᴅɪᴇ?"

"Of course you're not," replied Marti, not knowing whether she was lying to the child. "You're going to get well."

"How?"

Marti looked at Maria Hernandez. "Do you mean about the operation?" she asked.

The little girl nodded, her mass of black curly hair falling about her face.

"Well, let's learn together," said Marti as she took Maria by the hand to the corner of the playroom where the operating-room equipment and other hospital paraphernalia was kept. From nearby, Aileen Doud, one of the supervisors on the floor, was observing Marti as she first explained the syringe and then the needles to the child whose anxiety was visibly lessening as Marti removed the terror of the unknown.

"And this," said Marti as she held up a piece of green cloth, "is the mask the doctors and nurses wear during the operation."

"Why?" asked the child.

"To prevent infection. They don't want to breathe out or breathe in any germs. They'll also be wearing these gloves for the same reason. And a gown."

"Will I be wearing a gown?"

"Why sure. It's your party, so you should have your own gown," said Marti. "I hope it's pink. You'd look so pretty in pink."

"Marti, will you be here?" asked the child, the fear evident in her voice.

Marti knelt before the child, hugging her to her bosom. "We'll all be here. Your mama, your papa, the nurses, me. Everybody. Just waiting for you."

The child snuggled into Marti's warmth and as she did, Marti had to choke back her fear for the child and her desire to protect the little girl from anything that might harm her. The time before a child's operation was the most difficult for Marti. The staff had told her it would be.

"Maria, do you want to play doctor?" asked Marti, doing as her instructors in the Child Life Program had suggested. "Do you want to take one of the dolls and perform your own operation? I'll help."

Maria Hernandez shook her head. She would not like that at all, she said, but she would like to hear a story.

As Marti settled into one of the chairs in the F-7 playroom of Bellevue where she had been a volunteer on the children's ward the past two months, the other children congregated about her. Her storytelling had become famous. When she told of princesses and princes, it was one of the few times the seventh-floor children's ward was still. For Marti, it was her favorite activity. Her own children had been deprived of her stories as she had been too busy learning the stories of screenwriters who demanded she know their lines perfectly when she walked on the set. As she was about to begin, Marti looked about. She almost laughed. There she was, a real-life Pied Piper.

The past eight weeks had been happy for Marti, although the day-to-day realities of a hospital often upset her. She had come to Bellevue as a volunteer at Margaret's suggestion. Marti had forgotten, if she had ever known, that her great-aunt Augusta, the woman who raised her mother and Margaret, had worked at Bellevue as a volunteer many years ago. Margaret had recalled Augusta had loved it and had even gotten a doctor as a reward for her charitable efforts.

Had Marti wanted a doctor, many were available. The staff knew she was the famous Marti Tiernan who wished to be called either Marti or Ms. Ollson. They also knew she preferred to keep her relationships at the hospital strictly professional. She did not

7 7

encourage closeness except with the children. When the newspapers discovered she was a three-times-a-week volunteer, they besieged the hospital with requests for interviews. All were declined. Marti demanded anonymity and where it was possible, she received it. Although they did not understand and were extremely curious about her, the staff at Bellevue gave her both the instruction she desired and the distance.

Maria Hernandez was sitting on Marti's lap as she asked the children what story they would like to hear. Since it was nearing Easter, the most popular request was for Peter Rabbit. Within minutes, Marti had drawn her listeners into the story, making them part of the barnyard action. Maria was the voice of a duck; another little girl that of a hen. Marti's eyes were beaming. Perhaps as never before she was beautiful. But in a way far different from the days when she reigned as one of Hollywood's beauty queens. If someone had pointed out to Marti that she was once again using her considerable performing talents, she would have been annoyed even as she recognized the truth of the observation. Yes, she was performing, but whereas before she was playing a part, now she was living it. One was reality; the other was not. One gave Oscars and Emmys as prizes; the other gave hugs, smiles, and perhaps best of all tears when she left at the end of a day.

Some of the children die, she had been warned when she began. Keep an emotional distance, she had been cautioned. One way or another they all leave, it was explained. Marti wasn't always successful remembering the words of advice, perhaps because she didn't want to. In the past, with her own children, she hadn't always been able to draw as close as she would have liked and they may have needed. Now, although these children were not really hers, for the three hours she was there with them three days a week, she wished to be totally there. Besides, all would be well, Marti determined. Particularly with Maria Hernandez. Yes, she would be operated on the following morning and yes, she would leave the hospital one way or another soon thereafter, but *all would be well*. The child would be fine. After all, Maria Hernandez had promised, all seven years of her, to make fried plantains for Marti. That was one promise Marti refused to have broken.

Nelson was leaning against the huge elm tree whose leaves would once again be shading the two-story house on Ashford Street in a matter of weeks. The walkway leading to the house was short but to Nelson, after four years of silence, the distance seemed incredibly far to travel. It was Sunday afternoon which meant if his parents were true to form, they would be at dinner following the morning's church services. Afterward, they would walk the two blocks over to Spruce where they would have their dessert with his uncle and aunt.

As he stared at the new aluminum siding and the porch that had been built during his absence, Nelson wondered what else might be new in the house. Would his father still be the same? A thought came into Nelson's head making it ache. Was his father still in this house? Was he alive? There were other thoughts, as Nelson would later realize, that should have entered his mind before he attempted to enter their house and only later, through Jessamyn's off-camera proddings, would he understand why they had not.

Jessamyn had been prodding ever since they had left Toronto on the last possible day of Ford's clemency program. At the Canadian border, when he had been terrified to present himself to the officials, it had been Jessamyn who had assured him not one of the eighty-five hundred returning exiles had been arrested. Of course she had been proven right. His name had been checked off one list and placed on another. It had been that simple. In the rented van, they had driven into Michigan and through Flint. The city was as Nelson remembered: ugly. Despite its new high-rises, the general feeling was one of flatness caused by the long, squat, huge factories all bearing signs of belonging to the automotive industry. His father worked in such a plant and had hoped his son would follow in his footsteps. His father had always hoped he would in all things follow in his footsteps, which was why their clash had been so great. Nelson had been relieved when the van had sped north and on to Middleville, a twenty-minute drive away.

Nothing there had looked different. It was still as the Chamber of Commerce advertised: "Your average little city." Average indeed, if your Main Street was not only your main street but the one and only thoroughfare that boasted four stop lights over the length of it. Nelson was relieved to see Franklin's Pharmacy, Wheaton's Hardware, and Mitchell's Bakery all where he had left them. He was not surprised that the town still did not have a movie house, or a bowling alley. Not even a Burger King.

His anxiety had heightened when they had passed Middleville Central, the junior high school he had attended, and Clyde Frasker High, named for one of the town's leading figures of three decades back. It was a small town of small mind, and just how small leapt back into Nelson's consciousness when he thought of his high-school days and his bitter fights as one of the town's few antiwar protesters. Most of his graduating class—had he graduated—had done the expected thing: married or gone on to the University of Michigan, although many joined their fathers in the automotive industry. Most who were called to serve in Vietnam did so without protest, because no one protested in Middleville. Yet, as Nelson explained to Jessamyn, they were basically good people. They were just dangerous because they prefered blind acceptance to thought.

He had written his parents four times over the past four years, making sure his letter was mailed from a different Canadian province each time. Without a return address, he had heard nothing from his family. He had wanted to phone them once they had crossed into the U.S., but Jessamyn had wanted the surprise element for the camera. He had agreed. Certainly Norman Naismith, his father, would be surprised. They had battled bitterly about Vietnam. His father stood "squarely behind" Lyndon Johnson and then Richard Nixon. He made it clear he not only preferred but trusted his presidents' views to his son's. In fact, his son was the cause of increasing embarrassment at the Fisher Body Plant where he was a foreman. There, his contemporaries all held similar Vietnam views regardless of party affiliation. To them, Nelson was either a hippie, a commie, or a coward. Nelson had not been conciliating. He had attacked his father's and his father's coworkers' views constantly. The arguments in the house had been bitter.

"Nelson, it's time. Go on in," urged Jessamyn from the van parked at the curb. When she saw him hesitate, Jessamyn left the van and took Nelson by the arm, leading him up the walkway. In a moment, she would have what she wanted: the drama of parents facing a child they had not seen in years. That moment, that reunion, would be captured on film forever. It was drama. It was life. Or at least it was life as seen by Jessamyn. Jessamyn was high on life these days. Just before leaving Toronto, she had learned that Ron Carewski, the deserter she had followed from Winnipeg, where he had leased his house and abandoned his one-man trucking business in February, had been unable to find alternate-service work in Wichita, his hometown. Once there, he, and the camera crew she had left behind, discovered no one would offer him a job because of the action he had taken during the war. He had been forced to sell his truck to support his wife and family. The last she had heard, the crew was following him back to Winnipeg, despite the fact he had neither a house nor a job waiting there. It was the stuff of which good documentaries were made.

"Nelson, now!" said Jessamyn as she left him just before the steps leading up to the door. A cold drizzle was falling, typical for April in Middleville. Shivering, Nelson climbed the stairs and stood by the door. He was surprised when he rang the bell to hear chimes rather than the nondescript ring he had been used to for so many years. More changes.

The woman who opened the door wearing a plain but pretty blue dress with a print apron over it was no longer gray-haired as he remembered but honey blond. She stared at him through glasses she hadn't worn before. Confusion was etched on her face. She started toward him but was stopped when a voice from behind said, "Who is it, Delia?"

His father appeared alongside his mother. The first look that came over his face soon passed and was replaced by rage.

"You can't come into this house," he said, his voice choked by emotions.

"But, Norman," his mother protested.

"You are gone and dead by your choice. You can't bring further shame to this house."

The door slammed. From behind it he could hear his mother pleading. The door was flung open. His mother stood there torn between the boy before her and the man behind. Quickly, she flung her arms about Nelson's neck. She hugged him to her, kissed his face, and then turned back inside the house where his father stood. "Please. Don't come back again," he said softly. "You're not welcome.".

Quickly, Jessamyn ran from the van with the cameramen, calling for a closeup of Nelson. Closer. Closer still. She was not asking Nelson to speak. She didn't have to. His face was saying it all.

They were driving toward a motel where they would spend the night before meeting with the U.S. Attorney the following day in Flint when they stopped at Robbie's. The restaurant was one of the few open in Middleville on a Sunday afternoon. At the counter, two men were drinking coffee and sharing the remains of a piece of apple crumb cake. At one table, a family of five was finishing the Sunday special—roast chicken with dressing, cranberry sauce, mashed potatos, and peas—while at another table, a family of four was ordering it.

"Hi there, folks, what can I get you today?"

The voice was cheerful and it belonged to a round and rosy-red-faced man of fifty to sixty. "The food ain't much but it won't kill you, and besides, it's all there is in Middleville on a Sunday unless you want to come home with me for the wife's cooking and that *could* kill you." The man laughed, pleased with himself and, if the twinkle in his eye was any barometer, with his life as well. He turned first to Jessamyn. "So what's it to be, little lady? The special is just that." When Jessamyn had ordered the chicken dinner, the man turned himself and his order pad to Nelson. First he stared; then he spoke. "You're Norman Naismith's kid, aren't you?"

Nelson nodded. "How are you, Mr. Roberts?" When the man didn't answer, Nelson said, "I guess I'll also have the special."

"I just remembered. We're fresh out. Maybe down the road a piece you'll have better luck," said "Robbie."

""We'll just have some coffee then," said Jessamyn sweetly. "And some of that apple crumb cake," she added, pointing to the two men at the counter.

"Well it seems we're fresh out of that too. In fact, since you don't seem to get my point, where your kind is concerned, we're

out of everything. Now why don't you just git and take that commie with you," said "Robbie" as he walked by the door and held it
open for them. The two men who had been drinking their coffee
at the counter were now standing by his side ready to act as an
escort service.

There was a coffee shop next to the motel where they were
staying and as they were finishing their burgers, one of the motel's
gas station attendants entered and came directly to their table.

"Goddamn, if it isn't you after all, Nelson! When the hell did
you get in? Shit!" said the man, about Nelson's age, as he pulled
up a chair from another table to join them.

"Hey, Dan, how goes it?" said Nelson cautiously.

"Good. Real good, Nels. Damn, but it's good to see you. You
look good. Still skinny as hell, but it's better than the beer belly
I'm getting. It's the good life. Hey, you don't know I'm married,
do you. Shit, how could you? You've been away so long. So how's
it going?"

Nelson stared into the friendly face a foot or so away from his
own. "I've been in Canada."

"Yeah, well, I know. Nice place Canada. The wife and I are
thinking of going to Montreal next summer for the Olympics.
What brings you back, Nelson, and shit, man, where are your
manners? For that matter, where are mine? I'm Dan Mitchell,
ma'am. Your friend and I used to be quite the cutups in this here
town. In fact, most folks predicted we'd wind up no good."

Mitchell laughed as he shook Jessamyn's hand after Nelson
made the belated introductions. "So how *is* life treating you? Jesus,
Nels, I just never figured you to come back home. I don't think
nobody in this town ever thought we'd see you again."

"We just gave your Uncle Robbie a jolt," said Nelson. "My
dad, too."

"Oh, shit! Did you all stop at Uncle Rob's place? Man, I wish
I'd seen that. The old bugger means well, but he can be a real
horse's ass with that my-country-right-or-wrong shit. Well, it's all
in the past now."

"What is, Dan?" asked Nelson.

"Oh, you know, the gooks. Nam. Done and over with. I did my time but now I'm home. Shit. If I had had any brains I would have gone on to college and avoided the whole damn thing, but you know how dumb I always was. Well, as I said. I did my time and since everyone else has forgotten it, why not me."

"Your Uncle Rob hasn't forgotten it. Neither has my father," said Nelson.

"You're wrong, Nels. They have. But I guess you remind them of something they want to forget. And that's bad. Your father took a lot of shit down at the plant. He was as hard-headed as his hat. I don't think you heard that in 'seventy-one a lot of the younger guys there actually came out against the war. So did the United Auto Workers. It was damn tough for men like your father. Everybody was fighting everybody. And for what? That's what folks around here still can't figure out. Like my dad. He still can't get used to the fact that this big bad-ass country of ours didn't win the goddamn war. He can't understand why we just didn't go in and wipe out the bastards with our heavy artillery. Men like my father, your father, they just can't handle America not coming out on top as it always did. It's a shock to their system, man. And they got to blame it on someone. So it's the hippies, the commies, and the fags. One of them is you. It was also me until I cut my hair and did my time in Nam."

"How was it, Dan?" asked Nelson

"Well, shit, Nelson. Let's say it's a helluva lot prettier in Canada, *I am sure!* But I'm here with all my parts in place which is better than some and the same as most. Hey, I didn't mention. I got a little kid. A girl. Sue-Ann Diane. It rhymes. The wife's idea. She's a real killer. Nine months now. So hey, Nelson, if you're hanging around, come visit. We're on Spruce. We're in the book. Maybe we can grab a beer or two during the week. You staying at your folks?" asked Mitchell as he rose.

"No," said Nelson. "I'm not sure where I'm staying. I'll have a better idea once I see the U.S. Attorney tomorrow."

"Shit, Nelson. There's a helluvan easier way to fix a parking ticket." Mitchell laughed. "Well, I gotta be getting back to the pumps. Jessamyn, you come visit with Nelson. It's been nice meeting you. See you around."

"Yeah, Dan. I'll see you around," said Nelson as he drained the remains of his cold coffee.

*   *   *

By running the unedited film again and again, it was as if neither Nelson nor Jessamyn had ever left. Although only Nelson was seen on the footage, JJ could feel Jessamyn's presence. She was everywhere, achieving effects and emotions that would have eluded him. He still did not know how Jessamyn had convinced the U.S. Attorney in Flint to allow the camera into his office. When he had asked, she had smiled enigmatically and replied, "I walk a fence well." She did not describe how she had convinced Brett Wilkins that *her* documentary was the average American view of the draft resister and Ford's clemency program.

After having spent the past five days in Toronto, Jessamyn had returned that morning to Michigan to begin work as Nelson did. The house felt empty of the excitement her energy created. When they weren't discussing the shape their work was taking, they were taking of each other in bed. In both cases, Jessamyn was tireless.

Kay had come to the house when they had spoken with Nelson at the arranged time. He had been distant, as removed from himself and his emotions as he had been from them. Kay had been distressed by the phone call. She was even more distressed by the film footage when they had later viewed it together. She had left almost immediately upon its conclusion and, unless he had imagined it, JJ was certain Kay had looked at Jessamyn in a way he had not seen before and which he could not define. If Jessamyn had noticed, she made no mention.

Now, as JJ sat in his studio, preparing to view the film once again—this time to suggest where edits might be made and voice-overs added—he took a tight grip on the coffee mug in his hand and on his emotions.

A sign that read CHURCH STREET came into focus first. It was followed by a long shot of a two-story, yellow-brick edifice that proved in closeup to be Flint's Federal Building. And then there was Nelson, walking up the steps of the building and entering a white-tiled main foyer. Turning right down a long hallway, he

passes the marshal's office before entering through a door marked
U.S. ATTORNEY.

Two secretaries are seated behind a long black countertop.
Behind them, a huge window overlooks a four-story parking structure. One of the secretaries speaks with Nelson and then ushers
him into U.S. Attorney Brett Wilkins's inner office, where the
walls and carpet are of complementing blues. Wilkins is sitting
behind his large wooden desk. Behind him, the walls are lined with
lawbooks. Wilkins is a well-tailored man whose sideburns are as
short and to the point as he proves to be. Nelson's alternate service, he explains, has been arranged by Flint's Director of Selective Service and is to be at the Veterans Administration Hospital
in Ann Arbor. Nelson's face shows surprise. "But the drive is anywhere from seventy to ninety minutes, depending on traffic," he
says in mild protest, "whereas Hurley Medical Center and St. Joseph's are right here in town. Wouldn't they be easier?"

Wilkins's face remains impassive as he removes his glasses and
what till then had been a benign demeanor. Looking more at the
camera than at Nelson, he says: "You miss the point, Naismith.
No one is interested in making it easier. In fact, there are many
who believe you are having it made easy enough. Do I make myself
clear?"

Nelson stares at the man but doesn't respond. Wilkins picks
up Nelson's file, writes in it, and then says, "Good! We understand
each other. The hospital expects you a week from today. I suggest
you be on time. First impressions are lasting ones, and you
wouldn't want to get off on the wrong foot, would you, Naismith?"

The camera focuses on Nelson. He doesn't speak. Again, he
doesn't have to. Again, his face says it all.

JJ's heart was pounding and his hands were cold as the film
concluded. Methodically, he picked up his coffee mug and hurled
it against the darkened screen.

*   *   *

Skirts, blouses, and dresses were piling on the floor as Reese
raced from one end of her closet to the other, her hands fluttering
like the wings of birds as they landed on branches only to fly off
when frightened by a noise. Reese was frightened by many noises
but mainly by the beating of her pounding heart.

Too long. Too short. Too tight. Too drab. Discards. Rejects. The pile grew. Although there had been weeks to prepare, Reese had let the days slip by and past as she had hoped would the cocktail party celebrating the publication of Thomas's book in paperback. So many times during the past week she had wanted to tell Thomas to go without her. But she had lost the courage. What would people think that they weren't already thinking? How could the major's wife *not* attend his publication party unless she was . . . well, "sick" again.

She was sick again all right. Sick of the book and sick of the goddamn TV people who had cluttered up her home and her life for so many months. Never any peace. Never any privacy. Never any chance to hide where she couldn't be seen. And now it would be the worst of all. Now, this night, to coincide with the publication of the paperback—because one would sell the other—*The Thomas Ollson Story* was a "Movie of the Week."

Beige. Somewhere Reese had heard beige was slenderizing. Or was that black? No matter. She couldn't wear black. It made her skin look pasty. Where was that beige silk dress? It even had a little jacket that if she left unbuttoned cut her weight. Pummeling her way to the back of the closet, Reese found the dress on a hanger. She was about to slip into it and out of her bleak mood when she remembered why the dress had been relegated to the closet's recesses. Liquor stains. She had spilled her drink, or someone's drink, on it.

Kristan . . . she needed Kristan. Something cold for her head. And a Librium. Thank God her father had just sent her a new bottle. When had she taken the last? Lunchtime. Nothing since. The other pills? Aspirin . . . for her headache. She was certain of that . . . she thought. Kristan? Would you bring me my nerve medicine, Reese called out calmly. As she again began pushing clothes frantically back and forth in her closet, Reese felt the sweat begin to drip down her neck and under her arms. Kristan, please, dear, hurry.

The gray shantung! Of course. It's clean. It had to be. It was still in its plastic bag from the cleaners.

The zipper was broken. Either that or her fingers were. The damn thing wouldn't budge. Kristan, would you help me? Make it move, Kristan. You must make it move.

Thank God, the Librium was where she had left it—in a rolled-up set of pantyhose. And thank God that finally her vodka on the rocks was sitting on her dressing table. Better to drink it now when Thomas was still taking his bath. Once he was dressed, she would explain how she had tried but how there was simply no way she could attend this press party. And she *had* tried. Forever trying. All winter long trying to answer the writers' questions, trying to explain to the actress who was playing her how she had felt. They had wanted something from her, but she had the curious feeling that whatever she gave hadn't been good enough.

But I tried, Thomas. For your sake, I tried. But I have nothing to wear tonight to a party at the Beverly Wilshire Hotel. And please don't say that I planned it. Really, I didn't. I was so sure of the beige silk or at the very least, the gray shantung.

You go, Thomas, Reese said calmly to herself. It is, after all, your book and your life. Even *TV Guide* called your movie "a celebration of one man's courage in war and peace." She didn't have courage, which is probably why the magazine hadn't said a thing about her. Probably they were laughing at her. And why not? She was laughable. And pitiful. She knew that. Why kid herself? Why were they kidding her? She hated them. All of them. She wasn't courageous or a good little soldier or much of a mother and certainly less of a wife.

Kristan? The cold compress for my head, where is it, dear? The Librium felt stuck just below her throat. Happily, her vodka glass had again been filled. She drained it, grateful for the service that saw to her every need. Better! Much better. Back to the closet!

Again Reese rummaged about, throwing discards on the floor or into the bedroom. A pants suit. Did anyone wear pants suits anymore?

She remembered. White. Somewhere in the closet was a perfectly clean, perfectly beautiful white dress. She had been saving it. But why? Dimly she remembered its cut, its ruffles and lace, the mother of pearl about its neck and sleeves. It had been shortened. It was now a perfect cocktail length. Kristan, do you remember where I put the white dress?

It was hot in the closet. Terribly hot. When Reese realized she could no longer hear Thomas bathing in the bathroom, she panicked, growing even hotter. Thomas was almost ready and still she had nothing to wear.

Kristan, what should I do? *Kristan?*

The realization that Kristan was not at home and hadn't been since leaving early that afternoon to babysit for the Coveys hit Reese just as the vodka and the Librium did. As the room rushed to envelope her, Reese reached into the closet to hold on to anything that would support her. When Thomas later found her, she was curled up in the corner of the closet weeping as she clutched the white dress she had been looking for. It was the one she had been saving for Kristan, the one she hoped her daughter would wear with as much pride on her wedding day as she had on her own.

*   *   *

Although he had reluctantly left his own party in Los Angeles, Thomas was now defying the highway patrol and death as he more than exceeded the speed limit on the San Diego freeway. Within minutes, he would be nearing Rancho Santa Fe. Within minutes, he would be nearing a life that had to be resumed. Within minutes, he would be confronted by the situation that was prompting him to push the Mercedes to eighty miles per hour. As his hands gripped the wheel, his fingers as tight as the set of his face, Thomas fought the urge to slow the car. Home was waiting. When he had left it hours ago, he had left a wife, sprawled on a bed, sobbing convulsively, as one of their children administered to her. Had there been a choice—and in Thomas's mind there had not—he would have remained with Reese, but how does an author miss his own publication party?

The evening had been a series of explanations; first his, then theirs. To those who expressed surprise that he had come alone, he explained that Reese had the flu, probably the twenty-four-hour variety. Cramps, nausea, a slight fever. Everyone had clucked sympathetically. Too much so. Their suspicions lodged in their eyes. Then it had been their turn to explain. Yes, the press turnout was light, but he had to remember that he had seen most of the major columnists when the hardcover had been published. He knew they were withholding the truth, that press interest in him had waned with the lack of national interest in anything to do with Vietnam. He felt that daily in the job interviews that led nowhere. He would always be seen, but, as he sat at one end of the desk while his prospective employer sat at the other, he was seldom heard. They were doing him a courtesy but in essence his war record was an embarrassment to them. That was why he had given so much of his time to the making of the film. He had hoped it would not only awaken Americans but potential employers for Vietnam veterans.

Despite the poor press turnout, Thomas had enjoyed the evening. His editor had once again made playful advances and he, again, had dodged them, explaining he was a married man. Or, as she embellished, a married man who was really a married man. Thomas could not remember when he first realized he was not missing Reese. He was more relaxed without her, easier with himself and others when he didn't have to worry about where Reese was and how much she was drinking. That he felt safe and comfortable without Reese was disturbing, as Thomas had married Reese because she was the first person with whom he had felt safe and comfortable. But no more. Now, she added to his anxiety. When he awoke from his nightmares, he had still another nightmare to deal with.

As Thomas turned onto Las Planideras, he saw the house was aglow upstairs and down, an indication that something was even more wrong than when he left. As soon as he parked, the front door opened and Kristan came running toward him. At the same time, Thomas heard a car screech to a stop near him. The wail of a siren was growing louder as it grew closer. As Kristan talked, Dr. Dawson, his satchel in hand, pushed by him and ran up the stairs toward the master bedroom. The siren was atop them now, affixed to the ambulance that parked before his house. Suddenly it seemed as if all of Las Planideras was aglow. Windows and doors were opened. Concerned faces appeared as Thomas and Kristan disappeared into the house where Kristan had awakened to find Reese on the floor by her bed, an empty bottle of Librium next to the empty bottle of vodka on her nightstand, and the TV tuned to the channel that had just shown *The Thomas Ollson Story*.

"Run it again," said JJ, his voice tight from the control he was exerting over his emotions.

Although her thoughts sought escape, Kay sat immobilized as Jessamyn rewound the tape machine.

Jessamyn stood behind the machine and her work, proud of the effect she had achieved. It was pictorial journalism at its best. She had thought so then; she knew it now.

Her "then" came up on the screen in the form of a shabby small room which the subject is saying is his. The room is located in a boardinghouse on State Street, the thoroughfare that cuts through the University of Michigan campus. For his bed and bureau, the subject says he pays forty dollars a month.

The subject looks tired. His face is drawn and the fire that used to blaze in his eyes is extinguished. Yet, he speaks positively about his living arrangements. Ann Arbor, he says, is a pleasant town, and living near the university makes him feel a part of its life even though he is not. He frequents such student hangouts as the Fleetwood Diner and Mr. Flood's but he has not made friends. He explains that the students seem of a different world. Their interests are not his. "The women's movement is where it's at and Vietnam is long over. And since it was a drag, why drag up old issues?" Still, he repeats, he likes living near the campus, likes walking among its tan- and red-brick buildings with their many towers and parapets. Someday he would like to attend college here, he says, although he sees no hope of this in the near future. Not with what he is being paid at the V.A. hospital. No, he tells his off-camera interrogator, he receives no help from anyone, although his mother did visit. She brought him homemade bread and preserves. She promised to visit again but asked that he never phone the house. He has complied with her wishes.

Yes, he had tried to connect with his former friends. He bummed a ride into Middleville a few weeks ago and sat around the local bar. The reaction was mixed. Some of the guys were glad to see him. But they didn't want to talk about the past—not theirs or his. They acted as if nothing had changed. Others ignored him totally, their attitudes reflected in their turned backs. Yes, the experience had bothered him, he admits. Which is why he didn't go again. It was obvious he reminded them of something they wanted to forget—which was strange, as he didn't think anyone would ever want to forget what had gone down. He had said that to Dan Mitchell, who then chug-a-lugged his beer and said he had to get home to Sue-Ann Diane.

The screen goes dark. A second or two later it brightens with Nelson standing on a beautifully landscaped lawn before a nine-story, red-brick building. A sign identifies it as the Veterans Administration Hospital. This, explains the subject, is where he works, where he is doing his alternate service. Since the V.A. will not allow the camera into the hospital, when asked, the subject describes it as "your basic white-walled institution." He works the wards. When asked what kind of work he is doing, the subject stares at the camera and says in a voice devoid of feeling. "I empty bedpans, clean up vomit, shit, too, if someone is incontinent. I also distribute and collect food trays."

How does he feel about his work? his interrogator asks.

The look on the subject's face is one of contempt for the question. "Like the shit I'm carrying," he finally replies.

And how is he treated by the staff and the patients?

"Like the shit I'm carrying."

But he can stand the job, even the attitudes that come down on him, he says, if he keeps his mind on his goal. He will finish this service and then be free to pursue his life.

And what does that mean for you? he is asked.

Finishing high school and then attending college. Maybe pre-law as a major. "If I focus on this," he says, "then the shit doesn't stink so bad."

Again the screen goes blank. When an image appears, it is apparent from the steady downpour of rain that it is another day. Outside the V.A. Hospital, a half dozen people are picketing.

"Excuse me," says the off-camera voice, "but would you explain to our viewers why you are protesting?"

The procession of pickets stop. One of the older men wearing a poppy in his buttonhole approaches the camera and says: "We are protesting an injustice, one being perpetrated with our tax dollars. There is one draft resister and one deserter working in this hospital, which is a disgrace. Particularly in a veterans' hospital. These men shouldn't be given jobs but thrown in jail. They're traitors and it is criminal they are not only receiving pardons but our money as recompense."

"And why are you here," asks the off-camera voice.

A smallish man wearing a poncho and carrying a worn Bible replies: "To show those in power that there are still Americans who are against those who burn our flag, mock our Constitution, and show a disrespect for our country and everything it stands for. I served in World War II. I fought proudly for the red, white, and blue. Me and thousands of others thought it a privilege."

"And you, sir?"

"Korea," replied a heavyset man wearing a worn leather jacket. "Nobody much remembers that war, but I was there with my buddies. We served. We did our duty just as those of us here are doing our duty today. We are fighting for law and order. We are saying no to those who would make their own rules and tear apart this great country of ours. We are also saying no to these two men who are holding jobs that good, honest folks might have if it weren't for them."

The camera next focused on a small woman wearing a plastic raincoat and carrying a tiny umbrella over her simply combed, short, gray-flecked hair. "My son died in Vietnam. He died proudly. I am proud of him. He must not be allowed to have died in vain."

Again the screen darkens. The voice of Nelson is heard before he is seen. He is again sitting in his room in the boardinghouse. He is explaining how the half dozen were joined by others who then picketed the Federal Building. They also brought enormous pressure on the administration of the hospital. They enlisted the local newspaper and an influential radio talk-show personality to do this. "The hospital didn't lose any sleep over their decision to let me go, since they weren't all that thrilled to have me around."

"What now?" asks the off-camera voice.

The boy shrugs. He doesn't know. He has been told by the U.S. Attorney that jobs for resisters and deserters are hard to come by, as the V.A. isn't exactly cooperating with Ford's program even though they've been instructed to do so. The subject is hopeful that Wilkins can "scare up" some kind of work in a mental institution. "Imagine being hopeful over that," he laughs humorlessly.

"And if he does," the subject continues, "he says I can look forward to more harassment. So, it may be I'm better off where no one knows my story."

"How did they know it here?" he is asked.

The boy looks at the camera in disbelief. "I guess a little birdie told them; either one in the wards or in the offices. A little bird with a big beak."

"Are you all right?" the subject is asked.

"Do I have a choice?" the subject asks flippantly. And then the face changes. The boy emerges from beneath the façade of the man. "Sometimes it's tough to take. The loneliness is worst of all. It's colder than hell."

Jessamyn switched on the lights in the studio as soon as the screen went dark again, finding JJ coiled on the edge of his chair, his lower lip reddened from biting it. He was cracking his knuckles as he rolled his head about his shoulders to relieve the tension.

"They haven't learned a goddamn thing," said JJ angrily. "Nothing's changed. First they harass us into leaving the country and then when we return they harass us into leaving it again. And between the two events, they see no connection because they wear the flag as a blindfold. Christ, but the boy is suffering!" said JJ as he leapt from the chair and stood before the screen. "How do we make them understand? How do we effect the change?"

"When do you just give up?" yelled Kay, agitated. "When do you open your eyes and accept reality. Some things never change. Others take time before they do. But you can't understand that. *You* can't change any faster than the people and the system you so despise. If you really care, JJ, tell Nelson to give up and come home. Did you hear me? *Home.* He needs us. He needs *you.* Do you need to watch the tape one more time to see just how badly he needs you? For chrissake, JJ, see Nelson as a person and not as a goddamn subject for a goddamn documentary."

"Just what are you saying, Kay?" asked Jessamyn, annoyed.

"Exactly what you heard, Jessamyn. You're using the boy. Using him!"

"That is unfair and untrue," protested Jessamyn. "I'm a journalist, Kay. I have no room for sentiment in my work. A journalist keeps her emotions *out* and the facts *in* her work."

9 4

"Then get those facts, damn it," Kay yelled. "Get your all-American mother whose son died in Vietnam to explain what her son died for. And when she tells you in her sweet, sincere way that he died for his country, ask her *why*. Make her think. Make them all think, damn it. *That's* journalism."

"I'll be sure to apprise my graduating class of your views when I attend the alumni meeting this year," replied Jessamyn angrily. "And what a pity you weren't at Columbia to instruct us on our craft. I'm sure all of our work would be so much better."

"It certainly would have more heart," snapped Kay.

"I think your involvement eliminates you as a judge of my work," said Jessamyn.

"Why *my* involvement and not JJ's?"

"Because, best I know, JJ wasn't sleeping with Nelson," said Jessamyn angrily.

Kay looked stung, as did JJ. "Don't misunderstand me," continued Jessamyn. "Yours and Nelson's relationship is none of my business unless it affects my work. I have a job to do and damn it I'm doing it! The work is good and neither of you has acknowledged that. I've made it poignant and commercial, something JJ's work previously lacked. And whether you see it or not, it hits all the points. It just doesn't hit you on the head with them—which was my intent. Let me tell you something I did learn at Columbia, Kay. You spoonfeed the public on issues like this. You don't ram truths down their throats or they throw them up rather than digest them. I hope now that my intentions with this documentary are clear. For both of you," added Jessamyn bitterly.

"I wish I had slept with him," said Kay softly. "Maybe then he would have just one more warm memory to help him feel not quite so cold."

"Kay," said JJ, as he sat on his haunches before her, "Nelson's tough. He'll be okay. He knows we're here. Kay, we have to keep on fighting."

"For what?" demanded Kay. "There's a life here, JJ. An entire life. It's yours for the taking. It could've been Nelson's. But always in your mind is the fight."

"Kay, if we stopped, where would we be?" asked JJ softly.

Kay Andersohn picked up her coat. At the door she turned

and said, "Ask yourself that, JJ. The answer just might change your life."

*   *   *

Everything in the house was still except Thomas's mind, which raced as fast as the time did not. He had been awakened by his usual nightmare at four—the jangling metallic sound breaking through his sleep as it and the footsteps came closer and closer—and although the clock now read five-fifteen, it felt to Thomas as if days had passed as his mind moved from one possibility and decision to another. Some seemed viable. But to whom? To him certainly, but he wasn't the problem. The problem lay next to him inert, as dead to the world in sleep as she was when awake. Nothingness in the form of a wife. She ate, she slept, she wet. She even blinked her eyes. Depression, the doctors called it. Thomas didn't give a damn what it was called. He just wanted it to be cured and gone. Although he never showed it to those around him, Thomas was often angry. He was also often depressed. Sensing his distress, the children, other than Kristan, gave him a wide berth. Kristan seemed to understand and was soothing to him when he could no longer soothe the woman who lay like a dead one in his bed. They said she was alive but often he doubted it. They said he should be grateful but often he wasn't. When he wasn't hating her, Thomas was hating himself.

The story the hospital had released to the press coincided with the excuse Thomas had given for Reese's absence the night of the publication party. Thus it was believed. Reese had suffered a severe bout of the flu that necessitated her midnight ride to the hospital. Only the neighbors speculated on Reese's true condition. The neighbors and their children, as Thomas learned when Kelly asked if it were true, as she had heard, that her mother had attempted suicide.

No, it was not true, Thomas had all but barked. A lie. A malicious lie. Kelly had begun to weep under the force of his anger. Karl had simply stared into his plate and continued eating. And it wasn't true, as the hospital social worker, the first to gain Reese's confidence, explained. Reese had simply—"if the word *simply* here is not an oversimplification," taken too many Librium

9 6

with too much alcohol. The TV movie had depressed her, as had her inability to attend the publication party. She is still depressed. And ashamed.

"She's an alcoholic, isn't she?" Thomas had asked, admitting to himself for the first time what he already knew to be true.

"That's for your wife to say and not me," had been the social worker's reply.

But Reese was not saying anything. She had walled herself off from the world and entered it only through television. Her life revolved around game shows and situation comedies. More than before, the children were left to fend for themselves. He and Kristan took turns watching Reese. When she slept, Thomas slept, but even then with half an eye open, as he didn't want her slipping out of the house again, pawning something of value, to buy a bottle at the Rancho Santa Fe Spirits Shop where he had closed their account. Thomas resented being guardian and caretaker. He also resented the guilt created by the need for those roles. But most of all, he hated the chaos in his life and wished there was some easy way to put his house in order.

As he lay watching the first signs of morning illuminate the bedroom, Thomas heard Karl's door down the hall open and his son move stealthily down the stairs. In seconds, the front door would open and Karl would be off on his morning run. The boy had emerged as the star of his high school's track team. He was in constant training. He was also constantly absent from the house. At dinner, the one time of day when Reese would join the family, Thomas would often see her staring at Karl. Her eyes spoke of wants and needs that she couldn't or wouldn't express. If Karl saw them, he said and did nothing. Except run.

It was now past six and Thomas could hear Kristan in her bedroom, probably preparing for the final exams that were but weeks away. Not like Kelly, who would wait until the night before each test and then cram her head with facts as she crammed her stomach with Scooter Pies. A student Kelly was not, but she had friends. Lots of friends. Only recently had Thomas realized his own little Scooter Pie, as he affectionately called Kelly, never brought them home.

Thomas was fighting with himself to leave the safety of the

bed and begin the day. Of late, the fight was with the voice that asked: Why? To do what? The book had been written and published, the movie completed and aired, and still nothing had changed. Nor, if one was to believe the poor TV ratings of his life story, was it about to. People didn't care. That he did was obviously not about to produce a job.

"Thomas, I want to talk to you."

It was a voice from the past, and at first Thomas had difficulty identifying it.

"What would you like to talk about, Reese?" Thomas replied casually as if it weren't at all unusual that his wife was finally speaking. And not in a word but in a full sentence; one she had even initiated.

"I've been doing a great deal of thinking. I want us to go back," said Reese as she clutched the comforter to just under her chin. "Not to the way we were, because I know that's not possible. It isn't even good. But we can go back. Thomas, I want to leave here. I want to return to Boston. We were happy there, and we can be happy again."

Thomas remembered. They had been happy in the rambling brownstone on Commonwealth Avenue.

"Do you remember the night we scandalized ourselves by making love by the Charles River?" Reese giggled at the recollection. "I wondered if I had lost all my New England good sense, not to mention reserve, and you kept apologizing as if you had been solely responsible. Oh, Thomas, we were so happy—because it was so spontaneous. My God, but we glowed for days. Thomas, when were we last spontaneous? How long has it been since we glowed?"

Reese was sitting on the bed, her body propped by the headboard. "I had plans then, dreams, an idea of who I was and what I wanted to be. That seems to have gotten lost or at the least misplaced. Which is why I need to go back, to retrace my steps. Thomas, I have a feeling I'm somewhere along the Charles River. I'd like to think you are too."

"Why can't we be here, Reese?" asked Thomas.

"Because here the glare is blinding and everyone knows."

"Knows what, Reese?" asked Thomas cautiously.

"That I drink."

"You could drink in Boston," said Thomas.

"Yes, but I'm hoping I won't," replied Reese.

"It will take more than hope," said Thomas bitterly.

"There are A.A. meetings round the clock. And I already have a sponsor."

When Reese saw the surprised look on Thomas's face, she explained. "A few weeks ago, a psychologist on a talk show said there were no accidental overdoses but that there were real cries for help. I was crying, Thomas, and I heard myself. I don't want to die. Now I know I've made a mess of things, Thomas, and that it's been tough for you and the children, but I feel I deserve a chance. I mean . . . I was there for you all those years. Now I need you to be there for me. I've earned that. I just wish I felt I deserved it," said Reese as tears slipped down her cheeks. "If you choose not to go, if you feel you've had enough, I'll understand."

Thomas took Reese's hand in his. For several minutes the two sat silently before Thomas said: "I'll remain with the kids as it'll take time to sell the house and then pack and ship its contents. Also, it will give Karl the summer to compete in the All-Comers Track Meet in San Diego. He has his heart set on doing that, just as Kelly wants to return to Girl Scout camp. You can take Kristan to Boston. She'll be good for you."

Through her tears, Reese said softly: "No. I want Kristan to spend the summer with Ali and Mark at Marti's. I want her to have fun, to just be a kid. Marti's agreed to take her, by the way."

"But who will look after you?" asked Thomas, concerned.

"Me. It's time I learned how. Me and, as A.A. would say, my Higher Power. It's time we got to know each other better anyway."

When Thomas grew silent, Reese edged herself down and next to him. She took his face in her hands and said, "It may not work, but we owe it to ourselves to try."

From a very far off place, Reese heard Thomas say, "What will I do in Boston?"

"You can begin by forgetting there ever was a war. You've done your duty. Let it be so we can be. Thomas, in Boston, we can blend into the city, be as average and as private as we choose to be. I can be someone other than the wife of the war hero and you . . . Thomas, with your mind and your skills, with all the industry in the Northeast, you can be anything. But what I would most dearly love you to be is the boy I once knew who lived and loved me on Commonwealth Avenue. Do you remember, Thomas?"

He remembered. The girl and the boy. Maybe they would both be waiting in Boston and maybe one, if not both, would have the answer to some of the questions in his life, not the least of which was: What am I going to do next?

*   *   *

As Marti entered the children's ward, the nurse on duty said, "A JJ Ollson has been calling for you. He says it's urgent." As Marti took the pink message slip from Clea James's outstretched hand, her mind raced through the possible reasons for JJ's call. None clicked. JJ had never called at the hospital before, but then no one other than Reese had and that had occurred only during her early days in Boston when she needed a hand to hold, even at long distance, between her daily A.A. meetings.

More curious than concerned, Marti searched her shoulder bag for change as she searched the halls for a pay phone. Although the move to the new Bellevue had been more than two months ago in June, Marti still moved through its halls by rote rather than recognition.

The phone was answered on its first ring.

"JJ? It's Marti."

"Mart, am I glad you finally called. Listen. I've got a problem. You know my friend Nelson, the kid who was living here with me."

"I know *of* him. He's one of your subjects in the documentary, right?"

"Yes, but there's a problem. Marti, Nelson had been working at a mental hospital the last three months. Like you, in a children's ward. But unlike you, doing menial work with the Mongoloids and the other brain damaged. Anyway, the same damn thing that happened at the V.A. Hospital happened to him here. Some right-wingers protested, set up pickets, and the hospital caved in under the pressure."

As she listened, Marti wished JJ would hurry. What had this to do with her?

"Marti, Nelson's U.S. Attorney and the director of Selective Service haven't been able to find him another job since none of the government agencies, despite their orders, are cooperating. And Nelson, when he went back to the hospital to collect his things and get his check, well, there was some kind of fight and, from what I hear, Nelson messed up one of the guys pretty bad."

"And?" asked Marti, trying to rush JJ to the point so she could rush to see Maria Hernandez who was back on the ward looking more pale and gaunt than before.

"Mart, the last time I heard from Nels, he was real down, scared he was going to be arrested for assault and tossed into jail with the book thrown at him. But since then, he's taken off, gone, and no one knows where the hell he is. Not me or his friend Kay. And we're worried, Marti. He's just a kid. I mean, he's twenty-two but he's just a skinny little kid who's probably scared to death. Marti, if he calls . . ."

"What do you mean, *if* he calls," interrupted Marti.

"If he calls you. I gave him your address and phone number in case he ever got into trouble and needed someone."

"You what?" screamed Marti, anger and panic colliding.

"Marti, he may contact you," continued JJ, oblivious to his sister's reaction. "If he does, help him until we can get help to him. He could be in big trouble."

"Oh, God, JJ, what have you done?" screamed Marti. "How could you? JJ, it's my life. . . . Finally, it's ordered, in place. Safe. I made it that way and now you come along and throw it out of whack for somebody I don't even know. How dare you?" screamed Marti.

"For chrissake, Marti, what the fuck are you talking about?" asked JJ, his own annoyance and frustration evident.

"I'm talking about *me* and the peace of mind I've struggled to obtain. I'm talking about the threatening letters that finally stopped because of the actions and nonaction I've taken. And now you ask me to jeopardize everything for a stranger. It's beyond me. I don't understand. This boy, a resister, is already thought by many to be a criminal. Now he is wanted for assault. Do you know how it will look if he is found in my home? As if I am condoning his actions. I'll be harboring a criminal. And it will be in all the newspapers, which means I'll be at his mercy again."

"Whose mercy?" yelled JJ. "Marti, for shit sake, this is me! I'm asking you to help someone I love."

"What about helping me, or aren't I someone you love anymore?" cried Marti. "Oh, God, JJ, what have you done?" Marti repeated. "Well, I just won't let him through the door if he calls. I'm sorry, but I just can't help in this."

"Marti, listen, please. His parents have rejected him. Society has rejected him. He has no one. You're his only link. Unless he contacts me or Kay, and we think he's afraid to, for our sakes, he is all alone."

"I just don't understand how you could do this to me and to my children," said Marti. "I'll never forgive you for putting me in this position. Never!" she added as she hung up.

Leaning against the wall, Marti fought to collect herself, telling the anxiety that threatened to overcome her that it couldn't. Carefully she reasoned with her fears. Nothing had happened yet. Nothing had changed. She was as safe as she had ever been. Once before she had felt this threatened and she had handled it. Yes, the before was minor in comparison but it hadn't seemed that when Reese had called and had pressured her to come to Boston to see a house she wanted to rent on Marlborough Street. Reese had pleaded. The house, a four-story, red-brick town house, was but two blocks from the Charles River. But she couldn't make the decision alone. Marti had to help.

Two days of hell had followed. She wasn't ready to travel yet. She couldn't face being trapped in an airplane with Lord only knows how many people for an hour. It was fine for Reese to be making strides, going it alone in Boston, living in a hotel when she wasn't living at A.A. meetings. It was wonderful that Reese was overcoming her addiction and her fears. But that was Reese, and she didn't have to become swept up in any kind of competition with her for the mental-health title. If she wasn't ready to travel yet, then she didn't have to. And wouldn't. She had phoned Reese upon reaching the conclusion and Reese had managed just fine. Within the week, she had rented the house for September occupancy on her own. Nelson would manage also. People always do.

Petulantly, Marti thought how people wanted too much from her. But you encourage it, she told herself. You give mixed signals. On one hand, you're this big caretaker and on the other you want your own little world to be taken care of. Make up your mind.

I want both, she argued. Why can't I have that?

You can. But then don't get upset when your brother needs you. This man is important to him. He even said it's someone he loves.

Well, if he loved me, he wouldn't have asked.

It's because he loves you that he did.

Marti started to cry. Through her tears, she found still more change in the pit of her shoulder bag. This time it took several rings before the phone was answered.

"Hi. It's me again. Listen. I'm sorry. I overreacted. Tell me what you want done if Nelson calls."

There was a long silence before JJ spoke. "Marti, you don't have to take him in if you're frightened. Just set him up someplace. Get a hotel room, pay for it, and then for chrissake have him or you call me. But make sure he has some money, and that he eats. Mart, I don't think the guy's got a dime and it scares the shit out of me. Oh, damn, I didn't mean to cry on your nickel but he's gone through such a lot and it's so damn unfair."

"JJ," said Marti softly. "If he calls, I'll take care of him."

Again there was a long silence. "Marti, I know this is hard as hell for you, but there is no one else. There's just you. So thanks, Mart."

There were still tears in Marti's eyes when she entered the children's playroom overlooking the East River and found Maria Hernandez sitting in a corner, her hand clutching some crayons but making no move to color the blank paper before her.

"Hey, lady," said Marti as she sat down next to Maria. "Do you see the big space on the wall, the one between those two drawings? Well I'm counting on you to fill it. Billy took his picture home yesterday when he was discharged, so come on, girl, and color-up."

The child turned to Marti and in a clear voice said: "I won't be going home."

Marti felt her spine tighten. Quickly she searched her memory for the instructions she had received on how to respond to a child's feelings about death. She could remember none. Yet she could hear a staff pediatrician as he explained how some children often know they are going to die and accept that fact before the adults do. Marti could not accept Maria's calm in the face of death when she was so panicked by her own constant fear of it.

"Do you want to talk about it?" asked Marti, suddenly remembering what she was supposed to do.

Maria did not respond. Instead, she pushed herself off her chair and then crawled up and into Marti's lap. Together, they sat silently, staring out at the river, until Maria fell asleep. A male nurse took Maria in his arms and gently carried her back to the ward.

Casey Lhorman was sitting alone at a play table. Crayons and paper were before him as were balls of clay. The child made no movement or sound. From where she stood, Casey seemed to be hardly breathing. His face was still badly discolored about the eyes and cheekbones where he had taken the worst of the blows. His arms, too, had purple and blue discolorations. Whenever she looked at the child who was not yet six, Marti wanted to turn and run. She also wanted to lash out and hurt the person who had hurt the child.

Marti slipped into the chair at the play table facing Casey. When he made no move to reject her, she slowly pushed the crayons toward his hand. For several minutes the child remained removed from his environment. Then, without a word, he reached for the black crayon. Soon he was making angry slashes on the paper. First the black and now the red, crisscrossing, top to bottom, side to side. Marti encouraged Casey as he worked, speaking softly, almost crooning to him.

The man sat down at the table, observing Casey as he rubbed his crayon back and forth on the paper. The child never looked up or acknowledged that another person had entered his world. Suddenly, when there was no more space on the paper to color, he snatched up the paper, crumpling it as he did, before attempting to tear it to shreds.

The man to Marti's left looked pleased. She was surprised when he said softly, "That's okay, Casey. That's really okay. You're allowed to feel that."

The child began to cry. Little tears became great sobs. When the man tried to reach out to him, Casey pulled back and flung himself at Marti, crying and screaming as she tried to comfort him. A social worker came running. She tried reasoning with the child who kicked at her as he clung to Marti. Finally, he quieted and allowed himself to be led away.

A handkerchief was placed in Marti's hand. She looked at it uncomprehendingly until she realized she had been soundlessly crying. She thanked the man as she dabbed at her eyes.

"I'm not supposed to do this," she said apologetically. "It upsets the children."

If he heard, the man didn't respond. When Marti looked up, she saw his eyes were red-rimmed and watery.

"You're not a doctor," she said, responding to the man's emotions.

"I'm a psychiatrist. Matthew Strohl is the name," he replied.

"You're not treating the child, are you?" asked Marti of the man she had never before seen on the ward.

"No. I'm treating his father. Or was before this. Now, he's a patient on the psychiatric ward. He was admitted for observation after his arrest."

"For what he did to Casey?" asked Marti.

Strohl nodded.

"But why?" asked Marti, horrified. "I mean how does anyone beat up a child?"

"Too easily I'm afraid, Ms. Tiernan. It is Ms. Tiernan, isn't it?"

"It was, but now it's Ollson. Marti Ollson."

"Unfortunately Ms. Ollson, if someone has been abused as a child, feels as if he has been beaten up on by others, by the world, he often feels frustrated, enraged. And often the only way such a person can vent his rage is to do to another who is even less powerful what was done to him."

"God! To think such behavior can even be justified," said Marti disgustedly.

"Not justified, Ms. Ollson. Hardly that. Just understood," said Strohl. "Casey's father really isn't a bad man. He suffers from blackouts. They began to happen after his discharge from the war. The man doesn't even know his son is here."

Marti was watching Strohl's face. He was speaking to her as a

1 0 5

peer and not in the manner in which some doctors spoke to the volunteers and nurses—as if they were slow children to be spoon-fed no more information than their underdeveloped brains could handle. "You knew my name," she said awkwardly.

"I imagine half the world knows your name," said Strohl, laughing. "And we have met before, briefly, but it was memorable. I was at Udorn Air Base in Thailand when you visited the troops as part of Bob Hope's Christmas tour in 'sixty-seven. We were introduced briefly. Coincidentally, in 'seventy-three when your brother was released as a prisoner of war and I was the supervising medical officer at Clark Air Force Base, I gave him his psychiatric evaluation before his return to stateside."

"But you're no longer in the military," said Marti as she noted the blue blazer Strohl wore with his gray slacks.

"No, I'm in private practice now, but it often seems as if I'm still in the military. Many of my patients are veterans."

"Odd. I didn't think the military ever sought psychiatric counseling," said Marti with an hostility that surprised her.

"The head honchos don't, Ms. Ollson, which may be, as you're undoubtedly thinking, a pity. But the fighting men often do. Not by choice but necessity. As you may have heard," said Strohl, responding to Marti's tone, "war is hell. Casey's father is proof of that. As is Casey."

"Yes, I understand," said Marti, chastised.

Now it was Matthew Strohl's turn to stare. His hazel eyes studied Marti for a brief second before he said, "I believe you do. Well, I see time is running by and I've got to get back to my office. But I do have a few minutes. Could you tell me where one gets coffee here?"

"There's an employees' cafeteria on twelve," said Marti.

Matthew Strohl rose. "I enjoyed talking with you," he said. "Perhaps we'll meet again."

As Strohl disappeared down the corridor, Marti sat stunned by three things. One, that she had actually noticed that Matthew Strohl was tall, had just a touch of gray at his temples and a cleft in his jutting chin; two, that he hadn't asked that she join him, and three, that she minded, minded very much that he hadn't.

5

THREE THINGS PREYED ON JJ'S MIND: NELSON'S whereabouts, how the American public would react to his documentary *Homecoming*, and Jessamyn Giroux. All three were question marks, each an uncertainty filling JJ with anxiety. Neither he nor Kay had heard from Nelson in three months. Both shared a dread that something awful might have happened although neither spoke of their fear. Instead, they encouraged each other to believe the best. They also opted for the obvious: a private detective to locate the missing person.

The documentary was not troublesome, just frightening in that it would air in a month as a pre-Christmas special on PBS. JJ felt it was the best of his work and his associations. Jessamyn had caught the struggles, failures, and triumphs of the returning exiles, while he had captured the Canadian exiles' reaction to them. The documentary was a crosscurrent of events and feelings. It was provocative, and JJ was certain it would ruffle the feathers of hawks and doves simultaneously.

And then there was Jessamyn. The first time JJ had thought of marriage was late in June, when the mails brought the announcement that James Franklin Tiernan had been born to Este and Vinnie Tiernan. The second time JJ thought of marriage was the morning Nelson disappeared. It was an unexpected loss, one that all too recently followed the loss of a father, a country, and a way of life. Marrying Jessamyn would be insurance against a further loss. He had proposed in September, following a month in which he and Jessamyn had been indescribably close as they finished *Homecoming*. As they had neared completion, Jessamyn had become sexually insatiable, seeming to take more out of him to put into the work. She was demanding, often overwhelming, and always all consuming.

She had been stunned when he proposed. Then she was upset. Marriage was not in her plan. She liked their relationship as it was and didn't need the false security of exchanged vows. She preferred that they live together for so ever long as they chose.

He had been hurt. He wanted commitment. As meaningless as marriage vows, Jessamyn had argued. One is committed only for as long as one wishes to be. No vows or exchange of rings could guarantee commitment. Besides, she added, what would marriage add that they didn't already have?

And then it seemed to JJ they had less. As soon as the documentary was finished, Jessamyn withdrew, the energy and passion she had evidenced in bed as spent as she seemed to be as she moped about the house listlessly. She was depressed, she explained. She had delivered herself of a child and as yet there was no one to dote on it or her. JJ tried to be consoling but Jessamyn had remained unresponsive.

They had argued about Nelson; she, annoyed that he couldn't shake free of what she felt was concern based on needless guilt. Nelson was an adult, she argued, capable of making his own decisions. JJ's concern was obsessive, more than what a friend should feel for another. Nelson was alive and probably scoring as well in America as he had in Canada.

He had questioned her last remark and she had surprised him by saying Nelson was a hustler. He had hustled Kay and had hustled him. He was a survivor who used others to provide his safety. It was only his act to pose as a victim. She did not see him as such. Nor did she believe the documentary had positioned him in such fashion. Nelson was a man—not a boy as JJ insisted—who had made his bed and then had difficulty sleeping in it. JJ had replied that Nelson was a boy whose bed had been made for him and was then urged to sleep in it. Jessamyn had looked at him with annoyance and then said, "It's all a matter of one's point of view, isn't it?"

That had been their last argument. He would have preferred discussion and dissension to their current nothingness. Jessamyn seemed empty, devoid of fight and empty of life. He wished *Homecoming*'s airdate was sooner. Perhaps that would help. Something positive was needed to help her through what was obviously a difficult time. She was thinner, and her confident, often strident attitude was now replaced by silence. It pained JJ to see Jessamyn struggle. It pained him even more that she wouldn't burden him with her struggle. He wanted that burden, wished to help her carry it. He loved her, he said repeatedly. When she heard, she would touch his face with her hand but not respond. This was a Jessamyn Giroux JJ had not seen before.

*   *   *

Jessamyn had little sympathy for people who gave in to their depression and despair. Indecisiveness was not a quality Jessamyn admired. If troubled, act. If confused, find order. This was her credo. Thus, when weeks went by and Jessamyn realized she was easing herself gently but deeply into all the states she disliked in others, she took direct action.

Women's College Hospital was but a short walk to Queen's Park, where Jessamyn sat facing the Parliament Buildings following her exam with her doctor. Despite the wind whipping the snow about the park, Jessamyn wasn't cold. Actually, Jessamyn wasn't much of anything except contemplative. It was time for swift, intelligent action. There were several paths open to her. Only she could choose the right one.

She had thought her moodiness solely the result of completing *Homecoming*. Her despair, she believed, was rooted in loss. Like the postpartum blues. Upon delivery of the final edit, she had no place to go and no person to be. And it had happened so abruptly, as the last weeks of work on the documentary had been the most exciting. That Nelson had not been found only added to the pathos of the piece as a whole. That so few of those who had returned met with success was good drama. Whether it was sad or unfortunate was not for her to decide or feel. That was the viewer's option. *Homecoming* was a well-told story. That had been her doing. Whether one liked what it told was purely subjective and had nothing to do with the excellence of the work. She had done her job well. Too well, she now knew. She had allowed herself an involvement to the extent of forgetting all else. Mistakes happen that way. In Jessamyn's world, one always traveled with both eyes open and senses continually sharpened. She had been seduced by her work and by the opportunities it presented. Now there was a penalty to pay unless she could turn a wrong into a right, a seeming loss into a gain, which she now thought as she sat huddled in her down coat she could do. Jessamyn's decision was as cold as the November day. It was calculating, but, in her mind, correct calculations made for exact answers.

Basically, it was only bad timing, she decided. She had always planned to have a child, although that plan meant waiting until she was thirty or thereabouts and fully established professionally. So it would be sooner rather than later. If she had been more attuned to the changes in her body, it might not have been at all, since she would have known sooner and then might have been more open to abortion. Not that she had convictions one way or another on the action. If the father-to-be was someone other than John Ollson, Jr., she would have aborted no matter that she was in her tenth week. But that the father would be JJ made the difference. As she rose from the bench and began a slow walk toward her car, Jessamyn wondered why she had forgotten to use her diaphragm one night, or two. Was she seeking to recoup her losses? One child, her documentary, for another. A possibility, thought Jessamyn. And what better father than a man who not only wanted to marry her but had considerable clout in the industry in which she desired to work and who also had considerable monies, earned and inherited from his father and from Nancy Blanchard, a family friend who had bequeathed a sizable fortune in paintings to JJ upon her death last year.

As she revved the motor of her Datsun, Jessamyn laughed for the first time in weeks. She was her own object of derision. That she had wrestled with her decision for so many days now seemed ludicrous. That she had been depressed seemed destructive and dumb. The course of action was clear for the present and even into the future. She was actually a very lucky girl who was about to make someone feel as if he were a very lucky man just for allowing his woman to use her prerogative and change her mind.

*   *   *

They were walking through the Common when Carolyn suddenly remembered another time in Boston, thirty-eight years ago, when then, too, the family was the concern. Only then, she had caused that concern. Appearing in the out-of-town tryouts of *Shining Hour,* her first solo starring vehicle, she was living at the Touraine Hotel with the twins, infants then, when John had come to visit. Between her concern for her real babies, Thomas and Marti, and her other baby, the play, John had gotten lost in her attentions. She had proceeded willfully until John had returned angrily to New York, leaving her to sort out her priorities. And it had been a fight, particularly with her own self and her ambitions, to keep the family together. It had not been easy but certainly it was easier then than now.

As she walked silently by Thomas's side, enjoying the early evening frost and the lights of Christmas that haloed the city, Carolyn realized the situation was similar but hardly parallel. Thomas was not her and ambition did not play a part in the problem.

Carolyn had come to Boston ostensibly to visit the family in their new home but actually to effect a family reconciliation. So far, her efforts had failed. Now, with her plane to New York but hours away, she tried one more time.

"Thomas, I haven't put it this way before because a part of me thinks it ugly. But I'd like you to do this for me. I'll be sixty years old on the twenty-first. I would like the family together for the occasion."

"We will gladly come to New York at any time to celebrate your birthday," said Thomas as he held his mother's arm.

"Yes, but I will be in Toronto for my birthday, for Christmas and the wedding. All the same week. Thomas, it would mean so much. How many more chances will I have in life to see my family together?"

"If I'm not mistaken," said Thomas, "that's a line out of *Family Affair,* in which you played a Jewish mother."

1 1 1

"And quite well, I might add. I was awarded a Tony for that performance. Now, I'd settle for a Thomas," said Carolyn.

"Mom, if I could do it for you, I would. But it's impossible. I cannot set foot inside JJ's home, given how he feels and how I feel. This is a man who has defied the law. This is a man who tries to convince the world that his actions were justified. His documentary made it seem as if we who oppose him and others who share his actions and beliefs are the true un-Americans. It offended me."

"Thomas, at one time not so long ago, your actions, your beliefs, were also offensive to others. But they were there for you."

When Carolyn could see from the look on Thomas's face that he did not understand, she continued. "When you returned from Vietnam, landed at Travis Air Force Base, your sister, your aunt, and your cousin were all there to meet you. They put aside their own feelings and beliefs to be there for you. And, Thomas, you know how strongly Marti felt about the war. Margaret, too. And you and Vinnie never agreed on much of anything. All your relationships then were strained because of differing lifestyles and politics. But they put them aside. All for the same reason. Next to family, they seemed unimportant. Thomas, can't you bend just a little?"

"Mom, I just don't know if I should. Sometimes I think the world's gone wrong because we have all bent a little too much. I'm sorry. Honest to God, if I could do it for you, Mom, I would. I guess you think I'm hard and unfeeling."

Carolyn looked at her eldest son, so much the image of his father and so much like him in spirit too. She felt he was wrong but knew he was right, if not for her then for himself. His inability to compromise or be compromised was maddening, but it was also commendable. It was what made Thomas unique. "No, Thomas, not hard, not unfeeling. I guess where we differ is: at my stage of life I no longer feel it always matters who is right and who is wrong. I'm selfish. I just want my family together."

Thomas Ollson stared across the Common in the direction of the house on Marlborough Street. "That's all I want, Mom. Maybe someday we'll both have the answer as to why it has to be so hard."

---

1 1 2

Had Marti obeyed her impulse, she would have whooped and hollered, skipped not walked, from Lilyanne Bossinoff's office. As she walked from the children's ward toward the eighth-floor elevators, she was oblivious to the staff members who smiled in greeting as they passed. A telephone beckoned. Another impulse, to call her mother, was rejected. No, this was a triumph she would savor alone for the moment. She, Marti Tiernan, had been offered a staff position by the director, herself, with the Child Life Program. At eighty-five hundred dollars a year! Magnificent. Marti laughed, remembering how at the height of her film career she had earned that sum by the hour—but it had never brought the sense of accomplishment it would now if she took the job.

In the ladies' room, as she repaired her makeup and combed her hair, which she once again had grown to shoulder length, she considered whether she could assume a full-time position. Was it fair to the children? The children were never home, she replied. Not during the week when Mark had band practice after school and Ali, when she wasn't dabbling at modeling, was now dabbling at acting with the school's drama club. A laugh involuntarily escaped from Marti's mouth as she recalled Ali's debut last week as Lizzie in *The Rainmaker*. As the curtain fell, Margaret had stage whispered: "Congratulations. You have spawned the first totally untalented Tiernan in history." Which was true. Even Ali knew it was true and was unconcerned. "I am finding myself," she had said in defense. "Look somewhere other than the stage," Margaret had replied.

Again Marti laughed. Ali had simply shrugged and began talking about costuming as a career. No, the children didn't need her at home. They were self-sufficient from nine-to-five and since she would be home by five-thirty, the job would not interfere with her mothering. The question that remained was whether or not she wanted the full-time involvement. But it is lovely to be asked, thought Marti as she waited for an elevator, so lovely that I want to tell everybody, she decided as she entered the elevator and asked that someone press twelve.

She would begin with Matthew. Not that she would have to, as he would probably read it on her face before she could say a word. He always seemed to know what she was feeling, sometimes before she did. That was disconcerting, but then Matthew Strohl was a disconcerting man. After three months, she still couldn't read him but then, the man was not exactly an open book.

It had been two months after their first meeting on the children's ward that she had literally bumped into him one afternoon on line in the staff cafeteria. It was she who had asked him to share a table and from the look on his face he had shared her surprise that she had. And so it had begun. Coffee dates, although Marti doubted Matthew would have called them that, at her instigation. He was now at Bellevue two days a week, working on some special psychiatric evaluation about which he didn't speak. But then, Matthew Strohl seldom spoke about his work, although he often spoke about his field.

After her disastrous marriage to Philip Charper, Marti avoided psychological and analytical thought. But whereas Dr. Charper, the psychologist, professed to know and have answers for everything, Matthew only offered possibilities and suggestions. When she would discuss various children on the ward, he would make her search for interpretations of their behavior. He never diagnosed or made snap judgments from others' evaluations and was unimpressed to the point of being distressed with those who did.

For three months, Marti had been arriving at the hospital one hour earlier than her two o'clock starting time to meet Strohl, when he showed up, as theirs was a casual rather than a firm date. In all that time, he never suggested dinner or anything resembling a date outside the hospital, although once he mentioned a lecture at the New School on child abuse that he thought might interest her. It did until she realized he was not offering to take her. In fact he wasn't even sure he would be going but would *see* her there if he did.

Yet, he continued to meet her and their talks, although not personal, were. She knew how he felt about parenting, birth control, abortion, gun control, disarmament, Richard Nixon; the issues that were important to him, and yet, she knew nothing of his life away from the hospital. He could have been married. Or gay. The last possibility nagged at her. Suddenly she realized he never noticed what she wore or how she wore it. But then she thought of the gay men she had known and they always noticed what she wore and how she wore it. But still, the possibility remained that Matthew Strohl was gay. That disturbed her, whereas in the past others' sexual bents never had. On the other hand, he just might be shy. Or married. That possibility again entered her mind.

Whereas Marti sought to understand Strohl's behavior, she avoided her own. Not once had she questioned anything other than her attraction to the man and that she decided was based on the fact that he was intelligent, sensitive, and incredibly attractive. The last she admitted only under direct cross-examination by herself one evening and she was not pleased by her confession. Attraction had overtones Marti wished to avoid, and so she did.

Strohl was waiting at a corner table. She approached him casually, trying to rearrange her face into a blank. She was obviously successful as he said nothing; too successful as he avoided her eyes.

"Something wrong?" she asked, a statement beneath her question.

He looked up, his eyes pained. "Casey Lhorman is back on your ward," he replied. As Marti's hand covered her mouth in horror, she listened as Strohl explained. "The father again. It's so damn difficult to explain. He is not your typical or even chronic child abuser. It's been five months since the last incident. According to his wife, he goes crazy, suffers from some kind of flashback in time when he is under extreme duress. It's not just Casey but everyone he then perceives as the enemy."

Marti was watching Strohl intently, marveling that his sympathies could be with the abuser as well as with the abused. But then, he looks for cause as well as effect, she realized. In his eyes, both father and son are victims.

"How bad is the child?" she asked, moving to her own concern.

"No better but then no worse than he was the first time," replied Strohl looking even more distressed. "The poor kid is so hurt. Not physically. That he can handle. It's the other hurt that we have nothing for. Not yet anyway. How do you make a child understand what's incomprehensible to most adults?"

Instinctively, Marti reached across the table for Strohl's hand.

1 1 5

For a second, she felt him stiffen before he relaxed, allowing her a privilege neither had taken before.

"Listen, I have news," she said. "I know it may seem callous to be excited, actually thrilled says it best, at this moment—but here it is: I've been offered a full-time position with the Child Life Program."

Strohl didn't immediately respond. When he did, he slipped his hand out from under hers to touch her cheek.

"I've decided to celebrate," she said, speaking since he didn't. "I'd like you to come to dinner tonight. It'll be just the family."

There was a moment's hesitation before he said, "If you don't mind my arriving late, I'll be there."

No explanation of why he would be late and no apology. Just the statement.

"How late is late? Is it for dinner or dessert?"

"Eight o'clock. So you tell me. Are you early diners or late?"

"Eight it is," replied Marti, not responding to his question as she wondered what she could feed her children's faces to keep them quiet until eight. Normally, dinner was at six. But today wasn't normal. First she had been offered a job. Second she had asked a man to dinner. Third he had accepted. Not normal at all. Marti was pleased.

"Are you going to take the job?" asked Strohl.

"I don't know," replied Marti. "I haven't gotten past the flattered part yet to deal with the decision."

"You flatter them" said Strohl. "They're just doing what's best not only for them but for the children."

It was the closest Matthew Strohl had ever come to giving her a compliment, but Marti hadn't heard. Her eyes were riveted on a scene unfolding outside the cafeteria. A struggle was taking place with two uniformed security guards trying to hold on to a man who was trying to fight his way in. He was yelling and the words he was screaming in an anguished voice were her name. As he continued to yell for Marti Tiernan, Marti knew the bloodstained, mud-smeared man was a boy named Nelson Naismith. She knew because somewhere deep inside she had been waiting and she had always known her wait would not be in vain.

Jessamyn Giroux Ollson did not subscribe to the quaint old adage that maintained that a woman was never more beautiful than when she was pregnant. Jessamyn had only to look at her body to know neither it nor she was beautiful unless one was partial to protuberances. Nor did Jessamyn feel beautiful. Just pregnant. Pregnant and stagnant. In fact, in her mind the two words were synonymous. Still, Jessamyn was not depressed. Since she had no recourse other than to wait until the baby was born, Jessamyn had taken steps to ensure that the wait would not be in vain. JJ could bask in the glow of their excellent reviews for *Homecoming* and their impending parenthood but not she. She wanted something more.

Jessamyn believed in momentum. They had it, but JJ was losing it. JJ worked only when inspired. Since *Homecoming*, nothing inspired him other than Nelson. If there had been a way for him to have flown to New York to assist Marti in keeping Nelson out of jail, he would have. If he could have convinced anyone, which he could not no matter how often he had tried, that there was another film in what had befallen Nelson, he would have done that. He was, as she repeatedly told him, trying to whip a dead horse. He requested she use another phrase to express her lack of interest in doing anything further with Nelson.

In disgust, she had walked away from what would surely have been an argument. Nelson belonged to the past. He had served his purpose, as she had served his, well. He was now yesterday's news, worth at the most a small paragraph on page twelve or fourteen of the *New York Times*.

JJ had been appalled by what he termed her callousness. The boy had been thrown out of work, thrown out of his home, and had once again gone underground, thinking that if he surfaced the government would jail him for not having completed his two years of alternate service. He had struggled from job to job, one more demeaning than the next, until the last dragged him into the gutters of New York, never knowing his case had been closed by the U.S. Attorney when it became apparent to him there was no other alternate work available to the boy.

"And that's not a documentary?" JJ has asked when they had argued.

"No," she had replied coldly. "It is a fact of life. Dramatic,

117

ironic, but it is a piece by itself—and, as you taught me, a piece does not make a whole, particularly in a documentary."

His agreement became worse than his prior persistence. Once the idea of pursuing *la cause Nelson,* as she dubbed it, dissipated, so did his desire to do any kind of work at all. Jessamyn had to face the fact that her husband, when he wasn't talking to himself, which is what speaking out on unconditional amnesty was about, he was perfectly content to sit home and watch her grow larger and larger still. He doted on her, listened at her belly for any movement the child might make, and was in general an adoring husband and father to his unborn child. He made her crazy.

And then Tyne Philips appeared. Not uninvited or unsolicited, but in response to the numerous letters Jessamyn had sent as she grew larger and more impatient. Philips's letterhead read ASSOCIATED ARTISTS. Her client list numbered some of the industry's major writers, producers, and directors. Tyne Philips had viewed her work, as Jessamyn had requested, and was impressed. Tyne Philips would come to Toronto, as Jessamyn had suggested, to talk about representation and Jessamyn's future. Tyne Philips already had ideas for future projects for the Ollsons but, more important, in Jessamyn's mind, Tyne Philips believed Jessamyn Giroux (she had used her maiden name in signing her letters) had only to ask and it would be given.

Although four other agents responded to Jessamyn's letters, it was Tyne Philips Jessamyn decided to meet for lunch at the Chateau d'Orsi at both their earliest convenience. With the date arranged, Jessamyn relaxed. She had nothing further to do but to wait. For Tyne Philips. For the birth of her baby. For her life to renew. Jessamyn knew her wait would not be in vain.

*　　*　　*

He could not ask the receptionist for the key to the men's room again. She would think it odd, thought Thomas as he fought the spasms that signified yet another attack. Glancing at his watch, he saw he had been waiting only twenty minutes. It had seemed longer, much longer since he had walked to the Prudential Center from the house on Marlborough Street. But then, the last few months had been one long wait for something, anything to alleviate the emptiness of his life. Thomas was beginning to sweat. Best not to look at the receptionist. She might report he was acting strangely. But she was looking at him, inviting conversation. Thomas buried his head in the current issue of *Newsweek*, pretending to an interest in the magazine that he didn't have. As he felt his feet begin to itch, Thomas prayed the door to Ralph Hendryx's office would soon open and that he would once again be invited to enter. This was to be his second interview with the firm and his first callback in more than a dozen applications. Finally, he was being considered for a job he knew he could do.

Not that he could not have done the others. He could have, only they hadn't wanted him any more than he really wanted them. Still, he would have taken the jobs if any had been offered. According to his internist, he had to. He needed work to fill time and to bring a meaning that was missing to his life. Thomas had laughed at the notion that anything he might do again in life would have the meaning it once had and perhaps, he added bitterly, that was just as well.

But this job, thought Thomas as he again became aware the receptionist was openly inviting him through her side glances to begin a conversation, was a possibility. He knew about airplanes and flying. He could manage an airline. He could help it grow from a small inter- and intrastate carrier to an airline with both national and international routes. In his briefcase there were a half dozen ideas he had created since his first interview a week ago that would show management just how well he could earn the six-figure salary the job offered and its title of president. He wanted the challenge. Even more, he wanted someplace to go, something to do, and someone to be. The job would give him all that.

The advertisement in *Newsweek* featured a family much like his. They were smiling in their togetherness, feeling safe under the umbrella of insurance the man of the house had put aside for a rainy day. Two girls, a boy, a mother, and a father. But the resemblance ended there. As he turned the page, Thomas wondered when his family had stopped smiling together and when exactly he had lost control of their lives. Reese was seldom at home. Although she no longer attended A.A. meetings throughout the day, she did attend at least one. Then there was the part-time job she was doing "just for myself," she explained, as though everything she was doing was not for herself. Like her schooling. Two days a week, from late afternoon through the early evening, she was taking six credits at Boston University, preparing for the fall entry she hoped to attain to the school's master's program in special education. She was pursuing a lost dream, she explained, which was also why she was encouraging the children to follow their dreams, no matter how foolish or even detrimental.

Thomas could not stop Karl and, had he tried, it would have been from envy rather than concern. Karl, certain of what he wanted, sacrificed to obtain it. Through the Greater Boston Track Club, Karl had found an independent running coach who was training him daily for national meets in which he would run the five-thousand- and ten-thousand-meter events, among others. Karl's decision had made him an isolate at Buckingham, Brown, and Nichols, having rejected his new school's track team as it only offered crosscountry running and then only during the fall. Like his mother, Karl was seldom home. He was as much of an isolate in his family as he was in his school. Yet Thomas admired Karl's dedication to his avocation, which was not at all how he felt about Kristan. That was a nightmare and not a dream to be pursued as Reese blithely maintained.

Frequently, Thomas thought to put an end to this interference in Kristan's life before it had dire consequences. Modeling might be a life for Ali, but it was not for his Kristan. Angrily, Thomas often thought if Reese had not insisted that Kristan spend the previous summer at Marti's, she might never have been exposed to this Andreas person and his camera. It was obscene: a little girl just past fourteen being combed and coiffed to sell sex. And that's what it was, no matter what the dress, the jewelry, the cosmetic, or the rationalizations Reese attached to it. It was not a healthy environment for his Kristan. He would have preferred she be like Kelly, living a normal life with proper supervision in proper surroundings at Newton Country Day of the Sacred Heart.

Thinking of Kelly did not provide Thomas with the usual smile. It was no longer cute that she showed more interest in the boys at the neighboring St. Sebastian than she did in her studies, as the sisters maintained. Still, boys were a normal interest for young girls, whereas modeling was not. Nor was commuting to New York two days a week normal for a child. Yet, according to Kristan's teachers at Newton Country Day, her schoolwork had yet to suffer. But he had and he feared Kristan would.

Thomas focused on one of the pictures in the "Newsmakers" section of the magazine. It was of Marti, accompanying a haggard-looking boy into court. From TV footage, Thomas recognized the boy as Nelson Naismith. He also recognized the anguish in the boy from his eyes. He had seen that look before in boys who had given up and died in the camps. When Thomas had first read in *Time* and the *Christian Science Monitor*, a newspaper whose reporting he trusted, of Nelson, he had been appalled by the miscarriage of justice as he perceived it. Although he opposed amnesty, Thomas believed that once the government had given its word to grant it to those who accepted the conditions offered, then the government owed it to those men to honor and fulfill its commitment. If Nelson Naismith had agreed to alternate service, then the government should have supplied it no matter who protested. That the boy had been harassed and hounded from one job to another, from state to state, Thomas saw as a crime; not as grievous as the one Naismith had committed, but a crime nonetheless. To his surprise and even his annoyance, Thomas found his sympathies with the young boy whom the court had declared incompetent.

Thomas was not surprised that Marti had become involved, although he was surprised at his reaction. He did not object to Marti's presence in Naismith's life and thus the nation's press. In the distant past, Marti's press had created embarrassment. In his mind her exploits as a film queen and then activist turned quasi-feminist often bordered on bad taste. But the person today who walked past TV cameras and reporters, refusing comment as she did whatever she felt was necessary, had dignity. It did not surprise or bother him that Kristan spoke of her aunt with affection. It did bother him, however, that she spoke at all about Naismith, whom she had met on her last modeling excursion to New York. His daughter saw Naismith as a hero, and that did not please him.

As he closed the magazine and was about to thumb through another, Thomas realized he could no longer deny the barometer of his nervousness. With an embarrassed smile, he asked the receptionist if he could once again have the men's-room key, making what he hoped was a funny comment on the side effects of coffee and what was *really* meant when they said it was good to the last drop. When he realized the remark had an unintended vulgar connotation, Thomas was appalled. But the receptionist didn't take notice. Leah Winslow was too busy gazing into the very blue eyes of Thomas Ollson as her hand gently placed the key in his to be aware of anything but the handsome man standing nervously before her.

Ralph Hendryx was arguing with the two men with whom he controlled Revere Airlines. Hendryx was used to making decisions, money, and people do as he wished and was annoyed with the opposition he was encountering. The very thing Drake and Wilson opposed, he proposed: using Thomas Ollson much the way Eastern had used Frank Borman.

"This country knows the Ollson name," argued Hendryx. "It *reveres* it in many circles. Yes, the man has been controversial, but who the hell is going to remember the pros and cons of Vietnam a year or so down the line? What people will remember is the hero, the man who flew planes and was a leader. Between our publicity machine and our advertising campaigns, his face will come to mean reliability and integrity. I tell you, he is the perfect image for us. And he's hungry. My people tell me he's been kicking around for some time now. He needs us more than we need him. He can place us on the map and we can place him in a job."

"And you really think he can get the CAB to cooperate," said Wilson.

"If anyone can get us new domestic and international routes, Ollson's the man. Remember, he's respected. He is also establishment. These guys take care of their own," said Hendryx. "If anyone can get the CAB to budge, even fudge things a little, it's Ollson."

"I don't think Ollson is the type to have anyone fudge anything," said Drake.

"You're right," agreed Hendryx.

"Which is why he might be wrong for us," replied Drake. "Look, Ralph. This is a business. We need a hard-nose S.O.B., and not an ethics committee, to take us where we want to go."

"Gentlemen, I assure you. Within six months, Thomas Ollson will have established a fleet of Revere jets at a cost we can handle. He will have acquired a staff that will rival Continental and Piedmont. This man, if he has to tow the Boeings himself, will have us in and out of Washington, Philadelphia, and Buffalo within six months. He will not only manage but he will be doing, and the best thing he will be doing is using his name and his image to build us passenger traffic. I say we hire and use him to our advantage. We have everything to gain and nothing to lose except Ollson himself if he doesn't work out. And if that's the case, we're in no worse shape than we are now."

Thomas Ollson stood at the top of the steps leading down from the Prudential Building and saw sun where there was none on this day when a winter storm watch was in effect. He had his job. His wait was over. He was happy. Someone wanted him. An airline. He was to be their face and voice. Normally, he would have hated that intrusion into his private self but now, the idea that a corporation entrusted their business to him— that his face would be their fortune—was thrilling. He was no longer a nonperson. He was a *someone*, the president of Revere Airlines.

They had loved his slogan. Revere Airlines: We *revere* your time and space. And that's what *his* airline would do; that would be his guarantee. He would see that *his* passengers received the best service on the best planes *his* money could buy and that schedules *he* created were maintained. What he had been to the Triple Nickel, he would be to his men at Revere.

Thomas was laughing as he ran the steps two by two to the avenue below. He would secure the planes and pilots they wanted, the routes, too. He would make their ambitions, like their planes, fly. He would do all this and more. Just to re-earn his wings.

———————

As the blizzard conditions intensified, so did Marti's desire to leave Bellevue. It was late in the day and the afternoon had been difficult. Lilyanne Bossinoff wasn't making it any easier. As Marti sat facing the director of the Child Life Program, her eye was on the storm pasting flakes of snow to the office windows. Getting home would be difficult, much more difficult than the task at hand. Collecting herself, Marti tried again to explain.

"All my life I worked. Because my mother and my aunt did, I thought it was the thing to do. In other words, I didn't have a choice. Now I do, and although I'm thrilled you think me good enough to offer a full-time position, it's not something I really want."

"But Marti, you're so good," argued Lilyanne. "Seldom have I seen children relate to an adult so quickly and with such trust."

"Lily, I love what I do here. I like giving of myself, donating me and my time. I get more from my work and the children than you could ever pay me. The wonderful thing for me is that I don't feel I have to give or be more."

Seeing the cloudy look of noncomprehension on Lilyanne's face, Marti struggled for clarity. "Your job offer made me look at my life in a way I never have before. Suddenly I saw not only what but all I've done. Lily, I don't have to do or be anything anymore. I've done it all, been it all. For me, at this stage in life, to do less is to have more. I have two teenagers. Although they need less of my time now, they need more of me, the person. I want to do that. Also, to wax poetic, it's time to stop and smell the roses, but in my case the rose is a pot roast."

When Lilyanne didn't laugh, Marti explained. "I can't cook. I never could. I'm thinking what fun it would be to take a cooking course. Actually, it would be so much fun to do so many things *when* and *if* I feel like doing them. In other words, I want the experience without having to *be* anything, because I see clearly I already am. I just am."

"Well, I'm disappointed," said the director. "Not in you," she added when she saw Marti's hurt expression, "but in your decision. I can only accept it with regret. I am glad that you are staying on as a volunteer. The children need you."

Marti's thoughts wandered to Maria Hernandez who was facing yet another operation, about which Marti felt as drained of hope as the child was of strength. "And I need them," said Marti softly. "Although sometimes I must admit I wish I didn't."

A sudden blast of wind breaking on the window caused both women to stare at the storm. "May I use your phone?" asked Marti. "I want to call the taxi service."

Lilyanne pushed the phone toward Marti. The number rang repeatedly before a harassed voice answered and informed Marti that nothing was available, that the storm had traffic snarled throughout the city. He could not promise but he probably could have a taxi for her in forty minutes. Probably but not definitely.

"Anything wrong?" asked Lilyanne when she saw Marti's worried face.

"No, nothing," lied Marti as she collected her things. "See you Wednesday."

The elevator was crowded with people all talking anxiously of the storm and the likelihood of public transportation operating on schedules that would get them home to waiting dinners and families. Their anxiety increased Marti's own. The scene in the street heightened it more. Traffic was not moving on First Avenue and on every corner people were waiting for the beacon of light that would herald an empty taxi. As the cold gripped her, Marti considered the possibilities. She could walk home, normally a thirty-five-minute chore in the best of weather conditions but undoubtedly an hour tonight, or she could take the crosstown bus on 23rd Street to Tenth Avenue. That would leave her but a short but poorly lit block from the house. But she would be safe in the bus. In her hooded parka, she would be unrecognizable, which had been her intent.

As she began the walk to the bus, fighting the wind and the snow, Marti became aware of the crowds pushing by her. Suddenly, each person posed a threat. Despite the cold, Marti began to sweat. At the corner of 24th Street, she stopped at a parking meter and clutched it tightly, trying to anchor herself as she did. Despite the cold air that hurt her lungs, she breathed deeply, counting down from ten to one as she did. And Ali thought she was brave. Well Ali should see her now, terrified to be in the street and just as terrified to be taking public transportation. Oh yes, she had seemed brave when Nelson had been released by the court in her custody. He was free but she had felt trapped. She still did. Each day, before leaving the house, she checked through the draped windows to see if any strange persons were lucking about. Although her house and her life seemed to be running on their same schedules, she was in turmoil again. And yet, there was no reason. Yet!

She would talk to herself, Marti decided as she began her walk toward the bus again. She would deal with her fears by dealing solely with reality. Nelson Naismith had catapulted her into the news, but she hadn't been abused by either the media or the public. There had been no letters and no threats, despite her fears. That was all in the past, she told herself as she struggled against the wind and her fear.

Think of Nelson and not of yourself, she commanded. Think of his reality and your own will seem that much better. She had ensconsed Nelson in the apartment she had created for her mother when she had suffered her heart attack. The boy never left the house. He couldn't. He was too frightened, although he never spoke about his fears. His eyes and his involuntary trembling and weeping said it all. JJ had wanted Nelson sent to him but Matthew thought that inadvisable and almost impossible given the boy's condition. Marti had never seen anyone in the grip of a breakdown before, and although she hardly knew Nelson Naismith, she ached for him. Their experiences were dissimilar and yet Marti felt an empathy for the boy. To be that alone and that afraid was something with which she was acquainted.

Through Matthew, who was treating Nelson, and from the private investigator JJ and Kay had hired, Marti learned something of Nelson's existence as a fugitive living underground in America. And that's what it had been, an existence. Fearful of arrest, he sought no help from his parents, who would have refused it anyway. Certain there would be repercussions if he called JJ or Kay, he avoided involving them. And so he lived totally alone, sleeping in bus and train stations and in pay toilets. Work, even as a porter or dishwasher, was scarce, which meant eating on the run, figuratively and literally. He shoplifted from fruit stands when he had to, which was far too frequent for his own security. Towns and

1 2 6

cities and states were thumbed through as he thumbed his way crosscountry on highways and turnpikes, always fearful of an arrest. Which happened in Philadelphia. He had been walking about the Broad Street Station, trying to keep warm, when a plainclothesman arrested him for soliciting. A fight ensued. But who won and who lost and how he came to New York was something Nelson could not as yet remember. It was Mark who had explained how Nelson had come to Bellevue. He had been home early from school when there was a pounding on the door. The man outside kept yelling for Marti as he mentioned JJ's name repeatedly. Mark gave him the address of Bellevue and then called JJ for instructions. At Bellevue, Nelson created a disturbance as he shouted for Marti throughout the hallways. Before security could find him, Nelson was at the cafeteria where the struggle ensued.

The bus stop was in sight now. At first glance there seemed to be fifty people waiting. At second, a hundred, all bunched together. Marti was trembling, afraid to move toward the crowd but just as afraid not to. She focused on the court trial, a hearing actually, as she moved into the throng. The judge had dismissed the assault-and-battery charges brought by the hospital against Nelson when he recognized not only the facts of the case but that Nelson was incapable of standing trial.

Marti felt she wasn't capable of standing at the stop another moment. After a second bus had left her at the front of the line waiting for yet another bus to come, she was blinded by the wind that was chafing her face despite the scarf she now had wrapped about it. Then finally, she saw it, its headlights breaking through the wall of falling snow. Relatively empty, it was skidding its way toward the stop. Behind Marti, the crowd was like sprinters waiting for the gun. As soon as the bus would open its doors, they would be off, pushing their way into the warmth and the shelter it would provide.

The bus was moving steadily toward the curb when Marti felt the pressure on her back. At first it was light and then it hardened. She tried to turn about, to face the person, to make him stop, but the crowd was too dense and her feet couldn't find a firm footing on the slippery pavement. Quickly, the pressure became greater than her resistance.

1 2 7

The last thing Marti thought of as she was pushed before the crosstown bus was Maria Hernandez and how upset the child would be when Marti was not there for her operation. The screams of the crowd and the screech of the tires obliterated that thought and any others from her consciousness. Not that there were any. There was only the body sprawled face down in the street and the crowd that hovered over it.

As one woman held the other, ignoring the passers-by observing their grief, she looked beyond her sister's shoulder into the past. Once before, all too recently, they had clung together in just such a hospital corridor. Then, she had held her sister as death destroyed the neatly constructed corners of her life. Then as now there had been fear, doubt—and that was the end of the similarity, thought Margaret as she suddenly held Carolyn at arm's length.

"I think you should leave," said Margaret, her voice firm and her manner sure. "Ali and Mark need you at home, and frankly so do I. Look at you. White as a sheet. You're trembling. There is nothing more for you to do here except cause further worry. Go to Marti's. Make dinner. Keep the kids company and I'll be by as soon as all the details are completed."

As Carolyn made a push past Margaret and back into Marti's room, Margaret grabbed her roughly by the wrist. "Do you want to help her or not? The last thing she needs now is to worry about you. If you really want to help, put her mind at rest by taking care of the children. She'll feel a lot better knowing you're with them."

As Carolyn heeded the sense of Margaret's words, she turned and walked slowly down the long hospital corridor. Her posture, once that of the great star, a first lady of the theater, was now that of an old woman. Margaret felt the tears stick in her throat as she watched Carolyn disappear. On the verge of hysteria herself, she leaned back against the corridor wall to collect herself.

Marti lay still on the bed, afraid to move and yet afraid not to. Moving meant feeling the stabs of pain in her back and legs. Not moving felt familiar—too familiar, from a time when she couldn't move and was more dead than alive. Torn between her past and the present, Marti was remembering what little there was in her mind to remember of her other time in the hospital. It was the helplessness she recalled and hated. Then, she could do nothing other than wait and hope that someone would see to her every need. She had hated that dependence, feared it and feared being helpless. Never was one more vulnerable, she thought, than when one couldn't do for oneself.

That was not the case now, a voice reminded her. She could speak and she could move. X-rays, the doctors were certain, would show no broken bones. Nor was a concussion suspected. Her bruises would disappear, with her pain, in time, they assured her. But would her fear? Marti wondered.

The hospital room, as hospital rooms go, was pleasant, and Marti found it of some comfort to be at Bellevue where she had observed and thus trusted the routine. She did not remember being admitted, but then she remembered nothing other than the oncoming bus and the hand that had shoved her into its path.

But was it a hand? asked the same voice as moments ago. Could the pressure she had felt on her back growing firmer and stronger have been many hands, shoving shoulders, all anxious to board a bus that would take them from the storm and to their homes? Could it have been bodies and not hands, not *his* hands, at all? She couldn't be certain. She would never be certain, until it was either too late or it no longer mattered.

The doctors insisted she stay at least the night for tests. She wanted to leave immediately, leave the memories and the fact that she was injured, hit by a bus that was going no more than five to ten miles an hour at the time. Yet another part of her didn't want to leave, didn't want to go back out there again. The room was warm. The hospital was like a fortress with nurses guarding their stations and thus her.

"It's really too bad you haven't a book or a film to promote. You're all over the networks," said Margaret as she breezed into the room. 'Live at Five' had you dead at six and 'Eyewitness News' resurrected you at six-thirty. Not to mention that the *Enquirer* already has a back-from-the-dead story with you claiming to have visited the other side but refusing to stay because you couldn't find a Gucci."

Marti glared at her aunt.

1 2 9

"Spare me the scowls, please, particularly since I have spared you from your mother. She was about to enter this room and do ten minutes on how you should cross at the green and not in between when I sent her home. To your home by the way. The poor woman. She suffers so from a terminal case of proselytizis. Patients, strangers, saw her coming, and committed suicide by drowning themselves in their bedpans."

"Did they send you because Joan Rivers is subbing for Johnny tonight?" asked Marti, her voice revealing her annoyance.

"Well, so much for lightening the moment," said Margaret as she collapsed at the foot of Marti's bed. "So let's get down to it. How are you doing?"

Marti shrugged, aware Margaret was in tune with her darkest thoughts.

"Listen, m'love. You've had some hard knocks in your life, and you just had another. But you're still here. What's more, you haven't had it that much worse than a lot of other people."

"Are you crazy?" asked Marti, her voice rising in anger. "How many people have some madman trying to kill them?"

"I don't know. Nor do you. Nor do they. Furthermore, Marti, you don't know if it was a madman or just another mad moment in time."

"It could have been him," argued Marti.

"It also could have been Him," said Margaret. "Maybe there's a lesson in all of this."

"Now who's proselytizing?" asked Marti, annoyed.

"Me. But then I'm the one who has lived with death threats most of my adult life. Oh, stop looking so dumb. What conceit made you think you were the only one? Mine began with my position during the McCarthy era. I was very unpopular for not testifying, you know. Then my pen pals increased when I became known as that Scarlet Woman whose lover was not the father of her child. Yes, it was frightening. But I lived through it. Check my words, my dear, they are important. I said, I *lived* through it. Not 'got through it' but *lived*. My life went on as though nothing unusual was happening. It had to. So does yours."

"That's easy for you to say," said Marti as she clutched the top sheet to her chin. "You don't live with the threat of death hanging over you constantly."

"Of course I do," protested Margaret. "All people these days do, whether they know it or not. First, there's the button-and-the-bomb. You know that story, Marti. One push of the button and it's all over. For everybody. Then, too, there's the other threat that people my age live with daily. I'm sixty, Marti, not the ball of fire I once was and hardly a match for a mugger. I live in unsafe times in a city not always known for its benign states. Muggings and murders happen daily. To all people. Marti, everyone is a potential victim. Assassination takes many forms. Mugging is one. Rape is another. The nut who unloads his rifle from the roof of a building into a crowd of strangers is still another. As is the crazy who bombs airports and consuls and hijacks planes. My God, Marti, if we all took stock of the potential 'assassins' out there, we'd barricade our doors and never go out."

"Sounds good to me," said Marti dryly.

"If that's your choice," replied Margaret as she moved from the foot of the bed to a place directly by her niece's side. "But what happened to all those wonderful words of the weekend? 'Margaret, less is more. I don't need a full-time job because that's what living is.' What the hell was all that, Marti, edits from a Liv Ullman or Shirley MacLaine biography?"

"I meant it then," said Marti angrily.

"Well, mean it now, damn it. Nothing has changed. No! For once, shut your mouth and consider what I have just said. *Nothing* has changed. He's either out there or he isn't. He'll either get you or he won't. But before he does, you may. That was true before this evening and it will be true tomorrow. It's your choice. Less could be more or less could be nothing at all if you choose to make it that."

"Where are you going?" asked Marti as Margaret wrapped her "legendary lady" mink about her and strode toward the door.

"That was an exit speech, sweetheart, and since I could never top those lines I might just as well get off the stage. Besides, how this scene ends is in your hands."

"The scene but not the play," said Marti as she slumped back into the pillows.

"That, too, kiddo, whether you see it or not. You're your own playwright."

The phone rang just as Margaret exited, blowing kisses as if to a claque in a balcony. The tremulous voice asking her name was Nelson's. Through the receiver she could feel his fear and hear his concern. Nelson, who hardly ever spoke, was now talking to her, although more to himself. She answered. Words, sentences, phrases to assure him that she was alive. Yes, she would be home tomorrow. Yes, just some simple tests. Some simple bruises. Nothing really wrong.

As she made his world safe for him, Marti could hear the tightness in Nelson's voice lessen. His anxiety abated with her own. She was safe within Nelson's neediness. Seconds later, when Ali took the phone, spoke, cried, Marti felt the urgency of her daughter's need. Mark was perhaps the biggest surprise, however. The boy who seldom showed his emotions except through his music was revealing them to her now in sentiments of a child rather than an about-to-be man. She reassured him and as she did, she, herself, felt reassured.

His voice on the telephone surprised her. She had forgotten it was Monday and that he would be there to treat Nelson. He was asking about her, the caring apparent not just in the stumbling words but in the obvious feeling.

"I'm all right, Matthew," Marti replied softly. "I'm all right," she repeated as much for herself as to him. As she relaxed her head onto the pillow, the phone propped at her ear, Marti smiled as she realized just how all right she really was.

6

No, I'M NOT ALL RIGHT, DAMN IT," SAID JESSAMYN angrily, "but I do thank you for noticing. In fact, I'm truly surprised you did, considering how you've noticed precious little other than *your* work of late."

"Jess, either get off my back or tell me what the hell it is that's bothering you," said JJ, annoyed with the tension that had been constant for weeks in the house.

"It's you. All you. Not *us*, but you and *your* involvement with Amex. Your involvement with unconditional amnesty. *Your* life. There's no us."

"Oh, bullshit, Jessamyn," said JJ as he paced angrily about the sofa where Jessamyn was sitting. "It's all for us. Without unconditional amnesty, I can't take you and our child home. I'm stuck here, and although that doesn't seem to me any longer to be the worst of fates, it does seem so to you."

"I want a larger blackboard on which to write my name. I've told you that a hundred times," said Jessamyn. "But you don't understand. The very choice of your words proves that. *You're* stuck here but *we* don't have to be. How many properties, suggestions for films and documentaries, have been sent to us? And you ignore them all. Too busy, you say. And with what? Working with an organization that calls itself American Exiles, a fancy name for malcontents, leftists, and misfits."

"Damn it, Jess, I'm busy with the most important work of my life," protested JJ. "And with one of the most important organizations. What the hell do I care right now about some independent film or documentary when the work before me is the most meaningful."

"Oh, shit, but you can be a pompous ass," said Jessamyn bitterly.

"Look, Jess, I don't know what's gotten into you, but I wish it would get out," said JJ, more annoyed than he had ever allowed himself to feel with his wife's ever-increasing petulance.

"Me, too, and in two more months it will and then I won't be trapped by it or my body any longer," said Jessamyn, knowing her words would shock JJ.

"Do you hate the baby that much?" asked JJ, incredulous at his wife's overt hostility.

"When it is to the exclusion of all else, which it now has become, yes. But that's your fault. You've made the baby my entire life instead of giving me, or helping me to have, a life independent of the one I'm carrying."

For the first time in weeks, JJ stopped to really look at Jessamyn. Although she had gained relatively little weight, she was swollen, not just in the belly but in her face and her feet. There was a lumpiness that was as mental as it was physical to her. She was as close to being slovenly as he could remember. She was staring at him now, her dark eyes challenging him to challenge her last statement. She wanted to fight. He lacked the time.

"Jess, what would you like me to do?"

"I would say Think about us, but you'd only reply that's what you're doing," said Jessamyn as she slouched farther into the sofa. "We should be working. We had momentum going for us, and now we've lost it. Don't look at me that way. Sure, it means nothing to you because you've had it all before. You've had everything all your life. Well, I haven't. And I want it. This was my chance. I gave it my best shot and it was heard pretty much round the world. You could have compromised. You could've worked with Amex in the evenings, done your 'grass-roots lobbying' on time other than ours. But no. We were put on the back burner, and now the fire has gone out."

"We'll build other fires," said JJ. "We'll make plenty of money."

"Who cares about money?" screamed Jessamyn. "It's the expression, the outlet, I want."

"Jess," said JJ patiently, "we've been over this before and I don't intend to go over it again. Amex is the only organization that has clout, or to use your words, an outlet, an expression. I have to work through it. Sorry, but the issues involved take precedence over everything else. I thought you understood that. My career doesn't mean diddley shit next to what we are hoping to accomplish. The Democratic Convention is but three months away. Three, Jess. That's all the time we have left to affect their party platform. And we're close. We are as near to having them write an unconditional-amnesty plank as we're likely to get. And we can't let up. If we do, if we cease bringing pressure, we'll lose the plank. So I write my letters to grass-roots delegates and I make my phone calls and I hope to God that someone—since McGovern says he can't—will get through to Carter, who doesn't feel as an independent that he has to follow the Democratic platform. Now once more, Jess," continued JJ as though he were talking to a child, "I'll explain what that means. Carter is talking about an unconditional pardon. A pardon, Jess, for resisters. Not deserters, like me, but resisters. We object to that. You should, too, because it traps us here. We also object to the word *pardon*, as it implies guilt. As if we will be pardoned for our crimes. No dice. We are not guilty."

"And as I've told you a thousand times, you will never convince your countrymen of that," said Jessamyn. "You may eventually win your point, but you will still lose. You will always be seen as guilty as most deserters are," said Jessamyn vehemently.

"So then, you can see the battle we are waging and why," replied JJ.

And suddenly, to her amazement, Jessamyn could. Although she had heard JJ's words more times than she would have liked, even in more erudite sentiments, it was as if she was hearing him for the first time. She heard him so well that her skin began to tingle as his words took on ideas in her head. It would make a marvelous film. Not a feature but a short. One man's fight. One man's persistence, obstinacy, integrity, and stupidity. She would follow and photograph it from now through the convention and afterward. A slice of history recorded through her eyes. Her own. Not JJ's.

As the film took shape, so did Jessamyn's plan to board a plane the following day to take her idea to Tyne Philips in New York. JJ need never know and, given the intensity with which he was working, probably would not until the idea was sold—which Jessamyn was certain Tyne Philips could do. It needn't even be for theatrical release as it could snuggle nicely into a "60 Minutes" format.

For the first time in months, more than Jessamyn's skin was tingling. She felt alive and a visceral pleasure that her husband was embarked as passionately as he was on work he considered the most important of his life. Soon she would be sharing that feeling. Soon what was his would be hers.

*   *   *

As Reese sat rooted behind the wheel of her Volkswagen, she looked at the two-story, white Colonial house set back from the street and thought how nothing about it had changed. As in every spring, the azaleas and lilac bushes gave the house a greeting-card pleasantness. Remembering how she once had been responsible for the weeding of the garden behind the house made Reese tremble. Disgusted by her fear, Reese, despite palpitations, pushed herself out the open car door. If I can drive down from Boston, I can walk the remaining steps to my parents' home, she told herself encouragingly.

It was a perfect May morning. The sky was bright and clear and as Reese looked up and down Brooklawn Avenue and then again at the house before her, she tried to remember if ever, even when she was a girl, the day had seemed so crisp and new to her. It hadn't. There was in contrast a drab feeling about the house and her memories.

The face that appeared and then disappeared behing the lace curtains of the living-room picture window made Reese realize her parents might be as apprehensive about their meeting as she was. A long time had passed between visits. A lifetime, actually, thought Reese. She was a year sober this very week. A birthday. A celebration. Although the visit to her parents had been her gift to herself, Reese, with her finger poised on the doorbell, wondered if it were a mistake. Was anything to be gained by it? Her mounting anxiety answered her questions. There comes a time in one's life, Reese reasoned, when one shouldn't be afraid of one's parents or one's feelings about them.

Celia Tomlinson was also afraid, although she did not know it. The closeness she had once shared, or thought she had, with her daughter was past. When Reese had called two days ago to say she would be driving down, Celia had not been pleased. She was not a woman who liked surprises. Her life was always organized and Celia was always in control. But not this morning, as Celia had no idea why her daughter was visiting. And that was unnerving.

Celia Tomlinson had been watching Reese from the safety of her living room for several minutes. In a flat voice, she had announced to her husband that Reese had arrived, but Morgan Tomlinson did not move. Instead, he remained rooted in his club chair reading the *Wall Street Journal* as he did every morning when he wasn't either at the hospital or at his office seeing patients. Privately, Morgan Tomlinson wished his daughter would hurry so he could deal and dispense with whatever she wanted and he could hurry on to meet Tyler and Mills on the golf course as planned.

Reese saw the disapproving look on her mother's face as soon as Celia Tomlinson opened the front door. According to her mother's dress code, only children—and then, only those at play—should wear jeans. In Celia Tomlinson's world, a woman was judged by her dress. Good taste dictated skirts and blouses and ropes of pearls. It certainly did not mean pants, no matter what name the designer label bore.

The women greeted each other with an arm's-length kiss on the cheek. Reese noted there was no warmth to her mother's embrace or her skin. Celia was relieved not to smell liquor on her daughter's breath. "Your father has a golf date at one, so lunch will be at eleven-thirty. I trust that's not too early," said Celia as she disappeared into the kitchen before Reese could answer.

Although the house looked and smelled freshly painted, like its outside and its general feeling, nothing had changed. It was still "well appointed" as her mother's friends would say of the solid but uninteresting furnishings. The colors remained neutral. Mainly beiges and burnished golds. Morgan Tomlinson rose as his daughter entered the living room. In his gray slacks and a white cardigan sweater worn over a button-down oxford blue shirt, like the room in which he sat, Morgan Tomlinson also looked well appointed. At sixty-seven, the doctor, contrary to most men of his age, had not shrunk an inch from his six-foot frame. Perfunctorily, he kissed Reese on the cheek.

"So how are the kids?" he asked as he rearranged himself in his favorite chair.

Immediately, Reese felt as if someone had struck a match to her insides.

"And Thomas?" added her father. The flame became a fire. Morgan Tomlinson seemed unaware of his daughter's slow burn as she again answered his question with the single word *fine*. From the kitchen Reese heard her mother call: "Lunch in five minutes." The call had always been Celia Tomlinson's command to her family to wash before coming to the table. Some pull from the past urged Reese to use the upstairs bathroom. Before entering it, she looked into the room that once had been hers but was now a TV room and den. Her mother, thought Reese, had finally achieved her lifelong dream: To have a room that contained all the mess of everyday living while the rest of her house remained "well appointed." Reese was surprised at the hurt she felt when she realized the room she had so loved as a little girl was no more, but then, neither was the little girl. Abruptly, Reese was overwhelmed by a sense of loss for her childhood. As she wept, she realized the truth of the words her therapist had so often used in describing the hurt she still nurtured. It belonged to the past and was inappropriate in the present.

In the bathroom, Reese washed the irritation from her eyes, chanting as she did words she had so often heard at A.A. meetings. *There is only today.* In the full-length mirror affixed to the back of the bathroom door, Reese looked at her today. She was two years shy of forty, but at one hundred and three pounds she was the exact same weight as the day she had left this house to marry Thomas Ollson. Her hair was the same honey blond with only a few strands of gray to betray her age. Although still only five-foot-three, she appeared taller. Gone with the sixteen pounds she had lost over the past year was the slouch and the rounding of her shoulders. If she wasn't young, she was at least youthful. As she stared at herself, Reese appreciated her changes. They had been hard won and she could not allow anyone to diminish their gain. As she took control of herself, Reese thanked her Higher Power and the A.A. meetings she had attended at the Church of the Advent on Brimmer Street two days after she had arrived in Boston a year ago. Within that first month, that old, ivy-covered building was as much home to her as the one she had rented on Marlborough Street. Initially, the A.A. meetings were her day, her entire day, as she searched them out all over Boston. They and her determination kept her sober. Thomas, too, had helped with his support from afar, as had Marti. But it was mainly Thomas who had been a silent partner in the business at hand. For twelve months, Reese had been sober, but she had only been free of her addictions the past five. Until Christmas, she had "forgotten" to mention to anyone, including herself, that she was taking Librium three times a day; her supply replenished by the sample packets her father continuously sent through the mails. She hadn't thought of the tranquilizer as a problem until someone suggested, and that someone was Reese, that it was. If further proof was needed, Reese found it in her fear of giving up the drug. With her therapist's and A.A.'s help she did, and, as she did, Reese had become enraged.

Reese was feeling that rage as she came down the carpeted staircase and entered the dining room where her parents were sitting silently, obviously waiting for their daughter to explain her unexpected and uninvited visit. Celia Tomlinson had prepared her standard and simple lunch. Eggs, sausage, salad, corn muffins, and a pot of Postum. They ate quietly, her father seldom looking up from his plate while her mother frequently looked up from hers to assess Reese's face.

"I don't think you know I've been taking classes at night. In fact," said Reese, savoring the moment for her news, "I've been accepted as a full-time student this fall in the master's program in special education at Boston University."

"But who is looking after the children?" asked Celia Tomlinson.

The china cup in Reese's hand cracked in half as she smashed it into its saucer. "Damn it, Mother, I'm telling you I've been accepted into a prestigious master's program, that I'll be taking classes in learning disabilities and emotional problems—and you ask who is watching the children. Doesn't it mean anything to you that within a school year I will be taking care of many children, special children, children who need me?"

"You needn't yell, Reese. Your mother and I can hear you," said Morgan Tomlinson as he calmly sipped his Postum.

"Then say something!" pleaded Reese, annoyed with herself for the demands she had promised she wouldn't make.

"What would you like us to say, Reese?" asked Celia Tomlinson as she neatly folded her napkin and placed it in front of her plate.

"How about Congratulations or That's terrific, for openers," said Reese. "Something supportive for a change," she added, her voice both hostile and angry.

"Look, Reese," began Celia Tomlinson, her voice and manner assuming the tone of superiority Reese knew so well. "If you think you can barge into *my* home and abuse us, you're wrong. I will not permit it. Neither your father nor I intend to be victims of your diatribe."

"I am simply trying to talk to you, but once again you don't wish to hear one single thing I have to say. You never did, particularly if it differed from your point of view," said Reese, pained at the memories. "In your mind, in your world, I was always foolish or rebellious. Tell me, what is foolish or rebellious about wanting to work with emotionally disturbed or handicapped children? Particularly since that is all I have ever wanted to do."

"You might have started with your own," said Celia Tomlinson coldly. "Lord knows they could have used *something* from you these past years."

"You can't give what was never given to you, Mother," said Reese, hoping her words would act as a slap in her mother's face.

"Your father and I gave you every possible advantage. Public schools weren't good enough so we sent you to private schools. And at quite an expense, I might add."

"Yes, mine, if you remember. I hated it. I begged not to go. But would you hear me? No. It was always what you deemed best," yelled Reese.

"You were a child. An ungrateful one at that. You were privileged and what did you do with those privileges? You abused them. And you abused us. Yes, *us*. The shame you have brought to this house, to our name, with your filthy problem. Ever since that hideous story appeared in the *Enquirer*, your father and I haven't had a good day."

"And what about my days?" asked Reese as tears stung her eyes. "Do you know what it's like to have your life splayed across some terrible tabloid for all the world to read? People talk about you as though you're a thing and not a person. Mother, if it was bad for you, and I can understand how embarrassing it must have been, given the 'circle' in which you travel, then think of how it must have been for me. And for my family. Thomas was trying to find a job, my children their way in school, and suddenly they have to deal with the public knowledge that their mother is a drunk. And none of us know to this day how they got the story of my 'filthy problem,' as you so delicately described it. And how nice of you to be concerned," continued Reese, hurt and sarcasm connecting her every word.

"Since you seem to have forgotten, it was you who asked us not to come to Boston, you who rejected us," said Celia Tomlinson.

"I didn't want you to see me as I was. It was awful in the beginning, and I had enough difficulty handling me without having to handle you—which is what I have had to do all of my adult life," said Reese as tears blinded her vision.

"Reese, if you've come all this way to chastise your father and me for our failings, stop right now," said Celia Tomlinson, her face as stony as her voice. "We've looked into our hearts and we have clear consciences. As God is my witness, we did whatever we knew to do. We fail to see what we have done wrong or what we did to . . ."

"To what, Mother? To deserve a daughter like me?" asked Reese, finishing the sentence her mother regretted having started. "Then let me tell you. You were never there. Even when Thomas was in Vietnam and you came to California, you weren't there.

Not for me, anyway, but for you. To preserve some image of yourself and how your daughter should be in times of trouble. You brought gifts but you never brought yourselves. You tried to make me into some kind of *total* woman; total by your definition. The implication was always that I was incomplete and imperfect. You never encouraged me to be me. Just the opposite. I was stifled, smothered, pushed, and molded into being another you. It was always, Smile, Reese. Be a good little girl, Reese. My God, but it nearly killed me being what you and everybody from the nuns on to Thomas wanted me to be. Not nearly but did kill me. But in the past year I've been resurrecting that me, nurturing that bold little girl who thought rebelliously but couldn't act on her feelings. I'm defining me, and it isn't some incarnation of you or your sisters or your mother. But it's me and I refuse to bear one more ounce of guilt for not measuring up to who you think *me* should be."

Breathless, Reese knew if she didn't attempt to check her feelings, she would be sobbing and all control would be lost. Looking at her parents' faces she saw confusion. "Dad," she began, her voice softer and more conciliatory, "as soon as I walked in the door you asked about Thomas and the children but you didn't ask about me. That hurt. I'm your daughter. Don't you care? Dad, I told you the kids and Thomas are fine. I lied. Karl is a loner. I seldom see him and when I do he acts a total stranger. He runs, Dad. I understand he's very good, so good that his coach is talking about the Olympics. But I've never seen him run because he's never asked me to a meet. He's never asked Thomas either. He's probably afraid his father would criticize, would tell him to stand straight when he's standing as straight as he can.

"Kelly," continued Reese, her voice near a whisper. "I have no idea what I am to her. She will be thirteen in November. A most unusual child. Just a fair student but the most popular girl in her class. With the boys. She's a real jock. You know they call girls jocks now. Well, some girls anyway. Yes, Kelly is on all the teams at school and, from what I now understand, all the teams from the surrounding boys' schools are on hers. I had to have her fitted for a diaphragm just recently. But she is popular. Oh, very popular," added Reese as her parents sat captive, too horrified to move. "Her father knows none of this, by the way. He thinks his little Kelly is perfect but worries about Kristan.

"Finally, thank God, someone is worrying about Kristan," said Reese as tears rolled down her face. "You'll be horrified to learn your granddaughter has just signed a contract with a jeans manufacturer that will make her independently wealthy. Her father is ignorant of this too. He just damns the whole modeling profession but doesn't know exactly what it is Kristan does. Nor does Kristan. She just poses, smiles, struts, and then returns home where she excels at school and at homemaking. This is the best little person I've ever known. She gives so much and it hurts me so that in her brief life so few have been able to give to her."

Reese's face was buried in her hands as she sobbed. "You asked and now your know about my children. Now let me tell you about Thomas. Since February, he has been working as if his life depended on it, and indeed it may. Of course, at the pace he is going, the work may kill him—but that's a small price for having one's integrity, one's sense of belonging, returned. Thank God for the job. Till Revere wanted him, the famous decorated war hero was treated like dirt, even by our neighbors. My 'filthy problem' exposed in print had the same effect as a scalpel. It cut right through him. But he's recovering. He works twelve-hour days, sleeps, when he is lucky enough to sleep, since he is now an insomniac, four or five hours, and then plots and plans every last detail of his salvation and new toy. With the traveling his job requires, he's seldom at home and when he is, he's too tired to be a husband."

"Then how can you leave him to attend school?" asked Celia Tomlinson. "I don't understand. He needs you."

"Yes, Thomas needs me. The children need me. But I need me more. I have to do for me first if I'm ever to do for another person," said Reese. "Mom, I know I have done my children irreparable harm. I live with that daily. But I also know I didn't mean to, which is true of you, too. I know you didn't mean to hurt me —but you did. For years I drank because I couldn't support that hurt. My life, as it was, haunts me. My children, as they are, kill me. But what happened happened. I can't change the past. I can only try to make today better. To do that, I have to do things

1 4 3

for me. I'm not yet sure who me is but when I am, I'll be able to be there for others. Who knows? Someday I may be able to help other children. Maybe I can be for them what I couldn't be for my own."

Reese was crying silently, trying to reach the question she had come to her parent's home to ask, when Morgan Tomlinson said, "Reese, why did you come here today?"

"To see you, Dad. To understand. Dad, you knew I had a drinking problem. You knew I had emotional problems. Why then for God's sake did you give me Librium. Certainly you must have known or at least suspected the addiction it was creating."

"It was a medical decision," said Morgan Tomlinson impassively. "Some people can stand up to and survive stress. You could not. I felt you were disturbed."

"Disturbed? You bet you was, Dad, but I'd also bet not half as disturbed as you were. Imagine *your* daughter being a drunk. How humiliating! You bet it was humiliating, Dad, but much more for me than for you.

"Do you know what you did, Dad?" asked Reese, her voice rising in rage. "You made me an addict. Oh, you did. No two ways about it. Yes, I asked for the pills but you gave them. Over and over you gave them. Dad, instead of prescribing pills, why didn't you prescribe a clinic or some kind of treatment center? Alcoholism is a disease. Certainly you as a doctor must know that. So why, Dad? Was the Librium to quiet my nerves or your conscience? When I was kept quiet, were your nagging little voices kept stilled? Dad, tell me the tranquilizers didn't tranquilize your fears and guilt, maybe even your anger, more than they did mine. Tell me they also didn't dispense with your responsibility. Keep the kid sedated and maybe that way we can keep her and her disgrace off our backs and out of our lives."

"Everything you just said only proves to me that what I did was right," said Morgan Tomlinson calmly. "Reese, you're my daughter, but you're not only ungrateful but disturbed."

"Disturbed, I'm not. At least not in the way you mean. But ungrateful I am. What is there to be grateful for? Do you know," said Reese as she rose from the table, her eyes red and rimmed by tears, "I drove all this way because here I am, an adult woman, almost forty, and I want so much for you to be proud of me. I've started over. I'm accomplishing great things. It's wonderful, but what's so sad is neither of you can see it. And what's sadder still is I still want you to see it. And it's ridiculous," said Reese as she took her coat from the banister where she had placed it, "because if you couldn't do it back then, why would I ever think you could do it now?"

As she stood at the door, Reese looked at her mother, who was wearing her injured look like a medal. In that second, Reese knew it was over and done and that she would never again have this discussion with her parents. She had faced what she thought was the enemy and had found only people.

"I want you to know something," said Reese, "despite everything I said, I love you both. Someday, I hope you'll understand I came here not to hurt you but to help me. There's a very big difference between the two."

*   *   *

Nelson's eyes were riveted on the TV screen. To Matthew Strohl, it seemed as if the boy was projecting himself into Madison Square Garden and onto the convention floor. The moment on screen and off was tense. The NBC newscaster was explaining how Fritz Efaw, a draft resister exiled in London, had become a delegate to the Democratic Convention by using a ploy that allowed him to represent Democrats living overseas. Amnesty forces had cleared his attendance at the convention and Efaw had arrived at JFK to a press conference and an arrest that would be delayed until after the convention. Fifty delegates' signatures had been collected to nominate Efaw as a vice-presidential candidate.

Bitterness was deeply etched into Nelson's face as he heard how the procedures committee tried to block Efaw's nomination. Anger joined the bitterness when the newscaster explained that Efaw, about to be denied the nomination, had decided to nominate Louise Ransom, a Gold Star Mother, in his stead. Laughter made the face that of Nelson's again when it was explained that the Democratic Party then decided better Efaw as a candidate than a woman and allocated fifteen minutes for Efaw's nomination.

1 4 5

Matthew was concentrating on Nelson and Nelson on the TV screen when Marti entered the room with a pot of coffee and the German chocolate cake she had made that morning. Fascinated by the images in the room and on the TV screen, Marti sat on the floor to watch both dramas unfold.

The camera fixed on Louise Ransom. Her face and her words filled the nineteen-inch screen. "My credentials for addressing this convention have been earned in the hardest possible way. My oldest son was killed in Vietnam on Mother's Day, 1968. The only way we can give meaning to the lives of our sons, to guarantee that their deaths shall not have been for nothing, is to demonstrate that we have learned something from them and to ensure that never again will there be another Vietnam. Total amnesty would be a fitting memorial to the sacrifice of my son. Therefore, with pride, I put into nomination the name of exile war resister Fritz Efaw."

Nelson's tears were visible to both Marti and Matthew.

"He could be me," said Nelson softly.

"Efaw?" asked Matthew.

"No, her son. The one who died . . . for nothing," replied Nelson, "which is sometimes how I feel."

Matthew did not respond. Himself a veteran of the Vietnam War, although not of the active fighting, he felt conflicted. Although he had been treating many kinds of people since his voluntary retirement from service, Matthew had been unprepared for Nelson Naismith. This was the other side of the coin he had failed to recognize until it was placed for safekeeping in his hand. Although his feelings about American involvement in Vietnam were now confused, his loyalties to the military, his family for twenty years, remained fixed. To his consternation, he was seeing more and more veterans of the war in his private practice. All were disturbed but none of them were mentally ill. All seemed lost, confused, and angry. All could have been named Nelson. Like him, they were experiencing a loss of identity and ego strength. They felt alone and unsupported.

"I don't know that I could survive the loss of a child," said Marti in response to Louise Ransom.

Nelson stood up abruptly, his manner suddenly that of a wild animal seeking escape. Matthew, instinctively understanding what

Marti's offhand remark had triggered, stood between Nelson and the door. Nelson's parents had never called. Unlike Louise Ransom, they had given up their son for dead without a fight. Unlike Marti, they had survived the loss of their child seemingly quite well.

Matthew's arm reached out and touched Nelson's shoulder. It rested there until Nelson's face softened and with it, the body that had turned to stone.

As the camera panned the convention floor showing the crowd standing and applauding as the name Fritz Efaw was placed into nomination, Jessamyn trained her handheld camera on JJ as he watched the TV screen with the baby snuggled in his arms. So engrossed was he in the drama of the moment that JJ was oblivious to Jessamyn. That fact no longer disturbed Jessamyn, as she was now oblivious to JJ except as a subject for her financed film.

The delegates were barely resettled in their seats when Vietnam veteran Ron Kovic was wheeled to the podium. As JJ rocked the baby wrapped in blue, he unconsciously moved back from the TV as if to protect his child from Kovic's words.

"I am the living death. Your Memorial Day on wheels. Your Yankee Doodle Dandy. Your John Wayne come home. Your Fourth of July firecracker exploding in the grave."

The baby cried just as JJ thought he would. Kovic's words were as unpretty as his wheelchair; complementing but disturbing realities, thought JJ, of a war in which there were only casualties among those who fought and those who didn't. Was there really any difference between a Kovic and a Nelson? Weren't both crippled; one physically, the other emotionally? The only difference between the two was that one chose to fight as the other didn't. But was that true? asked JJ. Weren't both fighters and did either, given who they are as people, really have a choice? Could Kovic, given his background, have evaded the war and his wheelchair? And didn't it take a particular and even a peculiar kind of strength to follow orders and fight whether or not one believed in—if one even knew—the reasons for that fight? Why would anyone choose a wheelchair in favor of mobility unless there was no real choice?

Confused, JJ began to weep. Suddenly overwhelmed with a

sense of loss and loneliness, he clutched his son to him, thinking of the waste of war, the waste of men, and how his son had to be protected from such future waste. Last, he thought of a man he had not seen in years. There was, after all, a family resemblance.

As he stood at the bar in the Seattle airport, Thomas watched and listened as the chant "Welcome Home, Fritz" carried through the convention floor. To his amazement, only a very few of the delegates refused to be caught in what Thomas thought was madness. None was protesting. The same was true, he observed, of the people about him. Those that were watching the TV set positioned high above the bar, and most were not, watched it as he imagined they had watched the news from the jungles of Vietnam when it appeared with Walter Cronkite reporting: dispassionately, uninvolved, and as if it didn't concern them. A few people in the bar were applauding but no one was protesting. Perhaps the liquor had dulled their protests. Perhaps there were no more protests to be made.

Declining the nomination, Efaw spoke out for amnesty for resisters and deserters alike. As he did, Thomas's eyes searched for Kovic. He was both moved and yet revolted when Efaw left the podium, pushing Kovic in his wheelchair through the hall. It was Efaw who had spoken, but it was Kovic who had moved Thomas. What a waste, he thought, as he drained his Miller Lite. A waste of human potential. He wondered how he would feel if he had lost the use of his legs. Thomas's mind rebelled at the thought. It fought even harder when he asked how he would feel if his legs had been lost for little or no reason? Which is how Kovic must feel, thought Thomas.

With every ounce of strength, Thomas had to stop himself from pounding on the top of the bar, screaming at all those who were watching without seeing, listening without hearing. Look how much this man has given to his country and look how little his country has given to him. Where is his honor, his respect? Where is the applause, the national holiday, the monuments? He has sacrificed, as have others, in vain. War is insane, thought Thomas. It is always insane. It has no basis in reality. But even more insane is not fighting a war when there is one.

Thomas strode from the bar to the boarding gate, where his plane would first take him to Chicago and then to Washington. His meetings with Boeing had gone well. He could afford the price they were quoting for used jets better than the price he was paying standing around in some bar listening to criminal injustice. Tomorrow, he would begin negotiating for space at Dulles Airport for Revere. If none was available, he would do what he had done at Newark—rent from the airlines who did have space. Again, at a price he could afford. The phrase stuck in Thomas's mind. It reminded him of something Reese had said recently about his job, his health, and their marriage, but, try as he did, Thomas couldn't place it. His mind was too busy preparing his case for the Civil Aeronautics Board. In weeks, months, if he performed well, Revere would be performing throughout the Northeast corridor. Unless he did not obtain the Certificate of Public Convenience and Necessity. He could not allow that, let alone think it.

* * *

Their laughter caused others at nearby tables to turn in their direction. Embarrassed, the women looked at each other and then burst into giggles again. Marti took her napkin from her lap and dabbed at the mascara that was running down one cheek, fixing an eye on Reese as she did.

"You're staring," said Reese bluntly.

"I'm trying to decide if that's really you and if this is really me," said Marti. "We certainly don't seem like the same ladies who lunched a few years back at Patricia Murphy's."

"I'd say Let's drink to that, but it would get me in a helluva lot of trouble," said Reese.

"Then let's have dessert instead," suggested Marti. "Something really wicked and gooey."

"Are you crazy? I have finally dieted down to a size eight and you suggest dessert. What nerve! What gall! I'll have the Napoleon."

Again Marti laughed, her delight apparent to those in the Chelsea Tavern who recognized her.

"Easy for you to laugh, but you have no idea what it's like living with a daughter who is not only taller but thinner than you. It's the cruelest blow a mother could take."

1 4 9

"*I* have no idea?" said Marti. "Surely you jest, or else you haven't seen my very own version of Cher lately."

"Poor Kelly hates her, you know," said Reese. "Not Alison but Kristan. Kelly has my body, round and Rubenesque. I think it's called *zaftig* here in New York. Lord, the trouble we had finding her clothes this morning. Thank God, I'm spared from that this afternoon—only God knows what the girls will bring home. Do you remember the first time your mother allowed you to shop for your own clothes?"

"A pink poodle skirt with an angora sweater. I thought I looked gorgeous," said Marti, smiling at the memory.

"And I'm sure you did. I could never wear pink. It made me look like one of those elephants drunks supposedly see when they're on their way up or down," said Reese. As Marti again laughed, Reese continued. "I'm hopeful they'll buy nothing more than jeans. *De rigeur* of the day."

"I'm glad you came," said Marti as she reached across the table for Reese's hand. "It's so good to see you happy."

The silence that greeted her remark made Marti look closely at Reese, who was gazing off into the bar area where the brass fixtures gleamed in the wall-length mirror. "It's only a day. One. Hardly enough time to make up for years of neglect," said Reese softly. "But at least I now know where Kristan is filming and some of the people with whom she works. I feel a bit more relieved, although I don't know why. Some of that crowd seems awfully bizarre."

"She can handle it," said Marti as she picked at what remained of her chocolate cheese cake. "Your daughter is very level headed."

"She had to be," said Reese. "If she wasn't, who in that house would be?"

The remark, not the first of its kind since the women had sat down to lunch shortly after noon, again struck Marti as odd. Although Thomas had yet to be mentioned, Marti felt him everywhere.

"Reese," said Marti softly, "Kristan's okay. Honestly. We spend a lot of time together at the house and she relates so easily to everybody. She and Ali adore each other. In fact, I didn't want to tell you this before, but when Kris visited Ali at Phillips up at Exeter, a few weeks ago, both got confined to quarters—and Kristan's not even a student—for smoking."

"Isn't that rather harsh?" asked Reese.

"For smoking *pot*," added Marti. "My daughter was severely chastised and nearly sent home."

"Ali smokes pot?" asked Reese alarmed.

"Ali does everything once. Or almost everything. This summer my daughter discovered academia and boys, although I'm not sure that is the correct order of discovery. Which is why she wanted to go to Exeter for the summer. Not only does Phillips offer courses in journalism, which is Ali's latest crush, but precalculus and boys, all at the same time. I'm sure by next summer she'll be off on some other bent."

"Thomas would approve," said Reese. "He would think it very sensible. Your brother's not very happy about Kristan working and living here for the summer. He sees the modeling world as terribly wild and wicked."

"Perhaps it is, but Kristan isn't," said Marti. "She's an extraordinarily sensitive and sensible child. You should see her with Nelson. Better still, you should hear her."

There was another uncomfortable silence as Reese signaled the waiter for additional coffee. "They do come from very different backgrounds," she said finally, her voice strained.

"Reese, he's a very nice young man and, despite what you might think are his radical views, he's rather conservative. He's doing quite well now. Mother has made him the 'Maintenance Engineer' at the Tiernan Rep Company and from what I hear he all but keeps the building from falling down. He pays toward his room and board, which you and I both know I don't need, and he has worked out some kind of sliding-scale arrangement with Matthew on his fee."

"Do they see much of each other?"

Without asking, Marti knew the two people Reese was referring to. "Is this your concern or Thomas's?" she asked.

"Marti, it's hard for both of us. I am, after all, Thomas's wife."

The statement hung in the air with the stale cigarette smoke. "Nelson is not convincing Kristan any more than she is convincing him," said Marti. "But they do listen to each other. Your daughter is a true military brat. She is very loyal to her father, but she is open to discussion."

Suddenly there were tears in Reese's eyes. "I miss her, Marti. She's busy; I'm busy. We're all so busy in that house that we are all missing one another constantly. Even when we are there—which isn't often."

"Reese, I think what you are doing is incredible. To go back to school at your age is one thing, but to do it when one is also a wife and mother is quite another."

"Yes, I'm quite incredible," said Reese wryly. "I'm doing it all, or, as the expression goes, having it my way. But it has its price. Who's Matthew?" asked Reese, turning the conversation away from areas where Marti could sense trouble.

The question aroused surprising anxiety within Marti. Who is Matthew? she repeated silently and then wondered why it was she had never asked herself that question. "Matthew is a doctor, a psychiatrist, actually," she began slowly. "Coincidentally, he was the medical officer who interviewed Thomas before his discharge. He is treating Nelson, which is somewhat odd, considering his main practice seems to be with Vietnam veterans. In fact, he has some theory on stress among Viet vets which he is contributing to a study a John Wilson is making. I think it's titled *The Forgotten Warrior*."

It was Reese who was now trying to read through the various expressions that competed for dominance on Marti's face. "I've actually known him a year this month," said Marti as her mind drifted back to their first meeting and Casey Lhorman at Bellevue.

"Is it something serious between you two?" asked Reese, deciding to enter a privacy without an invitation.

"Oh, no," said Marti quickly. "We're just friends. I mean . . . well, that *is* what I mean, we're just friends. Good friends."

"That must be very nice," said Reese, her voice so plaintively soft that Marti was forced from someplace within herself where she had withdrawn to hear Reese. "It must be very nice indeed to have a man who is also your friend. Better still, think of what it must be like if that friend is also your lover."

"Reese, what's wrong?" asked Marti as she poured them both more coffee from the silver pot the waiter had left on their table.

There was a moment's hesitation before Reese spoke. "Thomas and I used to be each other's best friend. There was very little we didn't share. But that's all changed, perhaps because we have. Only I feel my changes are for the better. I'm not certain he would agree."

"But, Reese," Marti interrupted.

"I'm not talking about my alcoholism," said Reese. "He is as pleased as I am that each day that goes by without my taking a drink is . . . a day that goes by without my taking a drink. But I have another kind of life now, Marti, and I think it threatens him. As much as the children do, he needs me at home. But I can't give any of them what they need. It's impossible. Or it's possible but I'm not willing to give it. I have to give to myself first. So as I said before, we're all missing one another as we go on our merry little ways. Only mine is merry, Marti. I love school. I love what I'm doing. But I'm not obsessed with it. Thomas is busier than any one person ought to be. But I don't sense much merry coming from him. Instead, he seems driven. He is obsessed with the airline and making something of it. But it's not about 'It' but him. He is trying in some misguided way to resurrect himself and his image."

"The ads are wonderful, Reese," said Marti. "Thomas seems so self-assured. He makes me want to fly his airline, makes me feel my time and space would be Revered."

"Yes, in the ads, Thomas is this smiling, poised, and con-trolled man—the kind to whom you would trust your life. But at home, he has uncontrollable bursts of temper. He's moody and often depressed. His stomach is a mess. He pushes himself beyond endurance and he pushes the children when none needs to be pushed."

Marti thought back over the years. The Thomas Reese de-scribed was little different from the Thomas she had called Mr. Perfect when they were both growing up. He had always sought perfection, in others but even more in himself. Even as a child, when he was at his most insufferable, he was reliable, a leader, a boy whose manner made it clear you were safe in his charge.

"Marti, I worry so about him. About us, too. We're not as we once were, and we never can be again. He resents this. He resents me. He doesn't say it, but I feel it."

Reese grew silent. Nervously, she played with the silver buttons on the denim jacket that matched her denim pants. "We haven't made love in months. Not that our sex life has been all that great for some years—after all, a drunk isn't the most desirable of partners—but it was adequate. It was something. Now, he brings work home at night and falls asleep in his study. Marti, it's not natural."

Again Marti felt overtaken by anxiety. Her heart was pounding and her stomach was suddenly rejecting the shepherd's pie she had eaten. Unaware that Reese was staring at her, waiting for some kind of reply, Marti waved to the waiter, using one finger of one hand to write across the palm of another, her signal for a check to be delivered. The luncheon was now officially concluded and Marti wanted a similar conclusion to the conversation. She was not about to discuss sex with Reese when she had yet to discuss the subject with herself. Not that there was anything to discuss. Matthew was her friend, not her husband and not her lover.

Well, why the hell isn't he? she asked herself angrily.

She dismissed the question as rapidly as the thought that had entered her head weeks ago that something more might be required of their relationship. Sex was not a necessity. Nor was it a need, let alone a priority. Reese's problems with Thomas had nothing to do with her or with her and Matthew.

"Marti, it feels so awful lying next to someone who acts as if you aren't there," said Reese, her voice betraying the tears she was fighting back. "There have been some nights when I've reached out to him and he's pretended sleep. Oh, God, Marti, that is so awful. He makes me feel bad for wanting it and that's such a terrible feeling to have when you've worked so hard to realize there is something terribly right and good about sex with the right person. I think being sexually rejected is probably the worst thing a woman can be."

"I think many women would envy you, Reese," said Marti angrily. "They'd be relieved that their husbands put so little pressure on them."

"Marti, I've been in both places, and I know they'd be wrong," said Reese simply. "A woman needs to be held and loved. At least this woman does."

Glancing at her watch, Marti said: "Oh my God, Reese, look at the time. I'm due at the hospital in five minutes. Can I drop you anywhere?" asked Marti as she moved quickly toward the door. "Don't look at me that way. What do you expect me to say, damn it. I haven't known about sex in many years. I think that's the one part of me that doctors couldn't bring back to life after the assassination. I've relearned to walk. I've relearned to speak. I've even relearned how to live. No one has a right to ask for more miracles than that."

Reese took Marti's arm as they walked toward Sixth Avenue searching for a taxi. "Yes they do," she replied. "They really do. So don't be afraid. Ask."

*   *   *

Covered by just a sheet, her body warm and drowsy from sleep, Jessamyn reached across the bed for JJ. His absence brought the sounds of the shower into focus. As she lay quite still, Jessamyn imagined the water as it streamed down JJ's body. She pictured his hands as they would lather his neck, his armpits, and his groin. She then thought of his hands as they often massaged her and, as she did, her own hand worked what she felt were miracles.

At first, JJ was startled. With his eyes shut to prevent the shampoo from running into and blinding them, he couldn't see who was massaging his body, pinching a nipple with two fingers while the other was covered by both tongue and mouth. Only her little cries, part whimpers, half moans, identified Jessamyn. There was no need for him to do anything. Within seconds she had him pinned against the tiled wall, positioning them both in such a way that made her feel in control of all of him.

As the water washed over them, Jessamyn could feel his hands on her back and her buttocks, lifting her higher onto him. And then she was being carried from the shower to the bed which within seconds was soaked by their wet bodies. Their cries awakened the baby, but his cries didn't stop theirs until each had arrived at that place where there was nothing more to say or do.

1 5 5

Instantly, Jessamyn rolled off the bed and onto the floor, leaving JJ to tend to the baby as she began her morning exercises. Jessamyn was proud that after but ten weeks, her stomach was flat, devoid of the stretch marks she had feared and hated.

As JJ held David Blanchard Ollson in his arms, he marveled anew at Jessamyn's energy, enjoying the fact that she was active and happy again. Jessamyn's uninhibited passion never failed to arouse and delight him. And it was there constantly, not just in bed but in the work that occupied most of her day and often part of her night. Although she had refused to allow him to see any part of her uncompleted film, he could sense the excitement that served to feed his. The film, after all, was about if not him, per se, then those like him who were fighting in exile for unconditional amnesty. For the first time in their married life, Jessamyn followed him everywhere, often but two steps behind. He rather liked the attention, and the fact that she was often her camera did not disturb him.

From the first, it had been apparent that mothering was not Jessamyn's greatest talent. Although she did not neglect David, she certainly did not allow his needs to rule their home or her life. David was not fed upon demand. Nor was he changed when in need unless JJ did the changing. Jessamyn's attitude was: everything in its time and place, and David's time and place came second to her own.

JJ, too, had never been busier. Just after the convention, he and his fellow exiles in the amnesty movement launched a post-card campaign to press Carter into broadening his position on amnesty. This past week, after deciding they should go to the media rather than wait for the media to come to them, through Amex, he had participated in a mailing to some 350 radio talk shows offering himself and others as guests. Already there had been some positive responses. Within weeks, JJ would be talking for amnesty throughout the United States without ever leaving his home. He would be speaking out for and arguing his cause in open dialogues with Americans. He blessed phone-in radio for the opportunity.

Only Jessamyn worried about it as she wondered how to make talk-show radio come alive for her camera. There was one idea that appealed to her greatly: to create drama by in some way convincing Thomas Ollson to be one of the callers. Her efforts to reach Thomas at Revere, without JJ's knowledge, ended in frustration and rage. And after her mother-in-law's visit a few weeks back, a visit during which Jessamyn felt Carolyn's judgment and censure of her as a mother, she knew better than to ask any member of JJ's family for assistance. Instead, she pressed Tyne Philips for access to Thomas Ollson. Tyne knew Thomas's former editors. Certainly one would have his home phone.

Confident, Jessamyn not only looked but felt wonderful. Her film, a study of one man who represented many others, was taking shape. It depicted many aspects of the man, none of which was she about to discuss with the man, himself, for fear of losing his involvement. What JJ didn't know about what he thought was *his* film wouldn't hurt.

Particularly pleasing was the footage of Carolyn with the baby. Although she didn't have a signed release from Carolyn saying she could use the film, Jessamyn doubted any lawsuits would be forthcoming. Carolyn's inclusion was an important statement. Or so Jessamyn believed. The beloved "first lady" visiting her son and grandchild would provoke comment. As would Kay, who spoke logically and yet dispassionately about America and amnesty. She was an unexpected voice of reason who would create controversy without antagonizing.

It was all there, decided Jessamyn as she once again stepped into the shower, there on film and here in this house. It was a good life. Things were happening and the more they did, the more she felt alive. As she washed the sweat of the morning's activity from her body, Jessamyn heard JJ humming as he shaved.

"What time do we leave?" she asked from behind the shower curtain.

"As soon as everyone gets here. About eleven, I guess. Why?"

"Because I want to film it," said Jessamyn. "This is, after all, a big day," she added as she flung back the shower curtain, revealing her glistening wet body. "And get that look off your face, Ollson. One hour is not enough time for what you so obviously have on your mind."

"Why not?" asked JJ. "The leaflets are packed in the trunk of the car, the baby's formula is cooking. Your equipment is packed and ready to go and . . . so is mine," said JJ as he peeled the towel off his body to prove his point.

"Oh, shit. If this keeps up, I'm going to look like some god-damn prune," said Jessamyn as JJ turned on the water full blast.

Curled into a tight little ball, knees to chest, he was trying to breathe ever so softly so as not to disturb the silence. In vain. The all too familiar and terrible sound, metallic and harsh, broke into his consciousness as it broke the new day into pieces of pain and fear. As he waited, trembling, the sound entered his ear and drilled its way to his brain. And the door opened and he screamed as he flung himself into the darkness.

Thomas stood naked in the middle of the motel room, sweat pouring down his body as he fought to establish time and place. With the draperies drawn, the question of night or day was moot. Shaking his head, he delved to remember. Buffalo. He was in Buffalo. A combined business and pleasure trip. All was well. It was just another day, Saturday of the Labor Day weekend.

Buffalo. An ugly city but a possible profitable route for Revere. There was lots of traffic between Boston and Buffalo. Nothing to fear. Come Tuesday, he would find space at the airport as he had at the other airports in the other cities Revere intended to service. All was well, he repeated. His meetings with the Civil Aeronautics Board were behind him. He was certain he had successfully shown the need for supplying additional service with the suggested new Revere routes. And they had been impressed by his plan to position Revere as a low-fare, unique-route service, flying into small suburban airports as well as the major ones. He was absolutely positive, now that he had proven Revere's safety record, that the certificate would be forthcoming any day. He had been positive of this for many days . . . and weeks and soon into months. All was well, he repeated. Then why, he questioned, the pervasive feeling of impending doom?

The dream. He began to tremble as he remembered and once again heard the jangling metallic sound. He screamed as the door opened. The woman who stood for a moment in the entranceway was in shadows. As she came running toward him, he threw up his arms in defense.

"Thomas, it's me!" said Reese as she flung her arms about his waist, securing him as one might a small boat about to slip away from its moorings during a violent storm.

"I had a dream," he explained haltingly. "I guess I still wasn't totally awake when you came in."

Reese looked at Thomas's ashen face. Despite the night's sleep, he looked exhausted. Which is why she had suggested they take the Labor Day weekend as their own. He was tired; she was tired; their relationship was tired. Not that she had said as much, although she did state a need to be alone with him. And since he had to be in Buffalo and since neither had ever seen Niagara Falls, why not make it a holiday?

Thomas had not protested. After the children had been sent to Marti's for the long weekend, they had flown to Buffalo where they then rented a car for the sightseeing they intended to do. Their first evening alone had been lost as Thomas fell into bed shortly after they arrived and had slept even as she watched the late movie. But this day Reese had determined would be special. While Thomas had slept, she had driven to the local markets where she had purchased all one could need for a day's outing and picnic, including a red-checkered tablecloth with matching napkins. On the map she had gotten from the AAA, she had red crayoned their route for the day. First, they would drive up to the Rainbow Bridge, see the falls on the American side and then drive into Canada where they would picnic in Victoria Park. Afterward, they would drive along the Niagara River to Crystal Beach near Fort Erie before returning via the Peace Bridge to the U.S. According to her plan, they would return in time for a leisurely dinner before bed.

Bed. She had bought a new nightgown. Nothing obvious but something pretty. She would let him set the pace but she would set the tone. Although she was certain he would laugh, if not even ridicule, she had purchased some candles. To her delight, Reese was excited at the idea of spending a weekend alone with Thomas. Remembrances of Hawaii, their weekends, and weeks together, spent joyously, when he was on leave during his years in the military, reverberated in her mind.

"Are you about ready to leave?" Reese asked as she loosened her grip on Thomas.

"I need to shower," Thomas replied.

"Don't forget to take your trunks. And a towel. The guidebook says the swimming is good at Crystal Beach."

That he didn't reply, Reese interpreted as a sign of his willingness. Last night, on the plane from New York, he had fumbled for conversation as had she. They were awkward together, almost like two kids on a first date, trying to find a common ground that was safe and comfortable. Eventually, he talked about his work, Buffalo, and its meaning to Revere. He never asked about the master's program she would officially begin in two weeks and she didn't mention it. She had been disappointed but not surprised when he had fallen asleep but minutes after they had settled into their motel room.

From the shower she heard him say, "You know, I've always wanted to see the falls."

The tone of his voice, so similar to that of a boy she had known so long ago, brought tears to her eyes. He was there. He was all there and he was going to try.

It was a perfect end of the summer day, thought Jessamyn as she watched the Canadian countryside speed by as JJ pushed the van to sixty-five miles per hour. With David asleep in her lap, Jessamyn had time to review the morning and the work ahead. There were five cars carrying at least fifteen people, most of whom she had either met previously at Amex headquarters or at Grossman's. Most were exiles but a handful were sympathizers. She had filmed and interviewed as many as would permit it, and was particularly pleased with the impassioned speaking of the man who carried a placard reading AMNESTY NOW!

Jessamyn found it exhilarating that she would be both observing and participating, observing as JJ and others handed out leaflets but participating as she filmed the public's reaction to them and their message. Although she had read it before, Jessamyn again picked up the orange-colored sheet of paper. In bold print it declared presidential candidate Carter was falling far short in his position on amnesty. It attacked what it termed "the class and race discrimination" of Carter's plan, maintaining that the draft resisters whom Carter would pardon were basically white, while deserters were largely blacks, Hispanics, working-class, and poor.

The argument, thought Jessamyn as she folded the leaflet, was well grounded, but she doubted it would be well received. When she had asked, JJ could not say whether there might be interference on the part of the Canadian police. Nor was he certain how Americans on holiday would react to having an explosive issue thrust into their faces when they least expected it. But his enthusiasm for "taking the fight to the people" remained high. Soon, thought Jessamyn, all questions would be answered. Briefly she wondered if it had been a mistake to bring the baby. Suppose there was violence? There was no way she could handle David and the camera. And what if someone struck JJ while he was carrying David, papoose-style, on his chest as planned? Could she then objectively film that possibility without becoming emotionally involved?

"That's it up ahead," said JJ, his interruption of her thinking preventing an answer to her question. As he had predicted, Jessamyn noted that the bulk of the license plates were American despite their being on Canadian soil. His mission would therefore be accomplished. He had his captive audience.

Reese was speechless. Never before had she been quite so moved by natural beauty. The falls had surpassed her expectations and obviously Thomas's, too, if his silence, as they crossed over the Rainbow Bridge into Canada, was an indication. As they stopped at one of the many booths at the end of the bridge, dimly, Reese half-heard the questions.

Where are you from? How long will you be in Canada? What are you bringing into Canada?

Thomas's answers were lost as Reese focused only on the day and the hand that held hers even as he spoke to the customs officials. Finally, they were moving, moving slowly as they turned left off the bridge toward Victoria Park. From the number of cars in the lot, Reese judged that many tourists had come to the falls this Labor Day weekend. Momentarily, as she saw other families, she regretted not bringing her own. The park was pretty, grassy green with shade trees, although none were needed as the mist from the falls had turned a sunny day to one that was gray and damp. As she and Thomas each carried a handle on the picnic hamper, Reese resolved to return one day en masse, with Karl, Kristan, and Kelly in hand. Like a regular family.

The Horseshoe Falls was directly ahead. Again, Reese felt overwhelmed. Moving closer to Thomas, she watched the cascading waters with him and yet feeling very much alone. But comfortably so. It was the most peaceful she had recently felt. Until she saw the placard. Her initial reaction was to yell at the man wearing a workshirt and jeans, to demand his and his sign's removal from *her* day. She felt Thomas stiffen as he became aware of the man and his message. Throughout the park, people were muttering, some angrily, others merely annoyed by the intrusion into their lazy afternoon. Some people who had willingly taken the orange-colored leaflet that was being distributed, thinking it a discount for one of the many fast-food chains surrounding the area, angrily crumpled it into a ball and threw it at the person who had given it to them.

One lay at their feet. Thomas stooped, picked it up, and, after smoothing it out, read it in its entirety. Reese didn't have to. Somehow she knew what it contained. Quickly, as her heart pounded, she moved Thomas toward the parking lot. She could not, *would not*, allow this to ruin their day. She had taken the car keys and was gunning the motor, Thomas at her side, when she realized traffic was barely moving as cars tried to leave the lot. The reason became obvious as they neared the exit. A man with a baby strapped to him was distributing leaflets, stopping each car as it left to do so.

Thomas was staring straight ahead, his face a blank as he watched the tall, dark-haired man. As Reese attempted to leave the lot without stopping, the man poked his head into the open car window and started to speak as he handed them a leaflet but withdrew when he saw Thomas's face. The men's eyes locked.

Words began and ended on their lips. Anger and anguish competed for expression. Not believing what was occurring, Reese put her foot on the accelerator, leaving the lot and JJ behind her as fast as she could.

In the rear-view mirror, Thomas saw his brother standing in the midst of a pile of dropped leaflets. His hands were covering his face. Behind him, as she had been from the first, stood a woman with a handheld camera. Although the look on her face was confused, the manner in which she moved in for a closeup was not.

7

THE PHONE WAS RINGING BUT MARTI IGNORED IT AS she slowly removed her coat and hung it next to the others in the hall closet. The phone continued to ring as she walked toward the kitchen, insisting she pay it mind rather than the more pressing matters that occupied her consciousness. It wasn't until she had filled the kettle with water and placed it on the flame that she became aware the ringing had stopped. The house was still, the children at school, and the housekeeper gone as she was each day at three.

As her tea brewed in its cup, Marti sat at the kitchen table trying not to think, as the thoughts came one after another. She was fine, good as new, Dr. Charles had pronounced cheerily but minutes ago. The dryness and occasional bleeding of which she complained might be "senile vagina" but he doubted it as she was far too young for such a menopausal condition. More likely it was mental. Had she considered therapy? he had asked. No, only the therapist, she had replied to his confusion and even her own.

Matthew Strohl was for all intents and purposes out of her life, if not yet out of her mind. She had placed him there, although he had hardly protested. They saw each other only rarely and then only at the hospital. She maintained a distance that grew the more he respected it. They were friendly but nothing more. She wasn't capable of more, thought Marti bitterly.

For weeks afterward, remnants of her conversation with Reese continued to bother Marti. Who was Matthew Strohl and what meaning did he have in her life? None. None at all, she decided. The herb tea took away the chill. Marti missed Matthew but she did not wish to see him. She felt humiliated and rejected. He had dismissed her as easily as the doctor had, only one said come back in six months while the other said nothing.

There was something wrong with her. It wasn't natural for a woman to feel nothing even when she explored her own body in the safety of her bedroom. Not yet forty and dried up. And if she had no sense of her sexuality, why would another see what she couldn't?

She needed a change, she decided. She would get away, far away, farther than she had been for years. Next week, she would take the twins, Nelson, too, and visit JJ for Thanksgiving. He could tear himself away from papering Toronto with posters protesting Carter's planned pardon. To hell with the presidential candidate, let him entertain me. She would meet her new nephew and Jessamyn, about whom her mother had been less than enthusiastic.

The phone was ringing again, but Marti, as she mentally made her travel plans, chose still to ignore it. There was only one person she wished to talk to and ironically he was also the one person she wanted most to avoid.

*　　*　　*

Two years of agony would end, as would a major part of his life, once he signed the papers. They sat there on his desk in his office waiting for the pen, glued to his hand, to write. Matthew pushed away from his desk. The papers would wait. Cynthia would wait. But how long could he wait, he asked himself as he walked into the living room that also served as a place for his patients to wait. The heavy gray clouds hovering over the Hudson River prophesied snow even though it was only November. As he looked down on Riverside Drive, Matthew wondered when it had all gone wrong.

Two years ago, the "it" would have referred to Cynthia, but now it was Marti who was uppermost in Matthew's mind. Perhaps he should have been more honest, but he hadn't wanted to tell

1 6 5

her. At first, he was too untrusting. Later, he was too ashamed. When first they had met, she was *that* Marti Tiernan and the last thing he needed was to be another woman's trophy for her mantel. And he was not then interested in women unless they wanted to be the receivers of his anger and he had been amazed at how many did.

Matthew did not like remembering those days. They were filled with long nights of jogging up and down Riverside Park, defying muggers and other night creatures to bother him. But often, as he ran, he could not stop himself from obsessing over what was past but still so present in his life. And he would cry, big sobs coming from the child deep within.

Like most psychiatrists, Matthew was a realist. Unlike most, he was also a romantic. He believed in the marriage vows he had taken in Honolulu during which Colonel Marlon Mandis gave his daughter, Cynthia, to him to love, honor, and cherish. Which he had despite numerous opportunities during the eighteen-year, childless-by-choice *(hers)* marriage to scratch an occasional itch. But Matthew believed in fidelity and the intimacy that resulted from it. He understood that passion paled but that love and caring grew between two people as the years went by. He thought that more than an even exchange.

Matthew was not the first man to discover his wife had been unfaithful, but he was among the few to be totally unprepared for it. He could neither understand nor accept it, despite her insistence that it had meant very little *each time* it had happened. And the fact that he had never noticed or suspected proved, in her logic, how little it had meant.

As he paced his living room, not seeing that it was drab and in need of refurbishing, Matthew again felt the rage. Despite the past two years and the continuance of his own therapy, he still felt as if Cynthia had taken eighteen years of their life and humiliated them. He felt cheated. Something had become nothing. What had once been the foundation of his life was now reduced to rubble. It wasn't just his male pride that had been hurt—that he could have handled—but the part of him that trusted was destroyed. And she thought him foolish and had not wanted a divorce. Quite the contrary. She wanted to continue their lives as they once were.

What were they, Cynthia, he had yelled. He no longer knew. What had seemed real proved to be a lie.

As his lawyers discovered, despite her remonstrances that she did not want a divorce, she had her price. The list the lawyers received of her demands rivaled that of a spoiled child's at Christmas. Cynthia Strohl wanted everything and would take nothing less in exchange for his getting what he wanted.

Two years ago, when the proceedings first began, Matthew bitterly told his lawyers to give her nothing. She had already taken everything of value and could not have the house in Santa Barbara or either of the two cars and certainly not the boat. No. He had given up enough and would give up nothing more. If anyone was to get anything it was him. He wanted his pound of flesh, and according to his lawyers he could have it if he was willing to have his private life put on display. Yes, he was, he had said. He had nothing to hide. But how would it look to his colleagues and patients? He would win his battle in court but would lose so much more in the war. Which Cynthia knew—and so her lawyers refused to retreat. She was the woman who could have everything—her freedom, his money, and even his name if she just sat tight.

As the divorce proceedings neared their conclusion, Matthew, in a constant rage, withdrew, as he so often had, from Marti. His intent was to spare her. She was not to be his dumping ground. She was not his enemy even if there were days when it felt like she was simply because she was a woman. But he missed her now. Yes, there were colleagues to talk to and patients who talked to him, but neither could do quite so well as Marti.

With the first flakes of snow falling, Matthew smiled. Eighteen years of marriage were indeed over; finished, final, and on the road to being forgotten once he affixed his signature to the papers. And sign them he would. Not the house or the car or any *thing* was worth his balls—which is exactly what Cynthia had in her hand for as long as he fought her with the wrong weapons. The battle was over and both he and Cynthia had won; only she had tangibles to show for her victory. She would think her win was greater; he would know it was not.

As he picked up the pen with one hand, Matthew dialed the

phone with the other. He hoped this time someone would answer. If not, he would continue to call until she did.

*   *   *

As long as he doesn't ask to carry my books, it remains harmless, thought Reese as they walked from the Law & Education Tower toward Commonwealth Avenue and the subway she planned to take home.

"Can you manage?"

Reese laughed nervously. He *would* carry her books if she wanted. "I'm fine," she replied. "It's just difficult maneuvering on ice, particularly in heels. Which was sure dumb of me considering the forecast said it would freeze."

I don't think *dumb* is an adjective we can apply to you," he said seriously. "I think you're one of the smartest girls I've ever taught."

"Thank you for the double compliment," said Reese, her face flushed from more than the frigid nineteen-degree air that was making Boston very cold but Christmasy. "A girl I will never be again, although being back at school does make me feel like one. I recommend it for every woman whose chief concerns are no longer whether the surf's up or what to wear to the new 'in' disco."

"I admire you," he said, "admire what you're doing. It can't be easy at your . . ." He stopped, embarrassed by what he thought was about to be a gaffe.

"At my age? You needn't hesitate or be embarrassed. I'm not," said Reese. "Actually, I'm rather proud of my age—and don't ask because I'm not that proud of it. But you're right. It isn't easy, and yet in some respects it is. You see, I have an advantage over the others. I really know why I'm here. I'm not filling space at school or just thinking about a career in the field. I'm way past that."

"Yes, your work last semester showed that kind of determination."

"Oh, really? Then you should have given me an A instead of a B-plus," said Reese teasingly, wishing the words she was hearing were coming from another. This man was voicing an appreciation, even a respect, for her. She missed that. So often she had wanted just such a pat on the back and not received it.

1 6 8

"If your papers had been up to your tests and classroom participation, I would have given you an A. I wanted to."

He was looking at her and had she returned his glance she would have been embarrassed. As it was, she was fighting herself for just walking with a man who had been her former professor. Now she understood his friendliness, not just in class but in hallways when they met. At first, she thought she was imagining his interest. Today, she knew she wasn't and was uncertain how to react.

He is an attractive man, thought Reese. She estimated his age to be forty-five or thereabouts, hard to tell, she decided, given how teachers and students tended to dress alike these days. She tried to remember how he had looked to her last summer when she had taken his course. Even then she had thought he would look better if he had cut his rather long hair. What else did she remember? That she had never missed his class. Until now, she had thought it was for his lectures rather than him.

"How is it going this semester?" he asked, his interest seeming real rather than feigned.

"Good. With you I learned to assess a child's learning disabilities. Now I'm learning methods and management of those disabilities. God, but I sound like the college brochure, don't I?" laughed Reese. "But I do enjoy it."

"And it has had its difficulties."

Had she dared, she would have looked directly at him. Instead she said, "Yes, it has. It's impossible to be a full-time student and mother. I'm receiving A's in one—or in a few isolated cases a B-plus—and F's in the other. It's troubling."

"I'm sure your house is in order," he said consolingly.

She wanted to hoot, then cry. No house was ever in more disorder. Just how disordered gave her a chill that had nothing to do with the temperature. Karl was now coached by a professional who only took on those runners he felt had Olympics potential. Her Karl and the Olympics! Only he wasn't her Karl anymore, if he ever had been. Now he lived more with his coach and his family than he did with his own. Which was also true of Kristan, who spent more time in New York at Marti's than she did in Boston. And often earning the staggering sum of three thousand dollars per week! But still intent on maintaining her top-ten-percent average at school. Her two oldest children were like Thomas in their almost grim determination to succeed. Neither seemed young to her. Neither seemed to have fun. They were nothing like Kelly, who had no determination to succeed at anything but who seemed perfectly content and certainly the most happy of the lot in her undisciplined life. Kelly had fun and that's all she had.

"Your husband must be of great help," he said as he guided her into a coffee shop. She wanted to protest. He hadn't asked. She hadn't accepted. He had assumed. "Husbands cooperating and lending support seem to typify many marriages today," he added as he helped her to remove her coat.

Reese decided to leap into unknown territory. "Are you speaking from firsthand knowledge?"

"My wife works," he answered without hesitation. "She buys for Bonwit's." She expected to hear "We're separated" or some lament of the misunderstood husband, something that would explain why he was with her at this moment in a coffee shop, but no such remark was forthcoming.

"I see where your husband is finally doing something to revere our time and space when we travel," he said easily. "Lord knows it's about time and needed. I can remember when airline travel was fun and not a chore."

When the waitress arrived, he ordered a toasted English muffin with his coffee. The young girl taking their order seemed annoyed that Reese wanted nothing more than a cup of tea. In a petulant tone, she reminded Reese there was a dollar minimum per person when sitting in a booth. Evenly, he said he would pay it.

"Just what made you choose special education?" he asked as he settled into the red leather cushioned seat.

Again Reese wished the words were coming from a person other than this man. Not once had Thomas sought to share her life or to understand it. Not outside the house anyway. Often it seemed he was so engrossed in his own life that nothing else existed. And nothing else did. He took to his job the way a general takes to a battlefield, thought Reese. He considered all other airlines the enemy, and his days and nights were spent plotting ways, strategies, to beat them at their own game. He was so consumed in his ongoing battles that he couldn't see or hear anything else, even the cries of Kelly when he had slapped her harder than any parent should just because her stereo was interrupting his concentration.

"And," she continued, answering his question, "I always wanted to do something that would make me feel out of the ordinary."

"But you're not ordinary at all," he said, surprised.

"Oh, but I am, and I accept that now. I may be doing something out of the ordinary . . ."

"Extraordinary describes it best," he said interrupting.

"Perhaps. But it doesn't make me extraordinary," she replied. "I'm just me. Just another person. And content to be that finally."

Reese was not surprised when Stephen Larcher let her remark pass. In some way, she had been testing him, knowing that, had it been twenty years ago, Thomas would have picked up on her words and asked for an explanation. But Stephen wasn't Thomas and Thomas, she regretfully realized, wasn't Stephen.

"Are you going to be in town over the holidays?" he asked offhandedly as he reached for the check. "I ask because there are some lectures being given for faculty you might wish to attend with me. They're about creating a uniform structure for educating all types of children, handicapped and otherwise, in our school system. We're moving toward that, you know. Which is good for you. When you graduate, there is going to be a great need for special education teachers. I might be able to help you there as I do have connections at several institutions around the country."

"Thank you, but frankly, at the moment, everything centers about Boston. It's where the home is," Reese explained. "And the heart," she added softly as she slipped into her coat.

"You haven't answered my question," he said, his tone insistent. "Will you be in town for the holidays?"

"I don't know. We may visit my sister-in-law in New York. At least I hope to," replied Reese. As Larcher shrugged and turned to pay the check, Reese turned back to her frantic phone call to Marti of but days ago, asking her to arrange a meeting that didn't seem like a meeting between Thomas and Matthew. She was frightened, she explained. Thomas needed help, and Marti had told her that Matthew had just published a paper on stress and the Vietnam veteran.

Reese had been surprised by Marti's reluctance to commit herself. Although concerned about Thomas, particularly when she learned of his erratic behavior, the more Reese pressed, the more Marti had withdrawn. Their conversation had been inconclusive, with Marti stammering how she had to think about it. Mentally, Reese made a note to call Marti again tonight. If she was unwilling to have Matthew and the family for Christmas, perhaps they could think of another way, one that wouldn't arouse Thomas's suspicions, for he and Matthew to meet.

"Well, if you're in town and would like to attend the lectures, here is my card. The number is for my office at school. I should be there most mornings between ten and noon."

Stephen Larcher placed the card in her hand, leaving her with the responsibility and choice. Reese watched as he disappeared down Commonwealth Avenue, a tall, dark-haired man who walked like a cowboy, undoubtedly because of the pointed boots that made all men, no matter where they were from strut as if they were just off the range. As she approached the subway entrance, Reese dropped the card in the nearby litter basket. It wasn't until she was halfway down the steps that the incident that had prompted the phone call to Marti flashed in her mind. Thomas had just arrived home from one of his many trips about the Northeast corridor and was enraged from the moment he entered the house. The radio in his taxi had been tuned to one of those call-in shows and the guest had been JJ, "poisoning" the airwaves with his point of view, which the cab driver had actually thought valid. At that point, Kristan had come home, waving an advance copy of *Cosmopolitan*. Thomas had taken one look at his daughter on the cover and had railed against "this new sick morality that exploits children." As Kristan wept, Thomas had shredded the magazine with his hands.

It was the look on his face that Reese remembered as she turned, walked back up the stairs, and picked the card out of the basket. It was the glint in his eye that she thought of as she carefully folded the card and placed it behind her driver's license in one of the folds in her wallet.

*   *   *

Vinnie hugged her and then rushed into the street to find the near impossible on Christmas night—a taxi. At the door, Este, showing none of the effects of a miscarriage that determined she would never be pregnant again, was dragging a reluctant Jamie, who was dragging his kiddie car and Margaret. Neither looked the better for the wear. Shouts from the street announced Vinnie had been successful. Amidst many hugs and reminders that lunch would be Tuesday and dinner on Friday, they were gone. But *he* wasn't, thought Marti anxiously.

In the house, the children were collecting down jackets and sweaters for their annual trek to see the tree at Rockefeller Center. Thomas was collecting too, although from his sleepy expression it was apparent to Marti he would have preferred to doze by the fire where he had nestled shortly after Reese's coconut cream pies had been served for dessert. From the hallway, he yelled toward the kitchen that he would meet them at his mother's apartment. Then, they, too, were gone. And still *he* wasn't, thought Marti as her heart began to pound.

She could hear her mother and Reese in the kitchen, putting the finishing touches on dishes and silver the cleaning woman never thought to make so clean. She didn't want them to finish. She did not want to be left alone. Not with him. And he, pouring a small brandy into a very large snifter, was obviously in no hurry to leave. Now she was annoyed. She had been precise in her invitation. And honest. Not dinner but dessert. Not family but friend. The mission, whether it was his, hers, or Reese's, had been accomplished. Contact had been made with Thomas. So why didn't he leave?

And then she thought he was, but he had only donned his coat to rush into the street to find a taxi for Carolyn and Reese, who were yawning evidence of their exhaustion. More hugs, more promises to meet, more appreciative noises about presents received, and they were gone. But still *he* wasn't. He collapsed onto the sofa and picked up his partially empty snifter. She wondered if

1 7 3

he was mocking her as he raised it in salutary gesture. After he looked at his watch, he said without looking at her, "I know you'd like me to leave. Your discomfort is that obvious. But I think some explanations are in order."

"Matthew, I'm tired," hedged Marti.

"Me, too. Particularly of being frozen out. Marti, I think it's time you were honest with me."

"*Me*, be honest with you? You must admit there is a certain humor in that, since this seems to be the season or year of your dishonesty," she said as she paced before the fireplace, annoyed she was in a conversation she didn't want to have and yet grateful it was still on a level she could control.

"Why the hell don't you sit down," said Matthew. "It's damn hard speaking to someone who acts as if she's safer being a moving target. Are you afraid of me, for chrissake?"

She wanted to scream yes, that she was, but instead looked at him as though he had just spoken the day's dumbest thought.

"You're hanging me for a crime committed and paid for. You're using it and I want to know why. When I finally reached you on the phone, I explained why I hadn't told you about the divorce. In case you've forgotten, I was quite explicit about how I wanted that part of my life to be kept quite separate from my relationship with you. I explained the reasons for that when we had lunch at the hospital. Were you listening then? Are you listening now?"

"Don't yell. I hear you just fine. Or let's say I hear you," said Marti, fighting her urge to succumb to his sincerity. "I just have trouble understanding how you can be close to someone for a year and hide the most important thing occurring in your life. Do you know how that made me feel? I thought maybe it was me, as if I was lacking something you found in other women. Or boys. Even that crossed my mind. Now you say you were sparing me, and that you had feelings for me. What did you do with them? Send them to the dry cleaners for storage? I feel cheated."

"Who the hell are you kidding," said Matthew, his face flushed from anger. "For months you acted like the ice princess. Never a sign of anything more than professional interest or friendship. And then you finally invite me to dinner but act in such a way that you might just as well have worn a sign that read Hands Off. And as for honesty, when were you ever totally honest with me? And don't give me that big, wide-eyed look of innocence. You're hiding behind this divorce thing of mine, Marti. So I lied. Only I think it more an act of omission than a lie. And it's past. So why are you holding on to it. What are you protecting? What are you lying about, Marti?"

Chilled, Marti said coldly, "What makes you think I'm lying about anything."

"Because I know," Matthew said, his voice harsh, almost ugly. "I know how you get when you're afraid."

"How would you know that?" asked Marti bitterly, thinking of all the times she had been terrified but had not spoken of it.

"Because I know you. Because I know one can't go through what you did without thinking it could happen again. So ask *me*, Marti, how I felt when you slipped under that bus. Ask me how I felt knowing you didn't believe for a second you slipped but pretended you did. And then ask me about dishonesty. Ask me about frustration, about not being able to talk through a bad time with someone who is struggling, someone you care about. I know what you think, Marti. I know how all you Tiernans and Ollsons must think. I heard it from Thomas tonight. You're all potential victims. Worse, you make yourself victims when you're all such natural victors.

"Marti, have you any idea how helpless I felt when you were in the hospital? And cheated. I wanted to talk with you . . . be with you, lend you some of my strength. You shut me out, and so I had to deal with my fear alone."

"Your fear?" echoed Marti, confused.

"My fear for your safety and your sanity. Not to mention your new-found freedom. I don't want you to lose any of the three. And you needn't. Yes, there might be a crackpot out there, but frankly I don't think so. Nor do the colleagues I've consulted. Marti, we could have been frightened together."

"Just as we could have been through your divorce," she said bitterly.

"Yes, through that too." Matthew sighed. "Marti, my divorce kept us separate once. It doesn't have to now."

Marti's back was turned, but Matthew knew from the movement of her shoulders that she was crying. "I'm afraid," she said miserably.

From behind her, Matthew gently placed his hands on her shoulders. Misunderstanding, he replied, "Christ, Marti, I'm also afraid. We've both had bad marriages. We can either run the rest of our lives or we can risk being with someone and possibly getting hurt."

She turned to face him. "Matt, it's not that. I'm . . ." She hesitated. "I'm afraid of involvement."

"Marti, that makes no sense. It's a double message, and I'm not sure I'm receiving either one correctly."

"I'm not ready," she began weakly.

Again misunderstanding, Matthew interrupted. "No one's really ready. If people waited until they were, the world would be unpregnant and unpopulated. It would also be lonely as hell. Marti, what is there to be ready for?" he asked as he again held her by the shoulders.

"Matthew, I don't feel anything," she said in a whisper.

His face turned crimson and then white. For a moment he looked as if he were going to be ill. "That's a different story," he said. "You can't force attraction. It's either there or not."

"No, Matthew, you don't understand," Marti cried, seeing he thought it was him and not her. "I need time. There's something I must work out on my own. It has nothing to do with you."

"I'm not so certain from what you just said that it doesn't," said Matthew.

She could see the depression settling over him as clearly as if it were fog rolling in on a bay. "Matthew, it's me, not you."

"Marti, I'll respect the space you need. Maybe I need it too. Things have happened rather quickly lately. Maybe we both need distance."

"I'll call you," Marti said. "Just as soon as I feel I'm ready."

As he buttoned his overcoat against the December cold, Matthew Strohl smiled. "I have a life to resume. Neither it nor I can be put on hold for too long." And then both the smile and he were gone. When the door closed, Marti felt relieved. Safe at last. Safe and sad. In fact, as the minutes ticked by slowly, she couldn't decide which she was feeling more. When the crying jag began, she knew.

*   *   *

"It simply isn't good enough. We are bitterly disappointed."

Reynolds Trahey put down his pencil and clicked off his recorder. At the hastily held press conference, John Ollson, Jr., had not said anything unexpected in his response to President Carter's pardon. Trahey could not believe, given what he had gathered from Washington rumors, that Ollson had thought for a moment that total amnesty would be given. None in the so-called know believed Carter would initially pardon anyone but draft resisters and draft nonregistrants, and they had been proven right. It surprised Trahey that the look on Ollson's face confirmed his words of disappointment.

Unconcerned with the issues, Trahey had accepted his assignment as a follow-up to the interviews he had conducted almost three years before with the Ollson brothers. In Boston, he recently had met with Thomas Ollson and had been shocked by the physical change in the man. His face was drawn, almost haggard, and his visible agitation contradicted the calm spokesman who appeared in Revere Airlines' advertising campaign. This Thomas Ollson would not discuss politics and had obviously been carefully coached by his public-relations director as to what was "politic" and what was not.

No one had coached John Ollson, Jr., and he was more than willing to discuss the "pardon," which he called unconscionable and therefore loathsome. Trahey had noted the younger Ollson had also changed. Across his notes he had scribbled "battle fatigued."

"We are going on to Washington," said JJ to the assembled group of newsmen. "In February, in full view of the White House and the nation, those who can will participate in a series of veteran-oriented amnesty actions. A veterans' vigil picket line will be set up in front of the Veterans Administration Building and on February fifth, there will be a rally in Lafayette Park, across Pennsylvania Avenue, directly in front of the White House.

"The battle is not over," said JJ passionately, "and it will not be until we have won!"

1 7 7

Trahey noted the young woman known to the press corps first as Jessamyn Giroux and then as Mrs. John Ollson, Jr., turned off her handheld camera as a broad smile pleasured her face. Trahey tried to interpret the smile and the young woman's actions as she packed up her equipment despite the ongoing press conference. As she left the room, instinct told Trahey to follow.

Jessamyn was clearly surprised when Trahey stopped her in the hallway of the hotel chosen for the press conference. Yet she also seemed pleased. She was leaving, she explained, because her story was finished. For now, she quickly added. Yes, she believed hers was an extremely good story because no one had lived with the subject as she had. No, she could not yet reveal the nature of her story or when or where it could be seen but yes, she most definitely would let him know in advance. In exchange for pre-publicity.

With the terms of their deal arranged, Trahey allowed Jessamyn to depart, noting this was not only a clever but an attractive woman. He wondered what she had on tape that others did not. From the look in her eyes and from the manner in which she carried herself, Trahey was certain it was something out of the ordinary.

*   *   *

"What the hell do you mean it's finished? How can it be finished when we're still in the thick of the fight?" asked JJ, more stunned than angry.

"It's done, over, completed at the perfect juncture," said Jessamyn, so certain of her position that she never flinched as JJ stared at her in disbelief.

"But it's *my* story," he protested, "*my* fight."

"Your fight but *my* story," said Jessamyn coldly. "And as its author, so to speak, I deem it done. The rest is anticlimactic. Whether or not you win your total amnesty does not make my film any more meaningful or powerful. The work stands on its own as it is."

"But the issue does not. It's inconclusive," yelled JJ.

"Tell that to ABC," said Jessamyn smugly.

1 7 8

JJ was stopped. "What do you mean?" he asked, his voice reflecting his fear.

"That the network has bought it for the 'Evening News.' Beginning Monday, they'll air it in five five-minute segments."

"But how?" asked JJ, too stunned to group his thoughts for a paragraph that would state them accurately.

"Immediately after your press conference, the one which ended with you so eloquently and passionately stating, 'The battle is not over and it will not be until we have won,' I knew my work was complete. While you continued to speak that week at the Toronto Amnesty Conference, I flew down to New York and showed what I had to Tyne Philips, who arranged that very day to show it in rough cut to ABC. The rest is like a dream," said Jessamyn. "A great, big, wonderful dream come true."

"For you but not me. How the hell could you do this without consulting me? For chrissakes, you're my my wife," said JJ disgustedly.

"*Wife* is not a synonym for *indentured servant*," said Jessamyn, refusing to be bullied. "And why should I have consulted you? For months I've asked you to do something other than this amnesty thing."

"This amnesty 'thing'?" echoed JJ.

"You know exactly what I mean. I pleaded with you to develop other projects we could have worked on. Something to do as a team. But no. You had to proceed selfishly."

"Selfishly? I thought what we were doing was for both of us."

"Bullshit!" said Jessamyn. "Do you really think I give a flying fuck about amnesty? I'm not Kay. I'm not Nelson. That's your collective battle. Not mine. I leave the world-changing to people like you. I prefer to report it. God, the conceit of you Americans! Everything is always so 'big' in your eyes, including yourselves. We Canadians aren't at all like that."

"Good God, Jessamyn, but I don't believe this," said JJ as he sat down heavily on the sofa. "I feel used, betrayed, as if the last six months were a total lie."

"More bullshit. How were you betrayed? I did exactly what I said I would do. I made a film about a deserter and his efforts to win amnesty for himself and others."

1 7 9

"I guess my mistake was thinking you were doing it for me," said JJ.

"You're right. That was your mistake. I did it for me and if you and yours profited from my venture, so much the better."

"Why couldn't you have waited?" asked JJ, looking to Jessamyn for something that would make him feel better about her actions.

" 'Cause I've been waiting. Oh, God, have I been waiting. Ever since we did that documentary on Nelson I've been waiting. You gave no thought to me or my career."

"You didn't have a career until you married me," snapped JJ. "Damn it, you had nothing but your ambitions."

"And talent," yelled Jessamyn. "Don't forget that, please. Talent, and I want to use it."

"So you used me in the process," said JJ miserably, standing to pace as he spoke. "Jesus, Jessamyn, how the hell am I supposed to trust you again? Do you have any idea of the effect this could have on our marriage?"

"Yes, I do. But you'll get over it. We're both going to have time to assess who we are and where we are going," said Jessamyn as she eased into the place where JJ had just been sitting.

"What's that supposed to mean?" asked JJ.

"I'm going to New York for a week," said Jessamyn calmly. "The network is arranging a series of interviews to promote the segments, and Tyne is arranging for me to meet with several production heads, both at the networks and studios."

"And then what?" asked JJ.

"That all depends on what turns up and whether it is here, there, or someplace in between."

"And what's David to do all this time while his mother is away?" asked JJ.

"If such a question is soon to exist it's about how David manages without his father," replied Jessamyn. "I'm taking David with me, and, for God's sake, JJ, stop looking so upset. It's only for a week or so."

The sky was gray and the wind whipping the walkers as it whirled down Pennsylvania Avenue made the day that much colder. Still, Marti felt warm, and the expression on her face was in direct opposition to the weather. Nelson was at her side as she walked. Behind and in front of them were some one hundred others, mostly veterans and their families and exiles who had recently returned from Canada. The signs many carried read, TOTAL AMNESTY NOW! Passing in front of the White House, they crossed Pennsylvania into Lafayette Park where makeshift platforms had been erected for the speakers.

The scene was familiar to Marti, although she had never been in that particular park before. But in its postage-stamp size, it reminded her of the pie-shaped island at Lincoln Center where she and her father had been shot down. There, too, there had been a makeshift platform with a small sound system. There, too, she had felt proud and unafraid. Not then, not now, did Marti feel threatened, and silently she gave thanks.

Marti's decision to attend the amnesty rally in Washington was triggered by Jessamyn's five-part series on JJ on the "ABC Evening News." Infuriated by what she felt was Jessamyn's condescending and often snide approach to the man and his issue, Marti wanted to retaliate. When she heard JJ's impassioned battle cry, she was moved. Attitudes and actions, long suppressed, stirred within her. She remembered how she had hated the Vietnam War, had campaigned against it and for actions, like JJ's, that would render it impossible. She had never liked herself more than she did then; had never felt more vital, alive, and like her father's daughter.

She never felt more like an Ollson than she did that morning when she had flown into Washington to find Nelson camped in a church that offered overnight shelter to those veterans and exiles without accommodations. Nelson had not said anything when she found him but had taken her hand and gripped it with more emotion than words could have relayed. She had felt for JJ in that exchange and now, as they entered Lafayette Park, Marti was feeling for Thomas. Would he accept her presence here? She thought he might. She remembered his telling Matthew last Christmas of his pride in her; pride in that she had stood her ground, fought for

1 8 1

her country in her own way, and then nearly died, as he nearly did, serving her country. He applauded that. She had not deserted.

As she took her place with others in the park, Marti thought of what her parents had once said to the press. They had two sons, one in the service, one not, and they were equally proud of both. Then, she had thought it was merely lip service. Today, she understood their meaning perhaps even more than they did. Both her brothers were honorable men deserving of honor. Both had defended their country in their own way. Both were part of the democratic process. She wished each could see that in the other as clearly as she did.

She was picked out of the crowd, recognized by the local NBC affiliate. They wanted an interview or an on-camera statement. She refused, explaining she was there as a citizen and not as a spokesperson. Still, throughout the ceremonies, she could feel the camera training its lens upon her reactions. She did not cringe or attempt to hide herself in the hood of her parka. She was not that turtle anymore, she realized. For the first time since she had faced death, Marti faced life and found it exhilarating. Her skin tingled and she felt as if something within was about to overflow.

Hours later, exhausted but content, Marti was waiting at the Eastern Airlines lounge at Washington's National when she saw him. The walk was unmistakable. So few people walk with authority, she thought as she ran after him, calling his name as she did.

The man turned, raised his eyes in surprise, and then reacted with even greater surprise when she flung her arms about him in a big bear hug. For a second he held her. Then, remembeing his manners, he introduced the woman at his side. Like him, she was deeply suntanned. Like him, she was a psychiatrist attending a conference in Washington that Monday on delayed stress reactions in Vietnam veterans. Like him, she was surprised to see Marti. And like him, she said nothing more than amenities before each said their good-byes and exited in their respective directions.

There was a sense of loss that was even stronger than the disappointment Marti felt as she prepared to get on the plane. Lost in thought, it took her several seconds to realize she was the Marti Tiernan being paged at the Eastern ticket counter. The reservation clerk smiled as she handed the phone to Marti. Her hello was greeted with a request from Matthew Strohl for her to stay, to remain with him in Washington through the weekend. He did not beg nor did he repeat. He simply told her he was staying at the Shoreham Hotel and hung up after saying he hoped he would see her there soon.

8

As REESE APPROACHED THE CHECKOUT COUNTER,
she was startled by the familiar face in what was now an all too
familiar pose. Kristan, on the cover of *People* magazine, looking
far too beautiful for a girl whose sixteenth birthday was still five
months away. As she waited her turn, Reese thumbed through the
magazine, finding to her surprise a picture of Karl in Kristan's
layout. The caption spoke of his string of track victories and his
scholarship to Villanova University. It was amazing what she
learned about her own children each time she read one of those
articles, thought Reese as she replaced the magazine in its rack.
For a brief moment she wondered how Thomas would react to
this newest invasion of the family privacy.

She almost laughed. What privacy? There hadn't been any in
years, and now she doubted if there ever would be. If it wasn't
Thomas or JJ before the nation's eyes, then it was Kristan, and
soon, if she was to believe *People*, it would be Karl. Her heart
ached for Kelly, who lived in the shadow of her family, gaining
attention for herself in all the wrong ways. As though I'm anyone
to judge, thought Reese as she collected her shopping bags and
headed for the car in the parking lot. Like Kelly, she, too, had
needed attention. Only once she had received it, she had hated
it—which found Stephen Larcher grading her "puritanical" and
"provincial." She hadn't argued but agreed. Furthermore, she had
decided they weren't bad things to be.

Reese was still processing what she termed her "indiscretion," a term that Larcher also loathed. "It's an affair," he had corrected. For him. For her, it had been a mistake, a very bad mistake, considering the agony she had put herself through afterward. She could not have an "affair" while married and certainly not with a married man. Despite her actions, she was not that kind of woman.

The needs that had made a Stephen Larcher possible were obvious to Reese, but they still didn't make what she had done right in her mind. But in understanding, she forgave herself. She also reached a painful decision, one she planned to discuss with Thomas as soon as his latest Revere expansion move was completed.

The Boston Common was turning green. In a matter of weeks, as April matured, it would blossom forth in the New England spring colors Reese had so loved since childhood. She would miss that if she accepted the teaching position in Lawrence, Kansas. But the offer from the university was too good to simply dismiss. She would be learning her trade as she plied it. But it would mean changes in her life. Sweeping changes.

As she waited at an intersection, Reese realized her life, like her car, was waiting for a light to change from red to green. Still, she argued, one doesn't just walk away from eighteen years of marriage, particularly when one still loves the other person. There are obligations, not just to Thomas but the children. Still, she reasoned, two of the children would be gone. Karl, if she could believe what she read, would be at Villanova, and Kristan, after one too many abusive interchanges with Thomas, would be living with Marti come the summer. That left just Kelly; the two of them alone and yet living with a man who was seldom home and when he was, was seldom there more than physically.

She needed more, thought Reese as she turned the car down Marlborough Street. She needed affection and attention. Companionship, it was called. She needed to be married in the truest sense of the word, and Thomas had always been married to something more than just her. First it was the military and now it was the airline. His life was a constant battle and he was never the victor. In his mind, the war had been lost and now the airline was barely winning its battle over the red-ink side of the ledger—which

1 8 5

Thomas took personally, as if he had failed in some significant fashion. Often she was awakened by his nightmares. Equally often, she heard him struggling in the bathroom at night. Concerned, she had taken it upon herself to call Matthew Strohl, who had spoken with her at length about what Thomas might be feeling.

Abandonment and loss of control, first by his country and now by his children. Her, too. Matthew reminded her, now that she was for all intents and purposes independent of him and the only life he had to offer. Studies were finding these particular emotions often difficult for some POWs to handle, Matthew explained. Be supportive. Be there. Be the constant in his life. Matthew's words seemed to negate her and her needs. Still she said nothing and felt exceedingly grateful when Matthew said he would call Thomas and suggest lunch once Revere's "All-in-One" run was underway April 5.

That was tomorrow, Reese realized, but she doubted if Thomas would remember he had agreed to such a luncheon. She would make him remember. He would have to tend to his life, because she intended to tend to hers. He would talk to Matthew and she would talk to him. They would then talk to each other and get on with their lives.

When she unlocked the front door, Reese was surprised to hear conversation coming from the second-floor sitting room. After depositing her groceries on the kitchen counter, she climbed the stairs to find Thomas in front of the television watching Jessamyn Giroux being interviewed by Merv Griffin.

"She's a cunt," Thomas said coldly, "a real ball-busting, killer cunt," he added, unaware Reese was standing behind him.

Reese looked at Thomas with some alarm. His words were said with such hatred that the emotion shocked her as much as did the words themselves. Thomas Ollson did not approve of profanity and seldom used it. Quietly, Reese sat down to watch what had provoked such an outburst.

*　　*　　*

JJ decided against his usual morning coffee hoping the camomile tea would settle his stomach. Nervously, he was awaiting

Jessamyn's appearance momentarily on "Good Morning America." JJ had not seen the "Merv Griffin Show," although reviews, none good, had poured in from his associates. Not knowing who or what to believe, JJ had turned to Jessamyn for assurance, but none was forthcoming. Since leaving in January, Jessamyn had returned once and that was for but a day to exchange one wardrobe for another as the seasons changed. Tyne Philips, Jessamyn explained, was successfully "merchandising" her. She was a "hot property," in demand by talk shows all over the country. She did not agree that it would perhaps be best for David to be left with him while she was touring. The baby, she explained, gave her "roots and relatedness" in a strange country and in strange cities. She understood that he missed David, but she offered nothing to fill the hole she had dug in his life. Not even Marti's newly lent support could ease his ache. Nor could his continued efforts to press the Carter camp for an amnesty for all. He had not known what to think when Secretary of Defense Harold Brown, and not Carter, himself, a week ago told the press that details of the president's "Second Step" program for deserters and "bad paper" veterans would be announced April 5. Which is why Jessamyn Giroux was to be a guest on "Good Morning America." Who better to discuss the issues than the wife of one of the more famous deserters—and on the very day details of pardon or amnesty were to be revealed?

And there she was, or was it someone who only resembled her? She was thinner. Her hair was cut severely short, making her eyes look bigger. The suit was tailored but the blouse was ruffled. Her roughness had been removed. She had been honed and was just a shade shy of elegant. To JJ, this Jessamyn seemed a distant relative of the girl he had married. As he took a bite of his toast, Jessamyn took a bite of the first question.

"Of course I support my husband even though my political and even philosophical beliefs are somewhat different. But then, I fell in love with the man, not his beliefs."

He sat with toast stuck between his throat and his stomach. How could she separate the two? Wasn't he his beliefs?

"Whatever is declared today, an amnesty or a pardon, I do hope my husband will take advantage of it. After all, this *is* his country. He has put it and his beliefs, although not necessarily in that order—yet they are so closely entwined—before all else. It is time to forgive and forget, to let go, to perhaps be less dedicated, less compulsive, and more attending to the life that has been neglected—and those who share that life."

Her implications were vaguely hidden but there for the astute viewer, and, for a moment, JJ felt he was witnessing his own hanging.

"Whether or not I feel my husband has been somewhat misguided is unimportant. It is what *he* thinks that matters, and he truly believes that, by placing himself first, he was serving his country. His position could be defined, and has been by many, as patriotic."

JJ watched with fascination as Jessamyn, poised and assured, answered the questions with a double-edged sword. She was clever, JJ thought. She knew exactly how to manipulate her audience.

"Some see his desertion as cowardice; others as an act of strength. It's like beauty—in the eyes of the beholder. That my husband has risked much and suffered greatly is evidence of his strength. Yet we all know strength can be misguided. Not that I am saying his was or is. Each person must decide for himself what is and what isn't right."

She had led the interviewer into the trap, and the question presented to Jessamyn thundered across the tube from one country to another. "What is right for you, Mrs. Ollson? How would you have reacted in your husband's position?"

She hesitated just long enough before answering to suggest conflict. Then, after a deep breath, she replied: "I would have chosen other means with which to fight. My way of putting my country first would be to stay and fight. But not in the military. I share my husband's hatred of war, and I would have protested any kind of violent action in my way. Even from the stockades. In other words: I would have gone to jail. By doing so, I think I would have gained credibility with the people. My action would be loudly declaring: 'This is who I am. This is what I believe. And this is what I am willing to demonstrate for my beliefs.' I would have exchanged one kind of freedom in the hopes of obtaining a much greater one for mankind. But that's me. That is not my husband. What makes this country great is our right to disagree and dissent."

JJ listened, his stomach in turmoil, as she talked about citizenship for herself. Yes, she thought that probable. And was she prepared to fight for her country if needed?

"There are many ways one can fight, as my husband has demonstrated and as I have suggested. I would not want my son to go off to war. Few mothers do. I would want him, however, to support that which has nurtured and supported him. But there are many ways to do this. Carrying a gun is not the only alternative any more than desertion is. My son will find his own alternatives. Let us hope that the situation we are discussing remains now and forever hypothetical."

He sat there long after the program had ended, nursing his cold camomile tea and a hurt that deepened with every passing minute. She had been brilliant. Like her "ABC Evening News" segments, she had walked the line, straddled the fence, won points without losing any. For herself. Although she had never said words to the effect, JJ knew Jessamyn would not be coming home again. His wife had left and she had taken his son with her. He was alone. His life was empty, filled with a silence that not even the persistent ringing of the telephone could alter.

From her strained voice, JJ knew Kay had seen Jessamyn on "Good Morning America." She was hesitant, not at all the assured Kay who spoke her mind so readily. But it was not Jessamyn that Kay was avoiding but the news she was bringing. She had heard from her contact in Washington. The news would be broadcast in less than an hour at eleven. Gently, she explained that there was no amnesty, just another pardon, one more sweeping and inclusive than the last. Deserters with no military charges pending against them would be eligible to return to military control to be expeditiously discharged *less than honorably*.

She heard him gasp as she continued to read from her notes. Long-term AWOL, after being discharged, could apply along with four hundred thirty-two thousand veterans with general and undesirable discharges to have their "bad papers" reviewed under a Special Discharge Review Program. But the program, explained Kay, near tears, was really only designed for model GIs or those who had served in Vietnam, which means that it will be very difficult for you or any of the deserters to get your discharge papers upgraded. And, concluded Kay, the program would only be in effect for six months.

JJ said nothing as he returned the receiver to its cradle. The years of fighting were over. The "pardon" was unpardonable. So little was gained for the much that was lost. He could go home again but not with honor. Not in his country's eyes. He was pardoned, which in this case meant he was "forgiven" but not forgotten. His actions would forever follow him. From job to job and state to state. The tears that had begun a slow, steady trickle down his face collided with his anger. He would not be stigmatized. He would not be labeled. He would not give up. He would continue to fight for justice, for his child, for thousands like him, but primarily for himself. If there was pardoning to be done, it was not for them to pardon him but for him to pardon them—and they hadn't earned that yet!

*　　*　　*

Thomas was shaving for the second time in less than twelve hours when he heard the brief announcement on the radio.

Let Carter do as he will, thought Thomas, but I pardon none of them. Angrily, he stroked at his face with his razor. The announcement was just one more added annoyance to the day. Checking his watch, Thomas noted it was shortly after 2 P.M. He had but thirty minutes before he would personally supervise Revere's Flight 31 back to Boston. As he combed his hair, Thomas assessed himself. Visine would help his eyes' redness. Best foot, or in this case, best face forward, as it would be his face the passengers would see, just as they had that morning when Revere had inaugurated its Boston/L.A. All-in-One run. The idea had been his. A first of its kind for businessmen. A crosscountry shuttle. Back-and-forth service; dictaphone machines were available and staff would see to it that the letters were typed during the near four-hour layover in Los Angeles. There were even portable typewriters aboard for those who preferred that their own fingers do

1 9 0

the talking. It was, management had agreed, a brilliant idea and one that was easily executed and at a nominal fee for the passenger. It was also simple. Leave Boston at 8 A.M. Arrive in Los Angeles in time for a business lunch. Depart at three, which meant bed and board in your own home that same night.

But the air conditioning had broken down on the flight to Los Angeles that morning, and the passengers had complained throughout the near two hours it took the maintenance crew to repair it.

He had joked with the passengers, making light of the inconvenience, while internally he had felt like ripping out the hearts of those who had not checked each and every detail of their responsibility. As he put on his suit, freshly pressed by the Marriott Hotel's valet service, he soothed himself by reliving the flight's early arrival. The anger returned when he recalled how some passengers were inconvenienced when the baggage they had checked did not follow them immediately into the terminal as promised but suffered a delay "due to technical difficulties." Thomas slammed the door to his room. An airline that promised to Revere one's time and space could not afford technical difficulties, particularly on its inaugural run.

As the hotel's service bus took him to the terminal, Thomas thought about the announcement he had heard minutes back on the radio. More technical difficulties. More breakdowns in communications. Additional tribulations in Revering peoples'— namely *his*—time and space. That deserters were being pardoned was but part and parcel of the breakdown of this country. It was unpardonable, unconscionable behavior by the government in regard to Vietnam. But now that was expected.

Deserters would be discharged with dishonor. And how had he and thousands of others like him been discharged? Despite their "good papers," weren't they really discharged with dishonor? Didn't the nation, through the eyes of media, see them all as Mai Lai baby killers, spreaders of defoliants, napalm, and cluster bombs, drug addicts, malcontents, and criminals?

Thomas reached into the breast pocket of his jacket and found the Anacin and Gelusil tablets that would ease the upset in his head and stomach. He had asked that the return flight crew for

Revere be assembled in the Revere office at two-fifteen. He intended to speak with them just as he would have spoken to those he commanded in the Triple Nickel Squadron. This airline would deliver, damn it. It would be the best. It would just take dedication, determination, and discipline.

The passengers were restless. For nearly thirty minutes, the ground crew had struggled but still they couldn't get the plane door to close. As he strolled through the stretch jet's aisles, a smile pasted to his face, his sweat-laden clothes pasted to his body, Thomas could hear the jokes. If they couldn't get a door to close, how would they get a plane off the ground.

In his very quiet, controlled manner, he had threatened the crew. Intimidation solved nothing. He then asked for another plane to be brought in, forgetting Revere had no other plane available in Los Angeles. And then they were aloft, a perfect takeoff in perfect weather. He had begun to relax until he was informed there would be a delay in the dinner service as the ovens wouldn't heat. He immediately offered complimentary cocktails for all, hoping an open bar would appease real and imagined hunger pains.

To further compensate for the lack of services, he continued to socialize with the passengers, acting as a candidate for public office might. As he oozed charm, his stomach oozed poisonous gases. He was relieved when the crew began to serve dinner. Only service was exceedingly slow. Passengers in the front of the plane were clamoring for their coffee as those in the back complained because their meals had yet to arrive. In the galley, he castigated the stewardesses, reminding each that she could be replaced and that he would be watching them. He had wanted to yell, scream, hurl objects in his frustration, but he had confined himself to speaking in a tight, controlled voice which had frightened the girls more than his yelling would have. They were relieved when he finally collapsed in his seat at the rear of the first-class section.

When dinner was offered, Thomas refused it, preferring to do nothing but rest. As he settled back in his seat, his eyes closed, the plane's engines made familiar soothing, even lulling sounds. He dozed, that half sleep in which part of him was near at hand while the other was very far away. Even as he heard the now quiet, contented hum of passenger voices, he heard other sounds as he felt the burning in his gut. Drifting and dreaming, hot and then cold, he was somewhere between the then and now. He yearned for a deeper sleep. Comfort eluded him. The newly upholstered seat back suddenly felt like a pallet. His body felt thin, too thin to rest comfortably on such a hard surface. He wanted to sleep. He needed to sleep. Dawn would mean pain, more pain than he experienced during the night when the burning in his stomach meshed with the fear. He could feel that fear now as he lay, his back hurting, on his straw bed. It was coming closer, as were those awful, harsh, metallic sounds. Terrible sounds. Sounds that would awaken him then as they did now. With a scream and a start.

Bolting out of his seat and into the aisle, Thomas knocked the clattering tray of silverware from the stewardess's hands. It made terrible, harsh, metallic sounds as it bumped on the floor. The stewardess looked at him with terror and saw her look reflected on his face as he stared at and yet beyond her.

He was remembering. With his hands to his ears to drown out the horrible noise, Major Thomas Ollson was remembering the service, and in particular the wake-up calls, at the Hanoi Hilton. He would be half awake, anticipating the inevitable, when he would hear the noise coming closer. It rattled his insides as it rattled the locked door to his cell. It rattled because it was keys. Many keys making harsh, metallic sounds as they jangled on his nerves and his jailer's key ring. His door would open. There would be a dark form against the light who threatened to beat him if he didn't move quickly. Some days, he never moved quickly enough. And he couldn't cry or plead or do any of the things he wanted to do. He was a leader. He had to set an example.

He did not know how or when but suddenly Thomas felt himself strapped into his seat. The seat-belt sign was lit and his own had been securely fastened for him. The plane was losing altitude rapidly. Too rapidly. It was going down. He was going down with it. In flames. In enemy territory. Suddenly he remembered he was not alone. The name of his gunner flashed into his head. Pierce Dickey. And they were both going to die unless he could get them out of the plane. He struggled, fighting against the seat belt until he wrestled free of it. Standing, he spun about in turmoil until he saw the emergency-exit sign. He was fighting with the door and those who tried to restrain him when the pain spun him about and he toppled into the aisle. As he felt himself going down with his plane, Thomas closed his eyes, prayed that He would take care of Reese and the children, and then calmly waited for the explosion that this time would end his life.

BOOK TWO
1 · 9 · 7 · 7
IN TRANSIT

9

IT HAD BEEN A LONG DAY FOLLOWING A LONG NIGHT, but soon the ordeal would be over, thought JJ as he watched the hands of the clock near five. Through the barracks windows, he could see the waning light as the April sun dipped low on the horizon. Soon, thought JJ again as he crossed and uncrossed his legs impatiently. He was waiting his turn, the last of the half dozen to be interviewed by the Judge Advocate General Lawyer. Again, JJ's eyes found the clock. Was he imagining it, or was the man who preceded him taking twice the time of the others.

I want out! every part of JJ's seemingly composed body screamed. Although the past twenty-four hours had passed uneventfully, his panic, bordering on paranoia, had only somewhat abated. There was still the fear they would pounce on him, make him an example as they threw him in prison and tossed away the key. Methodically, JJ let his reason talk to his anxiety. To this moment, the military had been courteous and helpful. From the moment his plane had landed at Indianapolis Airport, and he was met, along with the five other returning exiles, by a soldier driving a government-issued car, events had proceeded smoothly.

He had been surprised when they drove on to Fort Benjamin Harrison. There was no security shack, no armed military police, and no major military display. With its manicured lawns. its shrubbery, and three-, two-, and single-story, red-brick buildings with peaked roofs, Fort Harrison could have been any of a number of towns JJ had driven through when he had seen-America-first after graduating from college.

They had secured him and the others for the night in an "open-bay" barrack. Without any partitions, there was no privacy, no chance for him to have collected himself before bedtime. In that respect it was much like Fort Dix, and as he had tossed through the night, covered by memories that produced a cold sweat, he remembered how much he had hated the military mind then and how much he hated it now. Those qualities he so much prized, his individuality and his sense of self, were exactly what the military hoped to destroy to further its own needs. His panic increased as he remembered his basic training. Throughout the long night, he waited for the raid that would result in his arrest. By morning, when it hadn't come, JJ was relieved but not reassured. He laughed when he realized his myth-makers would call him brave, never believing even if he tried to tell them of his fear. One week after Carter's pardon was approved, he had come to Fort Harrison to test the waters for the others. He would be the example. If he was unharmed, unhassled, and unharassed, so would they be. It was for him to return to Canada and sound the all-clear siren.

It had all been simple, thought JJ as he entered the Judge Advocate General Lawyer's cubicle. It had the feeling of being observed by a fraternity. Nothing was said. Just as little was insinuated by the "brothers." But still you knew you would not be pledged. They had been grouped at seven that morning to begin a long day marked by delays. Hurry up and wait, seemed to be the military's credo. The physical had seemed interminable. The various interviews, conducted in monotones by the military personnel, were for the countless records kept by the Pentagon. Or so JJ assumed. But no one had challenged him. Despite the uniform his interrogators wore, none was accusing or antagonistic. Throughout the day, JJ wondered what they felt beneath their façades about him and the others.

As the lawyer thumbed through his records, JJ thought of the plane that would take him later that night into New York and to the bed that once had been his for so many years in his mother's apartment. Tomorrow, he would see David as per the arrangements he had made with Jessamyn before leaving Toronto. Tears came to JJ's eyes as he thought of holding his son in his own country, perhaps even walking him as his mother had once walked him in Central Park.

Dimly, JJ heard the lawyer state that he would be receiving an undesirable discharge but that he was eligible through the Special Discharge Review Program to have his papers upgraded if he could meet certain criteria.

"Which are?" asked JJ, trying to keep his voice expressionless.

"Since you were not a conscientious objector, that you engaged in good citizenship while you were AWOL," was the reply. He could take his case immediately to the Special Discharge Review Board in Washington, the lawyer added as he rose, handed JJ his papers, and dismissed him.

I am now what they call a free man, thought JJ as he rejoined the others who were waiting to be driven to the Holiday Inn near the base where they would be reunited with their families. As he collected his overnight bag, JJ doubted if he would ever think of himself as free for as long as his papers were as "bad" as the feelings they created within him. He was thinking of the long-term effects of his discharge papers when the processing officer informed him someone was waiting just outside the main gate. He was surprised, as he had specifically instructed his family not to meet him so as to avoid any publicity.

The car in which he and the others were being driven was still a hundred feet away when he saw her standing just outside the base, surrounded by camera crews and others he instinctively knew were journalists. He wanted to tell the private to drive on by until he saw who she was holding in her arms. The car stopped. JJ climbed out and, as though walking through his own dream, approached Jessamyn and David. As the TV cameras recorded the moment, he reached out for his son only to find his arms filled with her. She was holding his son away from him as she entwined one arm about his neck and embraced him. Through his lightweight leather jacket, she could feel the tension in his body, a known sign to her that he was angry. She pretended otherwise. Laughing and chattering, making visible signs of welcome, she cooed at the baby as she placed him in his hands.

JJ was shaking as he held David to him. She had arranged all

1 9 9

this, but to what purpose? She had denied him his wishes, but why? The lights of the cameras were blinding him and frightening David. The child was crying as JJ hissed at Jessamyn to send the newsmen away. She looked at him helplessly and shrugged. Then she smiled, at him, at the baby, and at the cameras. She told America how happy she was that her family was reunited. When the newsmen beseeched him for a comment, she gripped his hand, digging her long fingernails into his palm as if to warn him against any words that might be considered inflammatory. He pleaded exhaustion and promised a statement later, but the newsmen were not to be denied. Yes, he finally stated, he was happy to be home but not with the "pardon" that had allowed him to set foot in his country. Yes, he would continue to right a wrong no matter how arduous the fight. The heel of her shoe bearing down on his instep curtailed any further words. Swiftly, Jessamyn steered him into a waiting chauffeur-driven car. In the twenty minutes it took to drive to the Hilton Hotel in Indianapolis not a word was exchanged. In the lobby where more newsmen were assembled, Jessamyn gripped his arm as they strode determinedly to the elevators. They were the picture of family bliss; he, holding David, while she held on to him as any dutiful and fawning wife might.

Once in the suite, Jessamyn's loving attitude came off with her coat. As she put David down in the crib in his room, she told JJ to make her a scotch on the rocks. When she returned, she was surprised to find her drink unmade and JJ, poised like a cat about to pounce on its prey, on the sofa.

"What the fuck is all this about?" he asked.

"It's about you and me," Jessamyn responded calmly. "It's about picking up the pieces of your life."

"Bullshit! That charade wasn't about me. What's in it for you, Jess?" asked JJ as he stared at the woman thought by the world to be his wife.

"Listen, JJ, and listen good," said Jessamyn angrily. "You're in no position in this country to show me or anybody else an attitude. In case you failed to notice, your image sucks. I just helped to upgrade it. The fond father returning to the bosom of his fond family. It'll look good on the tube. America loves family men."

"Get to it, Jessamyn. When I need public relations, I'll hire John Springer. In other words: a class act. Which leaves you out."

"I'm offering you an out, JJ, or maybe an in best describes it," replied Jessamyn. "I'm paying off a debt. You helped launch my career. I'm not ungrateful. I wouldn't be with the network today, given my own office and my own segments on their news magazine show, without having been trained by you. So this is the payoff, the wiping clean of the slate. I play the wife, you, the husband, and together we do one show and one only together. It reestablishes you, and then I split. Professionally as well as personally. I don't need you anymore. Frankly, you're a detriment."

"You sure have a way with words, Jessamyn. Christ, how do you stand yourself? Aren't you ashamed?"

"Of what? Of doing what most people wish they could do—taking what they want? No, I'm not ashamed. I'm damn proud. I've nothing to be ashamed about. When we were together, we worked well both professionally and personally. You were the only man who ever turned me on in and out of bed. But I wasn't your priority any more than you were mine. That makes us even by my calculations. Only I'm offering to pay a debt that might not even be owed. Take it or leave it."

"The only thing I'm taking is my son. We're both going back to Canada tonight. You're no mother, Jessamyn. You use David the way you'd use any prop, and I won't have it," said JJ as he stood to collect himself, his baggage, and his son.

"Make one move toward that bedroom and I'll call the police," warned Jessamyn. "And I will, JJ. That I promise you. Then see what awaits you. People frown on kidnappers much as they do on deserters and traitors. Combine the two and you have hatred. Do what you're thinking and you'll be stuck in Canada forever. Furthermore, you'll lose everything, and you'll never see your son again. That, too, I can promise you."

It was all in her eyes. JJ could see she would do as she threatened. For a moment, his anger almost overwhelmed him.

"And what you're thinking right now, I wouldn't suggest doing either. It's no smarter than kidnapping," said Jessamyn. "Bruise marks show on camera, and I'd be hard pressed to explain them. Other than with the truth, of course."

"This was all arranged for you to look good, wasn't it?" said JJ. "It was all for the record. The little woman meeting her husband with open arms. The perfect wife and the imperfect husband. All forgiveness and light. Jesus, Jessamyn, whoever is masterminding your public relations is fucking brilliant. What a stunt. It does make you look good, Jess. For now."

"You'll never touch me, JJ," replied Jessamyn. "People will always see me as the 'good one,' the one inside the law, while you . . . well, we know how you'll look, don't we. You've lost, JJ. Be gracious about it, and maybe you can keep what little you have left."

"What I have left, Jessie, you never had to lose. I pity you for that.

*   *   *

Laughter, tears, cries, and sobs. Caught in the throat. Released into space. All the same. Signs of life. Signs of her alive and living. Feeling. Never had she been so aware. Of herself and her body. Even as she was but dimly aware of time and place.

Time. How much and how little there was. The clock on the night table read eight-fifteen. But an hour. To live. To love. To dress and then drive to the airport to meet JJ. To bring him home. She felt herself coming home, closer every second, drawing near as she traveled avenues that had long been closed but were now open to her.

It was always time and there was never time enough. Always the need to rush to conclusion. More so for her. She needed the closure, a finish to something so exquisite it demanded completion. She was crying out now, abandoning all thoughts of past and future. There was only the now. Time throbbing through her body.

She stroked his head as it rested between her breasts. He seldom moved after their lovemaking but remained with her, taking comfort in her as he filled her with wonder. And fulfillment. Her eyes were closed as she drifted from thought to thought, riding each like a cloud until it vanished. Without a sheet to cover her body, she felt chilled but not uncomfortably so. The warmth within eradicated any discomfort, much like it had that day in

2 0 2

Washington. She had come alive that day, come together, found herself and those parts that were uniquely her just by *being* her. In all ways, as she had marched for others, she had marched to find herself where she had not dared to look. In action. In the living came life.

He moved. She groaned. He mentioned the hour and the possible traffic to LaGuardia Airport even at this time of night on a Friday. Not yet, she pleaded. One more minute of the hour to be together. Truly together. Entwined. As one. One more minute of an hour snatched from the family. She never remained for the night. She couldn't, not with teenagers at home. He resented that. So did she. Dishonesty didn't become her. It never had.

Again he moved, slowly now, trying gently to extricate himself from her grip. She squeezed and arched her body to hold him more securely. He responded. She smiled. Laughter, tears, cries, and sobs. Caught in her throat. Released into space. All the same. Signs of life. And as Marti gave herself to Matthew Strohl, she completely forgot about JJ and the letters that had begun to trickle in slowly but steadily ever since she had found life and herself in a march in Washington.

*   *   *

The cards meant to cheer only depressed Thomas. Whereas other patients in the hospital collected and displayed theirs, Thomas discarded his, wanting no further reminders that he had been ill. Had been but wasn't and would not be again, he had decided. He had received his "warning," as doctors referred to his mild heart attack. It was duly noted. The staff at Peninsula General near Kennedy Airport where he had been rushed immediately after his plane had landed saw to that with their electrocardiograms, physical therapy, and salt-free diets. Initially, they fed and bathed him, moved him about like a baby. He had felt like a vegetable in need of constant gardening. He hated the dependency. In the first forty-eight hours after his "warning," Thomas hated everything but mainly his physical self. When he wasn't angry, he was depressed. Junk in a junkyard, collecting rust as time and the weather continued to erode.

It had been Matthew Strohl who had turned his head around,

pointing him in a new direction. Matthew made him feel needed. And he was. There existed something he could do, someone he could be, as well or better than most. He wanted it. He would fight for it. That fight began immediately after Matthew's first visit to the hospital. Within the day, he was pushing himself, exercising his own body without the aid of therapists. Days before deemed ready, he was walking the hallway, slowly building stamina. This morning, after breakfast, when the hallways were still as they were apt to be on a Saturday, he had entered the stairwell and slowly had climbed up and down five steps. Just five, but a beginning. The price was exhaustion but a good one. As he semidozed, waiting for his lunch or the kids and Reese to arrive on the shuttle—whichever came first—Thomas's mind wandered. Without Marti's urgings, he would never have seen Matthew, but Marti, unlike the others with their worried faces, had been as annoyed as she had been concerned.

It was Monday or was it Tuesday, when she had first visited. He couldn't remember. He was alive and yet dead. His vital signs were responding but he wasn't. She had refused to tiptoe about him.

"At least I had someone else try to kill me, but you're your own assassin," she had begun. "Self-destructiveness takes all forms. Jesus, Thomas, aren't you tired of killing yourself? You've been doing it all your life."

As he dozed, Thomas smiled, remembering how he had then wanted to slap Marti. His baby sister chastising him rather than the reverse seemed much like kicking a man when he was down. He had told her to leave but she remained, sitting on the edge of the bed, holding his hand, a gesture that normally would have made him uncomfortable since it was so out of keeping with their past relationship.

"Thomas," she had said softly, "you have always driven yourself to perfection and others, I might add, to distraction. For what? You're not Mr. Perfect. I know that and I love you anyway."

He had been startled by her last sentence. She had never said she loved him before. But she did. He could feel that as she sat nearer to him than any woman other than Reese had.

"I want you to talk with Matthew. Now, I know talk is difficult for you," she had proceeded when she could sense his protest, "but Matthew understands, perhaps even what you don't."

He had been confused. What could Matthew tell him that he didn't already know? The answer arrived with Matthew.

Thomas remembered it had been raining that morning. Sheets of gray rain ricocheting off the windows and making his bleak outlook on life even bleaker. Matthew had taken a chair and placed it near the bed. "I'm really not a total stranger, not to you or the problem." He hadn't quite understood. What problem? Was Matthew also a cardiologist? The question was never answered as Matthew had somehow successfully gotten him to talk. First it was worries about his physical health and his ability to perform as head of the family and Revere Airlines. He felt both positions were threatened. He didn't understand his family, their wants or their needs. Kristan, the only one living in New York, had visited immediately. She had looked frightened. From his bed, he had stared at her, not believing the gorgeous child thought by most to be a woman was his own. She had stared at him, not believing her father, the man of invincible strength, had been cut down by a heart attack. With each not believing the other's circumstances, time had passed awkwardly. When she had left, kissing him goodbye, he had grasped her hand and held it longer than he normally would. She had pulled away in surprise, her face reflecting emotions he could not read. Since then, she had called but she had not visited again.

And Reese, he could not understand how she could have left him after that first weekend. Was school *that* important? he wondered. No, but your other children are, Matthew had said, reminding him of the others for whom Reese needed to care.

They had continued to talk, and eventually Thomas broke down, remembering how his plane had crashed in Vietnam and how he had been placed in a wooden cage until his captors could transfer him to Hoala Prison. He remembered the hating faces of the villagers as they poked their bamboo reeds at him through the bars of the cage. And he remembered the prison and the life he and the others had lived for far too many years. His anger over the war spilled out and as it did his color improved. Through the maze of medication, Thomas realized, as he spoke of emotions too conflicted and confused to elucidate, that Matthew Strohl understood. That meant more to him than all the life-support systems in the hospital.

As Thomas drifted between that rainy day and this morning when the rain was springlike in its soft persistence, he again smiled as he remembered how Matthew had preached as well as talked. At first it was all clichés. Words like "taking it easier" on himself, being more tolerant of others, making room for divergent opinions and lifestyles. And then it had turned to the past four years of his life, his frustration and his agony. It was as if Matthew had reached into his gut that day and released the valve that bottled the pressure. Unspeakable pressure that had caused restless nights and an even more restless stomach. He was not the exception, Matthew explained. The Vietnam War had produced many such casualties off the battlefield five and ten years after its participants had been discharged. Only now were doctors identifying these men as "war-wounded," and they were doing so in the face of opposition from the Veterans Administration and the Veterans of Foreign Wars. They and other organizations refused to believe the Vietnam veterans were in trouble, Matthew revealed, and they cited as evidence statistics indicating that there had been fewer field psychiatric casualties in Nam than in Korea. What they didn't realize, Matthew stated, is that the stress was delayed. Although it wasn't evident on the battlefield or even immediately upon the veteran's return, as the vet got further and further away from the experience, the stress began to skyrocket. Particularly when the vet came up against a wall of American numbness or worse, hostility.

"Are you saying I'm a little nuts?" Thomas had asked.

"You're suffering from a stress disorder," Matthew had replied, "and that is not a mental illness. Your case is similar to some but different from most. You weren't a field soldier but a flier, and an officer, and a prisoner, and worst of all—for stress—but best of all—for this country—a patriot. If there is such a thing as caring too much, you did. I'm not telling you not to care, but I'm here to tell you that you don't have to swim upstream when there is a boat to take you to your destination. It's an organization called the Disabled American Veterans, and they care every bit as much as you."

Thomas had wanted more but Matthew, afraid of overtiring the patient, had left, promising to return the following day. Which he did, bringing with him material from the DAV. If he was willing, Thomas could train to be a National Service Officer immediately upon receiving a clean bill of health. The salary was inconsequential in comparison to the benefits he would receive emotionally. He would be assisting other veterans, helping them to receive long-denied or delayed benefits, working with them on professional as well as personal problems. He would be fighting for the men who had also fought in the service of his country. He would be righting a wrong, perhaps many wrongs, making his presence felt. Contributing. It would be continuous forward action, perhaps slow but steady. He could win what had become an almost private battle for a handful of others like him. He could live with self-respect, dignity, and hope.

As he thought back to that day, Thomas started to clap his hands, applauding Matthew Strohl for both his passion and intelligence. Since then, Thomas had felt hopeful, often jubilant. He would do his "time" in the hospital, agree to its and his doctor's terms, and would then return to Boston to be at the JFK Federal Building, and the DAV's offices, with application and heart in hand. As soon as possible! He would put his house in order. He would be more of a father, more of a husband, and Reese could now be more of a wife. Life would resume, and it would be as it was before the war. No, he thought, better because I am better.

"Mr. Ollson?" From his bed, Thomas could see the white peaked nurse's cap before he saw the middle-aged woman. "I have a note for you. A gentleman asked that I deliver it," she said as she entered, waddling in white tennis shoes. "He asked that I wait for an answer."

The envelope, bearing the hospital's return address, had obviously been borrowed as had the stationery on which the note was written. The handwriting was not familiar.

Dear Thomas:

I'm at the nurse's station. I have a few minutes before my plane takes off. I didn't want to barge in as I know about shock. Also, I don't know how you feel about seeing me. Anyway, I'm here. I'd like to see you but if it's too much for you, I'll understand.

JJ

The hand holding the note became a fist, crumpling the paper as it did. Then suddenly it opened. Thomas looked at the paper ball that had once been a note, closed his eyes, and let the ball fall to the side of his bed where it remained as the nurse waited for him to speak.

10

It was but a moment in time, one for which she had waited more years than she cared to remember. As her gaze fell and then dwelled on each familiar face, Carolyn submerged in a well of contentment. To be surrounded by one's family is the greatest success, she decided, as she reluctantly excused herself from the table and walked slowly toward the kitchen, relishing the sounds of her family's conversation as it swirled behind her.

Margaret was placing the last of the candles on the three-tier, rose-laden birthday cake. Again it was but a moment in time and yet it was a moment that had been etched over the years and from many other birthdays their children had shared. So very many. Forty many. My God, thought Carolyn, if our children are forty, then how old are we?

"You know, I just remembered," said Carolyn wistfully as she sat down at the kitchen table near Margaret. "No one ever made me a fortieth birthday party."

"That's because you were never forty," said Margaret sweetly. "As I recall, you tried thirty-nine for a year but seemingly didn't much care for it as you were thirty-eight the next. And if memory serves me, you liked that one quite a bit as you stayed thirty-eight for an indefinite period of time. But, if it disturbs you," said Margaret as she rose to collect cake plates from one of the cabinets above the sink, "I could make you a belated fortieth birthday party.

I'm sure all your little friends at the old folks home would come. If they can find their teeth."

"Do you feel like Vinnie is forty?" asked Carolyn.

"No," said Margaret as she handed Carolyn a book of matches. "It's absolutely impossible for our children to be forty when neither of us is that old. They say I'm sixty-one which makes you sixty-two, but I don't believe it. In my mind, we're still the Tiernan Sisters, turning heads and hearts on screen, on stage and off. I still feel it's all beginning rather than drawing to an end."

"There are new beginnings, Margaret," said Carolyn softly. "All our children are grouped together under one roof. Yours and mine."

"I've never known the difference. Not really," said Margaret, her voice hoarse from emotions close to the surface.

"Neither of us has, which is what makes the day so special," said Carolyn.

"Do you think they feel it?" asked Margaret, handing one book of matches to Carolyn as she opened another and lit a match.

"I don't know what they feel," said Carolyn as she began lighting the candles on the cake. "Long ago I realized I couldn't program my children's feelings, so I deal only with my own. And I'm happy, Margaret. Truly happy."

From the look on his face as he spoke animatedly about his return to college and the work he would begin on his master's degree in psychology, Marti could see Vinnie was happy. One of the more apparent reasons for his happiness, Jamie, was sitting beneath the dining-room table where the family was grouped, running his kiddie car back and forth over her foot. Two other reasons, Este, looking pleased and plump, and newly adopted Lisa, ten months of gurgling, cooing baby with the brightest blue eyes since Kristan, were at his side.

It must be wonderful to be entering your forties with a new child, thought Marti, to be reliving life, to see it unfold anew and through the naïve and trusting eyes of a child. As her hand rested in Matthew's on his knee, hidden from the others by the long damask tablecloth, Marti realized she had her own wonderful and, for many, enviable way of entering a fourth decade: a new relationship, one based on reality rather than the fantasies of the young girl she once again felt herself to be. Matthew was not only her lover but her friend. Unlike the men of her past, she did not make him her caretaker. Still, she could not yet refuse those urging her to run next month for a delegate's seat to the National Conference of Women in November. Ever since her participation in the exile/resister march on Washington, there was a part of her that yearned to be more politically involved, but it collided with the other part that wanted nothing more than to spend an idyllic summer with Matthew. After all, it was not every woman of forty who got to be a girl again, thought Marti, even if it were but for a little while.

There had been other birthdays celebrated in this very room. Many other birthdays long forgotten. As he looked back, Thomas remembered how as a child he had resented sharing his birthday with Marti and Vinnie. Throughout his childhood, he had wanted a day all his own and had been denied it. That had been but one of the angers he had nurtured over the years. Then, he had felt little kinship, little sense of family, but now that had changed. His illness had changed most everything, but in particular much of what he felt about family.

Which is why Thomas had insisted despite Reese's misgivings on making the trip from Boston to New York. Although it had only been nine weeks since his "warning," he felt strong and confident. He not only wanted to celebrate his life but family. This was, beginning now, that year, this very day, a new life. Revere had terminated his contract by mutual consent and he was free to begin his training as a National Service Officer with the DAV the beginning of July. He had already visited their offices, and it felt as if he had come home. A home away from home, a place to be where he was wanted and needed. A place where his life would once again have meaning.

Thomas had wondered how he would feel turning forty. More than half his life had been lived and, had the DAV not taken on the aspects of a beacon shining through what till recently had been the darkness of his life, he would have felt near dead. Now, he felt rejuvenated. He wondered how many men his age received the opportunity to begin anew working at something they believed in. For the first time since his return from Vietnam, Thomas felt his life was on track. And he was not alone. With the DAV, he would get the job done. If for but no other reason, there was much to celebrate this birthday and, as he gazed about the table, Thomas realized there was no other place he would rather be. It was all here but for two exceptions.

As she listened and even responded to the various conversations, Reese's mind was adrift. As she felt herself to be. Not that her life lacked direction—but it had veered off course. Obstacles had arisen and still they could not be cleared. They would have to be or she would drown. Or suffocate. She could not allow that. She could not deny herself very much longer. Ever since Thomas's heart attack, her life had been on hold. She attended those classes necessary for her to pass her courses. The rest she skipped, preferring to give Thomas her time. He needed it. He also demanded it. She was the dutiful wife doing exactly what the doctors had advised. Their prescription for Thomas's recovery was indelibly etched in her mind. It was much like a mantra; to be repeated in times of stress.

She could hear them now as she absentmindedly looked about the table, avoiding the eyes of the sullen and drawn face she had last seen dispensing leaflets that Labor Day in Victoria Park. "Remember, you are in this together. You're a team and it will take team effort, team play, to win. This will be a time of adjustment for your husband. His body has undergone a shock. His lifestyle must adjust. *He* must adjust. He must accept his limitations. He will need sympathy, support, and understanding. In short: be there for him."

And she had been, but not without some resentment. As he was gaining, she felt herself losing. An identity about to be misplaced if she allowed it. Prior to his attack, she had planned to leave him. Now that wasn't a consideration, let alone a possibility. He had stood by her during her "attack." Therefore she would stand by him. Out of obligation and guilt. Also from caring. He had never been less than an honorable man. If he was deficient in some, perhaps even most, ways as a husband, he was nonetheless a provider and never had he given her reason to suspect he was unfaithful. Leaving him now would solve nothing but would add a further burden to her life. Besides, perhaps he would change. Perhaps they could live side by side instead of her being two steps behind as he seemed to prefer. She owed it to herself and to Thomas to see. Perhaps between their efforts, they could woo Karl and Kristan back to the family fold. But she could not and would not lose herself in the process, thought Reese. Not again. Comfort was not nestled within the bosom of the family but deep within her. Hopefully, she had only temporarily misplaced the map that took her there.

Ali was bored. Unlike Mark, who could sit silently as he did now, content with the music he composed and played in his head, she needed more active divertissement. Kelly, with her incessant babbling about boys and clothes, wasn't it. They were all full of shit, thought Ali angrily. Everyone noticed—how could they not?—but nobody asked where they were. What hypocrisy! No wonder Karl preferred to run in some dumb local track meet in the Boston area rather than attend the party. As for Kristan: if she were granted but one wish, she would wish herself with her cousin on the beaches of the Bahamas even if it did mean smiling your face off for some camera. Except, thought Ali, she could never miss her mother's birthday. But then, she felt different about her mother than Kristan did about hers and her father.

It was an awful feeling, one for which JJ had not been prepared. It was the antithesis of all he expected. He felt estranged, outside rather than within the circle. What he had hoped to recapture was lost forever. He was not that JJ anymore, and they were not that family he had idealized for so many years. Not that they were different, but they were. Certainly he was. Time had not stood still but moved on, leaving behind the boy he had been and the position he once had held within the family. He should have known. Any reasonable man would have thought it through prior to the experience and would thus have been protected. Now it pained him. It was something more to mourn. The sudden sense of loss accompanied by loneliness caused his throat to close.

Repeatedly, JJ reminded himself that these people were his family. If only they hadn't tiptoed around him, had made mention of the obvious. But they treated his presence and the fact that he and Thomas were sitting at the same table in the same room as an everyday occurrence. When it wasn't. He knew that, as did the woman seated next to Thomas, who continually looked at him with mistrust, as if his one word might put an end to the ceasefire in their hostilities.

He was tired. Too tired to think rationally anymore. He had arrived from Toronto that morning, leaving behind a number of past and future speaking engagements before those exiles who wanted firsthand information on what awaited at Fort Benjamin Harrison before partaking of Carter's pardon program. So many remained mistrustful, continuing to believe there would be, despite JJ's experience, some form of harsh disciplinary action taken against them, as if the undesirable discharge were not enough. In front of him loomed the Special Discharge Review Board in Washington. He had been anxiously awaiting a date for his hearing. He was prepared for the fight, certain he could prove his good citizenship and thus have his papers upgraded. Yet he wished he had a second in his corner, someone he could turn to when the infighting grew mean, as he knew it would.

JJ's thoughts were interrupted as the kitchen doors opened and Carolyn and Margaret, holding a candle-laden cake, came singing into the dining room. His mother's face, illuminated by the candles, was radiant. He watched as Marti, Vinnie, and Thomas grouped together as the cake was placed before them. Kelly was clinging to her father's hand as he made a wish and then bent with the others to blow out the forty-plus-one candles on the cake. The cheers from the others frightened Jamie, who had been playing under JJ's feet. As Carolyn began to speak, Jamie began to cry. Instinctively, JJ reached to pick up the child as he heard Carolyn say: "I dreamed about this day. It is I suppose what every parent dreams about . . . to be with her family, her children, on all theirs and others' special occasions."

As JJ looked from his mother's shining face to that of the child in his lap, the pain that had been sitting on his chest for most of the afternoon wrenched free. The sobs that erupted frightened them all but most notably the child JJ had been trying to reassure. As Marti immediately reached for Jamie, JJ ran toward his father's den, much as he had throughout his childhood whenever comfort was needed. Even through the door he closed behind him, his distress could be heard at the table where the family, stunned, remained still, not certain what to do. Slowly, Thomas rose. As the others began to do likewise, he motioned for them to sit. They did not question his unspoken command. There was something in his attitude that told them not to.

JJ heard the door open and close before he heard the voice.

"My son isn't here either," said Thomas to the back turned toward him. "For different reasons, but it doesn't hurt any less."

JJ's sobs stopped abruptly.

"You're going to find it's but one of the prices you'll pay for having taken a direction different from most," said Thomas softly. "And you'll receive little sympathy or support, because people will not understand. Furthermore, they won't want to. You're going to make them uncomfortable because you'll remind them of a time they want to forget. For a long while, you're going to feel lonely. You'll discover it's not just time you've lost but entire people. If you're lucky, you'll hold on to yourself."

JJ turned to look at the man talking to him. His expression was immediately interpreted and understood by Thomas.

"I couldn't talk to you that day at the hospital," he replied to the unspoken question. "I wanted to but couldn't. I hated your seeing me flat out. Down. Christ, I was sure you would think the war had done it to me and that you'd glory in that."

"It made me feel sick," said JJ.

"I wouldn't have known that then," said Thomas. "I couldn't see you clearly. I'm not saying I do now, but I can separate you from the position you took. You are my brother. You are not just a deserter. Sometimes when you hate, things mesh that should remain separate. I don't know if you understand."

JJ nodded. He understood and was surprised that Thomas had

been able to express so aptly the complexities of what he, too, had felt. "That day in the hospital sure was awkward," said JJ, a half smile on his face. "I said Hello, how are you, and you said Fine."

"I also said How are you, and you said Fine," reminded Thomas.

"Well, it was a beginning," said JJ philosophically. "I guess communication has to begin somewhere."

Thomas was silent. JJ's words made him think of Karl. "But how?" asked Thomas more of himself than JJ. Not that it mattered, as JJ was considering his own words and thinking of Jessamyn. "I want my son," he said finally.

"Yes, I know," replied Thomas. "Most fathers do, but we don't often admit it. Or show it," he added, his facial expression now a perfect match to the one worn by his brother.

* * *

JJ was standing on the bath mat, dripping wet both from the shower and the August humidity, listening to the phone ring and debating whether to answer it. Several premorning phone calls had already made him late. Kay would be arriving in minutes, and if he wanted the ride to the airport he couldn't keep her waiting, not when she opened her office promptly at nine. His own opened whenever the phone rang. And rang it did, and had, ever since his return from Fort Benjamin Harrison. Which was exactly why JJ had installed the special number in his home. He wanted every exile to have access to information only he had. That yes, he had indeed passed through the military installation without incident. The "hotline" was manned twenty-four hours a day, often by Kay when he was not available.

He had not been as available as he would have liked, but then he couldn't be in two places simultaneously. Since the U.S. Congress had not allocated funds to advertise or publicize Carter's pardon program due to their polarized feelings about the deserters, JJ and several others, with monies raised by various church and peace groups, were explaining the pardon program through advertisements, posters, leaflets, and interviews in the Canadian press. A pile of clippings from those interivews, from those cities in Canada to which he had traveled, lay on his desk, impressive to JJ only for the number of exiles he and they might have reached. Today he was flying to Sweden to acquaint the exiles there with the program.

Thinking of the trip again made JJ angry, as he recalled his efforts, all unsuccessful, to reach Jessamyn. He had wanted to coordinate his return with her, to return to Toronto from Sweden via New York so he could spend time with David. Jessamyn had neither taken nor returned his phone calls. He really would have to consult a lawyer, he decided. Or take matters into his own hands, as he had in June when he had last seen David. He had camped outside Jessamyn's high-rise apartment on East 54th Street after she had refused him entry and access to *his* child. She feared kidnapping and threatened him with the police again. But when she had been confronted with his presence in the street, she had acquiesced, not wanting a scene in front of the friend she did not introduce. And so he had spent the afternoon playing with David on the eighteen-foot terrace that ringed two sides of Jessamyn's apartment. The next day when he had returned, the doorman informed him Miss Giroux had left town. Furious, he had tried to brush past the man. A scene erupted, one he ended when he realized he could not afford bad publicity, not with "Judgment Day"—his day in court in late October before the Special Discharge Review Board—coming up.

As JJ let the phone ring, he mentally juggled his rage toward Jessamyn and the Review Board. The idea of a group of military men sitting in judgment of him infuriated him as much as Jessamyn did—just because she was *woman*, *mother*, having more rights to his son, than he, *man, father*. But he would win his wars. He was armed and impatient for the battle to begin. He had collected his data, his proof of good citizenship. In a file were all the reviews of his documentaries, the citations and awards he had received for his "good works." There were numerous letters of commendation from peace groups both foreign and American. These should bring him home with nothing less than what he had earned: honor.

He was dressed but for his shoes when the doorbell rang. . . . Kay. And he wasn't quite ready, he thought guiltily as he ran down the steps to the hallway. He flung open the door with apologies

2 1 7

prepared, but it wasn't Kay who greeted him but a suited man, perspiring only above his upper lip.

"John Ollson, Jr.?" he asked.

JJ nodded. The man thrust sealed papers into his hand, turned, and left. JJ stood stunned. Suddenly Kay was by his side. With her fingernail, she broke the seal. Simultaneously they learned that Jessamyn Giroux Ollson was suing John Ollson, Jr., for divorce. The grounds: desertion.

*   *   *

It was not without some sadness that Marti watched the sky shifting in colors and moods as it prepared for the new day's entry. In minutes, the sun would rise on the last of the fourteen days she and Matthew would spend together on Cape Cod, and an idyllic summer would end. Huddled under the blanket they had taken from their beachfront cottage, Marti, as she snuggled against Matthew, was oblivious to the predawn chill and the cold sand that had yet to warm from the heat of their bodies. This was a moment to savor. An end and yet a beginning.

That they had arisen early on this, their last day on the Cape, had been Matthew's idea, just one of the many that had further endeared him to her. From the moment they had left New York and Matthew, his responsibilities, he had been more boy than man. With his insistence on cookouts and bonfires, he had taken her back to her early summers spent on Nantasket. He made her feel that young again. Not once had he discussed his work, and as a result she never challenged her recent decision not to run for a delegate's seat at the National Conference of Women. She was happy. Beyond that, she was content. Never before had she been both in a relationship.

Never before had she seen Thomas seemingly so happy and content. From outward appearances, one would never guess he had so recently suffered a heart attack. On an impulse, she and Matthew had detoured en route to the Cape to visit with Thomas and Reese. On another impulse, they had arranged to celebrate Reese's hard-won master's degree at a local restaurant. It had surprised Marti to see Reese downplaying her achievement. Had it not been for her few private moments with Reese, Marti would not have known that she was about to begin student teaching that September. Certainly Thomas would not have told her, if he knew. He must have known, Marti had thought then and now, but even the next day, when he insisted Marti see where he "played," he made no mention of it.

She had been touched that he had wanted to share this part of his life with her. Over the years, Thomas had not been the most sharing of men, but at the DAV offices he welcomed her into his world with a spontaneity that previously had been lacking. He made jokes about the government-issue furnishings, the beige-and-brown color scheme that did nothing to alleviate the institutional feeling. He was "interning," he explained, and after his sixteen months of on-the-job training was completed he would be a National Service Officer. His voice made it seem like sixteen days. It was confident, exuberant, and youthful.

She had been surprised by the men who came for help. They were of all ages and all colors. They arrived in staggering numbers, lining up past the receptionist's desk and into the outside hall. Most were the age her father would have been or somewhat younger. Very few were Vietnam veterans. As Thomas explained with some bitterness, the VA had yet to acknowledge there was a problem with the men of that war and thus neither the men nor their benefits found their way into the DAV offices. But that would change, he promised.

It had been fascinating for her to watch how people reacted to Thomas. Although he was an intern, a trainee, she could see and feel the eyes that looked up to him. Even as he was being led, her brother was a leader. It amused her that the persons teaching him the ever-changing military regulations and procedures governing benefits for the disabled often turned to him for guidance. His was both the voice of reason and intellect. It had amused her in a wry way that Thomas was also learning to defend deserters. When she mentioned this he looked at her humorlessly. The situations were not comparable, he said. The men he would be defending had deserted under extreme duress. Usually there was illness or death in their families. She had not pursued the topic but she had pursued discussing JJ. Their brother was seemingly of little interest to Thomas, who listened to the details of the divorce

2 1 9

proceedings but offered little real concern. It was as if he had once again pushed JJ from his life, as if the afternoon of their birthday had not occurred. She had wanted to yell at him, to scream that if he, if JJ, if *they as brothers*, could not open and maintain a dialogue, bridge the gap, heal the wound, how could a nation? It was Matthew who later reminded her that a dialogue had indeed begun and that it would proceed at its own pace and not hers. Of course he was right.

As the first pink rays appeared on the rim of the ocean, Marti became aware of Matthew sleeping at her side. She debated whether to wake him, knowing he would be angry if she didn't but also knowing he needed the rest for the long drive back to New York, particularly due to the Labor Day weekend traffic. But she would wake him, she decided. She could not have this moment unshared, particularly now when she had reached a decision to share everything. That she wasn't afraid did not really surprise her. Eleven years had elapsed since her last marriage. Then, to spend time with a man meant spending time with him but none with herself. That was no longer true. With Matthew, she could feel her separateness even when they were the most together. And they had been frequently together. Even prior to their vacation, there had been many nights when he shared her bed and her house. There reached a point where she had been direct with Ali and Mark. She did not claim she and Matthew were "good friends," but simply stated they were lovers, a fact already known to both her children. There had been no questions but there had been one incident, not altogether unexpected. Mark had invited his "lady" to spend the night. Marti had been firm. Such an action was not permitted in her house. Mark had ranted about a double standard. She had not thought him totally wrong, but she had not reneged. Her argument that she was the adult and he the child did not soothe her any more than it did him. Worse was her stating that this was her house and therefore she would set the rules.

There had been considerable tension, particularly with Ali siding with Mark, until she admitted her arguments were weak but her feelings on the subject strong. That they understood and somehow accepted. The subject did not come up again.

As if knowing the moment was at hand, Matthew's eyes opened to the first glimpse of the sun as it edged its way onto the horizon. At first, it seemed hesitant, almost shy in its ascent. As if fearing to be too assertive, it didn't break into the day abruptly. Instead, it gradually eased itself into the life of the moment, giving everything and everyone time to adjust to its presence. As she lay next to Matthew, Marti likened it to the way a baby makes its entrance into the world, slowly, little by little and then just a little bit more. The imagery pleased her. Without thinking, although the thought had been in her head ever since their first week on the Cape, Marti said: "Matthew, I do want to get married after all."

It was the end of an argument, one she had repeatedly with herself ever since the question first arose in her head. "I would not lose a thing. I could only gain," she added.

His silence surprised her. "You did hear me?" she asked, her voice suddenly strident.

"Yes," he replied.

"But no response? I thought you'd be jumping up and down, crushing me in your arms with passionate kisses. Or is that my movie-mad mind believing too many bad pictures in which I, myself, was starred."

"Are you asking me to marry you?" Matthew said gently, still not looking at her but at the steadily rising sun.

"I thought I was accepting your proposal," replied Marti, suddenly anxious.

"But Marti, I never proposed. I never even hinted," said Matthew, his voice straining to remain calm. "The subject has never come up."

"Of course it's come up, Matthew. Damn it! We're not children. The minute two adults begin seeing each other exclusively, the subject is up. Like it or not, it's there. Unstated perhaps, but there. Constantly, I might add."

"Not for everybody, Marti," said Matthew firmly. "Not for me. Somewhere, you've gotten your signals crossed."

"Oh, no, I haven't," said Marti as she sat up, the blanket falling to the sand. "This is a signal," she said as her arm swept in the entire beach setting. "Coming here, asking me to spend the two weeks with you, was a signal."

"Marti, you're wrong. I've had a great time, the best, but this wasn't a test site or a proving ground for marriage."

"Spell out exactly what you're saying, Matthew," said Marti, her stomach now gaseous and hurting.

"I don't want to get married. I'm only recently unmarried, and the idea of doing it all again poses problems for me. Frankly, I never thought of you as a woman with a need to get married."

"I don't *need* to get married. That's one need I haven't felt in years. One can want to be married—even get married—without being in need of it, Matthew. What I need when I love somebody is to be with him."

"How much more can we be with each other?" asked Matthew.

"Oh, a great deal more," said Marti, furious that he was still lying there, seemingly calm, while she found sitting still an act of torture. "There are twenty-four hours in a day. I'd like to spend, if not all then, a major part of them under one roof with one man."

"I could move in if that's what you want," said Matthew.

"Live together is what you mean," replied Marti.

"Is what *you* mean?" said Matthew.

"No. That's not at all what I mean, Matthew. I'm much too old to just live together. Too old and too traditional at this point in my life. With me, it's all or nothing, because I'm an all-or-nothing lady."

"Marti, that sounds dangerously close to an ultimatum, and that's unfair. Whether we live together or not, I love you. My feelings don't change."

"But mine do, Matthew. I'm afraid they just plain do."

With the sun now firmly planted in the sky, Marti stared from it to Matthew. "So much for idyllic summers," she said as she rose and turned in the direction of the cottage. "It's over, and why not? It is Labor Day."

*   *   *

The sun was staring into Thomas's eyes as he began his final lap about the Common. With one hand, he brushed away the sweat that was dripping from his forehead. Suddenly the sweatband he so often had seen Karl wearing when he ran made sense.

Like most days, Thomas imagined Karl was jogging at his side. They were talking, about nothing in particular, but that didn't seem to matter. Only Karl didn't jog. He ran, and at speeds and for distances that excluded Thomas.

When the doctors had suggested either swimming or jogging, Thomas had chosen the latter, thinking it would give him an activity to share with Karl. That his son would refuse him had not entered Thomas's mind. Karl's logical excuse—that jogging would interfere with his training—numbed the pain of his rejection.

There are certain problems one cannot run away from, thought Thomas as he moved into a long-legged lope that would take him the final distance home. Karl was one, and Kristan another. He had read in the paper that morning that his daughter would be making her acting debut in an off-Broadway production late that fall. Enraged, he had hidden the paper, not wanting Reese to learn, as he had, of Kristan's new endeavor from a columnist rather than from the subject who was, after all, only their daughter. It was not right. It was also incomprehensible. But Kristan would have some valid excuse. There would be managers or press agents, a breakdown of communications—Kristan's favorite scapegoat—to blame for the unintended slight.

He should insist she return home, thought Thomas. He should give her no choice—only an order. Whether she would obey it or not was a question Thomas refused to contemplate. He wondered if Reese also felt a sense of loss. They didn't discuss Kristan often, or at least no more often than they discussed any of their children. It had to be particularly painful for Reese, decided Thomas, as she had been closest to Kristan. Still, she accepted both Kristan living in New York and her reasons for it. That it was professional and not personal was a party line to which they both willingly subscribed.

It was a typically cool September morning and Thomas wrapped the towel tighter about his neck as he neared the exit for Marlborough Street. The house was but a block up ahead. By the time he entered it, Reese would have left. Eight A.M. and gone about her day. That bothered him. Somehow, mistakenly, he had thought once she had concluded her schooling, she would not so soon have begun another program aimed at yet another degree, but would have contented herself with her home and family. He would have liked breakfast not only to have been prepared for him, as it was each day, but eaten with him. He needed her there.

Kelly, too, would be gone, her day, like Reese's, beginning early at school. He seldom saw Kelly. By the time he arrived home from work, she had concluded her studies and was ready after dinner to be out and about but home by ten. Although Kelly never missed her curfew, Thomas suddenly realized he had no idea where she went or with whom. He trusted that Reese did.

The house seemed much too still. As he heard his heart beating, Thomas took his pulse. It was good, perfect actually, considering the two miles he had just jogged. From the hallway, Thomas thought he could smell the freshly squeezed orange juice that awaited him on the kitchen counter. Next to it would be the bag of herbal tea Reese would have placed beside the clean cup. Even the instant oatmeal would be in a bowl, waiting only for the boiling water to be added. He had nothing to do but pour and stir and eat.

Thomas wondered if Karl would join him for breakfast. As he stripped off his jogging jacket, Thomas quickly took the stairs leading up to the bedrooms. At Karl's door, he listened for signs of his stirrings. Hearing none, he opened the door gently and to his surprise found the room empty except for the trunk and the two suitcases already half packed. Looking at his son's possessions piled in the trunk or on a chair waiting to be packed gave Thomas a sudden shock. What had once been such a source of pride—Karl's skipping a grade—now seemed such a mistake. Seventeen was too young for a boy to leave home. Suddenly what had been long planned seemed unexpected. In two days his only son would be gone from his house, a student at Villanova.

"Can I help you?"

The voice and its tone, as well as the tone of the question, were not inviting but accusing. They combined to make Thomas feel as if he had been caught trespassing. Karl stood in the doorway, his hair as wet as his sweatsuit, staring at him.

"I was just looking for you," said Thomas.

As if he weren't there, Karl stripped down, revealing a hard-muscled but thin runner's body, perfect in its proportions. It was not an act of father-son intimacy but one that seemed to obliterate Thomas's presence. Feeling confused and angry, Thomas stood there not knowing what to do.

"Was there something you wanted?" Karl asked as he wrapped a towel about his waist.

The question suddenly hurt more than all the combined beatings he had taken at the hands of his captors during the war. All that he wanted suddenly flashed across Thomas's mind. He wanted Karl to ask about his work, his health, his existence.

"How are you?" Thomas asked, embarrassed as soon as the words were spoken.

Karl's look was one of amused confusion. "Dad, it's okay. Just because I'm leaving for college, doesn't mean you have to do or be anything. It's not like I need to know the facts of life or anything like that. It's all right, Dad. Just relax. No role-playing is necessary."

Again Thomas felt as if he had taken a blow to the body. As he looked at Karl, Thomas tried to identify what if any weapon was being used, but the look on Karl's face said none. There was no rancor or resentment in the blue eyes that locked with his. Impatience, perhaps. Confusion, definitely. And something else. But what? thought Thomas. Suddenly, he wanted to leave the room into which he had yet to be invited.

"Dad, I don't want to hurt you, but let's face it: it's a little late to pretend to a big father-son relationship when there isn't any. I'm more sorry about that than you. God knows I wanted it. As a kid, I would have killed for it. But then you were gone and even though you returned from the war, you really didn't. Not to me anyway. Not for me. You were always so wrapped up in your life, the things that mattered to you so that I never did."

"But you did," said Thomas.

Karl waited for something more to be said. When nothing was he sighed. "Dad, you had a strange way of showing it. I never felt you had room in your life for me. I figured I just didn't measure up to your expectations. I just couldn't stand straight or tall enough."

It was the tears that appeared in Karl's eyes that made Thomas cringe. They were what he had feared, the unknown artillery that had lurked behind Karl's expression. They could kill faster than any gun or grenade.

"I was a leftover in your life, Dad. I ran second best to a war. I didn't understand that, Dad. But then you're not easy to understand. Like, the way people see you is a perfect example. Some think you're a hero; some a nut. Then there are those who don't know who or what the hell you are. And then there is me. I'm somewhere mixed up in all three, and I wish to God I wasn't."

Thomas looked at his son and saw a whole other nakedness, one that was much more revealing than the obvious one. A pain he had never felt before seared through him. "Well, I've got to be getting to the office," he said, turning toward the door. "I have a lot of work to do. A lot of people are depending on me. Let me know if you need anything before you go."

Karl stood staring at the back of the man who was his father, thinking of all he needed that the other simply couldn't supply. He then closed the door and turned toward the cold shower that he hoped would pump life back into his body.

*   *   *

"I want my son."

Henry D'Alessandro, the lawyer taking JJ's deposition, wiped his brow, then the lenses of his glasses before speaking. "Mr. Ollson. I urge you to be reasonable. Ask for what you might get."

"There is only one thing I want and that is custody of my son," said JJ firmly.

"My client," said D'Alessandro patiently, "also wants custody and she is determined her wishes will prevail over yours. And I believe they will. I'm sure your lawyer has already advised you that courts in this country rarely take a child from his mother unless it can be proven that the mother is unfit by some extreme cause. Can you show such cause, Mr. Ollson?"

As he considered the question, JJ looked about Henry D'Alessandro's office. It had the look of age and wisdom, with its highly polished wood-paneled walls and shelves upon shelves of books, legal and otherwise. No, he could not show such cause, JJ realized, not unless he could strip away the outer layers of Jessamyn

2 2 6

Giroux to reveal the nature of the person. Otherwise it would be difficult to prove she was unfit to be his son's custodian. Difficult but not impossible, JJ reminded himself.

"Mr. Ollson, I asked a question," said D'Alessandro gently.

"I heard it, Mr. D'Alessandro," snapped JJ, "and I'm not certain I will answer. Frankly, I think it's time your client answered to me."

"Mr. Remington, I suggest you advise your client this will get us nowhere."

Chase Remington, sitting to JJ's left, continued to twirl his Mark Cross gold pen as if he had not been addressed. From past experience, he knew this was just the beginning of hostilities. As the case progressed, so would the war. Inch by inch. This one would be particularly unpleasant.

"Mr. Ollson," continued D'Alessandro, "let us proceed in another fashion. Tell me, what makes you think you can provide a better home for your child than can your wife?"

"Because I am home. I am a full-time father. My child comes first, not my career. He *is* my career."

Henry D'Alessandro did not respond. No need to try the witness before the trial, and undoubtedly this case would come to trial rather than be settled out of court. The parties involved were too intense, too far apart, and far too bitter to settle amicably. But his client would win. Of that D'Alessandro was also certain. Jessamyn Giroux would appear to both judge and jury as a reasonable, sane woman. She was not asking for alimony. Nor was she asking for the house she had once shared with her husband. She simply wanted what most mothers want: custody of her child and financial support for that child from its father.

"I have no further questions, Mr. Ollson," said D'Alessandro as he rose. "I will be in touch with your attorney. I thank you for your time."

JJ watched as Henry D'Alessandro collected his papers and put them neatly into his briefcase. His wife's attorney was elegant in attitude and dress. Jessamyn had gone for the best to get the best. Chase Remington was nudging JJ's sleeve, signaling it was time to leave immediately. JJ, too, was eager to depart and then learn how Remington had succeeded that morning with Jessamyn when her deposition had been taken. Together, they would plan their strategy.

JJ had answered Jessamyn's subpoena with one of his own within three weeks of its receipt. He had secured the services of Remington & Wycoff, the family lawyers, and had been pleased when the youngest of the Remingtons, Chase, a man just somewhat older than he, had been assigned to his case. There was nothing of the Henry D'Alessandro about Chase. He was easy, comfortable, and without pretension. His attitude and approach often lulled the enemy into a false sense of security.

"It's not going to be easy, JJ," said Chase as they stood on the corner of Broad Street searching for a taxi.

"Given the fees your firm is charging, the difficult you should do right now. The impossible, I understand, might take a little while," said JJ as a cab screeched to a halt somewhere between them and oncoming traffic.

Chase Remington chuckled although he was not amused. He liked his client and did not wish to see him hurt any more than he already was. A court case and a trial by jury would only add to his grief. The newspapers would have a field day as they and their readers loved nothing more than custody fights between the rich and the famous. And JJ would lose, of that Chase Remington was fairly certain, although he had not as yet told his client. Remington had been taken somewhat off guard by Jessamyn that morning. From JJ's description, he had expected someone other than the charming, extremely attractive, and highly cooperative woman who had arrived at his office that morning without her lawyer. She exuded confidence and sexuality. She did not look or act the villain of this particular piece. Remington had frequently learned that in divorce cases there seldom is a villain except in the minds of those directly involved. He had taken Jessamyn's deposition without incident and although he could prove that she was not the typical mother, she did mother in some fashion. A governess and chauffeur/bodyguard were part of that fashion. If she were to be believed, David was never neglected. Still, she did not deny that her work often separated her from the baby for extended periods of time. Upon that admission, they would base their case. Remington wasn't hopeful. It wasn't just that their case was flimsy but that Jessamyn's was not. At least not now.

"There are certain things you must do immediately if you're to have any chance at all of winning," said Remington as he brushed his blond hair off his forehead. "First, no judge or jury is going to be pleased that you reside in Rosedale. You will have much less antagonism if your son, an American citizen, is being raised in an American environment. I suggest you relocate. And when you do, find a job. That you have been a successful film-maker and documentary maker is past history. You need to prove employment now. Or to put it more precisely: you need to prove stability in your life and that you can provide a stable environment for your child. And speaking of that, you can't. Not as you are now. You need a staff, a governess or caretaker. Remember. Because of who you are and what you have elected to be, no judge or jury is going to be sympathetic to you. We will, as they say, have two strikes against us before the court ever convenes. Now, are you still determined to proceed?" asked Remington as he carefully studied his client's face.

"I want my son," said JJ coldly. "I believe that answers your question."

*   *   *

"You're in good health, Marti," said Gerard Charles as the doctor closed the folder on his desk.

"How good is good?" asked Marti as she thought of the questions Margaret would ask as soon as she joined her in the waiting room.

"I can't answer the question you're really asking. Clinically, for a woman your age and for any person whose body has been through the trauma yours has, you are in excellent condition. But, you are forty and you have suffered a serious physical injury, and no one can hypothesize how this will affect your present condition. Nonetheless, I agree with your gynecologist that there is no current medical reason why you shouldn't have this baby if you so choose, and I gather that is your choice."

Marti nooded. "Yes, it is what I choose to do," she said softly. "My fear is not for me but for my baby. I want it born healthy."

"There are no guarantees, but there are tests to determine whether certain defects exist," said Charles.

"The amniocentesis test cannot be given until after the sixteenth week. Then I must wait four to six weeks for results. By then, the baby is fully formed. No matter what the test showed, I could not abort it then," said Marti.

"Again," said Charles, "that is a matter of choice."

The word *choice* must be a popular one with doctors these days, thought Marti as she recalled her conversation with Dr. Trebe, her gynecologist, when he informed her she was almost three months pregnant. He had instantly offered her an abortion. She had just as instantly refused. He had simply said, "That's your choice."

And it was, and it had been shortly after she suspected she might be pregnant. Had it not been for her swollen breasts and a minor degree of discomfort in the mornings, she might not have known what most women at least suspect far sooner than she did. But her periods had been irregular ever since the "incident," and the birth-control pills she resumed taking, when she remembered, when she began seeing Matthew, made them even more irregular.

Although Marti had been surprised by her pregnancy, she was not dismayed. Just the opposite. As she became accustomed to the idea, she found herself enjoying the secret she nurtured and shared with no one. There was but one complication, and Marti had not yet decided how she would handle him.

"Have you any advice, Doctor, any precautionary measures I should take?" asked Marti.

"If memory serves, the last time I gave you advice, Marti, it was to go out and live. Looks like you followed that advice all too well." The doctor's laughter was good natured and not derisive. It was without judgment. "But if I understand what you are asking me, I'd say I do not see any need for you to stay in bed or to change your life in any great fashion. I would go about it carefully but not obsessively so. As I stated, you are in good condition. Since you obviously want this pregnancy, my advice is to enjoy it."

As Charles escorted Marti to the door, he said, "You certainly prove the old adage that a woman is never more beautiful than when she is pregnant."

Although theirs had always been a formal relationship, when Charles extended his hand, Marti took it and then quickly kissed the doctor on his cheek. To her pleasure, she felt the pressure of the doctor's hand increase. "Good luck, Marti. It's going to be fine."

As she opened the door to the waiting room, the first face turned toward her was Margaret's. The other half dozen people in the room buried their faces in their magazines or newspapers, pretending not to notice there was not one but now two famous Tiernans in the room. Their determination to ignore such a phenomenon made theirs and the Tiernans' discomfort that much more noticeable. At the door, after Marti had wrapped herself in a bulky-knit sweater-jacket, Margaret turned and said to the assemblage: "Well, good-bye all. It's been lovely. Why don't we all arrange to meet here again in ten years. We can talk over old times and . . ."

Marti pulled her aunt from the office before her spiel was really on a roll. "But *you* didn't say good-bye," protested Margaret.

"You're incorrigible," said Marti at the elevator.

"Just nervous. It's godawful having to wait when you're dying to know what's going on," complained Margaret. "Next time— God forbid there is a next time—do me a favor and ask your mother. And now that I think of it, why didn't you ask her?"

The elevator was empty but still Marti felt strange discussing her mother in a public place. "I didn't know how she would take it. After all, I'm not married."

"Nor was Mary, I do believe, but your mother worships Jesus. I'm sure she'll do the same with your child," said Margaret.

"And I'm sure she'd faint if she had just heard your blasphemy. You know how mother is."

"Yes, I do, but I wonder, now that I'm listening, if you do," said Margaret. "Your mother has her religious convictions and her beliefs. They're hers and she doesn't foist them on me or anyone else. You have a short memory, Marti, either that or you're reverting to a little girl's behavior. Your mother has always stood by, no matter what you have done. She has always been there for you just as she has for all of us. Frankly, I do not find it amusing but annoying watching a woman who is a mother, and is about to become a mother again, be afraid of her own mother. Now enough! Tell me what the doctor said. From your face I'd say all is well."

2 3 1

"Well enough to let well enough alone be," replied Marti. "Dr. Charles thinks I have an excellent chance of having a normal pregnancy and a normal delivery."

"So you are going to proceed," said Margaret as she put two fingers in her mouth and whistled for a taxi.

"You sound like you disapprove," said Marti.

Margaret arched one eyebrow as she looked at her niece. "Disapprove? No! Question? Yes! Now, your place or mine?" she asked as a cab pulled to curbside.

"Yours. We'll be alone there," said Marti.

"I'm just worried," explained Margaret. "About many things, but mainly your well-being. Of course, I'm concerned for the baby. And for your other babies. Ali and Mark are liable to have feelings about this. Then, too, you are going to deal with the world. Like it or not, get ready for a helluva lot of press, most of it rotten I would guess, once word leaks about this. Actually, with you about to become an unwed mother, and JJ about to fight both the military and that awful Jessamyn woman, this would be an excellent time for me to have that sex-change operation. With the world focused on you guys, no one will ever notice."

They drove in silence for several minutes before Marti said, "I appreciate your concern, Margaret, and you know this isn't a haphazard decision. I've weighed all the possible consequences and I still want this child. I can't tell you why exactly because it's not an intellectual and perhaps not even a rational decision. It's deep down that I feel it. So who cares what the world thinks or says. This is my life and my decision. My baby, too."

"Oh, dear, you *do* make it sound like the Virgin Birth. May I remind you, Marti, that this baby has a human father," said Margaret as she clutched Marti's arm when the taxi swerved to avoid another at 86th Street.

Again Marti was silent. As she watched the leaves outside Central Park skip just ahead of the wind that made the mid-October day seem chillier than it was, she said: "I am not going to tell Matthew."

"He is the father, Marti," said Margaret noisily.

"And that's all he is at this point, and, if he knew, a reluctant one at that," said Marti miserably. "Margaret, before I discovered

I was pregnant, I asked Matthew to marry me. He refused. The man has no wish to be married. You could have fooled me. And he did. Since that time, things have been strained between us. We have seen each other less and less. By mutual choice. Again, as before, we don't seem to be communicating well."

"Shit! That's why I want the operation. Just for a day I'd like to be a man, like to know how it feels to do the fucking instead of being the one who gets fucked. And I mean that figuratively, driver, and not literally, so get your goddamn eyes out of the rearview mirror and back on the road."

"Trouble with Mr. Richards?" asked Marti.

"Never mind about me and Alden. Let's stick to you. I think you should tell Matthew, immediately. You not only owe it to baby Drusilla or Pierpont—whatever you call her or him—but to yourself. Marti Tiernan acts more responsibly. Vengeance never became you. With me, on the other hand, it gave that special glow. Your child will need a father."

"I did pretty damn well by Ali and Mark without one," protested Marti.

"Bullshit! You had Vinnie and your father as surrogate fathers during the formative years of their lives. Well, neither is available today and I refuse to have that sex change or walk around in drag to accommodate you."

"I know just what Matthew will say," said Marti, annoyed at Margaret's words, as they were the very ones she didn't want to acknowledge. "I can just hear them now."

*   *   *

"There are no accidents, Marti. None," said Matthew coldly.

"The gospel according to Sigmund Freud says there are no accidents, but I and a great many others, even those involved in analytical thought, don't agree," said Marti.

"But I do. Like Freud, I would say this pregnancy was dictated by your unconscious. It's known as unconscious motivation."

"Matthew, would you listen to yourself? I tell you I'm pregnant—with *your* child—and you're going on about an unconscious that gives unwritten and unheard dictation. It's ludicrous," said Marti, regretting her hasty decision to call. She had been

2 3 3

angry before he ever answered his doorbell. In the taxi, traveling through the park from Margaret's, she had chastised herself for giving in to Margaret's concept of "common decency" and "common sense." She knew he would not be thrilled with what she was about to tell him. Not that she had to. No sooner had he taken her sweater and hung it on the coatrack in the hallway than he said: "You're pregnant, aren't you?" She had been stunned. He answered her quizzical expression immediately. "Why else this sudden rush during my working day to see me. It doesn't take a genius to put it together."

His offhand approach had served as a further irritant. He was bothered by her and this extra intrusion into his life. It was then that she mentioned it was nothing she had planned, just an accident.

"What is it you want, Marti?" she heard him say as he stared out the window.

"Nothing. Absolutely nothing. This is my responsibility. I just thought you, as the father, should know."

"Marti, have you ever considered why it is you are suddenly pregnant? I'm speaking of cause and effect."

"Speak more plainly, Matthew, so that I can understand, and spare me any gratuitous analysis."

"I think you want to be married very badly, Marti. I also think you expect me to do the 'honorable thing.'"

She looked at him as if he were some stranger in her life. Her disgust took expression but no words. That he could say such a thing, let alone think it, hurt more than any words he had spoken that Labor Day. "I think I've made a terrible mistake," she said finally. "You're not the person I thought you to be."

"I never suggested I was," he said. "That was in your mind. I do the best I can do, and I damn well know it's not always good enough. That's what makes me human."

He was looking at her helplessly, the expression on his face now pained. He started to speak again, but she had taken her sweater from the rack and was gone, out the door and down the fire stairs, in too much pain to wait for the elevator.

Matthew Strohl stood in his open doorway unable to close his own door, fearful that if he did, he might be closing it on one of the more troubling but more rewarding times of his life. But Matthew, being who he was, closed the door, knowing that, like most, it could always be opened again. Or so he hoped.

*   *   *

Fletcher Hollister was being very precise, which is why Chase Remington had suggested that JJ employ him. The attorney, a former Army legal officer and a specialist in military law, knew exactly after studying JJ's case how he wanted to plead it the following week in Washington before the Special Discharge Review Board.

As he lowered his bifocals almost to the tip of his nose, Hollister said, "I've searched your induction contract for any technical inconsistencies that might have existed when you were drafted, and there are none. I also examined your medical records hoping quite frankly to find evidence of diabetes or some other nutritional problem that might have caused a chemical imbalance. Had one existed, we could have claimed that this imbalance acted upon your mind and motivated you not to serve. However, again, this is not a tool we can use."

"Mr. Hollister . . ."

"Be patient, Mr. Ollson. Let me continue. Nor can we use, not at this late date, the fact that you are indeed a conscientious objector. They would rip that one to shreds, asking why you didn't declare this before you were drafted or at the very least after you were inducted. A moot point, as C.O. status is only granted to members of certain church groups, like the Mennonites. So," continued Hollister as he ran a hand through his thick iron-gray hair, "we are going to establish you as a quality individual, a man of the highest standing, of distinguished parentage and background, citing your education at the Collegiate School and Columbia as prime examples."

"Look, having an undesirable discharge upgraded to an honorable has nothing to do with a scholastic record," interrupted JJ. "The point of this trial is for me to prove that during the war years I have been a model citizen, and I can do that. I have shown you the numerous awards and citations I have earned. I have also shown you, as we intend to show them, the countless endorse-

2 3 5

ments from columnists throughout the world. That is surely enough."

Fletcher Hollister looked at JJ, his expression that of a parent both amused and annoyed with an errant child. "Mr. Ollson, let me be perfectly blunt. As I have repeatedly tried to explain, the review board is made up of military men, officers dedicated to serving their country. Do not try to convince them that you were a model citizen because you spoke out against a war they endorsed, may even have been fighting. Military men do not consider what you did an act of model citizenry. They believe if you were what you are claiming to be, you would have fought in Vietnam. Now, if we can proceed with some logic, here is the course of action I intend for us to follow. We will basically be throwing ourselves at the mercy of the court. Without groveling, of course. We will take an intellectual yet an emotional position. After establishing you as I just previously proposed, we will say you are a human being and, like all human beings, prone to making mistakes. We will say you now regret not having faced the procedures that were open to you at the time—regret that instead of going to prison, which was one of those procedures, you went AWOL. We will then state that since you were indeed up to that time an exemplary citizen that you should not have to bear the mark of a hasty decision made *in your youth* for the rest of your life, particularly since it is a decision you now regret."

JJ was stunned. After weeks of phone conversations and two meetings, this was the defense his attorney had prepared. Wearily, he said, "But I don't regret it. Frankly, Mr. Hollister, what you propose is not only preposterous but insulting. To me and the men whose trust I have earned. This approach you would have me take is totally unacceptable. Can't you understand that I have no regrets? Nor should I. I *was* an exemplary citizen. I exercised my democratic rights. I dissented. I said no to an injustice, in this case an unjust war which, I might add, this very military lost. And a war for which they could not get the support of the majority of this country's citizens, men and women not far removed from me. And politicians. If anyone should have regrets, Mr. Hollister, it is the very establishment that is hearing my case. Now as my attorney I want you to present my case as I believe it should be. There will be no throwing me on the mercy of this or any other court. I have served my country well in my own fashion, which is the fashion of our Constitution."

"This is insane," blustered Hollister. "This is no defense, but an offensive attack that will surely fail. Mr. Ollson, as I already mentioned, you are talking to military men, many of whom have fought in previous wars. You signed on as a military man and they will feel you, as a military man, should have fulfilled your duty."

"I did, Mr. Hollister. That's the point, but I'm afraid you still cannot see it."

"You are right. I cannot, Mr. Ollson. I understand you think you have a defense, but you do not. If you persist in wanting your way, I'm afraid you must do so without me. I have a professional reputation to uphold. I cannot at this juncture in my life play or be the fool. You may do as you wish."

"Not as I wish, Mr. Hollister. But as I must."

*   *   *

It was a shock, and to feel numb or nothing as she did was permissible under the circumstances. No need to chastise herself. The mourners were many. Morgan Tomlinson had been a highly respected member of the medical community. That he had collapsed and died on the ninth hole of the country club golf course was in keeping with his style. There was no long lingering, no blood. Just a quick death, of mild inconvenience only to those who wished to play through that day at the Bridgeport Country Club. A well-appointed death, thought Reese, as the priest droned on.

She wished she could cry. Not for her father but for herself, for her loss. He had never understood what she was doing with her life. He had never watched her with the children at the Josiah Quincy School. He had never respected her for what she could do for herself rather than for him.

He had loved her as a child. Proud of her then not for who or what she was but how she looked. His "pretty little girl," he used to say proudly when introducing her to his colleagues. His "adorable one." But he had seldom spoken with her. He never knew who she was but remained content to think of her as the person he imagined or needed her to be. He was a lot like Thomas in that, thought Reese shivering, although the day was bright and sunny, warm for November.

But Thomas was intrinsically kinder. Or was it that she understood Thomas, whereas she had never understood her father. Few saw it, including her children, but Thomas was a kind man. People thought he had no feelings, but they were wrong. His were just buried as quickly as they rose to the surface. Somewhere, perhaps in his childhood when his feelings had been available to him, Thomas had turned inward, denying emotions that rendered him vulnerable. Outwardly, he seemed a man who didn't hurt. Inwardly, she knew it to be otherwise. She ached for him when he asked, "Were there any calls? Was there any mail?" It was his way of acknowledging his Kristan and Karl and admitting there was a lack in his life that a phone call or letter could erase.

He was standing next to her now, as duty dictated, and Thomas was a man who did his duty. There were other duties Reese wished he would perform, but Thomas did not see that they were as important as his presence at her father's funeral. But he did not know how to give to her, and she understood that one can't possibly give if one has never received. She often wondered where the breakdown had occurred in Thomas's early life. What had he not received that others had?

But he gave to his country. He gave to the men who sought his help, but he didn't know how to give to his very own. She no longer hated that part of him, but she continued to resent it. He had his work and that was paramount in his life. It, not her. Three nights a week now he was gone, learning medical terminology that would serve him during the day when he served those veterans in adjusting or claiming their medical benefits. He sacrificed his days and nights to help these men, never realizing she was being sacrificed in the process. She and their marriage.

As she stood next to her mother, Reese felt the bond of a certain kind of womanhood. Her mother had married a man similar in his singlemindedness to Thomas. Only her mother hadn't minded. The house had revolved around Morgan Tomlinson, his schedule, his desires, and his needs. He was the sun around whom she orbited. Her father had been her mother's world. She had never made her own. She hadn't seen or felt the need.

A sob caught in Reese's throat as she thought of her conversation with her mother the previous evening. She had driven in from Boston shortly after her working day and before Thomas to be with her mother. She found Celia Tomlinson at the funeral home, putting on a face for the world to see. There were no tears, no public display of grief, until she closed her front door and shut out the rest of the world who lived on Brooklawn Avenue and beyond. Then her body, like her spirits, collapsed and sagged. Reese had not known what to do. Her mother was suddenly a very old woman. Reese longed to comfort her but could not bridge the gap that had been created so very long ago. She wondered if there was ever a more complicated relationship than the one that existed between mother and daughter, knowing she had yet to succeed as either.

"Mom, what are you going to do?" she had asked, surprised she had verbalized what she was thinking.

"Do?" her mother had echoed. "What is there to do?"

"You could travel," Reese replied lamely.

"Don't talk foolishness, Reese. Where would I go, a woman my age?"

"Mom, you're not old. There are many other women out there—men too—who have lost their mates. They're all looking for companionship."

Her mother had looked at her in horror. "I'm not suggesting you date them, Mom, not at first, maybe not ever, but meet them. Make friends."

"I wouldn't know how," Celia Tomlinson had said softly. "Your father was never much for people. We had friends, but no one that we were particularly close to. We had each other."

"But what about you?" persisted Reese. "When Dad was at the hospital or at his office, certainly you had friends with whom you socialized."

"Yes, but not really. Reese, keeping this house for your father was a full-time job. He was a very particular man and he liked things done in a very particular fashion. I tried to please him. I spent my life trying to please him."

The words had cut through Reese. She had sat opposite her mother, bleeding for her and for herself. She, too, had spent major years of her life trying to please a man as best she could.

Particularly since his heart attack. Unlike him, she gave her work just so much and no more. Like her mother, she didn't encourage friendships as they infringed upon the time *he* needed. She, too, denied herself because her husband liked things done in a very particular way. He had never seen her school. He had never seen her with the children. He had no idea what it meant to student teach. He knew nothing of her plans to work with the physically and emotionally handicapped at the Dearborn School next semester and on. He knew nothing of her emptiness as weeks often went by between lovemakings. She needed the closeness he seemingly did not. She needed to be desired, which was different than needed. That part of her life was not over, even if he could pretend it was.

As she stood next to Thomas at the gravesite, she could hear her mother speaking as she had yesterday. "He's gone, Reese, and I'm alone with nothing to do and no one to be." She had not understood. "Mom, what do you mean, 'with no one to be'? You're you," she had argued.

"What's me, Reese? Me is Mrs. Morgan Tomlinson. I was his wife. I'm not that anymore. Once I was a mother but I'm not that anymore either. The only two things I ever was I no longer am. And I don't know how or what else to be."

"Mom, we could get you an apartment in Boston, near us," Reese had offered.

Celia Tomlinson had continued to rock herself as she cried. "And when would I see you, Reese, and what would we talk about? It's too late. We both know that. Here I have my house, my things, a lifetime of memories. There are people with whom I can pass the time in church, at the club, or at the markets."

It would be no life or at best a partial existence, but it was all her mother could do. Looking at her, hearing and seeing the life that awaited, chilled Reese. That still could be her twenty-five or thirty years down the road. A life that was no life at all.

As she stood between her mother and Thomas, Reese began to cry, overwhelmed by her sense of loss. But it wasn't, as the mourners thought, for her father, or for her mother, but for her marriage. It, too, had died, not suddenly like her father but after a very long illness.

11

WHEN MARTI OPENED THE DOOR, HE STOOD THERE hesitantly, seemingly not anxious to enter and leave the rain that was falling persistently. Impulsively, she took his arm and helped him into the house. As he handed her his coat, he was looking at her in that assessing way of his.

"You're not angry anymore," he said as a greeting, his face relaxing as he spoke.

He had always been able to read her. That was but one of the sensitivities that had so charmed her. "No, there is nothing to be angry about," said Marti. "Actually, I'm feeling good about things, mainly me but also you . . . us."

After having prepared for what he thought would be a difficult meeting, Matthew was now unprepared, not at all certain where to begin. "How do you feel?" he asked awkwardly as he accepted a scotch on the rocks she handed him.

"Good!" she replied as she patted her bulging belly.

"What did the test show?"

"The amniocentesis? I didn't have it. I felt it unnecessary. It's my baby regardless."

She regretted the words as soon as they were spoken. She had not meant them to sound so exclusionary, and he had flinched when she said "*my* baby."

"Marti, I'll come to the point. The baby needs a father, a real father, and I think we should be married."

"For the baby's sake?" she asked, trying not to let the anger seep into her voice.

"Yes," he replied guilelessly.

She had known this would happen, had known as soon as he had called shortly after her return from Houston and the National Conference of Women. Although she had not planned to participate, her pregnant presence had proven newsworthy.

Again she could feel him assessing her as he waited for a response. They were seated on the sofa and Marti turned away from Matthew as she spoke.

"I, too, have had time to think things through. I made some discoveries. Among them: I don't wish to get married."

"The baby needs a name, Marti," he protested.

"The baby will have a name, a very fine name . . . Tiernan. It is Tiernan, you know. I've had it legally changed again.

"Marti, it's my child," Matthew said softly.

Again she felt the anger seep into her words. "Matthew, it was your child two months ago when I first told you of its existence. You were in no hurry to accept it then. What's changed?"

"Marti, you're cutting off your nose to spite your face," said Matthew angrily.

"No, I'm really not," Marti replied as she once again turned to face him. "On Labor Day, you said you didn't want to be married. That hurt me then, but sometimes the truth hurts even when it's not meant to hurt. You explained quite reasonably why you were not interested in marriage. Had I been able to listen properly instead of reacting emotionally I would have realized then your reasons were valid. Just as my reasons for wanting to be married— or so I thought *then*—were valid for me."

"And what you're now saying," said Matthew impatiently, "is since then you've been through such great changes that you no longer wish to be married but I, not having experienced any such changes, do not know my own mind."

"That's not what I'm saying. Matthew, I want you to be the child's father. I will never stop you from being anything you wish to be when you wish to be it with our child. I would like our baby to know its father, to feel that it has one."

"Marti, why do I get the feeling I'm receiving some kind of

canned announcement," said Matthew, "So much of what you're saying sounds phony, as though it were rehearsed."

"Well, I've been rehearsing," she admitted. "I knew what I wanted to say today but wasn't sure how it would come out, so I practiced it. Obviously practice doesn't make perfect."

"So why don't you start over again," said Matthew as he added an ice cube and a fresh splash of scotch to his drink.

"Okay, Matthew. Do you really want to get married?"

His face said it all. Marti laughed. "Well, that's how I feel. I don't either. It turns out for all my talk of months ago, I'm no more ready than you are. But for different reasons. And to think I actually said to you: 'I don't need to be married.' Horseshit, if you'll pardon my French. I needed to but didn't know it. Thank God for Houston. It all sort of came together for me there."

Marti started to pace as she talked, excitement in her step and in her voice. "No matter what you saw on television, it was nothing like being there. Matthew, it was quite unlike anything I've ever experienced and maybe you have to be a woman to appreciate it. There were so many of us—they said fourteen thousand but there were more—and they came in all sizes, shapes, and colors. In fact, the only thing many had in common was gender and a desire to work through to some kind of understanding for themselves and for all women. The subject was equal rights, and under that heading were so many subtopics. We tried to hear and to understand one another. It wasn't always easy, not on an individual or a collective basis. Some issues were so very controversial, but when Betty Friedan spoke out for the first time in her political life for lesbian civil rights, my mother applauded. My mother, Matthew! A woman who is as fundamental in her religious beliefs as any fundamentalist. But she saw the point. I was so moved by her, as I was by all the women who had come to further themselves and a collective point of view."

He was watching her closely, observing the passion on her face as she paced and gesticulated.

"And that's when it changed for me, Matthew. Suddenly I was so angry that I, me, my decision had placed me in the gallery as an observer rather than on the floor of the convention as a delegate. That's where I really belong. And why wasn't I? Here's the point, Matthew, so listen. Because this fifties creature that I am, that part of me that still clings to the notion that I must be some man's little girl if I'm to have any real identity, was operating. I said I didn't need to be married—that I felt separate, enough of my own person to merge in marriage with another. True but untrue. I've learned how to be separate, to be on my own with my own interests, but I've always wanted to be that appendage because I was taught early on that I should be."

"We all need to feel connected, Marti," interrupted Matthew.

"Yes. I think being connected to another is all we have besides ourselves that's meaningful in life. But Matthew, I was again willing to deny my real self just to be this outdated vision. I'm meant to be front and center, out there, speaking freely. It's a lesson I thought I had already learned. I guess I needed some brush-up courses. So I don't want to marry right now, Matthew. I need something else. Like the thick of the fight. I felt that ever so strongly when I found myself suddenly eyeball to eyeball with the right-to-life people."

"You were good," said Matthew.

"You saw it?" asked Marti, pleased, as she sat in one of the side chairs facing the sofa and Matthew. "It was so unexpected, and yet the words poured out of me as though I had rehearsed them." Marti laughed. "I guess I do a lot better when I'm speaking extemporaneously. But suddenly this woman, a woman I totally dislike because she uses her rather keen intellect to subvert the issues, is claiming me as one of their own—a right-to-lifer because I'm unmarried and pregnant. It's ironic. First I'm labeled as anti-family because I support the ERA. Then I'm really an okay kid because I'm about to be an unwed mother. What garbage!"

The television interview flashed through her head. The reporter had come from the Astrohall where the spokesperson for the antiabortion forces had declared Marti Tiernan was really one of their own. The reporter had rushed to the Sam Houston Coliseum and asked Marti for a comment. Angrily she had replied, "I am pregnant by choice. I am carrying my baby by choice. That I am unmarried is the father's choice. I'm neither for nor against abortion, but I am for choice—for each woman's right to decide what it is she wants and does not want for her life. I see that as an unalienable and *equal* right, not just for women but for all people."

"I'm my father's daughter, Matthew. I'm a political person at heart. Matthew, you're the first friend I ever had in a lover. I hope that friendship continues for my sake and the baby's. We'll need you, as I intend to be a working mother. I owe that to my . . . to *our* baby. For its sake, I've got to be out there working for the passage of the ERA. Do you understand?"

Matthew was smiling. As he weighed her words, he was assessing her as she stood before him. "You said I was the first friend you ever had in a lover. You also said you hope the friendship continues. I'm about to make you an offer you can't refuse. How about two for the price of one?"

"My mother also said you get nothing for nothing and that you always pay in the end for what you get," Marti replied. But then, seeing the hurt look on Matthew's face she added, "My mother also said nice girls don't but bad girls do. And then she said there was a Santa Claus and a stork that delivered babies, so what the hell? Maybe I'll take your offer on approval. To be returned in thirty days if not fully satisfied."

*   *   *

January 3, 1978

Dear Marti Tiernan:

People like you can no longer be allowed to poison and pervert this country. You and your kind have already done terrible harm. Thousands like me suffer for the few of you. If God does not punish you, then He will designate someone who will. Evil comes to traitors and whores. I have warned you in the past but you have not listened. Listen now!

*   *   *

That the Tiernan Repertory Company was but a short three-block walk from the duplex apartment on West 43rd Street was convenient but not the reason JJ had rented it. Nor was the neighborhood—an oasis in the midst of Hell's Kitchen—a reason, as it would take years before the area surrounding the new Manhattan Plaza complex would be renovated. But the fact that Nelson was not only his neighbor but his super, the "wizard" who could supply

2 4 5

the perfect apartment when seemingly none other quite so perfect had existed, was the cause and effect. In the duplex, with its balcony facing the building's back gardens, JJ had a washer-dryer, dishwasher, and a cleaning woman named Marisha who came three times a week to watch the soap operas after she tidied what little mess there was. Having raised three children of her own, Marisha, when needed, would function as David's surrogate mother.

As he was about to turn right on Tenth Avenue, JJ saw the Sloan's delivery truck stop in front of his building. Luckily, Nelson was on the premises and had the three keys needed to open the various locks on his door. At long last, the modular sofa was arriving after the eight weeks on order that had stretched to twelve and then fifteen. Except for David, thought JJ, the apartment was now fully furnished.

The walk to the Tiernan Repertory Company took less than ten minutes, and each day produced the same anger. But the job, JJ reminded himself, was a means to an end. If he were to gain custody of his son, he needed both employment and a home. Finally, he had both.

JJ had arrived in New York in late October, his letters of application to the networks and various production companies having preceded him by several weeks. But it took just days for JJ to realize that, because he had been denied his upgraded discharge, no one was buying his services. Not that he was told that. They were not that direct but preferred a "We'll be in touch" to a more truthful if blatant rejection.

But the very reason he was not wanted on staff at the networks was the same reason he was an in-demand guest initially for TV talk shows: his former status as a deserter and exile. Despite Chase Remington's advice, JJ appeared on several of the more widely viewed formats in the hope of informing the most people about the inequities of the Carter pardon. But there was little viewer reaction. Neither he nor the issues he raised were of interest, and soon the spotlight into which he had again been thrust dimmed and then faded altogether. It was exactly as Nelson had said. No one cared, not about the war or those who either fought or deserted it. He, himself, had made his peace with that. To JJ's dismay, Nelson had abandoned his politics and was majoring in advertising at Fordham University, where he was enrolled in the Excel Program.

After weeks of rejection by potential employers, JJ had been approached by Margaret, who urged him to take the position of administrative director of the rep company. This would free Carolyn to do what she did best: teach, and to do what she enjoyed most: act, on stage, on screen, on TV, anywhere that wasn't near the rep company. It was a job for which he was qualified but unsuited. It was pushing pencils. Dull and unimaginative. But as Chase Remington had said: it was a job, a full-time, well-paying job that would look good in any court of law.

Six weeks had since passed. Daily he waited for a court date to be determined. Remington seemed neither eager nor in a rush. Nor was Jessamyn, who was frequently traveling, often with David and just as often as not, to various film locations where her interviews with celebrities were featured on the network's weekly newsmagazine show. It was apparent from the press that suddenly surrounded Jessamyn's every move that she had become as celebrated as those she interviewed. In her interviews, Jessamyn was careful and clever. Although JJ and the separation were frequently discussed, with Jessamyn sticking to her "Our marriage is another casualty of the Vietnam War" party line, he was never vilified. If anything, he emerged as an object of pity, a man semideranged by his fanaticism.

He saw David only when she was in town. Although their lawyers had privately agreed upon weekly visiting rights, Jessamyn ignored the rules when they inconvenienced her. Still, she had the nerve to ask Chase Remington to ask JJ to ask Marti, after Marti's representatives had already declined, for an interview. It was Remington's first indication that someone other than the woman he had first met when taking her deposition existed.

The building was still cold when he arrived, the steam heat yet to fully dissipate the dampness of the morning. JJ wondered why so many New Yorkers loved the month of April when he found it cruel in its indecisiveness. One day warm and the next, like this one, punishing in its between-seasons temperature. His office on the second floor was dark, the western exposure not bringing light until the midafternoon. Choosing his desk lamp instead of the harsh overhead fluorescents to light the morning, JJ thumbed through the mail the superintendent who had replaced Nelson had left on his desk. The knock on his door was not unexpected. It was the reason JJ was at his office an hour before the building officially opened.

Chase Remington hung his Burberry in the closet and then took two containers of coffee out of the paper bag he had been carrying. After setting one before JJ and the other near the ashtray he had immediately appropriated, he threw himself into a chair and his legs up on the desk facing it. "Now what's so important that it couldn't wait until a more reasonable hour of the day?" asked Remington.

"I want to go to court."

"Now tell me something I don't know," said Remington.

"I mean immediately, Chase. I'm tired of all the delays. I keep jockeying for position in a race that shows no signs of starting. I'm at the gate but Jessamyn's not. Nor do you seem to be."

"When are you due in Washington next?" asked Remington.

"What the hell has that to do with this?"

"Everything. Just tell me. When is the Special Discharge Review Board hearing your case again?"

"July seven," said JJ.

"And you feel good about your chances—that you have a real shot at reversing their decision?"

"You know damn well I do. I'm prepared this time. I've learned what their idea of good citizenship is. I can win."

"Then we wait, JJ. We do nothing until you've reversed the decision. And don't ask why, because you know damn well why. JJ, Jessamyn can kill you with that undesirable discharge. It's one of her most powerful weapons, and she'll use it."

"What does my undesirable discharge have to do with my child?"

"In the eyes of some, it makes you an undesirable influence on your child, an undesirable parent. Face facts, JJ. It will take a helluva judge to get past that. Look, JJ, Jessamyn's got a pretty good defense and a great offense. You'll have a much more difficult time proving she is an unfit mother than she will have proving you're an undesirable father. After all, you will be in an American court of law. If this was Canada, it might be different. The point is: the moment your discharge papers are upgraded, you're automatically upgraded in the eyes of the court."

"Then I wait," said JJ, biting his lip.

"It's just a little longer," said Remington consolingly.

"No. It's not just a little longer but a lot. Don't forget that, Chase, or you're neither my friend nor my lawyer."

The telephone ringing broke the tension in the room.

"Would you calm down? What do you mean, didn't I check with the answering service? For chrissake, I just walked in fifteen minutes ago."

Chase Remington watched as JJ listened as the well-known voice of Margaret Tiernan boomed in the room as though she were in it rather than on the phone. "I'm leaving now," he heard JJ say as he hung up.

"It's my sister. She's in labor, and there is some sort of difficulty."

*　　*　　*

It was Mark who had rushed for a taxi and Ali who had called Carolyn as Marti calmly collected herself and her things shortly after eight that morning. Her mother and her aunt were already at the hospital by the time she arrived, herself refusing to hurry, intent on enjoying every last minute of this birth.

From her bed, Marti had called Matthew, leaving word on his answering maching as he was already in a session. To her relief, Dr. Trebe had taken his life in his hands and ordered the famous Tiernan sisters, now doing their famous impression of Florence Nightingale, to the waiting room. From the look on their faces, Marti had seen neither had been pleased. But then, if they had experienced difficulty all their lives in taking direction from directors, how could they take it easily from a doctor?

Marti had not been nervous. Her pregnancy had been uneventful and, other than for the very visible fact that she was carrying a child, unexciting. She hadn't become big until her sixth month and then she became very big. Bulging big. Gross, as Alison had aptly described it. She had suspected twins but the doctor heard only one heartbeat. She remained unconvinced, pitying Matthew if he suddenly was the father of two when one was more than he had bargained for. Thinking of Matthew supported her through the first labor pains. After his initial hostility, he had been completely supportive through the remainder of her pregnancy, seemingly not minding that once she had entered the final stage of her pregnancy the physical side of their relationship became dormant. But his concern, less that of a lover and more of a husband, had surprised Marti.

When she had decided early in her pregnancy that she wanted to use the Lamaze method of natural childbirth, Dr. Trebe had been opposed, not in principle but for her, given her medical history and her age. But Marti had been insistent, up until the moment in her hospital room when the pains suddenly had become excruciating, nothing at all like the labor she had experienced with Ali and Mark. It was then her calm had been replaced with a sense of urgency bordering on panic. She wanted to have this baby and have it fast. But the baby would not comply.

They had given her a local anesthetic and although she was groggy, Marti was awake fighting to feel, if not physically, then emotionally, the birth of her baby. She had obliterated the danger from her mind. She refused to think of her dilated cervix and the baby that was in the wrong, feet-first, position. A large baby, said Dr. Trebe, too large for the vaginal opening as it was. An episiotomy would have to be performed. A surgical enlargement of the vulval orifice, Trebe had explained.

It was then she remembered what she had once read about babies in the feet-first position: that if they didn't come down the canal immediately, and if the umbilical cord was wrapped around their necks, they would suffocate . . . strangle. She began to cry. A nurse wiped the sweat off her forehead and the tears from her cheeks. Marti lay back, feeling nothing and worse . . . hearing nothing. Minutes passed or was it hours? She couldn't tell. As she lay there helpless, unable to assist, Marti felt an emptiness she had not experienced in the past nine-plus months. Empty and flat, physically and emotionally. And then she heard it, the faintest of a cry, not of outrage but of hurt, as if this baby was saying, how could you do such a thing at a time like this? Marti opened her eyes and saw the baby. In seconds she felt it as it was placed on her stomach.

"It's a girl, Marti," said Dr. Trebe, "a perfectly lovely, little . . . well not so little, but a perfectly lovely girl."

Marti squeezed the doctor's hand and then fell asleep, certain this birth was an omen. Her child had come through a difficulty and landed feet first. There was only one other person Marti knew who had come through life in that fashion. For that reason, she would name her daughter, Lynne, after her mother, the "fabulous Carolyn Tiernan" as her publicity often read.

*　　*　　*

Saturday had proven to be his most difficult day. Although the office was officially closed and he could sleep later, Thomas awakened earlier. Invariably, his stomach would act as a calendar, its tremors reminding him of the day. No matter what the weather, he never hesitated but leaped from bed into jogging clothes. Within minutes, he would be in the Common, lying on the damp grass doing his warm-up exercises.

He tended to sprint more than jog on Saturdays, and the extra lap he pushed his body through served to remove the remaining edge of his uneasiness. Exhausted, he would arrive home, ready for his shower and Reese who would arrive about ten to take Kelly for the weekend.

Although it had been months, Thomas had never adjusted to the silence of Saturdays. Once Kelly left, he would rush to find companionship in the empty DAV offices among the cases he reviewed for the following week's presentation before the various boards. Saturday nights passed, but if he were asked, Thomas would be hard pressed to say how. Sundays were also difficult. That day, the house seemed impossibly big and so he tended to remain in his bedroom among the newspapers and the Red Sox ball games. He found solitary confinement easier in one room than in a rambling house. It was more confining but less lonely. He tended not to miss anyone in a room barely big enough for one. Except Reese. He always missed Reese.

The weekdays were less difficult. Mondays through Fridays,

Mrs. McMahon would be watching "Today", breakfast prepared, when he returned from his run. She would sip her coffee and he, his tea, as they watched the morning unfold around the country and the world. He had wanted someone to breakfast with, and five days a week he had that someone in Mrs. McMahon, or Edna as she preferred to be called.

As he showered, Thomas remembered, as he did every Saturday morning, all that he wished he could obliterate or change. Six months of constant replay in his mind never revealed anything new. It was always the same, a shock even after all this time. He had been startled and disbelieving when Reese, shortly after New Year's, announced she was leaving him. That happened to others, not him. He had been a good husband. Never a hint of another woman. But infidelity was not the issue, she had said, although sex—their lack of it—was. As was their lack of communication and companionship. Their marriage, she maintained, wasn't fulfilling. She didn't feel nurtured. He asked, but she couldn't explain any further than she already had what she meant by that word.

She had not mentioned divorce but spoke of a separation; time to sort things through, to take stock and see who she was and what she wanted from life. But she knew. She had stated it. She wanted something more than what he offered, but he had no inkling what that something more was. She spoke of fun and again he did not understand.

He was upset that hers was not a rash or impetuous decision but one which was painstakingly made after many months. Which is how and why Mrs. McMahon had been employed. Weeks before leaving, days before speaking to Thomas, Reese had found the plump, red-faced and red-haired woman. He would need her, Reese had known, although she had not anticipated to what extent. That had surprised her far more than it had him.

As he toweled dry, he heard again the ugliness that confronted Reese later that day. She had planned to take Kelly, begin a new life in a small apartment in Cambridge near her new job at the Dearborn School. But Kelly, when told, simply said no. When Reese persisted, Kelly had remained obdurate, her words shaking what little foundation was left to their family.

"You can't uproot me again. I'm not changing my life just to suit you. What for? You don't give a damn about me. Long as I can remember, you've always been off doing your thing. Once it was liquor, then it was school. Now it's teaching. What's next? Well, you do your thing and leave me to do mine. I'm staying with Daddy."

He could still see Reese's face, her pain, and could still hear her response. "There's truth in what you say. Not the whole truth but the truth as you see it. Perhaps someday I can explain. Perhaps someday you'll understand. But now, given how you feel, maybe it is best that you stay with your father. If you need me, I'm always available."

"Then stay. Stay and be my mother," Kelly had screamed, for the first time in the conversation sounding and looking like the near fifteen-year-old she was.

"I can't. I just can't," Reese had replied as she began to cry.

And so Kelly had remained, filling a space but not the void in his life. He increased his work load at the office, remaining late at least three evenings a week once he was assured by Kelly she had her homework to do or friends to see and that Mrs McMahon was there if she needed anything. In two weeks, he would complete a year of his training. In four more months, he would be a National Service Officer. If rumors were founded, he would be busy, actively working for and with the Vietnam vet. *If* the rumors were true. He hoped; he prayed. It was work he not only wanted but needed to do. Desperately.

As Thomas entered the kitchen, still drying his hair with a towel as he considered the possibilities for breakfast, his thoughts were of the summer, and the month Kelly wished to spend with Kristan in Hollywood. He was against it, as he had been against Kristan's new career as a featured actress in a television series. Seventeen was simply too young for a girl to be on her own, not just in Hollywood but anywhere. That Margaret was often in town, starring in a TV series as the embattled matriarch of a family of machinating movie moguls was of some consolation. Thomas remembered all too clearly Margaret's flamboyant past, the rules she made up rather than broke. She was not the ideal guardian and yet no one knew Hollywood or its people better and, seemingly from Kristan's complaints, no one could have been more demanding on Kristan's behalf. As he poached an egg, Thomas wondered how Reese would react to Kelly's insistence that she be allowed to visit. She would probably think it fine. It often seemed to Thomas that Reese, like Margaret, lived by her own rules. At times, he wished his wife and daughter were still estranged. When Kelly had announced a few short weeks after Reese had left that she would be spending weekends with her mother, he had felt abandoned. Although Reese had done nothing more than stay in touch with her daughter, Thomas resented it. Weekends first; weekdays next. Soon she would have it all and he nothing.

Kelly entered the kitchen in her usual whirlwind fashion, kissing him on the cheek as she plopped her backpack on a kitchen chair and herself on his lap. Each Saturday, she would look at him earnestly and ask: "Are you going to be all right?" and each Saturday he would reply: "Yes." And then she was up, pulling Rice Krispies and corn flakes and Grapenuts and wheat germ from the cabinets as she looked for something that "looks thrilling." This morning it was yogurt and peanut butter, which he found hard to look at and even harder to imagine eating.

"Do you have any homework?" he asked, as he took a bite of his dry toast.

Kelly's look was one of loving condescension. "You're a broken record. Each Saturday it's the same question. Of course I have homework. I'll do it when I get home tomorrow night."

She, too, sounded like a broken record, as the same response greeted his same question every Saturday. He knew when tomorrow night came, she would be sitting with him in the den watching "All in the Family" and the "ABC Sunday Night Movie." But she would be home, at his side, which was not true of anyone else in the family. He would hate it if she went to California, Thomas thought as he watched Kelly spread the peanut butter on a chocolate cupcake. He would miss her mess and her noise. There would be none other's in the house, as Karl had opted to work as an athletics counselor in a summer camp.

Glancing at the kitchen clock, Thomas saw it was nearing ten. Again his stomach tightened. Reese would be arriving any minute now. "I'll be in the bathroom," said Thomas rising. "Should your mother arrive while I'm gone, tell her hello and that I'll see you both tomorrow."

"By the way, I have a date tomorrow night," said Kelly casually.

"But you had a date last night and Wednesday," Thomas protested. "I don't like it, Kelly. There's no reason for it."

"Yes there is, Daddy," said Kelly as she put her arms about her father's neck. "There's a very good reason. I'm pretty and I'm popular. Now stop worrying. I just want to have some fun, something I wish you would learn to do."

12

W<small>ALLS OF PEOPLE WERE MARCHING DOWN PENNSYL-</small>
vania Avenue past the White House and on toward the west side
of the Capitol Building where the rally would later commence.
Jessamyn listened as her coanchor excitedly described the wall as
a colorful parade of people. History was repeating itself, he maintained, as women once again took to the streets to demonstrate.
In 1913, the issue was a woman's right to vote. On this day, July 9,
the anniversary of the death of suffragette Alice Paul, the founder
of the National Women's Party, the issue was the extension of the
deadline for passage of the ERA.

The assignment was unusual for Jessamyn. She was not
known for her on-the-spot reporting but for her interaction with
people. But this event was about people, the network had argued.
Thousands of people, among them, the Honored Guests, those
celebrities of interest to millions of Americans.

As the marchers descended upon her, Jessamyn saw them
through the haze of heat and humidity that filtered up from the
pavement. Most wore tricolored striped sashes of purple, white,
and gold. Some wheeled baby carriages. Others walked with the
men who had elected to support their women in their demonstration.

To date, Jessamyn, in her own dealings with the press, had
dodged the ERA issue, hoping to avoid any controversy. Privately

she endorsed it, although thinking the movement was basically sluggish and uninteresting. Jessamyn believed in taking what was rightfully yours and asking for it later. Laws were needed only by the weak and the uncertain. She was neither. Nor was Tyne Philips. Between them, they had never allowed the basically chauvinistic policies of television network news to hinder her earning power. Since she didn't compete as a woman, Jessamyn demanded equal payment for professional services rendered and received it.

She was worried about her professional services this Sunday morning as she watched the marchers moving ever closer to her vantage point. Within minutes, she would be a foot soldier, mingling among the many, her only weapon the handheld camera another was carrying. She would wend her way among the Honored Guests, hoping to elicit some comment that would make the late evening news that much more exciting than the competitions'. Her network was counting on her clout and her nouveau chic among the celebrated to produce the heavyweights. Which is why Jessamyn felt anxious. She knew who the true heavyweights were among the Honored Guests, and for the first time in her professional life, Jessamyn wasn't sure whether they would fight in her class.

Marti felt joyous. Whatever doubts she may have had about her stamina, her ability to march so soon after Lynne's birth were dispelled. Even the normally hated humidity could only dampen her white dress, not her spirits. The exercise classes she had resumed four weeks after the baby was born had given her back both her body and her strength. The spirit of the occasion was also regenerating. She needed to be exactly where she was. That Ali was marching by her side was yet another source of joy. And pride. Her daughter, just weeks shy of turning eighteen, was as involved in the issues as she was, and she was taking that zeal to Yale this fall, where she would be one of very few women preparing for a career in law.

Marti reached across and took the arm of the man marching beside her, grateful beyond words that he was there in support of her, of Ali, and of all the generations of women to come. She had always felt a great kinship with this man. Beyond being biologically related, they were one of the same cloth in so many ways. Impulsively, her arm went from holding his to wrap about his shoulders.

There was something about people banding together, marching to right a wrong, exercising the democratic process, that never failed to move JJ. His decision to remain in Washington, to march for Marti as she had not so long ago marched for him, had been wise. It resuscitated and soothed him. Equal rights was possible after all. Not just for women but for all. As he looked over his shoulder, JJ saw the thousands weaving to and fro as the wall upon wall moved slowly toward the designated area. He felt overwhelmed with pride. *They* were the people. *They* were the government. *They* were the country. And they were never more so than when they took matters into their own hands, as they were doing this day, to peacefully demonstrate for what they believed in. Eventually, they would be heard. Eventually, they would win, which was more than he could say for himself.

The anger and the bitterness was there and JJ suspected they always would be. Once again the Special Discharge Review Board had not understood his defense of good citizenship. Nor had they understood how his dissent had been his unalienable right. They could not see how in his own way he had fought just as they had. Differing fights but for the same country. They had not seen it as part of the democratic process. He had been denied because, as they stated, he had not met *their* requirements. He could only have been a good citizen if he had remained in the Army during the Vietnam War. That, they insisted, was what he had obligated himself to do. No one who went AWOL could ever be a model citizen by *their* standards.

And so his undesirable discharge had not been upgraded. His case was closed and he was advised by one of the board members not to reopen it, as they would never reverse their decision no matter how many testimonials or awards he produced. To them, his actions would always be viewed as undesirable.

He had wanted to lash out, fight back, but there was no further means. It had all been a mockery. How could five men, all sharing the same point of view, be allowed to sit in judgment of him! Had a jury of his peers been his judge, the verdict would have been very different. But he had been denied that, and in a democracy that, too, should be an unalienable right. A democracy guarantees—or should!—equal rights for all. Which is why he had decided to march this day. He wasn't just supporting Marti but a belief that no Special Discharge Review Board could ever take away.

She could feel the hurt coursing through his body, but there was little Marti could say. JJ had said it all the night before. The undesirable discharge was something with which he would have to live. Given who he was, it might not affect him as deeply as it would another less celebrated, less educated, and less professionally proven. But it would affect him nonetheless. As he had admitted, it was doubtful now if any judge or jury would award him custody of his child. It was a fight that might best not be pursued. Marti ached for him. She could not imagine her life if Lynne was suddenly snatched from her and she was given but partial rights in her upbringing. Given JJ's experience, Marti was glad she had not done that to Matthew, that he had as much time with his daughter as he wished. It was with her father that Lynne rested comfortably this weekend. That knowledge made Marti feel safe and secure.

Only a short time ago she had stated she wanted more time to stop and smell the roses. She hadn't known then how much time there really is—if one wants to make it—and just how many roses there are. She was collecting a bouquet and the aroma was indeed sweet.

The marchers upon her, Jessamyn gathered herself and plunged directly into the midst, moving toward the one who invariably garnered the most attention. Their eyes met before they did. Marti Tiernan, seeing the network camera and the microphone in Jessamyn's hand, made the one decision sensible to her participation in the march. She was there to lend her presence,

259

support, and most of all her name to the ERA. If her appearance on any program, with or without Jessamyn Giroux, could sway one legislator's vote or convince one more woman to support the amendment, then that was what she must do.

"Marti Tiernan. Could you tell our viewers why you are here today?" asked Jessamyn, pushing herself in front of JJ as though he were not there.

"Because I believe the passage of the ERA is vital to every woman in this country."

"Critics of the amendment maintain it is antifamily. How do you respond to this?" asked Jessamyn as she walked by Marti's side, the microphone she held serving as both weapon and shield.

"My oldest daughter walks beside me, as does my brother. My mother waits on the speakers' rostrum, unable to march but able to lend her physical support in another way. My youngest daughter is with her father, who offered to care for her so that I might be here today. In short: we all support the amendment and we continue to be a close-knit family."

"But why you and the ERA?" asked Jessamyn.

"Because I want my daughters and my daughters' daughters to be protected by law, to have the same rights as men, to walk into a bank and get credit or a loan as any man might. Because I would not like to see them stripped of property and other resources, as they are in several states, because there is no will providing for their automatic inheritance. It's an amendment whose time has come."

And Marti was gone, her duty done. Jessamyn was already moving toward Marlo Thomas, ignoring the director who was screaming from the mobile TV truck into her headset: "For chrissake, what about Ollson? Ask him what he's doing there." But if Jessamyn heard the command, she decided to obey her own rather than it.

As she stood on the speakers' platform, Bella Abzug seated to her left, Gloria Steinem to her right, Marti looked into the sea of faces of those sitting on the huge lawn that sprawled before her. In the distance she could see thousands more standing, rimming the area. Many were holding hands. Her speech was outlined but not prepared. It was brief but to the point.

"In 1913, when the suffragettes marched for the womens' right to vote, here on Pennsylvania Avenue, they were spat upon, burned with lighted cigars, and slapped by angry bystanders. Today, as one hundred thousand of us marched, there was not one such incident. America, you've come a long way, baby."

The crowd roared its approval. Marti smiled and continued. "Some further history. Last year, when passage of the ERA failed in Florida, opponents rejoiced because they maintained passage would end support of wives by husband, force legislation of homosexual marriages, require the same public toilets be used by men and women, and force our daughters to the front lines should war be declared.

"Let me return to history, this time to the year 1918. Again, let us look at the position the great state of Florida took when it came time to endorse the Nineteenth Amendment, the one that gave women the right to vote. As the state declined to ratify the amendment, one legislator went on record to say—and I quote— 'No moral man would marry a woman who votes.' "

Marti stepped back from the podium as she let her words sink into her audience. Throughout, there was a sprinkling of laughter. As she stepped forward, a sly smile on her face, she said: "People, that sums up my case against the state of Florida and others who support their position, and *for* the passage of the ERA."

✳   ✳   ✳

As she focused her attention on the ceiling light fixture, thinking how the frosted-glass ball needed to be washed, Reese allowed herself to sink into her bed and her thoughts. Tomorrow, she would have to rise early. The laundry should be done before she left Cambridge to pick up Kelly. *If* Kelly was there. Last weekend, Kelly had neglected to mention she would be camping. Reese was certain her daughter's behavior was prompted by the divorce.

The divorce . . . it would change everything, or so Reese hoped as she shifted position on the bed. Certainly the separation had not. All it had done was place her outside what had once been her home but not outside the life within it. She wasn't free. She still felt married. Because she was. The feeling marred her social life. She couldn't date without feeling dishonest and even disloyal. Not that dates were all that available. Cambridge was not the ideal cruising ground for a woman almost forty, given the college-age crowd that lived there.

As her eyes drifted from the frosted globe to the TV and on to the other familiar objects in her bedroom, Reese thought how happy she was in her home. Mather Court was lovely, and her apartment in the six-story, red-brick apartment house faced the Cambridge Common. Across the way, distant and yet within walking distance, was Harvard University. The Dearborn School, at 36 Concord, was but a short hop from Number 1 where she lived. The apartment had been a find, perfect for one, with the sleep couch in the living room making it possible for two. Karl had slept there during the summer. His had been a perfunctory visit, and she doubted whether Karl would come again to see either her or Thomas during the school year. Unhappily, Reese realized as she watched the clock, noting the hour was growing later and later, she didn't much care. She hadn't enjoyed Karl and had even decided she didn't much like him, feelings she was sure he felt in return toward her.

Reese realized she no longer felt a failure with Karl or with Kristan. That they lived in the past was a problem they would have to solve. With her move from the house on Marlborough to the one here on Concord, she had moved into the present. Kristan was a stranger to her, even though she made an appearance in her home every Wednesday night at eight. A half-hour later she was gone, replaced, as another sitcom with yet another pretty blonde took her place. Kelly never mentioned Kristan or Karl, but then Kelly never mentioned much of anything, particularly since Reese had filed for divorce in August shortly after Kelly had returned from her visit to Kristan in Los Angeles. It was as if her youngest child was using silence as a punishment. It was obvious to Reese that Kelly, like Thomas, had thought the separation was but temporary, that eventually she would work things through and come home. Which was exactly why she had decided to file. A part of her had been thinking that, which was why her social life had been on hold.

The divorce . . . it was always on her mind, particularly at times like this, she thought. Not that there were many times like this, which again was the reason she had filed. It would take a year before it was final. Ten more months before she would be legally free of her married feeling. Reese wondered, as her eyes fell on the clothes thrown haphazardly about the room, how she had managed, brief and abortive as it was, to have had an affair with Stephen Larcher. Why had that been possible when one with a man as nice as Roger Ammis was so difficult, particularly when she liked Ammis and had never really liked Larcher?

Roger was single and solvent, unusual for an artist. His paintings, which she did not understand, were marketable, something else she did not understand. His bold black strokes with accents of red and green had caused critics early in his career to dub him "art's angry young man." His work still reflected that anger although on a personal level he did not. They had met quite by accident in the supermarket when her bag had busted. He had helped pick up her groceries and she hadn't realized that wasn't all he had picked up until she found herself seated across from him in a nearby doughnut shop. That had been two months ago in August. Her conflict had been instantaneous. She was a married woman. She could not be interested in an available and attractive single man. Which was why the divorce had become necessary. If she wanted a relationship, then she had to extricate herself legally from the one in which she was. Thomas had not protested or pleaded. Within the week, her lawyer was speaking to a Chase Remington in New York. Everything had proceeded smoothly as Reese asked for nothing but the divorce, although her lawyer insisted she was entitled to a great deal more. Thomas had agreed and offered a settlement of twelve thousand a year, which was two thousand more than she was earning. She took it, although it pained her. Thomas's acquiescence also pained her. She knew his silence meant he was hurting and that was hurting her. Even at times like this, she carried Thomas with her constantly and hoped that time and the decree would finally free her. In the meantime she tried just as she had that night. Roger had arrived at seven. A movie—and when had Thomas ever wanted to see a movie?—a late supper—Thomas hated eating later than six-thirty—and then home. It could have been idyllic, even romantic, had she been free. Truly free. Then, he would not be making love to her as he now was and she would not be looking up at the frosted-glass globe, realizing the specks at its bottom were dead insects that she would have to remove first thing in the morning.

In the morning . . . laundry to be done. Kelly . . . a weekend to be planned. And only ten more months before the divorce was final.

*   *   *

As he lay on the bed, his eyes closed, Thomas focused on sensations rather than pictures. He didn't like to think of images, not at this time, as only one appeared and that was the one he wanted to avoid.

The sensations were pleasant. Mindlessly, he allowed his body to peak and ebb as they did. He had never indulged himself as a child or as an adult when thousands of miles separated him from the source of such real pleasure. But others did. Vinnie had boasted of the frequency of such personal pleasure when they were kids. Even his fellow officers in the Triple Nickel had maintained that it not only kept them sane and free of disease but guiltless. Others, those who had put their fidelity on hold, had laughed at such thinking.

Had his doctor not insisted, Thomas would not have been lying naked in the center of his bed. But the pain he had been experiencing when he urinated and the milky discharge from his penis had proven to be signs of prostatitis, the disease of priests and studs as his urologist, Joseph D. Philipay, had explained. One developed the illness through either too little or too much sex. Knowing Thomas, he had not had to ask into which category he fell, which is why in addition to the prescribed tetracycline he had also prescribed twice-a-week masturbation—the antibiotic to be suspended after ten days; the masturbation not.

Thomas was grateful it was Saturday evening. It was the one night when he felt the most comfortable with his sensations, the night no one was home and he could be less ashamed of the act and the tears that fell as violently as his semen upon climax. For always, at the point when the sensations became unbearably pleasurable, his concentration would fade from them and to the pic-

2 6 4

tures that appeared as they did now in his mind. Fantasies, the psychiatrists would say. Always the same and always with the same woman, no matter that she was out of his bed and out of his life, although seldom out of his thoughts.

*   *   *

It was the nothingness that often overwhelmed him. Hours upon hours into days of nothingness. His job, which had always seemed pointless, now pointedly was without meaning or purpose. He had accepted the verdict even before the court convened. That was why he was not going to court. Custody would not be awarded to him. He had given up the fight and in doing so all the fight had left him. That was why JJ was sitting in his darkened office, trying to find a reason to attend the annual staff-and-student Christmas party. There was none, just as there no longer was a reason for him to stay with the Tiernan Repertory Company as its administrative director.

As he rocked in his swivel chair, JJ realized he hated his life and needed to change it. He needed to become involved. But in what? There were no outreach centers being set up for exiles and resisters as they now were for Vietnam veterans. He envied Thomas his new job and the chance for a new life now that his old one had fallen apart. And Marti, too, he envied. There was a place for her energies. She was everywhere and anywhere her presence might gain support for the ERA.

He would have to rouse himself, thought JJ, first from his chair, then to the party, and later from his depression. But it was hard, particularly when he was hounded by feelings of failure. Often, he felt as if he were lost in space or in some kind of limbo, a terribly lonely limbo where he was neither seen no heard. There were times when JJ, knowing of the inner circumstances of Thomas's life, yearned to talk to him, thinking that Thomas, alone, might understand how he was feeling. But even had he called, Thomas was on the road now, trusting his Kelly to Reese just as Marti so often trusted her Lynne to Matthew. But when Jessamyn traveled, she left his David with strangers. Only he in his family had but Sundays at three and holidays at two to see his child. Unless special arrangements had been made.

The knock at the door startled him. Before he could respond,

2 6 5

his mother entered. She did not speak but extended her hand. As he took it, JJ could feel her lifting both him and his spirits. In the hallway, her arm linked through his, she guided him down the steps and into the Augusta Monahan Theater, where students and staff were mingling and performing. As she took her place in the front, he sat toward the rear.

"Would you mind removing your hat?"

"I'm not wearing a hat," he said to the voice directly behind him.

"Then your head, please. I can't see."

He turned in his seat and stared into the largest pair of tortoise-shell glasses he had ever seen on so small a face. She was smiling at him as she waved him to a seat that wouldn't block her vision. Although he was annoyed, he moved. He was even more annoyed when she didn't say thank you but continued to laugh uproariously at the skit being performed on stage.

It was funny. It almost made him laugh. Had he not felt so depressed, it surely would have.

"It's really knocking you out, isn't it?" he heard the voice from behind say. "Laugh any harder and they're going to throw you out."

Again JJ turned and stared into the glasses-laden face whose eyes were riveted on the stage. "Would you get off my back!" he whispered.

"You should be so lucky," she replied also in a whisper. "Just my luck, I write a show and they bring in a busload of the clinically depressed from the Menninger Clinic to see it."

JJ chuckled.

"Now you're getting to me, kid. You know, some girls these days count orgasms, but I count laughs."

This time JJ laughed loudly.

"Face the stage, damn it, so they'll think you're laughing at the dialogue," she ordered. "You know, you have promise. Keep up the laughs and I just might share an eggnog with you later."

"I don't like eggnog. I'm not even sure I like you," said JJ, still whispering.

"Who are you kidding? You're crazy about me. Why else in a half-empty theater did you practically sit in my lap?"

"I never even saw you!"

"Oh, sure. That's what they all say. Now shut up. I want to hear the rest of this."

Immediately she focused on the stage and within seconds she was laughing again, acting as if the dialogue was fresh and unknown to her. When the skit ended, she applauded loudly and then moved from the aisle behind to the seat next to him. He was surprised to see she was tiny, a little fuzzy-haired blonde with green eyes and pink cheeks.

"For a little girl, you have a very big mouth," he said, imitating her tone.

"Oh, you sweet-talker, you. How'd you like a fat lip to match my big mouth?" she asked, smiling sweetly.

He didn't ask but acted, lifting the glasses from her face. His surprise reflected in his words. "You're pretty."

"I wonder if Columbus was as stunned when he discovered America. So I'm pretty. Lots of girls are pretty. You're not exactly chopped liver either."

"You're not an actress, are you?" he said, feeling stupid as soon as the words were spoken.

"I'm nuts but I'm not *that* nuts. Actors are very weird, you know. They can't speak unless God or someone tells them what to say. On paper. Double-spaced."

Again he laughed. "My mother might differ with you."

She looked at him closely, slapped her forehead with her hand in sudden recognition, and said: "I just remembered. I have to catch a train. The last one for Transylvania leaves in twenty minutes." She rose, but he pulled her back down. "What's your name?" he asked.

"Now that's a terrific question," she replied. "Really good. My name is Arline but don't call me that. It's an awful name," she added when he was about to ask why. "Nobody I know, or wish to know, is named Arline."

"What should I call you then?"

"How about Elvira or Clytemnestra. Forget Clytemnestra. You and every other chauvinist would call me Clyt for short. That's my problem, you know. The only reason I'm not a big success yet is because I don't have a name. Look at it this way. If you received a script from an Arline Ackerman, would you be lusting to read it? The name lacks personality . . . extravagance."

"You know, you may be the most ditsy broad I've ever met."

"I don't mind the 'ditsy,' but I take offense at the 'broad.' Don't use it."

"All right, you're ditsy."

"Now, that I like. It has a ring to it. Very preppy. A lot like those girls with names like Pookie and Bunny. Ditsy. . . . Yes, I do like that. Dits isn't bad either."

"I think you're better off with Ditsy," said JJ, matching her earnest tone. "People might find Dits just a little too cute."

"Unbelievable! The man comes from a family of Estes and Reeses, Alis and Martis—JJ is a real winner, too—and he thinks Dits is cute. All right, call me Irving. *That's* not cute."

But in her strange way, she was, and JJ, despite her purposeful arrogance, was charmed. They shared an eggnog at the party and then a basket of fish and chips at the nearby Landmark Tavern. She lived in Chelsea, near Marti, and when he offered to see her home, she refused, saying: "I've had a very nice evening. If I'm not too crazy for you, call me sometime. I'm in the phonebook."

"Under what name?" he asked jokingly, as he hailed her a taxi.

"You know what? I forgot. I've changed it so often that I'm not sure whether I'm listed under Potsie Plotkin or Lollie Lipke. Try both. If they fail, look under F. A. Ackerman. The *F* is for For-a-Good-Time-Call," she explained before the taxi pulled away and sped down Ninth Avenue.

Three nights later, he did call, asking for Irving. "What the hell took you so long?" was her instant response. "How many Potsie Plotkins are there in the phonebook?"

✳   ✳   ✳

She refused to sleep with him, explaining it was against her religion, which when he asked she defined as "latent lesbianism." He hadn't laughed but she did not acquiesce. He pursued; she resisted, and a month passed in which they saw one another several nights a week. He called her Arline. She called him John, refusing to even consider JJ as an alternative. John was a beautiful name, perfect for an attractive, mature man, which he was. It also had a solid ring to it, she explained. And a dull one, she added. Which is why it suited him. He was dull, almost to the point of boring, she would tease. Like his clothes. Like his lifestyle. "For you, a fun time is an earthquake, or fire, flood, and pestilence. You should have been Jewish. You suffer so well."

Her idea of a "fun time," he soon discovered, was having a good cry. When they went to the opera—at her instigation—she collapsed when Mimi did during *La Bohème* and cried with Rudolpho when Mimi died. She embarrassed him at the Regency Theater where Bette Davis bore her blindness and her death in *Dark Victory* better than Arline did. She even cried at pet stores when she realized all the puppies would never find homes. A lost or abused child wrecked her totally.

She had always wanted to be a dramatist. For years, she had seen herself as a Brooklyn-born, Jewish-raised, Chekovian genius. Her first attempts at playwrighting were received by her off-off-Broadway friends—"and the Drama Club at Brooklyn College is about as off-off-Broadway as you can get"—with great encouragement. They laughed and laughed, thinking what she had written was satirically brilliant and side-splittingly funny. It was then she realized whenever she thought sad, she wrote funny. JJ soon discovered she wrote funny a lot.

She loved to dance and dragged him to Studio 54. She was not upset when one of the young men there asked him to dance. He was. That made her giggle. She introduced him to little clubs where young performers, many of whom he had seen at the repertory company, tried to woo and win agents and producers. Many of the stand-up comics used her material. They never paid and she never expected they would. Not for years.

She became his own personal Yellow Pages. She knew exactly where everything was and at exactly what time one should be there. Sundays meant brunch at SoHo, a Mother Truckers ice-cream cone in the Village, and a slice of Goldberg's pizza when they went east to catch an early-evening movie. To his amazement, she knew the names and greeted several of the bag ladies about Manhattan. She explained when he asked that they were former sorority sisters, the best of her Brooklyn College graduating class.

He knew when summer came she would make him ride the

Staten Island ferry. She didn't wait for the summer. On the first Sunday in February, with an icy wind blowing in their faces, as he complained every freezing inch of the way, they ferried across the Hudson River to Staten Island, where they tramped around the frozen and deserted South Beach. That night, for her twenty-third birthday, she made him take her across the river again, this time to Brooklyn, and by subway, to the River Café. Later, on the IRT, somewhere between the Clark and Wall Street stations, she told him her life story.

Her mother had died when she was ten and her father, a traveling salesman, placed her with his brother and his family during the weeks he was gone. They were lovely, loving people. Except for Stanley. Her big, bad three-years-older cousin. He would sexually molest her and then threaten to kill if she told. Not that he actually ever did anything, but he did do something. He would put his middle finger into her vagina while he masturbated. She hated him. When she was older and her father had reclaimed her due to a promotion that found him working out of the home office, she threatened to expose Stanley.

"And you know what that creep did?" she asked, her voice a bit too loud, a result of the rich red wine to which she was not accustomed. "He laughed. The goddamn pervert laughed. He stood there like some hyena, screaming his head off. Who would believe her, he asked, since everyone knew he was gay. I mean . . . could you kill! I may be the only girl in history that ever got finger-fucked by a faggot. There's no drama in that, no pathos. It's ridiculous, just like everything else I do when I'm trying to be serious. And stop laughing," she added as she pinched his thigh until it hurt.

She was a survivor of James Madison High School, one of the few to make it out of that jungle without incident or injury. "Strangely enough, being the tiniest girl in class protected me. That and my mouth, which people knew was a lethal weapon. In fact, seeing the effect my mouth had, I decided if I could put those words on paper, I'd have a helluva career. In the Roller Derby!"

The day of her graduation from Brooklyn College, she was on a plane, "heading for the Coast. Oh, what excitement those words brought to mind. Heading for the Coast . . . going to L.A. Pure magic!" Only she hated Los Angeles. "People pretend to be laid-back there when they're really laid-out . . . as in dead. Retrospectively, I don't know why I went. I mean . . . I had already seen the movie. It was called *Imitation of Life.*" Now her energies were focused on Broadway, the stage, which is why she had taken the year-long course in playwrighting at the repertory company. "Do you know there are no funny plays being written by women? Or if there are, no one is producing them. And I'm as good or as bad as Neil Simon. I can cop out on an emotion, cover it with a laugh, as well as he does."

As he relived all the years he had missed in the space of eight weeks, he came to realize she knew herself well. She knew him just as well. "You should get out of this self-imposed trap you're in," she declared one night in between periods of a Rangers-Flyers hockey game that resembled a wrestling match on ice. She loved hockey and admitted to a secret fantasy involving Steve Vickers, one of the Ranger players. "And I don't mean out from just the rep company, but from your life. Do something you want to do."

He said there was nothing he could think of that would make him happy.

"That's the mistake, kid," she said seriously. "This thing you've got about being happy. Give it up. I was happy once. It was nice. Very nice. But frankly, I think it would be too great a shock for your system. Happy is not your nature. As I see it, you're making yourself miserable trying to be happy when you're happiest when you're miserable. So be miserable. Get involved with all the misery in life, all those scuzzy going-downs that make you so angry. Expose them. Protest them. Fight. Surround yourself with gloom and doom and believe me, kid, soon you'll have more happy than you can handle. For you the secret is to forget your happy and just get troubles and you'll chase all your blues away."

He had laughed, knowing beneath the attempt at humor she was being very serious. For him to be happy, he did have to be involved. He was much like his father that way and, as he thought about it, he suspected much like Thomas. The next day, he contacted Citizen Soldier, an antimilitarist group, and volunteered to help them in their public-service announcements, which were largely geared to alerting veterans to the perils of Agent Orange, a chemical defoliant used in Vietnam that was now thought to be causing cancer. It was yet another legacy of the war, unwanted by its victims and the government who used the defoliant and the chemical companies who manufactured it. Enraged at the apathetic attitude toward the killer and those it killed, he wrote a blistering editorial which the *New York Times* published. It caused comment. It created controversy. And a job offer. A very good job offer. Such a good job offer that it prompted Arline Ackerman to give up her religion that night, to convert, which had the effect, despite her urgings that it was not in his best interests, of making John Ollson, Jr., a very happy man.

13

As she heard the beginnings of her introduction, Marti also heard the now familiar beginnings of dissent. Just as in Tallahassee and then again in Gainesville, a small group of men and women dressed in the red, white, and blue were noisily running down the center aisle, their placards and chants protesting her presence, accusing her of being antifamily, anti-American, and anti-God. Her nose was in "family business." . . . "Yankee Go Home!"

The demonstration ended as abruptly as it started, with uniformed guards and local police pushing and prodding the resisting group from the hall. A punch was thrown, as was continued verbal abuse, but still Marti remained unruffled. Rather than concern herself with the hatred she saw on some of the faces, she focused her attention on the second row where Matthew was seated next to Vinnie, their faces turned upward toward her, their expressions approving and loving. As she heard herself introduced, Marti thought of Matthew, of Lynne, of the weekend they would now spend together hidden away at Vinnie's. She felt happy, pleased, and energized as two roles blended into one person, all Marti Tiernan. She concentrated on Matthew as she walked to the lectern. Matthew . . . always her friend; sometimes her lover. It was a winning combination.

He had never realized just how persuasive she could be. Her ability to put across her logic with passion was exhilarating. It was obvious she had been an actress. It was also obvious that had she chosen she would now be a much better actress than before. The woman on stage was real, likable, warm, and intelligent. She was someone, had he not known her, he would like to meet. She was forceful without being strident. Her animation as she responded to questions from the audience gave a different dimension to her beauty. She was something, *this* Marti Tiernan.

As he watched and listened, fascinated by this new yet not new woman, Matthew realized how he had initially undervalued Marti, not seen the total person or guessed at the depth that was lurking within the woman who was in as much of a transitional period when they met as he had been. Not until this moment had he been aware of the total statement she made as a woman and a person. Suddenly, it seemed real, not just a fact, that she was listed in the *World Almanac* as one of America's twenty-five most influential women. Obviously her passion aroused others as much as it was once again, now, at that moment, arousing him. Yet it wasn't quite the passion of his youth. It was tempered, and, without knowing why, Matthew knew it was better. Perhaps because it was comfortable and he felt comfortable with it . . . with her . . . with himself . . . with them. For a split second Matthew wondered if he were growing old. A smile crossed his face as he realized: not old but mature—and that there is a world of difference between the two.

*   *   *

She did not understand how he could still feel uncomfortable in the public eye. Kristan's own discomfort had nothing to do with the hundreds of gawking travelers crowding the Denver airport, but with her father. Ever since her Friday arrival for the Easter weekend, she had wondered how two people could be so near and yet so far.

"Do you have everything?"

Although his voice was gentle, it startled her. She yearned to reply: "No, Dad, I don't. I don't have you, not as a father. I never did and I doubt if I ever will." But she said nothing, not wanting to hurt or change his sense of well-being. Never had she seen him so relaxed, content, pleased with his life. From the moment she had arrived, he had talked almost with a passion of his newly assigned job, that of troubleshooter for the DAV's recently created Operation Outreach centers. She could feel his passion on the site of the Denver pilot program, in operation since January on Fox Street, on the second floor of a three-story, prefabricated concrete building that housed a ground-floor garage and the Colorado Veterans' Assistance Center. It had amazed her, as he spoke, that he, so uncomfortable in the public eye for so long, was now actually enthusiastic about being the face and voice, the media spokesperson, for the organization, the man speaking before various civic groups to enlist their financial aid. *He,* who had had so much difficulty reaching his own family was now reaching out to Vietnam veterans themselves, beseeching them to seek the centers for help as he also reached out to lawyers, employment counselors, and psychiatrists asking them to volunteer their services to the centers and the very men he hoped to help.

As he had spoken, Kristan had understood more about her father than she ever had. Smiling, free of the tension that had marked his face throughout her childhood, he was content. He was making it. On his own and on his own terms. But alone. That pained her. Guilt. Forever guilt. They had failed her, and yet she felt in some way she had failed them.

"I have everything," she replied to his question, rising, aware the crowd was parting before them as they walked together to the boarding area. She turned to face him, wondering when she would see him again. She wanted to touch his face with her hand but didn't. Impulsively, she flung her arms about him, hugging him as a child might her father. She felt him stiffen. His face was without expression when he said, "I'm glad you came. If you ever need anything, call." And he was gone.

"I'm glad you came." That was her legacy from her father. Something but not enough. But nothing would ever be enough. She must let go—must fill her life in the present and not think that the overflow could refill the past, she told herself. The past was just that—past and gone, except in her mind. She would have to be her own parent as she had always been. Like it or not. That could not change.

Seated by the window in the first row of the first-class section,

Kristan hid behind her oversize sunglasses and cried. Her mother had made a life of her own and so had her father. Now, with her own apartment, her own TV series, she had too, except for the fact that she had yet to make that psychological leap from past to present. See them as people and not as parents, Tricia Hill had advised. That way, they may delight or disappoint, but they cannot hurt you. Not as they once did. And that way you are free to like or dislike them for who they are and not for who you would like them to be.

She had seen him, the man, clearly that weekend and had liked what she saw. But had she seen it all? Abruptly, Kristan dried her tears and reached into her small flight bag. She found the article from the *Denver Post* her father had given to her upon leaving for the airport. He had been almost embarrassed when he suggested she read it on her return flight to Los Angeles. As she declined the stewardess's offer of a cocktail, Kristan began reading Dana Parsons's feature story, sorting through it for what was pertinent to her and what wasn't.

Vietnam. Many people won't read beyond the single word, so distasteful has it become. It reminds them only of wretched things, of a period of history that, strangely, now seems an eternity ago.

That was true. It reminded her of wretched things—her aloneness, her father's aloofness, her mother's alcoholism, and her own attempts to be parent to every single member of her family.

Let's forget about it, they say, because it is over. That is where they are wrong.

For a significant number of Americans, the war isn't over. For them, the memory of it still burns in their minds and in some cases greatly affects their everyday existence.

That was her father. Even now, his everyday existence was the war.

Some of the veterans brought their war wounds home with them in visible form. . . . With others, the problems are more

deep-seated. . . . Typically, the range of problems that emerge include depression, guilt, sleep disorders, alienation, periods of anxiety, difficulty in establishing intimate relationships . . .

That had all applied to her father, particularly with intimate
relationships. And because it had applied to him, it now applied to
her. She and Tricia Hill could attest to that.

. . . a mistrust of most people and institutions and a general questioning of the purpose and meaning of life.

No. That was not and never had been her father. His life
always had purpose . . . meaning. That is what made him impossible, often intractable, and someone she fiercely admired even as
she had nurtured her resentment. To her, he had always been a
hero.

Through tears that blinded her vision, Kristan, after reading
of the estimated half million Vietnam veterans who were currently
exhibiting delayed stress symptoms and how a half million more
could emerge by 1985, folded the newspaper clipping. None of this
pertained to her. As she was about to place it in her flight bag, she
suddenly realized she was doing what the country had done—
ignoring the issue, pretending it didn't apply to them. This was
what her father had been fighting ever since his return from Vietnam. Quickly, she unfolded the clipping and began reading anew,
determined if not to understand then at least to listen to the words
her father obviously deemed important.

Of those men who served in Southeast Asia, and were married before they saw duty, 38 percent were divorced within the first
six months after returning to the United States.

It hadn't been within the first six months, but it should have
been, thought Kristan, remembering all too clearly the lives they
all led in Rancho Santa Fe. Actually, it had been during the first
six months, she realized, only neither her father nor her mother
had been strong enough to admit it.

. . . and of Vietnam veterans under 35, there is a 33 percent
higher suicide rate than among the national average for nonvet-
eran males under 35 . . . a serious drug and alcohol problem . . .
an inordinately high percentage in prison, stemming from their
difficulty in getting work and being accepted by society.

She felt cold, clammy, and distinctly uncomfortable. When
she had visited the Fox Street center, she had seen its surplus
furniture, dingy carpeting, and walls in need of painting. Not until
this moment had she seen anything other than the externals.

. . . Although a significant percentage of Vietnam veterans probably needed some sort of counseling, the public has been misled as
to the nature of the Vietnam veteran.
Even of those who need counseling about the stress problem,
a majority are probably contributing members of society and
not violent. . . . The walking-time-bomb description that
has been used to describe veterans with emotional problems is over-
played. . . . The guy who's going to explode is the guy who has
tried all the legitimate channels to get his case heard . . .
Although many bemoan the lack of programs for the Vietnam
veteran, something is happening in Denver. The city is one of the
six in a pilot program sponsored by the Disabled American Veterans . . . the program is designed to assist veterans with legal, psychological, drug and alcohol, and unemployment problems. . . .

Carefully, Kristan again folded the clipping. Gently, she held
it to her breast. As if it were her father. In reading it, she had read
him. He must have understood that, which is why he had pressed
the article upon her in the airport. It justified and it vindicated.
But it didn't take the hurt away. As she placed the article in her
wallet next to her other pieces of identification, Kristan understood. And accepted. And as the tears once again fell from her
shielded eyes, she cared.

*   *   *

All across America, from Baltimore, Cleveland, and Denver
to Detroit, Atlanta, and Los Angeles—all the pilot cities for the
outreach program—Thomas heard the men, white- and blue-col-

lar workers, the upwardly mobile and downwardly trodden, speak the same words in the same almost awe-struck voice. "I heard your public-service announcements, heard the symptoms, and I knew you were talking about me." They would laugh but without humor. "And here I thought all the others had adjusted and that I was the only one who was alone, no one to hear my problems . . . going crazy." At the outreach centers they found a place to be both seen and heard: in the group-therapy sessions that proved to be the treatment of their choice.

He, too, had found his place to be seen and heard. He was totally involved. As he worked for others, he worked for himself. His work was all-encompassing, beginning at seven, when most of the storefront centers opened, and ending long after the official closing time of five. He never resented the hours spent coordinating the most minute of details, the names of professional organizations in other cities who might volunteer their services when the program reached them. His day overflowed into his evening and his night. He did his duty. On all fronts.

Every other weekend, he flew home to Boston. Only to see Kelly, to be a presence in her life. Until the outreach programs were fully functional, she was reluctantly living with Reese in an apartment barely big enough by his standards for one. But Reese had refused to move back into the house on Marlborough. She had cried when he persisted and he had not understood, although she had tried to explain, why a house—just the living in it, particularly since he would be gone—could cause such pain. Nor had he understood her anger when he had voiced his appreciation for her giving Kelly a home during his absence.

He had asked Kelly, as he had asked Kristan, and Karl, to visit him in Denver. Kelly had declined. Reese had explained when he had asked that Kelly was the typical teenager, wrapped up in her own life with her own friends. He had looked hard at Kelly and wondered what kind of a life did a child who was soon to be sixteen have? He determined to find out when he returned to Boston that summer to prepare for the opening of its outreach center. In the meantime, he had sent Kelly the same article he had given Kristan.

Karl had declined the same invitation, explaining in a terse note that now that he had decided against a running career in favor of one in sports medicine, he was too busy with his texts to travel. Thomas had accepted his excuse because it was easier than not accepting it.

The Los Angeles center had been almost as difficult to establish as the one in Denver. His public-service announcements reached just so many. What was needed Margaret provided. Unasked. One morning, she and other members of her TV series arrived to tour the outreach center. Press agents representing the show and its stars rallied the press. All that was missing were kleig lights, Shirley Eder, and Army Archerd to make it a true Hollywood event. Normally, Thomas would never have allowed a make-believe world to mix with his and his charges' reality. But this was Hollywood, where a star's appearance at such an event guaranteed media coverage. Margaret had urged him to use her. And he had. As the cameras focused on Margaret and members of her TV family, he spoke for six impassioned minutes on the five, then six, and then again eleven o'clock news. Within minutes, the center's phones were ringing and the familiar "You're describing me. When can I come in?" was once again heard.

Kristan called from Hawaii where she was filming a between-TV-seasons movie. She also sent him her love, which she had not done in more years than he could remember.

He was busy and he would be even busier if the sixty to seventy other outreach programs in other cities opened, as the DAV planned, within the year. All would need his expertise, his presence, and his dedication. He was so busy that he had no time to miss anything or anybody. And he was too busy to concern himself with the persisting prostate problems which he sometimes remembered but which he just as often forgot to do anything about. Given all else in his life, they hardly seemed important.

*   *   *

As Nelson stood at the altar waiting for his bride, he thought how this was to have been a small, quiet wedding followed by an intimate brunch. But the crowds and cameramen that had collected on the steps of St. Paul's had made it anything but small, and the few but vocal placard-bearing anti-ERA forces anything but quiet. It had amused and not dismayed him that it had taken

Atypical were the police that held back the crowds that threw insults and not rice at him and his "family." They had not forgotten. Again he and the others were encircled by a protective bubble of blue coats and nightsticks. As a group, they hurried into the sunny day, down the stairs, not seeing the tall, thin man dressed impeccably in a white suit break through the crowd, through the cordon of police and onto the steps before them. Backgrounded by a bright blue sky, he seemed unreal, a fantasy figure. He was talking directly to Marti Tiernan, his words loud, harsh, frightening even to the camera crews who recorded them. His hand reached into his suit jacket. There were screams, equally loud, equally harsh, as he withdrew it. More screams as the police and the crowds converged. Screams upon screams that could be heard even above the gunshots that echoed across Columbus Avenue and toward Central Park where the intimate brunch at Tavern on the Green was supposed to begin.

*   *   *

She opened her eyes, saw the sun through the curtained windows, followed a beam to the parquet floors and the blues of the Oriental rug, and then slipped back into a half sleep, secure in the knowledge that she was home and not still on the steps of St. Paul's church. As if from a great distance, she felt her headache. The weight on her chest prevented her from moving. Not that she wanted to move. She was content to remain hidden, safe, beneath the weight.

Further in the distance was yesterday. Again she heard the screams. A Greek chorus mourning a tragedy. She could almost see the faces. A woman crying as blood reddened her white dress and her day. Alicia, witnessing some rite, some ritual that was fast becoming as common as a wedding.

The weight shifted, bearing her down further. Yet, the fact that it was there, as it had been yesterday, lifted her spirits.

Half asleep, half awake, she was watching the pictures in her mind and remembering. Red on white. On a white dress, the one nearest the white suit. Screams. And the music . . . a party. Letting life go on.

It had felt like a dream; then a nightmare. And the man in

2 8 2

a cordon of police to move the wedding party from their limousines into the cathedral. Theirs would be the only wedding album among their friends' to include photographic stills from both the Associated and United Press services.

He was happy and sad, happy that his family of friends were there to give him away and sad that his own family was not. Through the years they had remained obstinate, unbending. In their minds, they had no son. On this, his wedding day, Nelson, for the first time in years, felt orphaned. He wished Kay were there and not in a hospital recovering from an emergency appendectomy. She said she would be there in spirit and, as his eyes searched the deep cerulean-blue ceiling with its painted stars and the clerestory stained-glass windows that rose above the massive columns of the church, he sought to feel her there. As JJ was. And Marti. The people who had parented him when others would not.

He had not expected asking JJ to be his best man and Marti to walk at his side, as she had from the first day he came to New York, to cause such controversy. And how his decisions had leaked to the press he would never know and could therefore never explain to his concerned fiancée who saw her wedding day threaten to become a national rather than a family affair. But Alicia Lorca was strong. She believed in him and their marriage and believed one married the man, not his family or friends.

He watched her now, moving ever so slowly down the aisle, her father a proud escort. Once again he was stunned by her Latin beauty. Nearing the altar, she smiled as she passed her mother, sitting on the aisle. Her fingers touched her father's arm gently as she left his side and moved to Nelson's. With her gloved finger, she brushed away the tears that were falling down his face. Throughout the ceremony, Nelson watched her, watching him. And suddenly, he was being asked for the ring which JJ handed to him. He placed it on Alicia Lorca's third finger, left hand, and spoke the words that made her his wife and he, her husband. He kissed the bride and as they were leaving in step to the "Wedding March," he broke away at Marti's pew to hug her and then Ali and Mark. Then, with his bride on his arm, her family walking behind, he strode toward the rear of the huge church.

The day was bright and sunny, typical for a June wedding.

white had stepped out of—or was it into?—it. And he was speaking to her. Angrily. Somehow, she had always known he would appear. She had thought she would be frightened, but she hadn't been. The hand thrust into his suit jacket. Coming at her so quickly. And then . . .

The ache in her head . . . from where she had fallen on the stone steps. Then too, a heavy weight on her chest, bearing her down, almost into the stone, hurting her ribs and back but not her. Smothered under the weight, she had heard the gunshots. *After* she had fallen. She was alive! And despite the pain, she was not hurt.

Marti's eyes again fluttered open. The clock read six-forty. The new day was still, silent, all the better to hear the sounds of yesterday. Music. The clatter of china and the chatter of those who ate wedding cake from it. The cries of the man in the white suit, shot from behind by a policeman who did not see that what the man had withdrawn from his suit jacket was a letter. Carefully typed, but nothing more dangerous than just another letter. In which he addressed his grievance to her because it was her "kind" who had made his wife leave him and their children to become liberated. She was gone, taking his peace of mind, his sanity, and more of his life than the bullet that had torn through his shoulder.

But he had had a gun, strapped to his waist, argued the policeman in his defense. But only the letter had been presented to her. Not that she had seen that. Not that she had seen anything but the man as he had stood threateningly near her. From the moment his hand had gone to the inside of his jacket, she had been thrown to the ground, pinned there, covered, protected by a body that was willing to take the consequences of his actions to spare her. Throughout the night, they had been together. Like this, his weight covering her own. A protective coating. Over and over as they reassured each other of life through the act of love, he had spoken her name.

Yesterday, his had been the first voice she heard, recognized when she had come fully to her senses on the steps of St. Paul's. Others were urging her to the hospital, home, or some other safe harbor. But he had said no, explaining there was a party she *must* attend. *Must*, he had insisted. She had understood. When one falls off a horse, if one intends to ride again, one gets up and back on again. Unless one decides not to take the reins ever again.

Matthew knew things. Particularly about her. But then he knew her, thought Marti. And loved her. And their child.

*   *   *

It started with a gurgle that became a giggle. Several giggles. Moments later, when JJ looked up from his own work, he saw Arline, sitting on the couch with her legs tucked under her and her fist jammed in her mouth. Reaching over, he pulled out her self-imposed gag, releasing a torrent of pent-up laughter. She kept pointing at the manuscript in her lap and trying to explain as she continued to laugh. Finally, when she had gained control, she began to read.

> Chantilly's limpid eyes glowed in the fire of his glance. The simple gold ring on her finger now said the inevitable, like her desire, so long felt and as often denied, was now permissible. She could feel herself trembling with anticipation as he walked toward her slowly, his every step bringing the moment nearer. Through his open shirt she saw his heart beating wildly, his huge chest rising and falling like stormy waves upon a virgin shore. Soon he would be her tides and she, his golden sands. Before Chantilly could speak, he pressed her to him, his lips urgent and cruel upon hers. She uttered the faintest of cries as he lifted and carried her toward the paradise she knew awaited at the top of the stairs. And as she soared, Chantilly thought: Eden at last!

The last words were barely audible as Arline, choking with laughter, rolled from the sofa onto the carpet where she continued to scream as she kicked her feet and threw manuscript pages all about her. "It's awful," said JJ coldly. "Just awful."

"Oh, yes," she gasped. "Thank you. Coming from you, that means so much." And she was laughing again. "Oh my, isn't it just the worst of the lot yet? It's so bad that it's good."

JJ shook his head in mock despair. It hadn't been until the spring, some four months after their affair had begun, that he had learned how Arline earned her living. It was ingenious if compro-

2 8 4

mising. Arline Ackerman, unsuccessful comedy writer by day, became Lydia La Rosamoré by night. Her first three romance novels had sold better than two million copies. Since the one paragraph he had just heard sounded worse than all the purple-passion prose of her other books, JJ was certain *Eden at Last* would keep Arline solvent and insufferably determined. Despite his offers, she would not take his help. She didn't want doors that had remained closed to her to open because the magic name of Ollson or Tiernan was used. As she explained, those very same agents who represented his family had steadfastly refused to see or read her when she was what she still was, except for her association with him, a nobody. Thank you, but no thanks, she had said. She wanted her own identity and her own emergence into the ranks. Remembering Jessamyn, JJ did not press but accepted Arline's decision, and not without some relief.

As she collected the pages of her manuscript, Arline, still giggling, announced, "I am now ready to face a grim evening. Imagine, a vigil. The very word is enough to make you dash off to Studio 54 and pray for the health of disco and Donna Summer's lungs. Those broads at NOW really know how to plan an evening of fun."

"And what's wrong with a twenty-four-hour vigil for the ERA?" he asked, annoyed that she wasn't in the spirit of the occasion.

"John, vigils are like Virgil or virgins. Archaic . . . extinct. Tell me. When was the last time you read Virgil or knew a virgin? Same as when you last went to a vigil I'll bet. Of course, with you," mused Arline as she slipped off her cotton robe and stood naked before her portable closet that filled a major portion of her living room, "the answer could be 'yesterday,' knowing your idea of laughs." She shuddered and JJ smiled, knowing her putdowns were always done with love and a certain measure of truth. "And let me tell you this: the last Saturday night in August is hardly my idea of vigil time. The entire *movement*—and the word itself is enough to make you barf—lacks humor."

"The issues aren't funny," defended JJ.

"But they could be," replied Arline thoughtfully. "Anything can and often should be, as it then becomes twice as effective.

Sometimes you must make light of things or they sit too heavily with people. And that makes them defensive and they turn off. And the *movement* turns off a lot of people who ought to be turned on. They're frightened by the Superwomen who seem to own it. It makes me furious. Every time I see that Bella Abzug dame, brilliant as she is, I want to say: In your hat, lady! If only she used some schtik, like slipping on a banana peel or taking a cream pie in that puss of hers, she'd score twice as heavily with the simple folk. Which is exactly what I've told Marti. God, I hope she uses the material I sent her for this evening," said Arline as she modeled a white picture-frame hat with a cabbage rose on it. "What do you think?"

"Of the hat or of your idea?" asked JJ.

"Both," said Arline as she pirouetted for JJ.

"I think you need something special to go with the hat. Like some clothes," said JJ. "Somehow that hat, particularly the rose, calls attention to the fact that you're naked."

"And to think some people believe men don't notice what a woman wears," said Arline gaily. "Next you'll want to know exactly what kind of schtik I gave Marti. All right, I'll tell you. Think of the fun she can have with these facts. In Massachusetts there are no equal rights, not for the sexes, not when only men are prohibited from making obscene phone calls. And in North Carolina, another cruel miscarriage of justice: only men are prohibited from being a peeping tom. In short, Tina can but Thomas can't. Unfair. And in Mississippi, only women are limited to a ten-hour working day. Do you get my drift? Peeping toms and obscene phone calls are issues people can relate to."

Her eyes were twinkling and he could see how pleased she was by the facts Marti could turn to the ERA's advantage. He understood without asking the amount of research she must have done to uncover just those three facts. She had taught him about a writer's research; just as she had taught him everything else about writing a column.

When the Kaplan Syndicate had first approached him after his letter had been published in the *New York Times*, he had been hesitant about accepting their offer. He was a filmmaker, not a writer. But Arline had scoffed at such limited thinking, insisting his documentaries were journalism at its best. Through film, he told his story in pictures. Now he could tell similar stories in words. He knew words, didn't he? she had asked. He could speak, therefore he could write, she reasoned. She would be his teacher, his editor, until he could edit himself. In exchange, he would teach her film, how to think in pictures, so that she could best put forth her own feminist philosophies but in sitcom form.

Her enthusiasm had been contagious. He had signed the Kaplan contract and his twice-weekly column was initially carried by but eleven newspapers. Within three months, that eleven had trippled, thanks in part to his "I Am a Feminist" column, which was likened, as it was meant to be, to JFK's famous "*Ich bin ein Berliner*" speech at the Berlin Wall. Now, his syndication had tripled again. His *Ollson Observes* was a voice that was often mocked, as often applauded, but heard, due in no small part to the way his "words" were presented. Courtesy of Arline Ackerman, who had served as his editor until his now famous column that attacked Carter's plan to reinstitute military conscription. He had titled that particular piece "A Draft on My Back" and in it, he had attacked those he called the "cold warriors," insisting that yet another generation would be torn apart by the draft and that draft resistance would be widespread. He argued persuasively that before long, once again, forces would be deployed to some remote or perhaps not so remote corner of the world to prop up a corrupt anticommunist tyrant heading a Third World country which some, just *some*, in power perceived as vital to U.S. economic and security interests. He foretold another Vietnam arising and proved, by quoting Selective Service Director Robert F. Shuck, when he admitted all eighteen-year-old males could be registered within five days despite the lack of mandatory registration, that the country could mobilize every bit as quickly in the event of a war with or without mandatory registration for the draft.

"At the heart of the matter," he had argued in his piece, "is the call for a more interventionist foreign policy. That we as a nation are considering a post-Vietnam draft is a symbol of U.S. willingness to play a more aggressive role in global affairs. And," he concluded, "a peacetime draft makes intervention easier."

When he had given the column to Arline to edit, she had

returned it with the following words: "Class dismissed. You have learned your lessons well."

JJ could hear Arline as she splashed about and sang in the bathtub, her thin but sweet soprano in sharp contrast to the often hard edge of her everyday speaking voice. There were at least two Arlines. One thought true wealth was having an ambulance meet you at the theater after you had just seen *Camille* for the thirty-third time and the other was the iconoclast who upon meeting Margaret suggested she, too, lighten up, in her acting, or risk becoming just another fag-hag. He laughed as he remembered the look on Margaret's face. He laughed even harder as he remembered Arline, oblivious to Margaret standing and listening as she looked down, very down, on Arline as she purused her well-meant point.

Arline continually surprised and therefore energized him. She had taught him how two people can have two separate lives and still share one space. Not that they lived together—that subject had never arisen—but they did share as much of their time as their disparate schedules permitted. He was the day person, slaving over his columns at the desk he had installed in his bedroom, and she spent the bulk of her evenings as Lydia La Rosamoré. Every Friday night, she put Lydia and herself to bed, Lydia in her apartment and she in JJ's. Except for those weekends when he had David. Then she and Lydia doubled up as he preferred to be alone with his son, except for those frequent visits to his mother's or Marti's. Whatever feelings Arline may have had about her exclusion, she did not voice them but used the time to work on her plays and a situation comedy that she thought would be perfect for Shirley MacLaine. She continued to say nothing when those weekends JJ spent with David became more frequent as Jessamyn's work took her farther away and for longer periods of time. Jessamyn Giroux was now internationally known and on a first-name basis with Everyone who was Anyone. Her interviews with elder statesmen and world leaders were often quoted in the *New York Times*, *Washington Post*, and other newspapers of similar esteem. JJ didn't share the current popular view of Jessamyn's work. He found it efficient but cold, lacking heart and humor. But then, so did Jessamyn.

Arline was anything but cold and often, to his annoyance, she had too much heart and humor. When she wasn't crying at every injustice in the world, she was laughing at it all. Her emotions were always visible and so he often found her exhausting. She was standing before him now, wearing a black shawl about her head and shoulders and nothing else. In her hands she carried a lighted candle. Seeing the look on his face she said: "Well what the hell else does one wear to a vigil?" He didn't answer but simply opened the front door, daring her to leave as she was.

They were almost to the street when she began laughing and then dashed upstairs to complete the rest of her wardrobe.

*   *   *

The clock read three-thirty and still Reese sat at her desk staring into the unlit fireplace whose presence made the school-room atypical. The first week of school had just ended and the seven eight-year-olds of various colors and learning disabilities had just noisily departed, leaving her very much alone. As she sat in her stiff-backed chair, Reese thought of the children in the Dearborn School. They were there because they could not function in a public setting. She shared that with them. She, too, was having difficulty functioning, publicly and otherwise.

Reese's depression had come upon her when she had least expected it. It had arrived in an envelope with her divorce papers. Although her lawyer maintained she was finally a "free woman," Reese had never felt quite so trapped by emotions for which she had been unprepared. She was no longer Mrs. Thomas Ollson but Theresa Tomlinson Ollson. She was cut off and adrift, a person in her own right who could come and go as she pleased. On her own . . . alone . . . which is what she had wanted, only it felt better in theory than it did in practice. Who was she now? What license did the divorce grant her?

Days followed in which she felt overwhelmed by grief. She mourned as if someone or something precious had died. The doubts and misgivings followed. Her marriage had failed, which made her a failure. Had she tried hard enough? Had it been her fault? Had she been too demanding, not understanding and unrealistic? Bombarded by these second thoughts, all the solid rea-

2 8 9

sons for her having wanted the divorce and her freedom suddenly felt vacant and unsupportable. Seeing Thomas hadn't helped.

He had returned to Boston in early summer to promote the outreach center that would be opening in Dorchester, a densely populated suburb. He had resumed residence in the big house on Marlborough with Kelly and Mrs. McMahon. His days and nights were as they had been from the moment he had joined the DAV: busy. But shortly before its August opening, he had asked her to view the Dorchester center and then have dinner. She had been hesitant, fearful of the encounter, until she reminded herself that the man was Thomas and he had been her husband for nineteen years. Still was until the papers arrived.

He was like a child demonstrating his science project. His obvious pleasure at what he had helped to create pleased her. His appearance did not. She had been deeply shocked by his changes. He looked tired and drawn. Yet, heads still turned when they entered the restaurant. The curious were unaware that in the past year, he had aged five. She suggested a vacation. He agreed but didn't say if or when he would take one, only that in the fall he would begin a new job with the DAV: seminars throughout the country, the goal of which was to assist people in the human-health field in understanding the Vietnam veteran. She listened, as she always had, as he explained the work he would be doing and with whom. And then they spoke casually of Kelly, as if her summer schooling to make up the algebra class she had flunked during the spring term was an everyday teenage occurrence. They applauded Kristan's success as though they were a part of it when both knew neither was. They mentioned a postcard from Karl who was hitching and hiking his way through Europe that summer on monies he had earned in his part-time job at the local hospital. Neither wanted to admit they did not know what that job was and so they said nothing of it and little of Karl. They spoke in generalities. Except when it came to her. Then they didn't speak at all. If she had closed her eyes, they could have been having dinner any night of the week in any year of their marriage. Nothing had changed.

Reese had wanted to cry then for the wasted years and the bridge he wouldn't cross. Only later had she realized she hadn't tried to cross it either. When the evening ended and she was back in her apartment, Reese had wondered not only what it had been about but why he had called. Two weeks later the divorce had been final and she had naïvely thought her life would begin anew; that she would be a born-again woman. But the expected excitement, exhilaration, never arrived. Instead, she fell into an abyss, from the bottom of which she could see no rope, no ladder, and no help. She was, as they said, hanging by a thread. Suddenly the apartment she had so loved and which had not seemed small even when Kelly was living with her, felt claustrophobic. Even when it rained, she preferred a walk through Cambridge or a drive up the New England coast to remaining in it.

And then mercifully, school had begun. But even there, tucked away in the converted Victorian homes, she found no mercy and no relief. The children unnerved her. Their tantrums induced her own; their grief triggered hers. She had called Roger Ammis in desperation, thinking perhaps now that she was this so-called free woman, she could give of herself more freely and thus enter into their experience rather than remain emotionally detached. But a woman had answered his phone and so she had hung up feeling even more rejected.

The janitor knocking at her classroom door brought Reese back to reality. As she collected her things, she thought of the weekend ahead with dread. There was only one place she wanted to be. She wondered if she went whether she would be welcome or if she were making a mistake. Suddenly it didn't matter. She would go. There were certain times, no matter what had been the relationship, that the person a girl wants most is her mother, even if that girl is forty-one and the mother of children herself.

*   *   *

Matthew wasn't asking but telling her. Which was his right, she kept reminding herself as she listened but heard only her own inner voice rather than his words. The smile on her face belied her true feelings, and he, so usually perceptive as to what she was feeling, this time, because of his excitement, was not.

Storefront centers. A goal of ninety-one, all to be located where the population figures indicated a concentration of Vietnam-era veterans. He would be developing the manuals to be used by the teams of trained professionals in the centers. He would be training and working with the staff psychiatrists and psychologists who would man the Veterans Administration's newly created Operation Outreach programs. It was greatly influenced by the success of the DAV's, he admitted. And as she dimly listened, she thought; Yes, and you've been greatly influenced by Thomas.

He was explaining that, as assistant to the director, he would be based in Washington, working in the V.A.'s Mental Health and Behavior Science Service Division. He would be an elder statesman—he laughed when he used the words; she didn't—using his in-service military psychiatric experience. He had been asked to participate because he was one of the first recognized authorities in his field to report on the delayed stress syndrome.

Matthew sat on the edge of the sofa waiting for Marti to respond.

"Will you be home for Christmas?" she asked, annoying herself with the shallowness of her response.

"I don't report until the first," he said, looking at her with his usual assessing eye. "Marti, this is something I want, something I need to do. Certainly you of all people can understand that."

She wanted to pump his hand, slap his back, applaud and congratulate him for doing what so few would—give up a lucrative practice to do something he deemed necessary, of value to others and therefore to himself. All on his own. Which is exactly what bothered her. She did not understand. Not his reasoning but her reactions. Inwardly, she heard herself, an accusing voice that wanted to know . . . how could he? That voice, *her*, wanted to accuse him of neglect, of selfishness, of putting himself before her and his child. Which is exactly what she had done in the past and was still doing.

She remained silent, lost in her reactions, surprised and then horrified that she could still feel so rejected and therefore worthless because a man was leaving her. No matter that he had every right to, no matter that there was something he felt he had to do, internally the voice said: if he cared, he would stay.

"Marti, I'll be here as often as possible. I could be a permanent weekend guest. And it's only for a few years." He paused, stopped, just as he was about to offer more encouragement. His face reddened as he said, "What the hell am I apologizing for?"

Still she couldn't respond. Not to him. Within she was maintaining a dialogue. Equality. Equal rights. For whom? Me but not him? Isn't what's good for the goose also good for the gander? I don't want equality, she decided. I never really did. Lip service. Somewhere within, buried and unadmitted, is that part of me, of every woman that wants to be protected, provided for even if it means taking a subservient role, even if that role is only in one's head. We trade in our selves for protection. And even when we break free of that thinking, we really don't. It's always there lurking in some corner, waiting to show itself in some new way.

Matthew's face reflected his anger. He had come to her in what was for him great excitement. And fear. Not of her reaction but of the decision he was making. He was changing his life, closing the door, at least temporarily, on his practice, and becoming reinvolved with the military. But he had never really become uninvolved. All these months, he had maintained constant contact with Thomas and found he was envying him. And when the V.A. had called because Congress was forcing them into their Operation Outreach program, he felt as if he had been given an additional decade in his life. Instead of turning fifty, he was again turning forty and he felt lighter, more youthful, and more exuberant than he had in years. Ninety-one centers for the Vietnam-era veteran. Not just those who had served in the war but any soldier, those in supply, those who had carried body bags—*all* who had served in the Southeast Theater from 1964 to 1975.

He had been certain she would share his excitement, that she would not only understand but be happy that he had found something that mattered so deeply to him. Hadn't she come to him in a similar fashion after her return two Novembers back from the National Conference of Women in Houston? Hadn't he understood, supported her decision even if part of that decision had been not to marry him?

"I'm sorry, Matthew," said Marti finally. "I'm behaving badly. It's just such a shock. How did it happen? I mean, how did it come about?"

"They came to me, Marti. Back in September . . ."

"September? But that's two months ago. Why didn't you mention it?" she asked, the voice inside now insisting she had been deceived after all, that she hadn't come first. But why should I have, she argued, disliking herself at the moment.

"There was nothing to mention at first," Matthew was explaining. "I initially rejected the idea as impractical. But they persisted, as did my conscience. And my envy. I've admired Thomas's dedication for a very long time now."

"And what about his life?" snapped Marti. "Do you envy or admire that too?"

Matthew looked at Marti patiently. "For some, life is something other than, or different from home and family. It may not be perfect or even optimal, but it is what works best at the moment for Thomas. It makes him feel good about himself, his life. He is contributing, or if there is such a word as 'retributing', he is doing that too. He is fighting back, making the years that were spent in a useless war useful."

"His 'usefulness' to others has only estranged him from his children and his wife," said Marti, annoyed, again more with herself for her argument than with Matthew.

"Which makes him all the more admirable," replied Matthew slowly. "It is all the more difficult for Thomas because he has lost so much."

"And you have nothing to lose?" asked Marti, instantly horrified by the implied threat in her question. Who is this person making me speak so? she wondered.

"No. You can only lose what you can't find," said Matthew. "I have a daughter. I know where she is. I know my feelings for her. I know what I can and will be for her. And you, you're a part of my life as important as any."

But not more so, she wanted to cry but didn't, allowing the thought to remain in her head where it belonged.

"Marti, things will not be all that different. With your appearances about the country, your speeches, your fund raisers, weekends are usually all we ever have together anyway. That may not change. All that much," added Matthew when he thought of the number of cities he would be visiting beginning in January with Los Angeles.

"I hate this damn war. It never ends," said Marti. "It killed my

2 9 4

father. It damn near killed me. It killed both my brothers' marriages . . ."

"That's bullshit, Marti. The war does indeed go on, and it may go on for years to come—but it isn't war but people who cause the failure of relationships. You, actually, were one of the lucky ones. People cared about your involvement, your wounds. They also cared about your father's death. That's more than what can be said of the men who served and those who died in Vietnam. They are nothing more than statistics. But they exist, Marti, and because they do, I must. My statistics are no different from yours and they deserve the same equal rights. Don't you understand?"

Marti looked at Matthew and then had to look away. She had failed him. Her emotions had blocked her intellect, making her not be what she would have wished for him. "Give me time," she said quietly. "I just need time. I truly know what you are doing is not only important but right for you. I just have to understand that it is really all right for me. I'm sorry, Matthew. I know I must be a great disappointment to you, but believe me, no more than I am to myself."

*   *   *

If there was one thing Arline Ackerman had, it was an impeccable sense of timing. In her work, as in her life, she always knew when to end a scene. In her comedies, characters came and went, never overstaying their welcome and thus never losing their interest. It was one of the qualities Shirley MacLaine had most admired about Arline's projected TV series; that and its subtle but decidedly feminist point of view. With banana peels and cream pies. That she had rejected it had nothing to do with the quality of the work but the fact that she simply didn't want the grind of a weekly series.

As she drained yet another glass of white wine, thinking and talking to herself for entertainment, Arline once again understood MacLaine's position. All too well. If there was one thing she had recently come to hate, it was a weekly or a daily grind. It impinged on one's creativity and generally made one feel constipated.

The evening had been stultifying, thought Arline as she gazed about the room, a grind, a TV season all in one night. Despite the balloons and noisemakers JJ had provided at her insistence, it looked less a New Year's Eve party than it did the First Annual

Meeting of the Deeply Depressed. Arline was certain that at the stroke of midnight, it would not be Father Time chased about the room by the New Year baby but the guests. By little men in white coats. With butterfly nets.

Only JJ could put together such Chekovian drama on New Year's Eve, thought Arline as she took yet another glass of white wine. Only he would fill a room with his sister, her "ole man" who would soon, as in tomorrow, not be her "ole man" with any regularity, his brother—another Mr. Laughs—and Nelson and Alicia Naismith. Talk about your fun people! Arline shuddered. To think JJ had preferred this to the late show at the Ritz or dancing at Xenon was as amazing as it was annoying.

Of course the ingredients for a lively evening were here, thought Arline. A man, a now-famous columnist, attacks the Congress for providing money to establish outreach programs for Vietnam veterans when it does nothing, gives nothing, to those "soldiers" who served by resisting and deserting. That column comes under all sorts of fire from both the right and left. Enter into this columnist's life, and on New Year's Eve, his brother and sister's lover—both of whom are involved in the very concept the columnist has attacked. Human drama if ever there was any, thought Arline. As she sipped her drink, she wondered how she would handle these people if they were characters in one of her plays. The answer was immediate: put them all on a bus and drive them off a cliff, thus ending theirs and their audience's misery quickly. She laughed. Which drew stares. Arline shushed herself. Laughing was definitely the odd thing to do this night, or any night actually at JJ's. He confused the sound with the plumbing and complained to the super. There would be nothing but quiet at the super's tonight, thought Arline as her eyes again took in the guests. If anything, there would be a crying jag before the evening was out and an old acquaintance to be forgotten. Glancing at her watch, Arline saw it was much too early to pull the curtain down on the human drama that wasn't unfolding. This was one play, she decided as she downed her drink and rose from her chair, in which the body language was louder and more informative than the dialogue.

JJ watched as Arline weaved unsteadily toward the stack of records Alicia and Nelson had brought with them. He knew she would chose something loud, intrusive, and divisive, separating people from their thoughts and one another. He would hate it, even though it might be a welcome intrusion. The music, like so many things Arline introduced into their lives, demanded attention. Time wasters, they took him away from his work, shattering the seclusion in which he lived even when surrounded, which was often how he felt, by Arline's considerable presence.

As he looked about his living room, JJ realized it was strange having Thomas there. It was even stranger that Thomas had elected to be there. On his own. Marti could not have twisted his arm any more than she had tried to twist his own when she asked if she might bring Thomas with them. There had been an awkwardness as they shook hands at the front door and that awkwardness had remained throughout the evening, as no one acknowledged.the past and to a lesser extent the present that kept those in the room in divided camps.

Throughout the evening, JJ found himself staring at Thomas and wondering who this man was. It was not an enemy he faced, but a man who seem determined and yet tired, old behind his still youthful appearance. And sad. Most of all that. Which is how Marti looked, and that pained him.

Marti had underestimated his importance in her life. Not a husband. Not a lover. Something in between and still undefined. She had grown to depend on him, not for anything in particular but just for being there. And not in some passive way that typified so many marriages. True, his presence was a comfort, but again that was but half of what it was. He made her feel secure not because he was a man but because he felt that within himself. Tomorrow, thought Marti, no matter how Matthew insisted nothing need change, something would. For both of them. They would be on their own. She would feel alone and, despite his reassurances, she would feel rejected. Which she was. No matter how he argued the point, or how she argued it with herself, he was rejecting her in favor of something else that took precedence.

That she had once done the same hardly made it easier. But she would be all right, she told herself. Within her was the real security. She would nourish and sustain herself. It was a pledge Marti recited repeatedly, as if in the repetition could come the belief.

Marti checked the time. An hour to midnight. The party must be grim if she was hoping for a phone call from her babysitter suggesting she return home because Lynne had a slight fever. Lynne, the love of her life, and the fun of it. She missed her daughter horribly when she was touring for the ERA. Now, with Matthew away, she would either tour less, and just when the movement needed her more, or she would take Lynne with her. Not a viable alternative. Lynne did not travel well. Perhaps her mother would do yet another tour of grandmother duty. If she wasn't busy at the theater or at the church. Her mother, like Ali and Mark, had her own life and was, Marti kept reminding herself, entitled to it. The thought made her search out Matthew, who was talking to Thomas but looking at her. She smiled even as she thought she might cry.

He knew that expression. But then he knew her. What he didn't know was whether their separation would alter their relationship. That depended on her. There was no need for a woman as beautiful and as accomplished to be alone. She would have her choices and she would make them just as he had made his. He loved her, not enough to stay but more than enough to "forsake all others," without being asked or promising to do so. He was much like Thomas in that respect. He honored his commitments and found them hard to break once they were made.

There was something haunting about the two girls dancing. Although their names were Arline and Alicia, it could have been Kristan and Kelly, thought Thomas as he remembered when his girls had danced together in his living room on an occasion such as this. He had wanted to see how JJ lived, which was why when

Marti extended the invitation he had accepted. Not that he understood why it was suddenly important to see JJ in his surroundings. On the surface, it didn't seem that his brother was suffering from any of the symptoms he had now seen in so many men who had served in the war. Not he or his friend, Nelson, the man he had once feared would take Kristan from him in body and spirit. But it hadn't been Nelson who had done that.

Uncomfortable, Thomas wanted to leave but had no place to go. New York had seem preferable to Boston when Reese, after he had asked, had said it was none of his business what she was doing New Year's Eve. And what business had Kelly that she preferred it to him when he offered to spend the evening with her?

He wanted to warn Matthew. He wanted to explain about the work. It had its pulls. All away from home and any semblance of a normal life. There was as much chaos in peacetime as there was in war. His own new tour of duty would take him many times across the country and back. But to where? Home was now a lectern on a podium, informing influential people who shouldn't have needed to be informed how the Vietnam veteran had helped the community by going to Vietnam and how it was now time for the community to help the veteran. The films and slides he presented of *his* veterans, in combat both on the battlefields of war and on the battlefields of their everyday, often jobless, unfocused lives, were indelibly etched in his mind. Like the pictures of their families some men carried in their wallets.

Once again, Thomas looked at JJ and was surprised to find his brother looking at him. Thomas wondered what pictures JJ carried next to his heart and if they, too, caused him as much pleasure as they did pain.

The music had become insufferably loud. Even louder was Arline. JJ hadn't meant to snap or even to bark, but suddenly he heard himself ordering her to stop. The room silenced. Arline responded by turning up the volume and increasing the frenzy of her dancing. He pulled the plug from the wall and the record ended with a screech. She stared at him and with the back of her hand she swept everything off the buffet table, drinks and dips

2 9 9

colliding as they fell in a mess on the carpet. Within seconds she was atop the table, glaring at JJ, loudly humming "Tea for Two" as she tap-danced, something she had just learned in the classes he had refused to attend with her.

Suddenly Alicia remembered she had promised her sister that she and Nelson would arrive before midnight. Their exit was hasty, with Arline not bothering to come down from her perch. Miraculously, but minutes later, Marti received the phone call she had wished for from her sitter. But it wasn't Lynne who was unwell but the sitter. And within seconds, JJ and Arline were alone in the room, their respective silences putting an end both knew to more than the old year.

A year ago, thought JJ, he would have found her dancing silly fun, charming, a crazy thing to have done—which would have made her all the more endearing. A year ago, when he had been young again. Now, he found it and much of the behavior he had once enjoyed annoying. Somehow, within the year, he had become too old and she too young.

"You bore me, too," said Arline as if reading his mind. "I'm young, damn it, and although you are, you won't act it. I like being half woman, half child. I wish you could be half man, half boy. The potential is there, but the ability is missing. That boy in you is gone, lost somewhere, perhaps in Canada. I thought maybe I could bring him home, but he remains a prisoner of some kind of war which defeats me. I can't take it anymore."

She was collecting her things, preparing to leave, and although JJ felt he should stop her, he knew he should not. Involved as each was in his and her own thoughts, neither saw the man standing in the bathroom doorway.

"And you've hurt me," continued Arline. "Oh, God, how you've hurt me. Not that you meant or mean to. You just do."

JJ was staring at her, his face reflecting concern and confusion.

"Yes, you! You hurt. You're so horribly rejecting and you're so unaware of it. From the beginning, you excluded me. Why didn't you take me to Nelson's wedding? Why aren't I included in your Sunday activities with David? Why wasn't I at your mother's on Christmas? And you don't even realize that these actions speak louder than any words. Well, I hear you and I don't like what I hear. Now hear me. You're selfish, unthinking, and for all your bleeding in that wonderful caring column of yours, you are un-feeling. You're half dead and I'm tired of trying to pump some life back into you. I want something more. I need something more. It's called fun."

She was at the door and he was following, wanting to say something that would make her realize that he cared, had even loved much of what she was and what she had been to him. But words wouldn't come.

"Well, kid, should old acquaintance be forgot and all that jazz." At the opened door, she turned again to face him. "If only you weren't such a terrific guy this would be a helluva lot less painful and I'd have a better exit line than out-with-the-old-and-in-with-the-new. Somehow that doesn't sound funny. Just sad."

And she was gone, although the sounds of her sobbing could be heard even after he had closed and locked the door. He was surprised by Thomas, rooted in the doorway of his bathroom, surprised mainly by the compassion he saw in his brother's face. Thomas was staring at JJ, not quite believing that what he saw in his brother's eyes was what he most avoided each day when he shaved, brushed his teeth, and combed his hair—a reflection of himself.

*   *   *

She was trapped. Somewhere to go but no way to get there. All exits blocked. The phone call had made her a prisoner and, with nothing but time before her, she considered her crimes. She was guilty, of being here and not there where she was needed. But I was needed here too, she pleaded with her internal judge.

Had Marti left the gala and her seat on the dais, it would have drawn attention to her and away from the fact that the Who's Who of Hollywood had assembled to celebrate the thirteenth anniver-sary of California's National Organization for Women.

She had received the phone call many times before, but prior to this night only in nightmares. Then, as now, the call came when she was away from home. The message was always the same:

Lynne or Mark was sick. In the dream, as today, there was never a way for her to fly home immediately. Always she awoke from the dream battered emotionally but otherwise unharmed. But this time, thought Marti as she played with a swizzle stick, it was no dream. There would be no merciful awakening. Her baby daughter was sick, running a temperature of one hundred and four for no apparent reason. Her mother, after trying all the conventional procedures, had rushed Lynne to New York Hospital.

And she was waiting. In the Los Angeles Room of the Century Plaza Hotel, before seven hundred celebrants, with a smile pasted on her face and her heart threatening to break through the sheerness of her gown, she waited for another phone call. She had left explicit instructions that if her mother called, a message should be taken and passed to her at the dais. No matter what its content.

The waiting was the worst, that and the fact that with the time differential, she could not leave for New York until the following morning and not arrive until late that afternoon. A lifetime. Hers and her daughter's. And what would she do during that time and space between coasts when she would be deprived of all communication?

Marti wished Matthew was with her or, better, in New York with Lynne.

What? Yes, of course, she said as she passed the butter to Jane Fonda seated on her left. Fonda was looking at her curiously, but how could she confide to a stranger that she was crazed with worry because her daughter was ill? Marti brushed a stray strand of hair from her face. She was tired. Within the past week she had made two trips to Los Angeles for the ERA. On Monday, she had taped "Dinah" with Carol Burnett. She had decided to return to New York to spend the remainder of the week with Lynne before flying back to Los Angeles for the Sunday evening NOW event because so much of her month of March had been spent on the road stumping for the amendment. Marti needed to sleep but doubted if sleep would come this evening unless Lynne was out of danger.

Lynne had been her usual bouncy and demanding self when she had left that morning for Los Angeles. Far more bouncy and better than she had felt in her exhausted state, thought Marti. In the past three months, she had shuttled between coasts and cities, never permitting longer than a forty-eight-hour separation from home. Not unless Matthew was there, and Matthew was seldom there—what with his concerns for his own project. She had been left alone to manage and it had proven difficult, so difficult that *she* should be one of the recipients this evening of NOW's Women of Courage awards. Only, where is my courage now? asked Marti as her stomach continued to churn. She was in danger of coming apart; she could feel that in the tightness in her throat. The emotions were caught there, threatening to come out in a scream or a torrent of tears.

In order to survive the evening, she decided that she would focus on anything but her problem. Her eyes found the crystal chandelier that dominated the room and it made her think of Jayne Meadows's earrings. And Meadows, particularly her laugh, made her think of Carol Burnett, the "Dinah" show that past week, and the woman in the audience who saw ERA as a license to "draft our daughters and send them off to war." Marti had gently pointed out that Congress already had the power to draft an army and to designate who shall serve: men or women. And then she had asked the woman, again gently, if she had a son. The woman did. And she had said of her own son, of her Mark, that if he went to war, if he were killed, she would mourn him no less, no more, than she would her daughter. The woman had not wished to understand until Marti had asked . . . "Why is it we don't protest the drafting of our sons but we do our daughters? My son is no less precious to me or expendable." They had all understood that and had applauded her words.

Another woman then blamed the breakup of the family on ERA and quoted from that section of the Bible that maintained woman was created to be man's helpmeet.

She had been very careful not to offend the fundamentalists. Again gently, she had stated that no law can maintain or ruin a family, that families are held together by love and understanding, and that when a family unit splinters, the reasons are much deeper than the ERA. But *should* that unit break apart, she maintained, then the wife must be as protected, afforded the same rights under the law as the husband. Lastly, she had taken the most controversial point of the issue and had boldly declared that "any religion that requires woman to be subservient to man cannot stand in a culture where almost half our workforce is now female." There had been an audible gasp, but there had also been applause.

She had felt so sure of herself that day, Marti recalled. But if she had, why then did she look with such wonder at Carol Burnett who Arline felt would be perfect for the series Shirley MacLaine had rejected? The role demanded a middle-aged woman who was strong yet vulnerable, attractive and sexual without being blatantly so. Marti thought Burnett could play it as easily as she played all her other roles. Marti had wanted to ask how she did it—combining work with the raising of three daughters, a marriage, and a life.

A hand suddenly covered Marti's. The smile on Jean Stapleton's face was generous and Marti returned it as best she could. She began to tremble, frightened by the reality of her situation. Her daughter was ill and she should be there, not here. The "should" was that of voices she had heard since childhood, a race memory of what a woman should be and do. Children come first, it said, and Lynne would, Marti vowed. Even more than she already had.

The message was passed from Joan Hackett to Della Reese, and, as it made its way to her, Marti knew the trips for ERA around the country had ended. She would find another way to guarantee that Lynne would never be a second-class citizen or a "helpmeet" or made to think of herself as either. Every problem has its solution. How often her mother had said that.

The envelope was in her hands. She looked at it for a moment before using her nail to slit its seal. The message was short but very sweet.

Fever broke as did the gum where the new tooth made its appearance. Come home soon. Love. Your mother and daughter.

*   *   *

"I hear noises and I jump for cover . . . hide in the basement . . . fall flat on the floor. Sometimes I think I'm going crazy. . . . I can't sleep at night. I keep getting up, checking to

3 0 4

see if the doors are locked. . . . Nothing makes much sense anymore. I can't seem to relate to anyone or anything. . . . I think about the people I killed and think maybe I should have done things differently. So many women and children dead. I know if I hadn't killed them, the booby traps they carried would have killed me. But still . . ."

Above the noise of the 747 jet's engines, Thomas heard their voices chattering incessantly. They were often with him long after the group sessions. They lived with him from city to city and it was their voices that spoke with him in hotel board rooms and medical schools when he addressed doctors, lawyers, psychologists—all those involved in the human-health field. From Gillette, Wyoming; and Boise, Idaho; to Knoxville and Nashville, Tennessee; to Winston-Salem and Columbia, North Carolina; he had in his seminars introduced these voices to their fellow Americans. Their voices and his own.

"You must look at the veteran not as a felon or a victim but as a man who fought for his country. You must be aware the veteran will test you and ask things like 'What were you doing during the Vietnam War?' But mainly, mostly, you must learn to separate any feelings you might have about the war in order to look at our veteran clearly."

He hated that part of his speech. He hated pleading his case before an incompetent jury, hated pleading a case that should not have needed pleading.

"The treatment goals involve: rebuilding trust, giving the veteran time to grieve for a buddy killed, restoring pride in the individual, learning how to treat the woman partner."

The last always caused him to pause. "Women also experienced what their men did: isolation, helplessness, feelings of worthlessness. The veteran has to understand that his comment, 'Everything would be all right if my wife understood', has no bearing on his case. The veteran must learn his wife has needs of her own."

The woman partner. . . . No matter how often he spoke the words, Reese's face came to mind. As it did now. He had been attending a seminar in Hawaii when she called. Their Hawaii, the place where they had spent his military leaves from Vietnam ser-

3 0 5

vice. His surprise at her phone call was nothing in comparison to his surprise at her demand that he return immediately.

He did not know what to expect, but as Thomas heard the landing gear lowered, he knew what he feared: A confidential talk during which she would explain about 'Him.' It didn't matter who 'He' was, just that 'He' was and that she would be marrying again. But why not wait until he had returned, since he managed to be home several times each month? What was this sudden urgency. Unless. . . . Thomas's stomach knotted at the prospect. Could Reese, at her age, be. . . . He couldn't finish the thought. Even now, he rejected the idea that Reese was having sex. To consider another man sharing her body was impossible.

To have shared his own body with another had been almost impossible. Almost. He continued to regret his encounter with the social worker in Houston, although he did not ask himself, and therefore did not know, why. She was a mature, attractive middle-aged woman who had actively pursued and seduced him while maintaining the pretense of his courting her. Which he had not done. He had been flattered by her attention and grateful for her company. Still, he had never thought to take her to bed until they were there, in her apartment, and he, for the first time since his marriage, was physically engaged with another woman. More than once. For the week he had been in the city.

He had felt nothing except an increased feeling of loss and separation. She did not seem to notice, which he found surprising since she was a social worker and as such he thought she would be attuned to another's reactions and feelings. They had parted without ceremony; she, casually suggesting he call when next in town, and he, saying he would when he knew he wouldn't—be in town or phone. She was a "perfectly lovely woman" for whom he had felt nothing.

As the jumbo jet circled Logan International Airport waiting for the clearance that would take them down through the spring rain and into Boston, Thomas wondered what he would feel for Reese when confronted with her face to face. As the plane dipped sharply, causing several passengers to gasp, he hoped he would feel as little as possible.

Unable to sit, Reese was pacing by the landing gate, anxiously waiting for Thomas to appear while hoping he would not. It wasn't fair, she thought. She should be as divorced from him in feeling as she was in fact. She should no longer be concerned with him but with herself. Why was that so very difficult? Guilt. And more guilt, making her feel heavier and heavier, no matter how thin she became. Once married, once a mother, never free, always burdened, always guilty.

She had not felt this anxious or upset even this past winter when she discovered she had gonorrhea. Nor had she been particularly anxious or upset—just disgusted—when she realized she did not know which of the three men she had been dating, two fairly frequently, the other, an eyes-across-the frozen-food-section-of-the-supermarket encounter, had given the disease to her. It had been awkward asking. Neither of the two men she had been steadily seeing were infected. Neither had taken it well that she was. Both stopped calling. She had expected they would.

But she had known exactly what to do then; she, the ampicillin and probenecid the doctor had prescribed. She had only just healed emotionally and now this. Only now there was no certainty about what to do. Thomas would take it badly. What he would say or do she couldn't predict. He might refuse responsibility. If he did, she would assume it. Not gladly or even willingly, but as part of what her personal integrity demanded.

She saw him just as he saw her. Should she hug or kiss him? Shake his hand? He looked tired; he always did. But he also looked worried, less confident than usual, almost scared. He didn't know it, thought Reese, but he had good reason to be.

Thomas found her in her room, lying on her bed between magazines and half-empty boxes of Oreos, the TV tuned to one of the late-afternoon reruns. From her uncombed hair and the housecoat she wore, Thomas judged she had never left the house that day. Without lipstick, without coloring of any kind, she was very beautiful. His little girl . . . beautiful. His littlest girl. She did not acknowledge his presence as he sat at the end and edge of the bed facing her. He said nothing but reached out to hold her ankle.

"Mother told you?" she asked, the tremor obvious to his ears.

3 0 7

He nodded. "What are you going to do?" she questioned, fear now as obvious as the tremor in her voice.

"It's not what I'm going to do but what you want to do," he replied softly.

She looked at him and at the hand that so gently held her ankle. She had expected him to yell, to perhaps even hit her as he once had when he was enraged. She had expected all kinds of punishment, undefined in her imagination, which made it all the more frightening—but not this. She started to cry, softly at first, and then loud, terrifying, terrified noises coming from deep within.

"Why didn't you tell me?" he asked.

"I was afraid," she replied and then, seeing the expression on his face, added, "Yes, afraid. Of you. We were all afraid of you."

"But I'm your father. You're my daughter. I love you."

She looked at him, stunned to hear words he had never before spoken. "I never felt you really loved me. If you did, why did you leave then? Why have you left now? You never loved anything but yourself and that stupid, stupid war."

"I hated the war!" he exploded. "Hated it then and hate it even more now. And no matter what you thought or felt, I always loved you. You and your mother and your sister and brother. Why else did I do it? *All* of it. It wasn't just for me then or now. I didn't sacrifice part of my life, my family, to indulge myself but to give you something—an inheritance more valuable than money."

She looked at him without understanding his words but feeling he was giving something he had never had before: a large part of himself. His hand was covering his eyes and, from the way his body was shaking, she understood he was crying. She flung herself at him, curling into his arms as she had when a child. He rocked her as he stroked her hair and made sounds that had no verbal meaning.

"Daddy, what should I do?" she asked when her own tears had subsided.

"What you want to do. Your mother tells me you're four months pregnant, late but not too late for an abortion if that's what you want," said Thomas, hating, as opposed as he was to that possibility, the words he was speaking.

"I want the baby," said Kelly, sounding not at all like a little girl but like a grown woman. "I want the baby," she repeated. "I want something of my own to love."

Her words hurt more than the ones Reese had used to tell him of Kelly's pregnancy.

"We will have your baby," he said, rising from the bed. "The question is where. You need someplace where you will not have to deal with anything but you and your baby. Just give me some time to work things through," said Thomas as he continued to hold his daughter, to stroke her hair and calm her fears. "Your mother and I are here," he said. And as he spoke, it almost seemed to Thomas as if Reese was there with him in Kelly's room instead of in Cambridge where she, too, was lying on a bed, shivering, alone, wishing desperately that there was someone to gently hold her ankle, or her hand, in support and love.

BOOK THREE
1·9·8·1
ARRIVALS

14

THE CURLY-HAIRED CHILD WAS STANDING BEFORE THE TV screen staring into the familiar face. "Mama?" he asked.

"Yes, David, that's Mama," replied JJ as he watched mother-and-son together, although separated as they frequently now were by miles of TV wire and assignments that spanned the globe. David patted Jessamyn's face with his hand, leaving jam imprints on the TV screen, and then resumed his play with the Erector Set. Within minutes, JJ knew David would bound up from the floor again, look out the frosted windows, and ask if they could now do their usual Sunday tour of the docks where both could watch the Day Line boats coming and going along the Hudson River. But the day was typically January, bitter and biting, and made even more so by a swirling wind that pushed thick, gray clouds through the overcast sky.

As he sat watching Jessamyn and the week-long hysteria that had gripped the country, JJ's hand absentmindedly stroked David's head as the boy played at his feet. His son delighted him. He was bright, inventive, and affectionate. He seemed more comfortable with his dual living arrangements than did either of his parents. It had surprised JJ that Jessamyn was leaving David more frequently, and with him and not with his governess. It also surprised JJ that, according to David, "Mama cried" each time she left. Such concern and its accompanying emotion did not blend with JJ's image of Jessamyn, who was even now remaining dispassionate in the face of mass patriotic hysteria.

". . . and on Tuesday, the fifty-two, escorted by Algerian diplomats, left Teheran where they had been held hostage by the Iranians for four hundred and forty-four days. Their flight to freedom began this past Tuesday when an Algerian airliner flew them to Algiers where two U.S. Air Force planes then took them to Wiesbaden, Germany, for debriefing, rehabilitation, and a meeting with former President Jimmy Carter. And now, within minutes, the moment millions of Americans have been awaiting: the landing of *Freedom One*, the VC 137 carrying the fifty-two hostages, here at Stewart Air Force Base. It is an emotionally charged crowd that awaits. For more than the fifty-two, for millions, this will be a joyous homecoming indeed."

Although Jessamyn was only reporting and not making the news, JJ's anger directed itself at her. Why didn't she or any of her TV brethren point out the disparity? Couldn't they see it, or did they chose not to report on what was so very obvious? Fifty-two innocent people had been taken and held by force and, in doing so, a small nation had taken a major worldwide power and controlled fifty-two parts of it and more, like so many puppets on very many strings. The people of that major power, after years of passivity, raised their voices as one and demanded justice and retribution. In the end, they settled for a "moral victory" in a not-quite-war they hadn't won. But what of that other war that hadn't quite been won? Where was its "moral victory?"

He had raised these questions in his column. A decade ago, millions had been taken and held by force by their own government in a not-quite-war that now seemed very far away to most, but not all. Then, too, a small nation dangled a major power on strings that stretched across oceans, pulling people in varying directions. That not-quite-war had never been resolved; its participants, on and off the battlefield, ignored, not honored as those fifty-two were about to be. The emotion for the hostages, JJ had maintained, was misplaced and undeserved. His position produced his most abusive and threatening mail. It also caused seven of the now one hundred and thirty-eight newspapers that carried his column to discontinue their support.

For his efforts, he had received unsolicited advice from, of all people, Jessamyn. Normally when he collected David for his weekends, Jessamyn was either not at home or not available, preferring that her secretary or housekeeper deliver last-minute instructions or cautions to him. But this weekend, she had appeared with David. After a quick hug, she sent the child to wait downstairs with the doorman, a most unusual occurrence, JJ had thought, given Jessamyn's almost morbid preoccupation, a current celebrity malady, with kidnapping.

"You're digging yet another ditch for yourself," she had said without preface. He had known exactly what she was referring to, having heard similar words from Marti. "You had just begun to build up credibility with a sector of this country and now you're destroying it." At that moment, he had wanted to destroy her and all the self-righteous smugness she represented. "I'm not arguing with the efficacy of your words but with the words themselves. Nobody is interested. You're whipping a dead horse, and guess who that dead horse is? You!"

"But thousands like me—thousands—not fifty-two—were held hostage by force and by our own country. And outside our own country. We were never made to feel welcome upon our return."

"And you never will be," replied Jessamyn coldly. "And if you weren't still such a child of privilege—a Tiernan, an Ollson—so used to asking and receiving—you would give it up, leave it behind. But you persist like some godawful spoiled brat who wants what he wants when he wants it. Well, you can't have this, JJ, now or ever. Accept that. You cannot rewrite history or change it any more than you can ever really change people."

"My critical commentary is about change, or there is no purpose to it," he had argued.

She had looked at him with amusement. "Always the crusader and always so fucking pompous. And naïve. Or is it just plain dumb? JJ, you have a brilliant mind. You write a damn good column. But you don't know people because you've lived far too long inside yourself. The public needs this homecoming. It needs this celebration. Desperately, I might add. If you attempt to take it away, it will take away much of what you have created for yourself and I assume for David."

It was only after she had closed the door behind him that he had wanted to ask: What's in this for you? But there was nothing. He could see that. It was unsolicited but straight-from-the-shoulder advice. It had cost nothing to give and it had come from one of America's most admired *and* trusted voices. Begrudgingly, as he watched Jessamyn on camera, standing before the airstrip where *Freedom One* would land, JJ admitted she was good. With her reputation secured, she was now heartless in her own interrogations of facts and fancies.

JJ was watching Jessamyn as though she had never been his wife, which he sometimes doubted she had been. Other than David, there was no bond between them, no memories that caused either grief or pleasure. It was as if all emotion, even the anger, had been erased by that great pain reliever . . . time. Jessamyn no longer interested him. Few women did. Since Arline, his life had been about work and little else. Occasionally he wondered about this half-life of his but with the weekends came David, and his wondering ceased.

". . . and the U.S. agreed to return eight billion dollars in Iranian assets frozen since the November 1979 seizure of hostages in the American embassy in Teheran . . ."

He was not stupid. He knew his own assets were frozen; in part if not in whole. He did not need Jessamyn to point out that people were more important than issues. He knew that, but he just couldn't feel it. He could only feel the weight of what he felt was his responsibility, hanging heavily from his neck and on his shoulders. He was vulnerable only to David, and it hurt him that he could not write about, because he could not feel, the human experience.

". . . and now . . . I've just been informed. . . . Yes . . . the approach of *Freedom One*. Within minutes, the ordeal of fifty-two of America's men and women will have officially come to an end."

How lucky for them, and how unfortunate for me and all others like me, thought JJ bitterly. How very unfortunate indeed.

"Come on, David," JJ said suddenly. "Let's not let a little weather stop us. The boats are waiting."

". . . More than twenty thousand people are lining the seventeen miles of road between the Air Force base and the Hotel

Thayer in West Point where these fifty-two men and women will be reunited with their families. And Tuesday, ten times that number is expected to greet the hostages when they visit President Reagan at the White House. As the scores of yellow ribbons here attest, a nation remembers. . . . It cares."

Thomas felt a hand squeeze his shoulders as he watched the live telecast. It rested there silently, saying as much in its way as the nation's symbolic yellow ribbons.

". . . President Carter had reported after his meeting with the hostages earlier this week in Wiesbaden that they were subjected to acts of barbarism and mental and physical abuse. But today, those wounds are being cleansed by a grateful nation . . ."

His own wounds reopened as the years of his own mental and physical abuse swirled in pictures and feelings within his head.

"Are you sure you want to watch this?"

Thomas signaled he did not and Vinnie released his hand from Thomas's shoulder in order to move toward the TV. Thomas was no longer surprised by Vinnie's sensitivities. Intuitively, he had known this was the place to bring Kelly, the place where she could have her baby and herself in peace. Somehow, he had known Vinnie would accept without condoning or condemning as he had been to many of the places Kelly had seemingly been and had successfully returned.

As Vinnie led the way to the patio where the sun was beginning its afternoon slide across the pale blue sky and into Biscayne Bay, Thomas was again awed by the beauty of the setting. The house was nestled between the bay and Bay Road, hidden from public view by huge iron gates and tropical trees and flora that towered over them. The waters of the glistening bay rose to the dock where Jamie and Lisa, bundled in light windbreakers, were playing under Este's watchful eye. Thomas, Jr., or Teej, as Kelly insisted on calling the baby, was sleeping in his carriage, gently and absentmindedly rocked by Este's free hand.

His grandson, thought Thomas, his perfectly formed, perfectly beautiful grandson. Four months old this day, which as far as he was concerned was far better cause for celebration than the one the nation was observing. Annoyed with what he felt was his meanness, Thomas wished he could feel something more for the hostages, while knowing the antipathy he felt was not really directed toward them. He understood they had been victims, sufferers, but he was bitter. If he could only do as Matthew had suggested: see beyond his own loss and concentrate on his new goals—the memorial and Kelly.

The memorial in Eagle Nest, New Mexico, soared in his thoughts much as it soared skyward toward the towering peaks of the Sangre de Cristo mountain range. Thomas could never think of the gull-like structure, built out of and up from a hillside, perched like a great bird about to alight in heaven, without becoming emotional. It was what a memorial to the men in Vietnam should be, and he was glad he had been reassigned by the DAV to his new job as chief fund raiser for its perpetuation.

It lacked public support mainly because it lacked public awareness. Part of his job was to correct this. It was a job Thomas relished. He was moved by Dr. Victor Westphall and his decade-long struggle to erect and maintain a monument in honor of his son and other casualties of Vietnam. The chapel had been built almost with Westphall's own hands as well as his money. It had not been until 1977 that the DAV, aware that many of its members made pilgrimages to the New Mexico memorial, pledged ten thousand dollars yearly to maintain it. From Thomas's personal observances, he had seen that money was woefully inadequate.

The one unfortunate aspect of the new job was its travel. Now that he was determined to be with Kelly the bulk of his time, Thomas resented his frequent fund-raising trips to the sixty-eight DAV offices around the country. But that was where the contributions were made, "at the heart of the matter," as Thomas had explained to Vinnie, and not in Washington where the government had finally decided to erect a Vietnam memorial of its own. Where it belonged. Or so they believed. Several DAV members disagreed. It was the seat of government . . . Washington . . . that had not cared for or about them during the Vietnam War, so why give them that honor now? Thomas skirted the issue by deciding two memorials were better than one and far better than the none that had existed until now.

"Thomas? Watch the kids, will you?" called Este. "I'm going to make some coffee. You guys want a beer or something?"

"Tea," called Vinnie. "Make it a pot," he added when Thomas signaled tea, too, was what he wanted.

There was no doubt that Florida had been the best place for Kelly, thought Thomas again as he watched Vinnie light a long-stemmed pipe. No one had known her here, and her privacy had not been invaded. More important, no one had acted as her judge or jury. Both Vinnie and Este had been exactly to Kelly what she needed: friends.

As he watched the sailboats on the bay, Thomas again questioned why he had expected Reese to leave her job to be with Kelly. If the idea had crossed Reese's mind, she made no mention but was content that Este was willing to serve as her surrogate. At first, Thomas viewed Reese's behavior as neglect, but as the weeks went by and as he learned of Reese's nightly phone calls to Kelly, he understood it was not neglect but something for which he had no explanation or definition. And then when the baby was born. . . . He remembered how Reese had cried in the waiting room all the time Kelly was in her labor. She had also sobbed afterward. And the look on her face when Este for the first and last time called her "Nana Reese" was something he could neither forget nor decipher.

Kristan, too, had called frequently, and when the baby was born had sent a check for five thousand dollars. But she had not attended the christening that all concerned agreed was wise, as her presence would only draw press attention to Kelly. Karl had remained Karl, aloof, electing to send a savings bond rather than bring himself.

The smell of brewing tea awakened Thomas from his thoughts. "It's hot," cautioned Este as she placed a tray with cups and a plate of chocolate chip cookies before him and Vinnie. "And no seconds," she cautioned. "Dinner is at six and I want appetites, not apathy." Vinnie smiled and, as Este turned to leave, he patted her rump appreciatively.

"Listen, you dirty old man," she snapped. "That, like dessert, comes later and only after you've eaten all your vegetables."

Thomas was uncomfortable each time Este spoke openly about sex, but he could see from the delighted smile on Vinnie's weatherbeaten face that the same was not true for him. Vinnie

3 1 9

was indeed Margaret's son, while he was his mother all over again. Which is why he had elected to send Kelly to Vinnie and not to his mother. He had feared his mother's religious beliefs, her moral convictions, would unintentionally add an extra weight to Kelly's overburdened shoulders. His daughter needed support, not sermons. Morality wasn't the issue. Having the baby comfortably and then adjusting to it and readjusting to life was.

But his mother had surprised him. When informed of Kelly's pregnancy, she said little but did much, sending pretty maternity clothes for which she personally shopped. The gifts always included a handwritten note that said nothing and yet everything about his mother's feelings for her granddaughter. And when the baby was born, she flew down on the first plane and into the hospital to see her first great-grandchild. He had watched her with the baby, had seen the tears sliding down her cheeks as she rocked Teej, cooing to him in a voice he thought he almost remembered. Thomas had been quite unprepared for such a declaration of love without sermon or strings. He was also unprepared for Margaret arriving at the christening in a floppy red hat worn with a red oil slicker as the September rains had hit Miami with the same force as had Margaret. She had immediately established a trust fund for Teej and refused to be thanked. In a private moment, Thomas had observed Margaret holding his grandson and looking much the way his mother had.

Marti and Matthew had also attended the christening, despite Lynne's sudden case of chickenpox, which necessitated their leaving her with Mark for the day. The support touched him. It also freed him. No longer did he feel he must be the sole protective shield between Kelly, Teej, and the world. They had family.

As always with Kelly, it was the noise he heard first and then the person. This time, Kelly announced her arrival with little whoops of pleasure and pain as she concluded her daily jog up and down Bay Road. She arrived on the patio dripping sweat but smiling.

"Made it to three miles today," she said as she snatched a cookie from the table.

"Good for you!" said Vinnie as he snatched it back. "Now, where is that resolve, that will power?"

320

"Hidden behind the remaining seven pounds of fat that refuses to come off," puffed Kelly as she continuted to bob up and down, boxer-style, moving in that strange way toward the carriage where Teej was resting.

"And how's my little man?" she asked as she picked up the baby and held him to her breast. The sun framed the picture and Thomas thought his little girl looked so much like a beautiful young woman.

"It feels cold to me. I think I'll take him in," said Kelly as she hooked Teej under one arm while the other wheeled the carriage into the house.

Thomas watched her leave and Vinnie, as if reading his mind, asked, "Are you still determined to return to Boston with her this week?"

Thomas nodded, knowing from a previous discussion that Vinnie was not in total agreement with his thinking.

"Thomas, she's happy here," began Vinnie.

"That's not enough. It's too temporary. She must grow up."

"She could do that here," replied Vinnie. "Thomas, Kelly is an adult."

"Kelly is a mother," replied Thomas quickly. "That doesn't automatically make her an adult."

"She'll be eighteen this fall," pursued Vinnie.

"It's just an age, a number. It has little to do with maturity."

"Thomas, it's *her* life."

"And look what she's done with it to date. No, Vinnie. I understand your concern, but I'm concerned that my daughter has a full life, not a partial imitation of one. Kelly needs to go home, needs to face her fears and her demons. She has no future until she faces her past."

"What you mean is she must face facts and rumors and innuendoes," said Vinnie.

"Exactly," replied Thomas. "My daughter is a good person. I want her to stand up straight, to walk tall. Just because she made a mistake, there is no need for her to hide from anyone or anything."

"Thomas, she is not you. She may not have that kind of courage."

It pained him to hear Vinnie say that. Kelly would have everything he had to give her, plus her own very special strengths.

"Someday, Thomas," said Vinnie gently, "you must learn to let go."

Thomas looked into the sun now setting in pink-purples on the bay and replied: "And just what do you think I've been doing ever since the war's end?"

*   *   *

The alarm's buzzer was insistent. Through half-opened eyes, Marti acknowledge the ultrasophisticated digital computer clock near her bed. Monday, March 30. Six-thirty. A ghastly hour, she concurred with the groggy and grouchy self that dominated the first hour of her waking day. The bed was as cold as the room, an indication that Matthew had left earlier than planned for Washington. For a moment Marti thought to set the snooze alarm for her "fifteen minutes of sensuous sloth," but, remembering it was Monday and that she would be meeting Arline in the office, changed her mind.

The bathroom was spotless with only a wet towel proving someone had recently used the facilities. Matthew's studied neatness always brought annoyance and resentment rather than pleasure or relief to Marti. Often she felt a prisoner in her own bathroom when Matthew was home, afraid to leave things about. This morning, for the hell of it, Marti, after brushing her teeth, left the cap off the toothpaste.

As she showered, the sudden reduction in water pressure announced Tisa Bannington had just flushed the toilet in her bathroom above. The governess arose at the same time as Marti but did not make an appearance until Marti had left, a direct request of the "mistress" who could not stand to make conversation with anyone first thing in the morning. Instead, she preferred to organize both her personal and professional stock—a sort of time for reflection and meditation. Her last fifteen minutes before leaving for work were always spent with Lynne, just as her lunch hours and her breaks were.

"It's all working," thought Marti aloud, still amazed even after three months that it was. She had solved old problems without

3 2 2

encountering any that were new. A four-day workweek and a daughter who visits on the job. She was lucky. She had it all. Only luck had little to do with it, she argued pragmatically as she blended her usual breakfast of protein mix in soy milk with wheat germ oil, brewer's yeast, and honey. No, luck was not a factor. I've worked for this, Marti thought proudly. Including the bomb and death threats.

The former were annoying as they demanded a work stoppage and that the premises be cleared while the bomb squad searched for the work of a madman. Nothing was ever found, which was almost as upsetting as if something had. Then there would at least be a reason for the inconvenience. The letters were all too familiar, thought Marti, cranks, according to the FBI who continued to analyze her "billet doux," from an increasing claque who obviously thought her voice was coming in too loud and clear. They had increased in number after she had increased her visibility following the Republican National Convention last summer. She had actively campaigned against both the party and Ronald Reagan when the Republican plank had dropped its forty-year endorsement of the ERA. She had been equally vocal in her criticism of the party's proposed amendment prohibiting abortion.

Although the letters had arrived from all parts of the country, a handful bore a sameness Marti had come to recognize over the years. The postmarks of these were from the New York tristate area and it seemed to both Marti and the FBI that there was one person out there, near her, who hated her, had hated her during and after the Vietnam War, and whose hatred had increased over the years with Marti's visibility. This person, a middle-class white, according to FBI analysis, blamed her for the decline of morality in the country and wielded the Bible as a weapon of destruction.

Marti was advised by the FBI to take caution. She had laughed at such a suggestion but had listened when Matthew insisted a limousine take her each workday to and from her destination. It was a caution Marti hated because it called attention to her in a way she found embarrassing. She was not that kind of star, she maintained. The public and the press said otherwise. She was indeed a star, a bigger one now than she had ever been, and that mattered only because of the access it gave her through TV and magazines to peoples' homes and therefore their minds. Best of all, it was a manageable stardom. With her four-day week, and only one of those days stretched from twelve to fourteen hours if necessary, no one—not Lynne, not Matthew, not she—suffered for it.

Lynne was dressed and about to be fed breakfast by Mrs. Bannington when Marti entered her daughter's room to kiss her good-bye. Each morning, Marti was amused by Lynne's blondness, something she could only have inherited from her grandfather, as Marti and Matthew were dark complected as were her mother's and Matthew's sides of the family. Lynne, Marti observed, was being more dark than blond this morning, acting in a fashion Marti recognized and thus respected. Her daughter, too, was not a morning person and, as Marti used to joke, "wasn't civilized until she had her morning milk and pablum." Then she became her usual inquisitive and talkative self, seeking constantly to outwit and outrun the very patient and very reserved Mrs. Bannington.

Marti hugged Lynne lightly—her independent child also hated to be clutched and fussed over in the mornings—and announced she would see her later. Lynne begrudgingly said bye, making it clear she was more interested in food than fond farewells. This, thought Marti, will be a very interesting little person in a few years.

The morning newspapers were waiting in the limousine. The headlines announced more planned Reagan budget cuts affecting childcare and family planning. If only there was a way to make those issues funny, thought Marti as the Cadillac drove uptown toward the offices behind the Ed Sullivan Theater, realizing if there was a way, Arline would find it.

Marti always met with Arline an hour before the staff and crew arrived. It was their time to discuss current events in the world and in their lives that might be fodder for "The Marti Tiernan Show." The title was not theirs but just one of the many concessions they had made to the network. It was a small price to pay. The series had premiered in January and had been an instant success, proving Marti's enthusiasm for the project had been justified.

It had been on a return flight from Los Angeles exactly a year ago that Marti had read Arline's script more out of boredom than curiosity. By the time the plane had passed over the Continental Divide, Marti was making notes in the margin of the script, notes about *her* character, Donna Dayton, the situation—widowed life with a twenty-one-year-old daughter—and its possibilities. It was exactly right for her, Marti had decided by the time the jumbo jet was circling New York, a message show disguised in humorous situations. The possibilities for comically presenting every issue pertinent to older and younger women were there, whether they be professional, personal, or sexual. It was delicious, had thought Marti, particularly because mother and daughter were north and south, east and west, day and night. Total opposites in their generational attitudes about men, marriage, and sex. Their impact on one another was yet another delightful facet of the show. On a larger scale, through the guise of schtik, it attacked former forbidden TV taboos, poking at open wounds and a few that had closed but not healed. No wonder, thought Marti, as she stepped from the limousine to the curb, that there were lots and lots of letters to match the lots and lots of viewers who had ensconsed the show in the top ten from its opening week. If there weren't, then there would be something far more wrong than just a handful of death threats.

*   *   *

Arline's head ached. Sunday night through Monday morning were her worst times. She seldom slept the night before her workweek began but spent the time tossed between fear and panic. It was too much too soon. Too fast for the too inexperienced. And yet she was a success, she would argue in the third person. But for how long? Every show *had to be* funny, meaningful, and yet nonoffensive. A neat trick of tightrope walking for which she had no experience. Not even Lydia La Rosamoré did.

Slamming shut the week's script on her desk, Arline despaired. It would need a rewrite. It always needed a rewrite. And as story editor, that job fell to her—usually on long weekends, the ones Marti had provided contractually so that all involved on the show could have a personal as well as a professional life. As she had mentioned to Marti, she could not remember when she last had a personal life or when a man had tried to get personal with her personals.

She was unprepared for the job. In over her head. She wrote dialogue, not scripts; snappy lines, not plot. Of late, the scripts reflected this. So did the latest ratings. For the second week in a row they had proven vulnerable to the opposition's special. Not a good sign. If only there had been time to work it all through, but what was only a dream one day was reality the next. It had happened that quickly once Marti decided to do the series. A pilot was shot in August. An order for thirteen shows had been placed by the network in mid-November. An end-of-January airdate was announced but weeks later. Bang. Bang. That quick. Bang. Bang. She was dead. Lots of pressure; too little time. Lots of good ideas; precious few executions to match the ideas. Too many ingredients but no recipe. Not true, thought Arline, so stop doing this number on yourself. If anything, the reverse is now seemingly true. You know exactly what you're baking, but you're missing one of the key ingredients. Or so the demographics and the ratings maintain. But what, damn it?

As she plunged her doughnut in her coffee in frustration, splashing the black brew onto the cover of the script, Arline sighed, realizing she was once again participating in her now usual Monday-morning quarterbacking even before the week's game had been played. A key turning in the lock turned her despair to hope. Mama was here. Marti, the entire crew's port in what was one continuous storm, had arrived to take charge, looking quite wonderful and not at all in need of the vacation all would take when the show went on hiatus in May. Marti, Arline knew, was vacationing in England, while she, as she offhandedly explained, was torn between the Menninger Clinic and Aunt Fanny's Funny Farm. She was leaning toward Fanny's because of the padded walls in its disco, its strait jackets—with their Calvin Klein labels —and its clientele of half the people she had met in the executive offices of the network.

The stage, where but minutes ago the cast had concluded its first readings of the week's show, was dark. In the orchestra of the

Ed Sullivan Theater, Arline and Marti sat without speaking, each reflecting on the work to be done. As Marti stole a glance at Arline, she saw her face was as lined and yellow and as thought-filled as the pad she held in her lap.

"That woman is driving me crazy," said Arline finally.

"Which woman?" asked Marti, wondering which member of the writing or acting staff was giving Arline problems now.

"Your woman. My woman. Donna Dayton, the queen of flip-flop. If only she would stay put. If only she would make up her mind and be something for more than a week."

"You could be my conscience." Marti laughed. "Donna can't stay put, Arline. She shouldn't. And that's your intent. Donna is evolving, first emerging into something new after many, many years of representing and being the old. She's caught between her mother's and her daughter's generations. She's also caught between her own visions of what she is and who she would like to be."

"You're more certain of who she is than I am, and I created her," said Arline.

"But I've lived her and still do," said Marti. "Donna is me just as she is so many other women of my age. Only I have more patience with her than I do with myself."

"Oh, please, spare me the difficulties of being Marti Tiernan, particularly today," said Arline, rising. "At this point in the afternoon, when I consider the disparities and differences in our lives, I'm liable to throw up. In envy. You have a life; I have none. Only that's not true either," said Arline as she paced the aisle. "I have a terrific life, only it's a bit lopsided. I want what every woman wants but which we're no longer supposed to: a man, a relationship. I'm this great big success, and I've no one to share it with.

"Do you hear that, world?" yelled Arline as she ran up onto the darkened stage and then turned to face the sole person in her audience. "Arline Ackerman wants a man. And a marriage. God help her, but she may even want children! Which makes her a failure, folks, a wimp."

"You're wrong. It makes you human," said Marti softly.

"Oh, Lord, Marti, you always know the right thing to say," said Arline as she climbed down from the stage and returned to where Marti was sitting. "It all comes so easy to you."

Marti laughed, although she wasn't feeling good humored about what Arline had just said. "Very easy," she said dryly. "Arline, when I look at my life, my past, I just laugh. At me! Talk of your queen of flip-flops! I'm a vacillator and I hate it until I rationalize that there is nothing wrong with experimentation. And there isn't. Only it is a rationalization. There's a part of me that believes a woman of my age should be complete. My mother at forty-one wasn't searching for herself. She knew exactly who she was."

"Of course she did," snapped Arline. "Things were defined for women then, particularly their roles, which in themselves created boundaries. That's not true today."

"But somehow I'm stuck with the feeling that I should be complete, unswerving in my directions," said Marti.

"Women your age are not used to having options," replied Arline.

"Women *my age*, as you so indelicately put it, are therefore much more like Donna Dayton than the Marti Tiernan of media. I am not Superwoman. The Marti Tiernan most people lionize is a fraud, an impostor."

"Would you tell me how this conversation has gone from my identity crisis to yours? How typical of you star ladies. You just can't stand to have the attention diverted from you for a second."

"Oh, shut up and sit down. And spare me the injured look. If but a handful of the men in your life spoke to you in the same fashion, you'd have that relationship you think is so important."

"*Think* is so important? Is your tone telling me yours isn't?"

"It both is and isn't. During the week, when he's not here, I miss him. But if he were here now that I'm working, I'd resent it. He'd be an intrusion, an inconvenience. Weekends are wonderful. I leave all this to be something else with him. Whether it is better or just different, I can't decide. See? Again I'm vacillating. I'm not anything completely."

"Maybe that's good," said Arline earnestly.

"I don't know. Yet, when I recall my mother's marriage, it wasn't all that different. She was no more committed to it than she was to her career."

"So how does that differ from you?" asked Arline, her tone implying it did not.

"It feels different. It feels so compartmentalized."

"Probably because they're not integrated. Maybe you think of them as two sides of you, separate, rather than part of a whole. I bet that's true of many of you in-between ladies. *In between*," explained Arline as she noted Marti's puzzled expression, "as between generations—your mother's and your daughter's. I bet Alison doesn't feel compartmentalized."

"I'm not sure what Ali feels. Nor is Ali. If vacillating is inherited, she most definitely is her mother's daughter. God only knows what she is doing in Europe now that she's dropped out of Yale."

"Why are you so hard on yourself?" asked Arline impatiently.

"Because it's damn tough being thought of as one person when you're quite another," replied Marti, her agitation growing. "Do you know I've started reading that crap they write about me in the women's magazines. I thought maybe I'd discover something everyone knows but me. I mean . . . who is this woman the world fusses over. Why can't they see the coward who once was afraid to leave her house or the woman who was so certain all she wanted to do was smell the roses, or the pot roast. And the caretaker, the mother of all. And the woman who wanted to marry and then who didn't want to marry. Ad infinitum. Ad nauseam."

"But that's exactly what I admire about you: your ability to make changes, to take risks, to jump into things. Sure you fall down, but you also bounce up and come at 'em again. You have done whatever you've needed to do at whatever time in your life. And that's what it's all about, or at least that's what it should be."

"I wonder if my children or Matthew would agree," said Marti thoughtfully.

"But do you? That's all that really matters."

As Marti considered the question, a smile gradually eased its way onto her face.

"You do, damn it, you do," said Arline excitedly. "How nice. So now another answer, please. Since you feel so close to our Donna Dayton, what the hell is wrong with her?"

As they bundled up against the early spring cold that would greet them once they left the theater, Marti replied, "That may be the problem, Arline. I'm just too close to know. I suspect we both are, just as I suspect the answer is right under our noses."

They never left via the stage door on 53rd Street but preferred to exit on Broadway where the limousine waited in front of the theater. This time, the car wasn't there but a meter maid was, signifying the chauffeur was circling, as parking at that hour on Broadway was not allowed. People scurried by in their usual preoc-cupied state, unaware of the celebrity within their midst or even of the city in which they lived. Typically New York, thought Marti. Arline ran to the newsstand on the corner. She returned with the paper folded under her arm.

"Do you really think I come on too strong, that men should tell me to shut up?" she asked, her large eyes questioning and not defensive.

"I think more men should tell you what they really think, and then you should do exactly what you feel," replied Marti. "I sus-pect men find you intimidating. You make an awful lot of noise for a little person."

"Is that good or bad?"

Marti smiled. "It seems to me I just answered a question sim-ilar to that. What do you think?"

"It's me," said Arline. "Why should I change?"

"I'm not saying you should. Only you can decide to do that. But many people change or shape their personalities to be more pleasing to others. Women more than men, I think, but then men are more fragile."

"What a sexist remark!" said Arline, feigning indignation.

"But it's true," replied Marti. "So few men have the vaguest idea who they are. Only a notion of who they *think* they should be. We're much luckier. We now know who we shouldn't be and are beginning to grasp who we really are. Men are stuck with the old values about women because they're stuck with the old values about themselves. When they give up their images of 'maleness,' they won't need us to conform to some fantasy."

"You make them seem very unattractive," said Arline as she unfolded the paper to look at the headline she had ignored when she bought it.

"I don't mean to. I merely wished to suggest that certain kinds of women—the overtly strong ones—may have to tone it down some if they don't want to scare off their men."

Marti looked at Arline to see if the message had been received. One had, but Marti could tell from Arline's expression that it wasn't the one she had just delivered. "What is it?" Marti asked. Arline held open the newspaper she had tried to hide. The headline screamed: REAGAN SHOT!

The people continued to scurry by, oblivious to her, New York City, and this latest assassination attempt. The meter maid continued to write tickets. The limousine turned on 54th onto Broadway. Nothing reacted; nothing changed. It was no longer the unexpected or the unacceptable. Arline was staring at Marti— an overtly strong woman, one who often toned it down to achieve what she wanted. The Superwoman of the *Journal, McCalls,* and *Ms.* was silent, letting the convulsive shaking of her body say it all.

*   *   *

The areobic dance and calisthenics classes had redistributed her weight, and her body, more shapely than it had ever been, was more that of a young girl than a woman. She was pleased by the reflection in the full-length mirror. No one would ever think she was a grandmother.

Sometimes she had to laugh, particularly at herself. She had become a master of disguise. With just a little more misguided effort, she could be ludicrous, one of those women forever looking to be looking forever young. It was all ludicrous; the boys—no matter what their ages—pretending to be men, and the women pretending to be girls. So much pretense, so little reality. So many lonely people.

She was one of the lonely many. As she checked her hair, once again cut short, Reese wondered what happened to all the older men who had seemed so attractive in their maturity when she was young and unmarried. Had they then been a dying breed or had they existed only in her mind? The "mature" men she met today did not want a mature woman, and certainly not a grandmother. They wanted a girl in bed and a mother out. They needed more than she wanted to give, but no more than she would have gladly given had Thomas ever needed it when they were married.

3 3 1

Thomas . . . remembering the marriage made her recall its responsibilities. She could never just be some man's wife today, not now when she had her own visibility. Her professional life was good and she had been well rewarded both by the love the children lavished upon her and the praise of her employers and peers. A paper she had written for one of the journals specializing in special education had been published and the attention it received brought her even more attention when media brought its cameras to focus on her and her work at the Dearborn School. To her surprise, only once in each interview had she been identified in part as the former wife of Thomas Ollson. She was Reese Tomlinson Ollson now and proud of it.

But not proud of that part of her that refused to accept facts. She *was* a grandmother. All the aerobics classes in the world could change the appearance but not the history, past or present. It wasn't that she didn't love Teej, as he was impossible not to love. But he was a reminder that the years were not just passing but had passed, and that that part of her life she had missed could never be recaptured no matter how many new beginnings each new man brought with him.

The kitchen was hot from the oven, and even the open window did not help. The day had been unusually warm for early May, which had made it perfect for Sunday strollers but not for Sunday diners eating in cramped apartments where the central-air-conditioning system would not be operative until Memorial Day, several weekends away. Thomas would be arriving soon. With Kelly and Teej. He would like her blouse—Thomas liked pale, frilly pinks—but he would make no mention of the designer jeans which looked better on her than on Kelly. He would also like the casserole, chicken with fresh vegetables, cooked in the style of *nouvelle cuisine*. Reese was glad he had agreed to take dinner with her rather than the usual, which was her ritually attending Sunday dinner at the house on Marlborough. It was an acknowledgment that she did indeed have a home away from his home. It was also a way to broaden Kelly's horizons. Although she had agreed to the return to Boston, Kelly had yet to begin a life away from her child or from the child she was to Thomas. Her daughter was still her daddy's little girl. Given the men Reese had met, she could not blame Kelly.

She met them through friends, at conferences, at evenings at the Boston Pops. Most were stereotypical: interested in sex and money. But a few others were quite nice: men alone, divorced or separated, or just surprisingly single. But to date, each had lacked a certainty of purpose. They wandered through their lives, without commitment, something she had come to expect in a man. They took up space rather than filled it. Their lives lacked passion. They were undefined. None made a clear statement as to who he was and none seemed the least bit mindful of that fact. And so she was quickly bored and thus quickly terminated whatever it was she had begun with the new man.

A car door slammed. From her window, Reese saw Thomas in the roadway holding open Kelly's door. He was dressed casually in khaki pants and a sports jacket. His shirt was open at the collar and his eyes were shielded from the afternoon setting sun by mirrored sunglasses. Passers-by turned to look, some in recognition, others merely in response to his good looks. As if he was aware of the attention, Thomas reached into the car for Teej. He held him aloft toward the sun before nestling him comfortably in his arms.

Reese was quite aware that she measured each man she met against Thomas. That they all fell short had initially surprised her. But no more. The very qualities that had irritated and infuriated during her marriage were now the very ones she admired. There was no doubt that Thomas Ollson filled his space. His voice would be heard as he protested the design finally selected this past week for the Vietnam Memorial in Washington. Wrong or right, he would take a position, make a commitment and make it passionately.

He was coming toward the entrance now, carefully negotiating the distance, the visible pride on his face making it clear to anyone who was watching that he was what she wanted to hide— the grandparent of the eight-month-old baby boy he was carrying.

*   *   *

The bed was soft and embracing and as Arline breathed deeply, she could smell the summer night through the open windows. Only the sound of the occasional passing car broke the stillness. Each night, shortly after she had slipped into the queen-size bed and before she slipped into sleep, Arline giggled at the realization of where she was and how many would envy her being in Marti Tiernan's bed. A national fantasy through the years, thought Arline. As a little girl growing up, even she had dreamed of knowing Marti, of crawling into her bed to share sandwiches and secrets. Girl talk. Arline missed Marti now, although her presence was felt daily.

It had not been easy housesitting for Marti while she was vacationing in London with the family. The house was big and its loneliness was immense. Arline greatly preferred her own "nest," small as it was. She knew its every creak, and when the phone rang she knew someone would always be there to respond to her greeting. Not so with Marti's telephone. It rang; she answered and, often as not, there was silence although she could feel the presence of another on the line. It was unnerving. Yet, she had worked well in the house, as though Marti was there for counsel and support. In Marti's room, where she had established home and office, the coffee table was covered with notes and suggestions for future shows. None seemed to solve the overall problem. A key ingredient was still missing.

Arline was beginning to drift, to feel herself being lifted into another realm when she heard the sound sneaking up the stairs to her room on the second floor. Only the fact that it was there in the silence made it jarring. When it came again, louder and more insistent, she was awake, listening, aware the sound was not only intruding on her sleep but the house, itself. Someone was wrestling with the locks on the front door, trying to force entry. Terrified, she dialed 911. Busy. Controlling her panic, she reached the operator and quickly breathed her fear into the phone, giving the address of the house and the nature of the disturbance before hanging up. She heard the front door open just as she finally thought to close and lock her own. Only there was no lock on her door. A weapon, she thought. As she was about to reach for an andiron from the fireplace, she heard the footsteps on the stairs. Without thinking she yelled, "Whoever you are, I just called the police."

The footsteps stopped as did all sound except that of her heart pounding.

"Who the hell is that?"

The voice sounded as frightened as her own. "What do you mean, 'Who the hell is that'?" she replied. "Who the hell are you?"

"Arline?" asked the voice outside her closed door.

The door opened and JJ stood on the threshold awkwardly, a suitcase in his hand.

"For crissake, couldn't you call first?" Arline asked, more angry now than relieved.

JJ was staring at her, laughing. She followed his glance. To her breasts. Her bare breasts. With her erect nipples, something that occurred whenever she was aroused or frightened. She crossed her arms to cover her nakedness until she realized she wasn't partially but totally naked. Throwing her arms in the air as a gesture of defeat, she said, "What the hell, modesty is a little late and more than just a little ridiculous at this point in our relationship."

As soon as Arline spoke the words, she was embarrassed. They had no relationship, hadn't for well over a year. They had seen each other but a handful of times and then only at the studio when JJ was visiting Marti. Their meetings had been strained.

"I'm sorry I frightened you. I didn't know you were staying here. I just got in an hour or so ago from El Salvador and found my apartment a mess. The place still reeks of paint fumes and I couldn't face another hotel," said JJ.

"No problem," said Arline. "You've got your pick of the palace. Only the queen's chambers are occupied. Are you hungry? The freezer is loaded with Swanson frozen dinners."

A sudden banging on the front door startled them both. JJ looked to Arline as though she might have an explanation. After a moment's hesitation, the flat of her hand thumping her head told him she did.

"The police. Christ, I better get down there before they break open the door."

And she was down the steps, opening the front door before JJ could stop her.

"I'm grateful you came, but there's been a mistake," said Arline to the two uniformed men before the door was fully open. "You see I'm housesitting for a friend and I thought this man was an intruder when he is actually my friend's brother and he had his own key so everything is really all right and I'm sorry that I disturbed you but there was no way I could have known and I was frightened."

The policemen said nothing but their eyes, staring, boring holes through her, said it all. When she realized what they were staring at, Arline closed her eyes as if that offered some protection from her own nakedness. She could neither speak nor move, and she was grateful when JJ attempted to guide the men from the hallway back into the street. They stood firm, demanding identification and further explanation. They insisted she remain where she was until they were satisfied. But with what? she wondered. Finally, they left, but not before one said in passing: "Good-night, miss. It's been nice to see you. A real pleasure."

Arline stood there in the hallway with her back turned to JJ. Her voice was small and choked as she spoke. "The only reason they let us off so easily is because anyone could see I had nothing to hide. I mean . . . obviously this wasn't any cover-up we were engaged in."

It was more than understanding her humor. It was knowing her. "Arline, if you feel bad, cry," said JJ softly.

And she was sobbing, hitting the wall of the hallway as she did. "I *hate* it when a man looks at me that way. It's so dehumanizing." He slipped his arms around her and held her tightly against him. "I feel so humiliated," she whimpered. Her body was soft and warm and it was raising old feelings within him. Quickly, he held her apart from him, his hands on her shoulders, steadying her. She understood.

"I'm flattered," she said. "Thank you." And she was crying again. She waved him back, her body language insisting she was in control. "It's just a reaction to the whole. Just minutes ago, I thought I was settling into a good night's sleep, and then you arrived . . . and Christ, if we're going to talk I should put some clothes on. Why don't you pour us some brandies and then meet me in my room."

JJ had thought about Arline frequently. He liked her. He particularly liked what she had tried and almost succeeded to awaken within him. He loved her more now than he had when he was supposed to. But not as a lover. In retrospect she had become a friend.

She had combed her hair and slipped into jeans and a sweatshirt when he entered her room with the two snifters of Grand Marnier. She took one from him with both hands extended, as a child might reach for a mugful of cocoa. He laughed. "You're cute," he said in explanation.

"And you're in a good mood," she replied.

Again he laughed but this time the sound was hollow. She recognized the difference. "Jet lag?" she inquired.

"Well, it is a lag of some kind, but it has nothing to do with jets," said JJ cryptically. "I'm just running late."

"For what?" she asked confused.

"My whole life," he answered as he swallowed half his brandy in one gulp.

"I'm glad it's nothing serious," Arline replied mockingly.

He sat awkwardly on the sofa facing the fireplace, his hands playing with the stem of the snifter. Arline could see he was reluctant to talk. "Shall I leave so that the two of you can be alone?" she asked. "I can see you are in deep thought and I don't want to intrude."

"It's awkward," said JJ. "We haven't exactly been close in well over a year, you know."

"I know very well," said Arline, "and I've missed our closeness. Not our relationship as it was but the closeness we shared. That was real. And that never changed for me. I've always liked and admired you, JJ. In my eyes, you're some kind of hero. You've got guts and integrity. Now tell me what you like about me."

He laughed, knowing how she needed to break an emotional moment with comic relief. "You were a good friend. You always talked straight. I trusted you. Perhaps most important, given my rather bleak nature, you made me laugh. In this rather awkward post mortem let me say what perhaps I never made clear: I like you, Arline."

Little tears were running down her face. "I'm glad," she said. "Very glad. But gladdest of all that you could say it. You never did before."

His shoulders dropped. He again looked tired. Something she

had just said had disturbed him. "There are lots of things I never did before," he said finally. "I think I have to go back and do them."

"John, did anything happen in El Salvador?" she asked after a long silence.

"Yes and no," he replied enigmatically. "Yes, in that I made a discovery. Some things never change. Salvador is Vietnam all over again. Reagan's position could be Nixon's or LBJ's. I give you a direct Reagan quote: 'We are sending aid and advisers into El Salvador to halt the infiltration into the Americas by terrorists, by outside interference and those who aren't just aiming at El Salvador but at the whole of Central, and possibly later—South America and . . . eventually North America.' T'aint nothing new there. The beat goes on. Only without me. Suddenly I don't care. It's just a story, one to fill several columns. But the trip was unnecessary. I'm not like Jessamyn. The thrill of the chase doesn't interest me. I'm not an investigative reporter. I would have been happier recycling one of my columns on Vietnam."

Arline was listening intently, trying to understand what it was that JJ was having difficulty explaining.

"I'm giving up the column. It's like a goddamn albatross around my neck. Always looking for issues at which to throw stones. Where the hell is it written that I should be the conscience of the people? What kind of conceit breeds such a grandiose idea?"

"John, slow down. Where is all this coming from?" asked Arline. "It all seems so sudden."

"It comes from Jessamyn. I have her to thank—and I do thank her—for it. She made me look at something. *She* of all people made me realize my feelings have died. I'm issue-oriented when I used to be about people. Or thought I was."

"Then care about the people," said Arline.

"To do so, I have to care about me first," said JJ. "And it's almost a cliché to say I don't know who me is. Thirty-four and confused. Do you know I've been protesting one thing or another since I was sixteen. The march on Washington . . . the riots at Columbia . . . civil rights and Vietnam. Always protesting. When did I laugh? When did I ever relax and just let life be? Let *me* be?

I'm going to bed," said JJ abruptly. "I can't believe I've gotten into all this at this hour and . . ."

"With me?" asked Arline, finishing JJ's sentence.

JJ shrugged. In the dim night light he looked tired and extremely vulnerable.

"Arline, can I sleep here with you, tonight?"

The question shocked her.

"Sleep, Arline. That's what I said; that's what I meant," said JJ.

She understood. Quickly, she took another pillow from Marti's closet and placed it next to hers on the bed. They were lying together side by side, fingers touching, when she heard JJ say, "Arline, I want to be happy, but I don't know how to be. I can be happy with David. *He* makes me happy. Just as you tried and often did. But I don't know how to be happy by myself, for myself."

Arline did not answer, content to listen even though she hurt for JJ.

"I've never taken the time to just be, never asked what I really wanted to do. I just go on fighting windmills. I don't want to fight anymore. Does that still make me some kind of hero in your eyes, Arline?"

Her hand tightened on his. "More than ever. Talk about guts and integrity. How many men can admit to doubts and fears, to questions about where they've been and where they are going?"

But JJ didn't answer and, had he, Arline would not have heard. She was lost in her discovery. The missing ingredient for her series had been found and Marti had been right. The answer had been under their noses the entire time. Under their noses and in their beds. They had only to get beyond themselves to find it.

15

THE LOBBY OF THE SAVOY WAS EMPTY AND AS MARTI passed through it unnoticed by the early morning staff at the hotel's service desk, she momentarily wondered if she should leave Matthew a note in the unlikely event he should awaken before her return. Not necessary, she decided. He would know she was once more strolling along the Victoria Embankment, drinking in the sights and sounds on this, their last day in London.

It was typically foggy, which pleased her. Wrapped tightly in her trenchcoat, Marti, despite the gentle mist that moistened the air, found the morning perfect. Just as every morning had been ever since Matthew's arrival ten days ago. His first vacation in years, their first since they had last been at the Cape. Marti smiled as she remembered that Labor Day, smiled even as she remembered its aftermath. They were very different people then. Both had come a great distance—with more than just one detour—to be where they were today.

The Embankment was deserted. Although she could not see it in the fog, Marti began walking toward the Tower of London, breathing deeply of the Thames as she did. Although some reviled it, Marti would have bottled the scent, labeling it Eau de Thames and endorsing it for fellow Anglophiles. Arline's predawn phone call already seemed hours ago, and New York felt many more miles away than it was. That night, she would be returning, the same and yet different from when she left. There would be an "addition," a new consideration which was new no matter how many times each said nothing would change.

Arline's excitement had been delicious to hear even if it had taken her out of a dreamy, semiconscious state. How strange, but wonderful, that Arline, too, should have found the missing ingredient. She had both known and felt it from the moment she and Matthew were alone; he, separated from his outreach centers and she, separated from every other aspect of her life but him. Even now, as she thought of the barriers they had broken in the past two weeks, she smiled. It was that final inch, the extra step taken to understanding the other person.

The bench Marti selected was wet like all others but still she sat, wanting to savor the morning, the moment, and what the day would bring. She wondered why she wasn't anxious. It would be normal if she was, but she had never felt less anxious and more assured. It was right. Her world was right. Arline was right. Each had to mature in her own way to see, feel, and know it.

Their series needed men and not foils to illustrate chauvinism, professional and personal. It needed "male persons," as Arline defined it, who were struggling with their own feelings, their own growth, in changing times. It needed to depict the new yet old man and woman caught but trying to separate from the tangled web of old concepts into new relationships. It needed men like JJ, men like Matthew. Only there were no men like Matthew, thought Marti, aware that that was how most women felt about their men.

She had never thought of Matthew as being her man before. To have done so would have acknowledged that she was his woman, and that would have bothered her. She had been so intent on becoming her own person, she had not realized she could be both with one not injuring but bettering the other. It felt somewhat strange to Marti coming to this point in her life just days after her forty-fourth birthday. She wondered fleetingly if it would at all change once they had recrossed the Atlantic and both had reentered their everyday and very separate lives.

It would change. Of that she was certain. But she was equally certain it would return as they returned to it at other times in their lives. There would be other vacations, other respites, times together, that turned them inward toward one another rather than outward toward the world in which they both functioned caringly.

Big Ben announced eight o'clock. Ali would be preparing for her flight to London from Paris. Mark would meet her later that morning at Heathrow Airport. She would not think of Ali now. Not this morning. Ali would find her own way just as she had. Marti just hoped it would be sooner. She hurt for her daughter on a day when she wanted to feel nothing but joy. Her day. A family day. They would all be together. Not all actually, but enough. A small family gathering for a small, private occasion. And suddenly Marti was crying. She wished her father were here. By her side until Matthew took his place.

He had only brought his gray suit, not knowing it would be a perfect match to the light gray dress Marti had elected to wear. She was beautiful in gray, thought Matthew—but then she was also beautiful in green, blue, black, and beige. She had turned toward him, her eyes laughing as though amused by the position they now found themselves in. And there was humor in it, thought Matthew. His answering smile denigrated his nervousness. This, he reminded himself, was not a hasty decision. Actually, it wasn't a decision at all. It was something that was suddenly—but was it suddenly?—right. It took no discussion, no deciding. It just took doing. And what he was now pledging was no more than what he had already done. Love, honor, cherish . . . none was new. Not with this woman. Each had fought; each had won. It was only as he slipped the simple gold band on Marti's third finger, left hand, that Matthew fleetingly wondered what the battle had really been about.

*   *   *

The sign was clear. Straight ahead, the Detroit/Windsor Tunnel and Canada. Despite his intentions, JJ pulled the rented Datsun off the road and into the McDonald's parking lot. He could not do it, could not face further despair and defeat. Toronto might be a rerun of Memphis, Dallas, and other cities and small towns through which he had taken his sentimental journey. It could be just as chilling, as numbing, but even more unsettling.

The blast of hot, humid air that greeted him when he opened the door of the air-conditioned car was typical of end-of-July weather in Detroit. By the time he entered the restaurant, JJ's shirt was wet from perspiration. The smell of meat frying at the still early hour of the morning nauseated him. His appetite vanished, not the first time he had suffered such a loss on this trip. But at least his loss had only been of an appetite, he thought.

His fist smashed on the Formica table as he remembered those he so recently had left. Several people in JJ's immediate area looked at him and then quickly resumed their breakfast or lunch, dismissing his behavior as not that far removed from the norm in fast-food chains. Their faces reflected no interest. They, too, did not wish to be involved.

When he had left New York the Fourth of July weekend, JJ had not known what he was searching for other than the men he had known when they were all in exile. Only as he entered Baltimore had JJ realized the purpose of his trip was to learn, to see how others had gained an acceptance, a peace with resolution and dignity. He wanted to resolve and put aside his anger and have this "fun" he saw as a carrot dangling before him, always short of his reach.

Officially, his syndicate informed their subscribers that he was on vacation and that his column would resume in the fall. Their optimism was not based on contractual agreement but on their experience that even the most disillusioned writer returns to what he does best and hates most. It was no surprise to JJ that the syndicate wanted his return. His columns made money, although features on exiles did not, which was why the syndicate had expressed no interest in his summer plans. Not that JJ had any intention of writing about the family reunion to which he was going unannounced and uninvited.

It was a widely scattered family that never came together no matter what the occasion. Nor did they reach-out-and-touch, although there was every reason to. But there were no means, no organizational pulls, no DAV or VFW to offer psychological help or to act as a mutual bond or to instill a feeling of pride. No monument was planned to honor them. The world took no interest, and their lives reflected that. Except for a few. Like Zack Linahan. One of the more active and vocal among the exiles in

3 4 3

Canada, Linahan, a writer, was still active and vocal in Baltimore, writing for those newspapers that would use his free-lance services. Linahan was still burdened by the stigma. Three times he had fought and lost with the Special Discharge Review Board to have his less-than-honorable discharge upgraded. He was bitter, and that bitterness was reflected in his writing, which made it less acceptable to the mass markets. It was also evident in his lifestyle. Linahan lived alone. Totally alone. No woman, no dog, no friends that JJ could see. Linahan's phone did not ring the entire time JJ was there. His life seemed almost hermitlike. The experience had depressed JJ. Only now, as he looked back, did JJ realize Linahan had been the least depressing of his experiences—which was a helluva commentary.

Aaron Pressman had stunned him. The man bore little resemblance to the boy who once held rhetorical court at Grossman's Café. His long blond hair was cut as short as his temper was once known to be. His eyes were dull and, to JJ, Pressman seemed like a wild animal that time and circumstance had domesticated for living in southern "comfort," provided by his wife, Ruth, a Savannah beautician. Her southern hospitality did not extend to JJ. Her hostility was unmasked. She did not want her husband speaking of the succession of odd jobs he performed for a succession of employers who weren't concerned where he had spent eight years of his life, only that he accept the minimum wages they offered.

But was Pressman's passivity preferable to Kyle Drexler's militarism? JJ wondered as he dawdled over his Coke. Drexler had greeted him in Chicago dressed like a Cuban rebel. He was alive and kicking . . . furiously. Two years ago, after he had helped to organize the National Antidraft Teach-in project, he was expelled for his radicalism. It seemed Drexler, in addition to visiting college campuses and developing opposition to the newly proposed draft and to the administration's return to a more interventionist foreign policy, had been planting bombs in and around Chicago's financial districts. It had taken less than an hour for JJ to realize Drexler was still "involved," but to the exclusion of all else. Drexler had protested his wife's desertion, but as best as JJ could determine, protest was all Drexler did with his life.

Whether that was better or worse than the others—those like

Nelson who had wrapped themselves in protective layers of middle-class values—JJ could no longer say. These men. lulled by the American dream, slept soundly. Even when they were awake. They had forgotten or falsified their pasts and forged new identities. They had not been pleased by JJ's visits. He was an unwelcome and uncomfortable reminder of who they had been and, if they were not careful, who they would always be.

Others, too, had no pasts and no futures but were mired down in the present in menial jobs and mean lives in small towns scattered throughout the country. They got by, asking little and receiving no more than what they asked. Some had families, but even those who did tended to be reclusive. Wherever JJ went, whoever he saw, he was accosted by the alienation, the inability to speak of what once was. No one wanted to look back. They all just wanted to "get on" with their lives.

They lived as though they were lepers, and in many of their minds that is exactly what they were. At first, he had ached for them, pitying their circumstances. The forgotten men, not just by their country and all those who championed "human rights," but by themselves. Which is what had angered him. He remembered their questions, one in particular: What had it all meant? Their question was no different from that of the Vietnam veteran. A near decade later and a generation of men were no closer to an understanding.

What *had* it all meant? The question staggered JJ because the answer was so apparent. These men, these "family members," had helped shape politics for years to come. Not easily could Ronald Reagan send forces to El Salvador. Not easily could he conscript men to fight a war that sounded terrifyingly familiar and similar to the one fought in Vietnam. Because of what the exiles had demonstrated years ago, they were role models: men who had fought and won a larger war than the one in Vietnam. The position they had taken was one that masses of people—men and women—could now, and *would now*, take against sending themselves or their children to kill other people. They were the victors. That's what it had all meant. Their lives had mattered. *They* mattered, but they were not allowing themselves to see that. That was sad, but it was also annoying. And dumb.

3 4 5

He was angry and glad of it. You had to be angry at such treatment. Unless you didn't like yourself—which was sadly true of too many of his "family." But he did like himself. No matter what he had told Arline that night, he now saw clearly that he, John Ollson, liked and admired himself. He would never be sweet or docile, never be the "fun kid" others wished him to be. He was who he was and he would fight to preserve that. If he felt a little lost sometimes, there would always be maps, signs, and roads that would eventually bring him someplace, which was a lot better than *no*place.

He would not drive to Toronto, JJ decided as he settled into his car. He wanted to remember his life and the people he knew, Kay, as they had been and not as they now might be. Besides, that was the past and, as of this moment, he was no longer living in it, although it would always live within him.

*   *   *

As JJ stood with one foot on the curb, the other in the street, trying to flag down a taxi, he silently abused Marti's decision not to take the limousine. On such a steamy night, and at seven-thirty—the heart of the theater-district rush—the limo would not only have been more convenient but more comfortable. And considering how exhausted Marti looked after the day's rehearsal, she could have used some air-conditioned coddling. But no, thought JJ, frustrated as yet more occupied taxis sped by, Marti had chosen not to draw attention, not where they were going.

Suddenly, the yellow miracle appeared. As miraculously, it slowed to a halt as it drew near JJ, who waved to Marti and Arline, waiting in the Ed Sullivan Theater lobby, to join him. The driver recognized Marti immediately, addressing her by her first name, and congratulating her on her marriage. It was a familiarity Marti had come to expect and accept from strangers. That was the power of television and that power was what had interested her in it, not for herself but for the sake of issues that needed presentation.

Once settled in the back seat, cramped in the close quarters, Marti rolled down the window and gulped the humid and fetid air as though it were antacids. Her color, a pale green, did not change. Beads of perspiration lined her upper lip. Arline, carrying

3 4 6

the week's script and the pages that needed immediate rewrite, was turned off and tuned out with her Walkman glued into her ear. She was finger-popping noisily as the cab turned toward the East Side.

As he glanced out the window at the ABC Building and past it to CBS, JJ was reminded of when he and Marti had last combined their efforts on a TV project, *Soldiers: A War of Their Own*, filmed when he was still in exile in Canada. With Marti, they had traveled throughout Europe interviewing men who had been AWOL through many years and many wars. Their efforts had won JJ an Emmy. He wondered what might result from this evening. His syndicate had been correct: he was ready to write again, to be heard, through the printed word and other forms of mass communication. He was open to suggestion. That was why Marti had urged him to attend the evening's memorial for Hiroshima victims. Marti's interest in Helen Caldecott and the Physicians for Social Responsibility had been keened when she heard the doctor speak in May at the Cathedral of St. John the Divine in New York. Caldecott, and her worldwide organization of twelve thousand doctors, were for nuclear disarmament and against any further nuclear buildup. A freeze, explained Marti.

JJ's views on disarmament were embryonic, involved as he had been in what he had thought were more important issues. Although aware of the weapons buildup, he had not truly comprehended its significance, an attitude not peculiar to him, he now understood, but to most. "Ostrich-ism," the ability to hide one's head in the sand in the face of danger, was fairly common when it came to the public's consciousness of nuclear war.

Marti reached across and grabbed and thus silenced Arline's fingers as they had continued to snap in rhythm to the rock music blasting in her ears. Arline pulled off the earphones and stared at Marti.

"The noise was driving me nuts," explained Marti.

"You're an old fart," said Arline, annoyed.

"Just a tired, not an old one," said Marti sweetly. "I worked today if you remember."

"If you can call reading my lines work," replied Arline airily. "It should be a joy."

347

"And there should be peace on earth and a chicken in every pot, but there isn't," said Marti. "Your lines, pearls as they all may be, still take repeated rehearsals and a helluvan actress to bring them to life."

"Then I suggest we have a talent search and find that actress immediately," replied Arline.

"Oh, God, when will I learn not to engage that mouth in any kind of verbal warfare, It's deadlier than any intercontinental ballistic missile."

JJ smiled as he listened to the women's banter, thinking of smiliar verbal jousts between his mother and his aunt. The relationship between Marti and Arline surprised JJ. Despite the difference in their ages and backgrounds, they were like two young girls, often giggling and clucking together like teenagers. There were even times when they accompanied each other to the bathroom. It was Arline who had suggested JJ collaborate on a script—perhaps even a two-parter—in which Donna Dayton and daughter take opposite sides on the disarmament issue—with humorous yet meaningful results.

"How much longer?" asked Marti as she checked her watch. "It starts at eight."

They were at Third Avenue and 59th Street. Marymount College, where the memorial was taking place, was but minutes away at 71st. Marti relaxed, resting her head on Arline's shoulder, when she was reminded that Jane Bartlett, the evening's organizer, had promised to reserve three seats for them. As she rested with her eyes closed, Marti wished her nausea would disappear.

"I think in this heat we'll have the entire place to ourselves," said Arline. "Even Dr. Bartlett thought the attendance would be light. I guess potential nuclear anihilation doesn't draw much of an audience, particularly on Tuesdays when it's on opposite 'Happy Days' and 'LaVerne & Shirley.' "

With her thumb and her index finger, Marti tried to push the headache from the front to the back of her head. The headaches often accompanied the nausea, and they occurred at all hours of the day. They exhausted her. Normally, given her work schedule, Marti did not make commitments for during the week, but the issue of nuclear disarmament nagged at her. It wasn't a search for some new cause now that the passage of the ERA seemed doomed, but something that felt even more important than that issue: survival, not just of women but of all people. Matthew insisted she was overreacting. She had been furious with his complacency. Marriage had not drawn them any closer politically. Neither he nor Thomas doubted Caldecott's sincerity, but they did not agree with what they termed her "idealistic, unrealistic thinking." Both took the military position that the best offense is a strong defense and that the stockpiling of nuclear weapons, warheads, was the single best deterrent to nuclear war.

She had bristled at such reasoning, insisting nations do not build weapons not to use them.

Thomas had looked at her calmly and asked, "Marti, if I have a gun and you have a gun, and both of us know the other is armed, what is the likelihood of our using our weapons on each other? The threat of retaliation is a strong deterrent."

She had looked at Thomas just as calmly and replied, "Ever hear the expression 'trigger happy'? There's always the possibility of someone or someones who decide to strike when their particular irons are hot. The world cannot risk that, not when there are already eighteen thousand strategic weapons that if detonated could kill ninety percent of all Americans and Russians. And, I might add," she had concluded nastily, "bombs do not distinguish between adults and children." It had been the one statement that had changed the set expressions on Thomas's and Matthew's faces.

"We're here," announced JJ. Marti looked up to the red-brick façade and realized she had passed the college many times before without realizing what it was. As JJ paid the driver, Marti used a tissue to wipe the mustache of sweat from her upper lip and to dab a few drops of cologne on the back of her neck, hoping it would cool and soothe.

At the front door, a security guard directed them past the lecture halls to the Great Hall where doctors, physicists, and other speakers for the memorial had assembled. Although the clock in the main hallway read a minute to eight, there was no way they or anyone else could hurry. Crowds headed in the same direction moved slowly. Marti held tightly to JJ for support. Arline, up ahead at the door to the Great Hall, gave their names to the usher who signaled their seats were at the very front of the high-ceilinged room. There were people and makeshift seating everywhere. In the room designed for two hundred, three times that were in every space available. Despite the huge windows, the heat rose in waves. As did Marti's nausea. Signaling JJ to wait, Marti fled to the bathroom.

She was leaning against the tile wall, holding on to one of the sinks, when she heard an authoritative voice command: "Sit on the commode." Marti did as she was told. "Now put your head between your legs." As she did this, Marti heard the sound of water running. Seconds later, a cold compress of toilet tissue was placed at the back of her neck and still another at her wrists. When the feeling of faintness passed, Marti smiled at the attractive woman standing before her and asked: "Are you a doctor?"

"Only if you're a French poodle or an Irish terrier."

When Marti looked blank, the woman laughed. "I'm a veterinarian. My name is Kay Andersohn. And I used to be a good friend of your brother's.

*   *   *

The most intelligent thing JJ had been able to say when he saw Kay appear with Marti was "My God." She had laughed and hugged him lightly, extricating herself quickly from his clumsy embrace to introduce the person who had suddenly appeared by her side. It had taken JJ several seconds to realize the person was a man and not just any man but one of the doctors speaking that night. The proprietary way he held Kay by the elbow was in itself oratorical. The message was clear.

In the rush to find their seats, JJ had heard her respond "the Sheraton" to his question. Phone calls to all three hotels of that name had finally produced her at the Sheraton Russell in Murray Hill. Her phone had been answered by *Himself*. He would tell Kay JJ had called when she returned.

As he sat in the sun-drenched pocket park on West 57th Street, enjoying the twenty minutes before he was due at St. Paul's, JJ realized he had never thought of Kay with a man. With boys and animals, yes, but with a man, no. She had her work and he had somehow assumed that would be enough. For reasons he could not explain, he felt betrayed that it had not been.

She had returned his call the following morning, speaking casually and impersonally. She expressed hope that the weather would cool for the christening Sunday. He had not replied. She grew silent. Suddenly he remembered. Kayce Naismith was to be christened at St. Paul's that Sunday morning. He had received the invitation shortly upon arriving home after his month-long sojourn. He had not connected Kayce with Kay, and it had not occurred to him that Nelson had obviously named his daughter for the woman who had mattered in so many ways to him, so long ago.

He would of course be at the christening. Good! she had replied. She would see him then. He had felt dismissed and only when she had added, "If you're free afterward, perhaps we can lunch," did his anger lessen.

As he began the short two-block walk to the cathedral, JJ regretted accepting her invitation. The idea of being a third person, a single party to a couple, was an unacceptable and uncomfortable position. Still, he was curious about Kay, particularly since she had so recently been on his mind. JJ wondered if Kay's attendance at the memorial had been for her or for *Him*, as JJ tended to think of the graying "gentleman" who not only looked but acted the part of the noble physician. As he entered the church, JJ regretted not taking David with him. If nothing else, David would have made a lively fourth. He also would have proven that he, too, had a someone in his life.

The cathedral was cool and comforting. It took JJ's eyes several seconds to adjust to its darkness after the glare of the midday sun. Toward the altar he saw Alicia's family assembled en masse. Nelson, in a white suit, looking robust and successful, was epitomizing the proud father. The baby was being held somewhat awkwardly in Kay's arms. Kay looked awed and decidedly ill-at-ease, as if the baby was about to break or bite. "I'm better with puppies," she said in greeting when she saw JJ. *Himself* was not present, which puzzled JJ through the short ceremony and the walk from the cathedral to Tavern on the Green, where JJ had made luncheon reservations for the Crystal Room. But he didn't ask and

Kay didn't say. Nor did he ask where her luggage was but assumed that *He* was taking it to LaGuardia where she—they?—were catching a late afternoon flight to Toronto.

It was a strange thing to notice and reflect upon, but it captured JJ's attention: Kay looked right in the elegant setting of the Crystal Room. Her pale blond hair was pulled severely back from her face and knotted at the top of her head. A strand of pearls was the only accessory she wore with her white linen suit. It shocked him that she no longer was the pretty young girl, so midwestern farm-fresh in appearance. She was older. More attractive than pretty, it was her attitude that had turned heads when they had entered the restaurant.

It was her attitude that was causing him discomfort now. It was slightly mocking. Her eyes were fixed on his face as if she were waiting for him to say something momentous. He could barely think of anything except the five-day forecast which he had heard just before leaving the apartment.

"It's hard to believe we'd ever have difficulty talking," she said.

"It has been a long time," JJ replied, relieved she had not only opened the conversation but broken through the barrier with her one statement that carried an entire history with it. "Times change. People often do, too," he added, coming straight to the point of his uncertainty.

Her face studied his as she ordered a glass of white wine. "Sometimes for the better, and sometimes not that much. You know, JJ, you were a very good friend to me."

"I, a good friend to you?" He laughed. "I think the reverse would be far truer. You were a great girl."

"*Were?* Watch it, buddy. I still am," she said, laughing. "I'm absolutely all the things I've ever admired in a woman: strong, independent, motivated, intelligent—definitely that!—and self-sufficient." She was still laughing but it wasn't derisive. "Of course, my marriage failed . . ."

"You were married?" he interrupted, surprised he had not received an announcement.

"For exactly eight months and sixteen days. It was within the first sixteen days that he discovered all my flaws and faults. It took him eight more months to decide I was incorrigible." When JJ looked at her appraisingly, she added: "I am many things, but here is what I'm not: a homemaker, a cook, a 'little woman' who stands behind her husband in every way, the second in command. It resulted that I was much too strong, independent, motivated, intelligent, and—what was the other?—oh, yes, self-sufficient, to make my marriage work."

"You don't seem crushed by the experience," he said offhandedly.

"Were you crushed or relieved when you were free of Jessamyn?" Kay asked. He didn't respond. They both knew the answer.

"My son is wonderful," JJ said. Kay followed his progression from marriage to fatherhood. "He's my proudest accomplishment," he added. She looked at him oddly. He shrugged, somewhat uncomfortable under her scrutiny. "I'm not as sure of myself as you are. I'm a helluva lot better than I was but I still have these dark doubts about my life, whether I've made the most of it." She continued to look at him oddly. "Not still guilty, I hope," she said finally.

"Oh, no. Not that. I did what I had to do. It's just sometimes I wonder if I did it for too long and whether there were other measures I might have taken that would have been more productive."

"More productive?" she echoed. "What more did you want?"

JJ shrugged.

"No one gets one hundred percent, JJ. And to think because you didn't that you failed is childish," said Kay. "You've represented the minority view, and often that view has been part of the solution. It was the protest groups, small as they were initially, that eventually stopped the war. You were part of those groups as was I. It was protest that achieved amnesty, and we were among those who led that protest. So it wasn't the exact amnesty we wanted—but it was an amnesty and *we* fought for it.

"Oh my, all that and on but a half glass of chilled wine," said Kay, laughing again. "Some things never change. I still do run on."

"Then run. I'm listening," said JJ. "What about your work . . . your life," he added, meaning the unmentioned doctor.

"My life is simpler than yours," said Kay as she buttered a dinner roll. "My differences, the ones I make, are perceptible. I treat sick or injured animals. Either I succeed or fail. The results are usually obvious quite quickly. I love my work. I have a thriving business—in fact I had to take on an intern—and I have a lovely apartment in Toronto and a wonderful retreat in Gravenhurst. It's in the Muskoka Lakes region," said Kay as she saw JJ mentally try to place its location. "A not-so-rustic cabin—I had a dishwasher, washer/dryer installed—in a woodsy area. It reminds me somewhat of my father's place on the lake in Wisconsin."

"No regrets about having left America?"

Kay stopped midway into a bite of her lobster salad and replied, "I did have a few years back but no more." She could see from the look on his face that he was waiting for elucidation. "The bubble burst. The honeymoon ended and the job of day-to-day living took over. In short: I discovered Canada has its own problems, many not so far removed from those of the U.S. In 'seventy-nine, the inflation rate was past nine moving up to ten percent. The unemployment was a staggering eight percent, quite high for Canada. Exorbitant tax increases were proposed at the same time as government cutbacks on health and unemployment insurance. Then the problems with the black population emerged. Canada has its own racial problems. There is terrible discrimination. And perhaps the worst for me personally to handle was what the government did with the Akwesasne Indian territory rights. As you know, somewhere down the lineage line, I've got some Indian blood and . . . well, when the Canadian government engaged in a three-month confrontation with the Indians—the police moved in and it was frightening—I was ready to pack it in and return to America. I mean . . . it was all so strangely reminiscent, as though I had been there before. Wounded Knee revisited. And then the animosity toward the boat people . . . As you can see, not that much changes from country to country, even in a democracy."

"What did you do?"

JJ's question was asked easily, but it was pointed. And loaded.

"I ran for local office . . . alderman . . . and lost, and by a very wide margin," said Kay. "Not that I ever expected to win. The most I hoped to achieve—and I did—was recognition. To make some noise as I made my points."

"Get the ole minority view heard," interrupted JJ.

"Exactly," replied Kay. "So in that respect, our lives have paralleled. Only I rejoice in those who hear while you seem to dwell on those who don't. You can't be dissuaded by those who would dissuade."

Her face clouded and a for a long moment there was silence between them.

"Your husband?" JJ asked intuitively. She nodded. "If there is a hearing equivalent of tunnel vision, he had it. We couldn't communicate. Too much static. I was more than he expected. Or wanted. He thought of my practice as just that: a practice and not a profession. And then, how many veterinarians turn politician? Strangely enough, I met Dieter through him—Dieter is the doctor you met earlier in the week—and he introduced me to the disarmament issue. Which took me even farther away from the person, Carroll—that was my husband," Kay explained as she saw the look of confusion on JJ's face from the sudden onslaught of names— "thought I was or would be. But why he ever thought I was that person I can't imagine. Certainly I gave him no reason to, I *think*," she added, laughing, turning her attention once again toward her seafood salad. "Do you ever miss Canada?" she asked suddenly.

"I've never thought about it," said JJ honestly. "It was not a happy time in my life. I don't have good memories. Yet I'm very grateful to the Canadian government, to the people, for allowing me to live. But I wasn't really living, was I? I have such little remembrance of the country, itself. I was always so busy, seeing some things far too clearly and others, like my immediate environment, not at all."

"I doubt if I could ever leave Canada," said Kay. "I love my life, and the issues that now concern me are larger than just being Canadian. The possibility of nuclear warfare, and thus the need for disarmament, affects not one country but the world. I studied for many years to learn how to treat, to save, living things. I cannot allow madmen to destroy those living things or any of the others I hold dear."

JJ was staring at Kay, his expression revealing nothing of his feelings.

"As I said, I do run on," said Kay. "But remember, you caused it. From one of your questions, I had the distinct feeling I was being tested."

"I'm sorry," said JJ. "It's just that there have been so many changes in the past four years . . ."

3 5 5

"And you wanted to see if I, too, had changed. Well . . . have I?"

"Yes, but not like the others. You're here. All here. Even when you don't speak, you make a statement, as everyone in this room will concur."

"I think that's a compliment. At least I'll take it as such," said Kay, not even pretending embarrassment.

"Some part of me keeps thinking we should talk about books we have read, movies we've seen, vacations we've taken. Something to lighten the moment," JJ said awkwardly.

"And be who we are not, at least not with each other? We never sat around making small talk, JJ. We were always rather heavy in our conversation. I'm sure we bored three-fourths of all who knew us, but we didn't bore each other."

Again there was a long silence. He waited for her to say something, anything, about this Dieter and if together they bored three-fourths of those who knew them. But Kay said nothing. When she finished her coffee, she looked at her watch with some alarm. "A plane to catch," she said as she rose. They were standing at the entrance to the restaurant, waiting for the doorman to find a taxi that would take her to LaGuardia, when they once again became awkward with each other.

"When will you be in New York again?" asked JJ.

"I don't know. I have no plans to return. It's actually very difficult to get away, with my practice being what it is," she replied.

Once more JJ had the feeling he was being dismissed. Until Kay, as she stepped into the taxi turned her head to say: "But you could always come to Canada."

It was the way her voice had underlined "always" that made him feel much much better. "See ya," he said as he closed her door. She smiled, waved, and then gave the driver exact instructions on how she wanted to travel to the Sheraton Russell and then on to LaGuardia.

* * *

The phone rang as she was rushing to leave the house. The voice that responded to her salutation said simply: "I've decided to meet you." The connection disconnected before Marti could protest. She had thought the issue had been settled the previous evening at dinner following the taping. But nothing it seemed was ever settled when two strong women held differing positions and one was just the least bit hesitant about her own.

The mailman was negotiating the steps of the brownstone as Marti came down them, mindful only of the lateness of the hour. Their near collision produced a smile on his face and the mail in her hand. She thanked him, hoping there was something pleasantly distracting within the packet.

The morning was clear and cool, as if summer had decided to leave town the week after the people returned to it following the Labor Day weekend. Once the limousine driver deposited her into the cushiony interior of the Cadillac, Marti examined the mail. Her "friend" ran true to form. Every Monday and Friday there was a letter. The writing was now known to her although the stationery varied as frequently as the postmark. No longer did these letters upset Marti but then, no longer did she read them, preferring to send them directly to the FBI, who analyzed them and then logged them with the others.

More than two weeks and there was still no letter from Ali. She would call tonight unless she was upset. And she might be. Suddenly, Marti began to cry. Alone in the back seat of her oversized limousine, she felt lonely and frightened. Twice since the evening of the memorial, she had fainted. It was Arline who had insisted she see a doctor, but it was Margaret who actually made the appointment when she had learned during one of Marti's weaker moments that she was feeling ill.

A part of Marti strongly suspected the cause of her distress, but the major part did not want to deal with it. Instead, she concentrated on Ali, her peripatetic daughter who couldn't seem to settle down into anything or anywhere. No longer was Ali in Paris but in London, living with Kristan, whose defection from her TV series rivaled Farrah's from "Charlie's Angels." But at least Kristan was making a film, doing something, which was more than what could be said of Ali, thought Marti.

As the streets passed by her smoked-glass windows, Marti wished Ali was with her. In the protected, unreal life of an oversized and overstuffed back seat of a limousine, they could cuddle

3 5 7

and the world would seem so much farther away as they drew closer to each other. As tears trickled down her cheeks, Marti recalled the many times she and Ali would snuggle on the sofa by the fireplace in her bedroom. How close they were then. How distant they seemed now to be.

Marti sighed. She wondered if she would ever adjust to the fact that Ali was on her own, too soon and too late for anything other than regrets. How do you tell your child, Marti wondered, that no matter what the physical or emotional distance, she is always loved and always had been.

Absorbed as she was in thought, Marti was unaware the rear door was open, the driver waiting for her to emerge, until he gently called her name. She took his outstretched hand and found herself standing in front of the Park Avenue residence with the doctor's office on the ground floor. Margaret rose as Marti entered. No hello, no questions asked, just a vigorous hug before she sat down, trying to be unobtrusive among her magazines as Marti adjusted her hair in the mirror above one of the couches in the waiting room.

A buzzer broke the silence. A second later, the nurse said, "Dr. Trebe will see you now, Mrs. Strohl."

*　　*　　*

The examination took less than thirty minutes. Although the tests would take both hours and days before they would nullify or confirm his suspicions, Trebe was fairly certain of his diagnosis. As was Marti. She iced as she listened to the doctor speak of the dangers. She was, he droned, forty-four years old. He was not trying to scare her, he maintained, but there were things to fear realistically. Her intellect agreed, although a part of her resisted. He was wrong. Statistics told partial truths. There are alternatives, the doctor said calmly, remedies to the situation. Marti knew them all.

Margaret took Marti by the arm when she exited Trebe's office. Marti's silence was intimidating. "If you're still angry because I've yet to give you a wedding gift, remember, I, your aunt, your friend, a star, was not invited to your wedding. To the one man, of all the men you've married, that I heartily like."

"It's fairly certain that I'm pregnant," said Marti as she stared out the open window of the limousine. "About nine or ten weeks, the doctor estimates. Or, just before or after the wedding I did not invite you to because I wanted something small and simple, two adjectives that are not synonymous with anything that has to do with Margaret Tiernan."

Margaret was assessing Marti's face, looking to see how her niece felt about the possibility of pregnancy.

"It comes at an awkward time. They will have to write around me for the last shows of the season. And there is some danger," continued Marti, "mainly to the baby." Her voice broke. "And possibly to my marriage."

"For God's sake. This is where I came in. Now why would you say a thing like that?" asked Margaret.

"Because Matthew and I never discussed having more children."

"So it was an accident," said Margaret.

"Matthew doesn't believe in accidents. Oh, God, I don't know what to do," sighed Marti as she lay her head back on the cushioned seat. "About Matthew," she added belatedly.

"At the risk of repeating myself once every four years, talk to Matthew. Tonight. As soon as he returns from Washington. It's enough you may be carrying a baby, so don't make your load any heavier," said Margaret as she took Marti's hand in her own. "Damn! Now I not only have to worry about a wedding present but a baby gift. Tell me, how much did you spend . . . forget that. How much are you intending to spend on my birthday present *this* year?"

*   *   *

His suitcase sat at the foot of the steps in the hall where he had left it. Normally, immediately upon his return for the weekend, he unpacked and then showered, but this day he sensed her mood as soon as he entered the front door. Her kiss was unresponsive and her hug was restrained. She had taken him by the hand into the living room where he fixed her a sherry and himself a scotch and water.

"Matthew, I'm pregnant," she said softly, her eyes seeking his for a reaction. "I realize we didn't discuss having another child and that a baby may not be something you want at this stage of your life, but nonetheless I'm pregnant. I could say I didn't plan it and that it was an accident, but you wouldn't buy that and frankly, thanks to your force-feeding of Freud, I don't buy it either. I guess I simply on purpose forgot to take my birth control pills."

She sat down next to him on the sofa. He could feel she was upset but determined. "I think I wanted to have your child. Even more this time than before. I think in that great deep unconscious mind of mine, I see having a baby now—and pardon my prosaics here—as the flower of our love. I mean . . . it makes it, us, complete. I know that this is archaic thinking, but I'm stuck with it. I also like it. I don't apologize for it. The thought is not new or unique. Thousands of women have felt it before. Matthew, I want to carry our child."

As she sat nestled against his side, the silence seemed interminable. "What are the risks?" he said finally.

It was a question she did not wish to consider. "An abnormal child," she said simply.

Another silence was followed by yet another question. "And the risk to you?" Matthew asked.

"I don't consider there being any. Look, I was forty-one when I had Lynne. They advised against it then. They were wrong. My pregnancy was not difficult. It should not be difficult now. I'm older but I'm every bit as healthy. I'm undoubtedly in the best shape of my life. I should have no problems from pregnancy to delivery."

"But there are no guarantees," said Matthew.

"None," said Marti flatly, an edge of anger creeping into her tone.

"Marti, tell me the truth. Should I be afraid for you?"

She looked up into his face, saw concern and not anger, and fought to control the tears. "No," she said softly.

"And for the baby?" he persisted.

"No! It will be a fine baby."

"And if it isn't?" he asked.

"That will change nothing. It will be a baby, *our* baby. I will love it regardless." She thought silently for a moment. "But I can't ask that of you, can I? I can only hope for it."

"And what of Lynne?" asked Matthew. "What of the effects upon her if her brother or sister is different in some way?"

His choice of words affected her deeply. He didn't say *deformed* or *destroyed* or *retarded* or *abnormal*. He simply said "different." "I've thought about that a greal deal since I saw the doctor today. Lynne will adjust as we all must to those things in life that are different and thus often more difficult."

"No amniocentesis?" he asked.

Marti shook her head. "No. Not for me. If I'm to have an abortion, then I'll have it for you, for us, but not because my baby might not conform to the standards of normalcy or beauty." She started to cry. "I'm wrong. I couldn't even do it for you or for our marriage. I believe in a woman's right to decide what's right for her life and her body, but I could not destroy a child. That would destroy me. So don't ask it of me, Matthew."

"I want the baby," she heard him say in a choked voice. "God help me, but I want it more than I should. I don't know how I would have felt had you said you wanted to abort it. We're a family. We will manage. I will love this child in a way that I could never love Lynne.'"

She was shocked and hurt for her child. "But you love Lynne!" she protested.

"Yes, and I always will. But this baby is more mine. I always felt Lynne was yours and that I just had the rights of a father. That's not your fault but mine. You decided to have her, you carried her, without me. I pretty much relegated myself to the background. But this child is ours. Together we made it. Together we'll share it. It's a part of me and I, it."

She understood. Together, on the sofa, they clung to each other. She began to cry when she realized that, for the first time in her three pregnancies, the man who had fathered her child would be with her from beginning to end.

*   *   *

It did not escape Reese that if the roof were removed from the house and the world allowed to peer in, they would seem to see the average family at home on a typical Sunday. In the living room, newspapers spread out, the TV tuned to the beginning of "60 Minutes," sat the father. Upstairs, bathing her baby, preparing

3 6 1

it for bed, was the fair-haired daughter. While she, an apron covering her denim jumpsuit, was in the kitchen chopping onions and red peppers for the salad she would serve with her lasagne.

Reese smiled. She felt cozy within the stereotypical image. Ever since her return from Europe, she had slipped into this casual and comfortable Sunday existence, one that often spilled over into Wednesday and Friday nights. It was a place to go, to be and belong, after the workweek, a home that eclipsed "the Sundays," as she referred to the day she found the most difficult. Time took forever on a Sunday, passing slowly no matter how late she retired on Saturday night or how thick the Sunday paper was.

Reese had also found her summer had taken forever. The tour of Europe she had taken in July with a group of teachers had been boring. Only the price had been right: special rates for a not very special group of people. She had been constantly disappointed in them and in her own expectations. Suddenly being thin, as thin as the college girls who were everywhere, didn't matter. Youth did. At least it did to the European men. That she was an older woman was evident from the company she kept. The tour was for old ladies, even those under thirty. They complained about the heat, the lack of sanitary facilities, and constipation. They clung to one another, afraid to venture out on their own after dark, fearful more of life, thought Reese, than real dangers.

She had broken free in Rome, removing herself from the group except to travel and share a room with one of the teachers. On the first of her three days in the city, she had been wandering through the Borghese Gardens when she suddenly found herself engaged in conversation with a man watching a young boy and girl kick a soccer ball about the sun-parched grass. His grandchildren, he explained. That he was attractive was Reese's first awareness. That one could be a grandparent and still have that kind of appeal was her second. He was babysitting while the children's parents were on holiday. His wife, too, was on holiday, a very long one of twelve years. He did not know where she was and since Italy did not recognize divorce, it didn't matter. He had been pleased to ask her to dinner. She was pleased to accept. He had been pleased to then ask her to lunch and then dinner again. But he had not been pleased when she refused to accompany him to his apartment afterward. He had not understood. He felt hurt. They obviously liked each other, so why not share the intimacy?

She had been surprised by her response. And then what? she had asked. Why share what was most important in life when there was nothing to be gained from it?

Except the moment, he had countered, believing his words.

But it was not moments that interested her, she realized. Not anymore. She had had her moments and found them to be like Chinese food. She now needed true intimacy to share the most intimate parts of herself.

He had not understood. But she had. She was looking for a future and not a past.

She had arrived back in Boston feeling differently about her life. Suddenly, it had a shine to it. She looked forward to the resumption of school and the life she had carved for herself. She still smiled at men in supermarkets, but she was less quick to date any who responded once she talked to them. The desperation had passed. She had changed and she was not alone. In the month that she had been gone, Kelly seemed older. Reese admired her daughter. She never whined or complained. Teej had matured rather than aged her. Yet the little girl was still there, and she brought forth Reese's maternal feelings.

As she tossed the salad, Reese thought about the next day and worried for Kelly. It would not be easy trying to resume a part of one's life that had already passed. Yet, just as the baby had made it more difficult, his presence in Kelly's life would make it easier. He would anchor her. Whenever she had doubts about what she was doing, Kelly need only to look at Teej to understand its importance.

She heard Teej's baby laugh floating down the stairs into the kitchen. The moments before Teej was put to bed were always spent with Thomas. Once she had walked in on their play and had been amazed, wondering who was the man bent over the crib, tickling a child with his finger and funny voices. The father of her children, once so remote, now rolled around the carpeted living-room floor with his grandson, playing . . . like a child. He also talked. To Kelly, particularly. Thomas was to Kelly what he had been incapable of being with anyone else.

There had been moments, strange moments, when she had felt jealous of her own daughter. She had never had that much of Thomas. Yet even that was changing. Often, to her surprise, she found herself in an exchange, with him telling her of his work and she telling him of hers. And he listened. Furthermore, he reacted. But then so did she. She now understood more than the motivation for his work but its necessity. She applauded it. Sensing this, he had casually mentioned how nice it would be if the "family" would visit the memorial at Eagle Nest next summer. She had been touched, but then she was frequently touched by Thomas these days. And by Kelly. And by herself.

The article in the *Boston Globe* was factual and informative. As he settled himself anew in his club chair, Thomas contemplated the controversy. He agreed with the twenty-eight Republican congressmen who felt the Vietnam monument planned for the nation's capital made "a political statement of shame and dishonor rather than being an expression of our national pride and courage, patriotism, and ability of all who served."

The words were mealy-mouthed but contained all the angry and bitter feelings Thomas and many veterans of Vietnam felt about the planned Washington, D.C., monument. Thomas put down the newspaper and breathed deeply. The smell of lasagne replaced that of baby in his nostrils. The young designer of the monument had said her work was "not to honor the war but rather to honor the sacrifices of the Vietnam veteran." He had been offended by her statement. He felt it discredited the war. Not that war shouldn't be discredited—but not just this war. To do that discredited the men who had believed in and fought it.

Again he examined the published pictures of the proposed monument. A big, black slab of stone rising gloomily from a trench. It had no American flag, no symbol to make it a living rather than a dead statement of war and peace and those who fought one to create the other. He would not publicly attack it but neither would he endorse it. His silence would work in his favor. Its deficiencies would help him in his fund raising among the DAV chapters and those companies and foundations sympathetic to the organization and all that *their* memorial at Eagle Nest represented. Tomorrow he would be traveling on its behalf again. It was not the best day to leave home, considering the circumstances, and yet perhaps it was. If Kelly could make it on her own tomorrow, she would make it on her own the rest of the way. And if she didn't, then she would try again the following day, and the day after that if necessary. But make it she would. He had determined that.

Once again Kelly checked through her closet, mentally sorting through her wardrobe for just the right clothes to wear the next day. She needed to blend, to conform, fade into the norm and become one of the many. Nothing in the closet seemed appropriate, particularly when she knew she wasn't one of the norm and furthermore didn't really wish to be. She never had—which is why she had discovered during her long talks with Vinnie that she had been footloose, too loose, and too fancy free. It had been her way of competing with Karl's athletic achievements and Kristan's everything, her way of gaining attention.

She had not thought then that she had other resources. She did not think she was particularly bright. Nor did she think she was particularly pretty. Vinnie had said if she changed her thinking, her life would follow suit. She had believed him then. Now, she wondered.

Teej was asleep in his crib. As she heard Reese call her to dinner, Kelly covered her baby lightly with the cashmere blanket Kristan had sent from London, and she wished for the moment that she could crawl in beside Teej. She would be safe behind the crib's bars, safe in the knowledge that her daddy was downstairs to keep the world outside her door and her own world safe.

All too well Reese understood Kelly's inability to eat. Too clearly she remembered her own first frightened steps into the world. So long ago, yet yesterday. She remembered something she had once heard at an A.A. meeting: new beginnings make for weak stomachs but strong people. She had been annoyed then by the mouthful of words. Now, she wanted to repeat it to Kelly and assure her it was true.

Kelly was sitting motionless at her place at the table, her hands at her side, her lasagne untouched before her. Reese impulsively reached out to touch her but Thomas's expression of warning removed her hand before it could reach Kelly's.

"What's happening, Kelly?" asked Thomas casually, as he continued to eat.

Kelly's mouth quivered as she tried to form words. Unable, she ran from the table, her sobs wrenching at Reese's insides as she made to follow. Again Thomas signaled her to stay put. He wiped his mouth with his napkin and then slowly followed Kelly up the stairs. For a moment, Reese sat at the table, doing as she had been told. Then, flushed with anger, she flung her napkin on the table, rose, and walked quickly up the stairs. Kelly was her daughter, too, and this was a family matter. She belonged in the room. Or so she thought until she caught their reflection in the mirror on the wall facing where they were sitting on Kelly's bed. Her daughter was cradled in Thomas's arms, crying softly as he rocked her gently.

"I'm afraid," Reese heard her say as she leaned against the wall just outside the bedroom. "I can't handle it."

"You can," said Thomas firmly.

"No, *you* can, so you think I can too. But I'm not you. No one is you. Everything is so easy for you."

"This isn't easy for me, Kelly," Reese heard Thomas say softly. "When you walk through those doors tomorrow, I'll be walking beside you. If you fail, I fail. If you succeed, I succeed. If you try, we've tried."

"Oh, Daddy, why couldn't I have taken a correspondence course to earn my diploma. All this for what?" asked Kelly, her voice fearful.

"All this for you," said Thomas quietly. "For your dignity, for your life. For your sense of self-respect."

"But why that school where everyone knows me? Why not Boston Latin? Here, they'll all be staring, judging me."

"Not half so much as you are judging yourself. Kelly, make peace with who you were and who you are today and nobody can touch you. Run, hide, and it will always be lurking, ready to engulf you. Don't give it that power, Kelly. Free yourself. If you can face yourself tomorrow at school, you'll face anything else life has to offer. You owe that to yourself, Kelly."

"You make it sound so easy," said Kelly bitterly.

"I know it isn't. I just know it can be done."

"How would you know?" asked Kelly, the antagonism evident in the tone of her voice.

"From having lived with your mother. From having observed her struggle, her fight to free herself. Your mother picked herself up when everyone else—including you, me, too—put her down. She was a drunk and everyone knew it but no one better than she. But she faced the fact. She faced the problem. And it wasn't easy, Kelly. Not even when we moved here. After the *Enquirer* got the story, her life was an open book. Still, she persisted. She showed her face and damn it, she did it. Conquered her alcoholism and made it through school. Your mother accomplished something I want for you: a life of her own. And Kelly, it must have taken more guts than you and I can ever imagine. She didn't have, as you do, people to fall back on. But look at her today. You can be like her, Kelly. It just takes that first step."

Reese presssed against the wall, tears burning her eyes.

"Dad, why can't you stay another day; just be here when I get home?" asked Kelly plaintively.

"I'd love to be, Kelly. It's what I want—to be with you and Teej—more than anything. But I know better. First, I have a job to complete: the memorial. That matters to me. Which is why I want you to see Eagle Nest. Somehow, the memorial is like freeing my own self. It gives me a sense of completeness and the peace I have been seeking. Secondly, Kelly, I have to get on with my life. Just as you must learn to make a life of your own, in some ways, so must I. It would be too easy for me if I just gave in to myself and set up house with you and Teej. But that's not the answer. Not for you or me. On your own, Kelly, you'll make your own life. Maybe you'll want college, or a career, maybe even marriage. But whatever you decide, someday, you'll be gone."

"Oh, Daddy, who would want me?" asked Kelly, near tears again.

Reese could feel the anger in Thomas's response. "Don't ever say that, Kelly. Not to me. I know you, and you're a terrific person. So full of life, of living, you sparkle. You bring joy. You always did. I admire you so, because I never had your qualities. You inherit them from your mother, the pert and perky Reese Tomlinson."

Reese slowly sank to the carpeted floor in the hallway, her back supported by the wall. She was crying quietly, half in pain for the waste of years and half in joy for what was.

"Dad," she heard Kelly say softly, "how come you don't hate me for what I did?"

"Hate you?" echoed Thomas, his voice reflecting disbelief at the question. A silence followed, during which Reese heard movement.

"Why did you bring me Teej?" she heard Kelly ask.

"Look at him," said Thomas, his voice firm, almost angry. "Look at him sleeping in your arms. Tell me, Kelly, no matter what he did, could you hate him, or would you hate yourself for whatever you did that might have caused him to act in such a way?"

Sobbing, Reese crawled away from the wall and into the entranceway of Kelly's room. "Damn it, Thomas Ollson," she yelled. "Just damn it! You did the very best you could do. We all did, under the circumstances, and anyone who can't see that can just go to hell!"

16

THEY STOOD AMID THE PILES OF SHAVINGS AND PLAS-
ter looking up to the balcony that ringed the semicircular living
room. Each was lost in his own thoughts. A pale sun drifted into
the room, doing nothing to take the cold from it. Their hands
were linked as each imagined what the room would look like once
it was furnished with children and other familiar loved objects.
The antique fireplace was larger than the one in Chelsea. It drew
you into the room. Marti liked it.

Matthew's arm slipped about Marti's shoulders, drawing her
nearer to his body's heat. He did not want her catching cold or
even a chill. Not with *this* pregnancy. Despite the doctor insisting
there was only some concern but no alarm about Marti's persistent
staining, Matthew worried. Marti was pale. Early in the pregnancy, she had lost weight that she had just barely regained. She
scoffed at his fears, reminding him she had just completed twenty
weeks of a TV season in nineteen, enough to make anyone look
haggard. He would worry less in this house. A new beginning. A
new address. Old mail to be forwarded only to him. No more
letters from the anonymous ones. No more threats, real or imagined from a telephone that rang but didn't speak when answered.
But these were not the reasons for his wanting to move.

They had discussed it in October. He had told her exactly
how he felt. The house in Chelsea had a history that did not

include him. The house was hers and despite their marriage could never be his. He wanted a place that was their own, one they would choose together, one where he truly was the man of the house. She had understood. A week later, they had found the brownstone on West 76th Street, just a few doors off Central Park. Together, they had designed the renovation, and she had been pleased that he had thought to design the basement floor as a separate unit for Mark, an apartment with his own entrance. To their relief, Mark had been delighted. Leaving the house that had been his home since childhood was not to be a problem.

As in previous weeks, they had come to see how the renovations were proceeding and to settle in, to feel that the place would soon be their own. Just as the baby grew within Marti, their house grew weekly before their eyes. Both baby and house were scheduled to be ready in March. From the paper bag Matthew had carried with him, he extracted the two containers of tea they had purchased on the corner of Columbus Avenue. He motioned to Marti to sit on the stairs leading up to the second-floor master bedroom. Easier said than done, she laughed as she held her bulging belly and lowered herself carefully to the step.

Marti cupped both hands around the container, hoping to draw its warmth into her hands. Despite the cold, she didn't want to leave. She motioned to Matthew, who was examining the restoration work on the hand-carved molding, to sit beside her. Huddled on the bottom step of the landing, they felt warmer.

"Would it be decadent to make love on this staircase?" she asked.

"No, but it would be impossible in your condition and mine—which is blue from the waist down."

She laughed, snuggling deeper into his arms. "Well, as they say, it's the thought that counts."

"I don't know who 'they' are but *they* are full of shit. I know. I had many of these 'thoughts' in Washington, and believe me, they don't count."

Again, she laughed. "I think you've gotten more randy since our marriage."

"It's the final flush of youth before senility sets in," he replied as he stroked her hair.

She grew silent, realizing it was the second time he had made an issue of age that morning. Earlier, in the taxi, driving up to the brownstone, he had explained his startling decision. "I'm past fifty," he had said. "That's not old but nonetheless it's not young. People have been known to die in their fifties." She had been shocked at the nonchalance with which he spoke the words. "Marti, at this point in my life, I need permanence, need to be in one place. With you and with our family."

Which is how she had learned he had resigned his position as an assistant to the director of Operation Outreach. He had not consulted her, rightfully feeling, she now realized, that the decision was his.

"What do you plan to do after the first of the year?" she asked suddenly.

"Drive you stark raving crazy," he whispered into her ear, "and not by passion but by being underfoot, by cleaning up your bathroom, visiting your set, interfering with the order of your life."

She screamed and slapped at him, wondering how he had done it again, read her mind as though she was nothing if not transparent.

"Do you think you can stand it?" he asked teasingly, his hand rubbing the inside of her thigh.

"Your actions speak of one thing but your words refer to another," she said, pushing his hand away. "No, I don't think I can stand it. I will probably go crazy. I'm used to a lot of space. Yet, it will be nice to know you are around, through the week and through the day."

"I'm setting up shop, you know. In a little office on your set. In all my years of practice, I never saw so many crazies running free as there are in television. One man even thinks he's the NBC peacock."

"Don't tell him he isn't," said Marti. "We make fortunes on his feathers."

He laughed and stretched. "Let's go. I don't want you sitting here in the cold for too long."

Marti looked up, but Matthew had already moved away. What he took for granted, she was just getting used to: his caring. His total, all-enveloping but nonsuffocating caring.

3 7 1

"Matthew," said Marti as she arranged herself with mock seductiveness, her body supine on the stairs, her skirt hoisted to her thigh, one hand cupped under her head, "how blue is blue in a world where they say all things are possible?"

*   *   *

The plane was but half filled; the day after Christmas proving to be an unpopular travel day. David was sitting on his knees, staring out the window of the jet, counting clouds. At five-and-a-half, he was a seasoned traveler, having logged more flight time with his globe-trotting mother than most adults do in the course of all their years.

Kay had wanted them to come for Christmas, but JJ had refused, not wanting to separate David, or himself, from the family. It was not without some bitterness that Kay had noted not so long ago the only family JJ had was her and Nelson. JJ had been firm in reminding her that times change and with them so do people. She had apologized.

It was not the first time Kay had to adjust, accommodate to David. A planned ski weekend before Thanksgiving was canceled due to David's tonsillectomy. The readjustments taxed Kay. She was not used to dealing with the well-being of a child, only animals. One required some caring; the other a total commitment. She soon learned JJ was totally committed to his son. She also learned that beyond her resentment was a deep respect for that commitment.

Since August, they had seen each other five times, all in Toronto, as Kay's own commitment to her practice prevented any long trips unless she could obtain coverage at her animal hospital. They stayed at her high-rise apartment in Toronto, he on a sofa bed she made up for him. He had been confused by her action, assuming when he had agreed to visit that they would be sleeping together. They were, but in different beds. When he protested, Kay was adamant. Where else should a friend sleep? she had asked. But wasn't he more than a friend? he had replied. Since neither could answer that question satisfactorily, Kay gave him an extra pillow and a thermal blanket and retired to her own bed.

Their weekends passed quickly and without difficulty, once JJ realized sex was not in the offing. Mainly they talked and seldom was it trivia. Most of Kay's friends were either in politics or were political. It took only a weekend to see that Kay had changed in but one respect. She now gave orders rather than carried them out for others. People, as involved as she was with the burgeoning antinuke issue, looked to her for leadership, which she provided without making an issue of it.

Their first visit to her cabin in Gravenhurst had made for changes. The professional person remained in Toronto, replaced by a girl in jeans and a parka whose hair was worn loosely, unstyled about her face. Although she wore no makeup, her cheeks looked as if she had overdone the blusher, her natural reaction to the Canadian cold. She had insisted on crosscountry skiing and then, as a reward for his aching muscles, had revealed her "pride and joy and great personal extravagance"—a snowmobile. They had spent the better part of the afternoon swooshing through the snow. The play was a side neither had ever seen in the other. When they discussed it later that evening before the rather crude fire JJ had built under Kay's amused eye, she had admitted play was not often there in her life. She spoke without regret. "Some people have fun in the traditional ways. I don't. Long ago I discovered my work, my interests, were fun. Otherwise, why would I do them?" He had looked at her and felt that another piece to his own puzzle had been put into place.

She did not make up the sofa-bed that night. Or any night thereafter. Their friendship had progressed to yet another level.

"Daddy?"

David's questioning voice interrupted JJ's musings. His son's back was still to him as he continued to stare out the plane's window. "Why are we going to Canada?"

"I've already told you, David. To see a friend."

"Kay," said David solemnly.

"Yes, Kay," repeated JJ, knowing his son was about to unload both barrels and shoot some very heavy questions at him.

"Why?"

"Because I like her and I thought you might like her, too."

"Is she your girlfriend?" asked David, turning now to face JJ.

"She's not my anything or anyone else's," said JJ, knowing his answer would not be understood or satisfying. "She is a woman I have known for a very long time. A very nice woman. I like her. She likes me. She wants to meet you, and since I like her so much, I want you to meet her."

"Do you love her?"

The question stunned JJ. On two counts. How did a child know what love was? Too much Kermit and Miss Piggy, JJ suspected. Did he love Kay? Funny how he had to be asked that question by another before he could ask it of himself.

"Yes, I suppose I do love her," said JJ slowly.

"The way you love Mama?"

JJ looked at David, trying to assess where his little mind was going. "No, David. I don't love your mama anymore. I did once and because I did, we had you. Which made whatever happened later between your mother and me unimportant. The bottom line is: we made you."

"Why don't you love Mama anymore?"

JJ sighed. "Because people change; one person goes one way and the other, another. Love doesn't always last forever—which is why we divorced."

"Could you divorce me?"

The question tore at JJ. His son's fears were revealed.

"Never, David. We will always be father and son. You're stuck with me, 'cause I ain't ever letting you go. David, the reason grownups stop loving each other has nothing to do with their children. It's totally separate. And because they stop loving each other doesn't mean they could ever stop loving their kids. If anything, you love them more."

"Why?"

JJ considered the question. "Because they're really a part of you and often, because they are the only sense of what otherwise was senseless."

"Daddy, are we getting married again?" asked David as he climbed onto JJ's lap.

JJ laughed: "Not unless you've got some girl stashed away somewhere. Have you?"

David giggled and grew still. JJ's answers had obviously satisfied him, more than they had JJ. Why hadn't he thought of marriage? What was it he wanted in a relationship? As important, what did Kay want? He would ask her, and, knowing Kay, she would tell him.

*   *   *

Reese and Thomas were at the kitchen sink, neither speaking as one washed and the other dried. A plate slipped from Thomas's hands and broke the silence with its crash. As Thomas picked up its pieces, Reese continued her scrubbing.

"You're going to wear a hole in that roasting pan," said Thomas as he looked over Reese's shoulder into the sink.

Reese turned off the water, wiped her hands on her apron, and sat down in the breakfast nook. Thomas followed. "I thought we were done with this years ago," he said as he sighed, exhausted.

"It is God's judgment and our penance," said Reese dourly. "Because we skipped out on it the first time around, He is making it that much worse this time."

Thomas didn't respond. He was thinking. "Do I impose a curfew?" he suddenly asked.

Reese looked puzzled. What demands can a parent place on a child who has a child of her own? "Yes," she decided. "Tell her tomorrow is a school day—for her and for me—and that we would appreciate it if she would be home at . . . say a decent hour. That's better than giving her a specific time."

"A specific time for what?" asked Kelly as she burst into the kitchen, a bundle of blond wrapped in lavender silk.

Neither Thomas nor Reese could immediately respond. Both were trying to remember when they had last seen their "little girl" in a dress and shoes with three-inch heels.

"Do you know where he is taking you?" asked Reese casually.

"To dinner and a disco," replied Kelly as she stuck her finger into the jar of peanut butter she had extracted from the refrigerator's recesses and proceeded to lick it.

"Oh, which one?" asked Thomas.

"Daddy, would you know one from the other if I told you?" replied Kelly. "Now look, you guys. I'm nervous enough without having to deal with your nerves."

"Wait until it's your child. Then you'll know what nervous is really like," said Reese.

"I still don't understand why he is not coming into the house to pick you up," said Thomas crossly.

"Because I asked him not to," said Kelly. "Dad, the boy is shy. It took a month before he would ask me out. Matters don't need any further complicating. Best he doesn't know who my father is . . . yet. You'd scare the hell out of him."

"I wouldn't do a thing," protested Thomas.

"You wouldn't have to," explained Kelly. "Your name, your image, would do it all. So let's give the kid a break. Both kids. Him and me."

"But you don't know a thing about this guy except he jogs with you every morning," continued Thomas, still unhappy.

"And that he attends Boston College and is cute as a button. That's enough for a first date. And on Valentine's Day. Now leave me alone before I come undone but totally! You would think from the way you two are carrying on that it was you going out on your first date in more than two years."

"Well, it is," said Thomas grumpily. "Frankly, I'm too old and too out of practice for this kind of thing. What time will you be home?"

"Early," said Kelly, "and don't you dare be waiting up downstairs. I might want to ask him in."

A car horn honking in front of their house sounded the mass alarm. Kelly couldn't find her pocketbook. Then she couldn't find the sleeve in her coat. Not even with Reese's help, which proved to be more of a hindrance. In the confusion, Thomas opened the front door and, despite the cold February night, strolled to the waiting car nonchalantly and was proceeding to play Inquisition when Kelly breezed past him and into the car, leaving each to wait as they told one another there was nothing to worry about. Once again in the kitchen, Reese said if Kelly had survived school she would survive dating. Whether they would or not was a totally different matter, she added as she poured each a fresh cup of tea.

"Suppose he gives her a bad time about Teej?" asked Thomas, hitting the source of their anxieties.

"Worse if she gives herself a hard time about Teej," replied

Reese. "Come on, get the cards. I'll give you a chance to win back the twelve thousand, six hundred and thirty-eight dollars you owe me from the night Kelly went out with the girls from her class for the first time."

"Twelve thousand, six hundred and twenty-six. You knocked with six points the last hand and I only had three," said Thomas as he shuffled the cards.

"You deal. I want to check on Teej," said Reese. "But if you dare look at my cards while I'm gone, God will get you."

"You have a very suspicious mind," groused Thomas.

"With good reason," replied Reese. "I've played gin rummy with you before."

Had it not been Arline's first party in her new condominium, Marti would have remained at home. It was difficult enough finding a dress to cover her rather remarkable girth these days but even more difficult to move that girth from one place to another. But Arline had pouted and Matthew had insisted it would do her good to get out. The only thing that would do her good to get out was the baby. All five hundred pounds of it. Only Matthew was enjoying her pregnancy at this point. Five weeks before post time and he still found her belly—now the size of a Sahara sand dune, she estimated—sexy.

Marti was watching Matthew—*her* Matthew, he of the three left feet—dancing with Arline to Michael Jackson's "Off the Wall." An apt title, thought Marti, as she surveyed Arline's bare apartment. Other than a futon mattress in the bedroom, the chair Marti was sitting in was it. The rest of the furniture was on order, and thus, Arline had declared, the place was perfect for a St. Valentine's Day massacre of their own.

Marti was bored. She wished it was she and not Arline dancing with Matthew. She hated being tied down, something she had been more with this pregnancy than any other. Rest, rest and more rest. With five weeks to go, she looked like a well-rested elephant, right down to her gray complexion.

When the music stopped, Matthew returned to her side with a plate of cold salads and meats. Her first bite was followed by the first stab of pain which caused her to sit up and breathe deeply. She was not frightened. She had experienced these pains the past two weeks. They always passed as quickly as they came. The second, however, caught her off guard, and it toppled the plate from her lap to the floor. The blood rushed from her head. Her body was wet, clammy. She clutched Matthew's hand. He squeezed it reassuringly, adjusted as he had become to the various discomforts that had troubled Marti's pregnancy.

"Matthew," Marti gasped, as another pain tore through her, "if I'm not in labor, I'm giving a damn good imitation of it."

He helped her from the chair, saw the puddle from her own water, and began giving explicit instructions to those who had assembled about Marti in concern. The doctor was called, as was the doorman who was sent to find a taxi. Arline wrapped Marti in a blanket and, with Matthew, moved her slowly out of the apartment toward the elevator. Tears were streaming down Marti's face. "It hurts," she explained as the elevator doors opened. "Please, call my mother," she asked as the doors closed behind her and Matthew, leaving Arline speechless for perhaps the first time in her life.

"You now owe me one hundred and thirty three thousand dollars," said Reese, as she cut the cards. "Will this be cash? A check will also do."

"Where the hell are they? It's almost past eleven," said Thomas as he once again got up from the kitchen table.

"Past eleven! Oh, my God, maybe we should call the police. Imagine, a girl past eighteen out after eleven," said Reese mockingly. "Would you hear yourself? Thomas, she's okay. She knows who she is. She's doing exactly what you wanted her to do— making a new start. She'll manage. Just as she has managed everything else."

"She has done well, hasn't she?" said Thomas, calmer now than he had been all evening.

"Take a bow, you deserve it," said Reese. "Now, before I sit down again, how about something to eat?"

"Reese, we've already had waffles, then ice cream, and, no more than ten minutes ago, some fruit."

"If that's a hint, forget it. All that stands between my becoming as bananas as you is a banana. Or a peach. Or a cookie. Except there's nothing left in this damn refrigerator except half-empty jars of peanut butter."

"I like you heavier," said Thomas suddenly. "You no longer look like a plucked chicken."

"It's only five or six pounds," said Reese, knowing it was ten and not caring—something that surprised her.

"It makes a big difference," said Thomas. "Listen, you're not planning on driving home tonight, are you?"

"Why? Do you think I'm too fat to fit behind the steering wheel?"

"It's just that it's late."

"It's not that late," said Reese, pretending to be annoyed when she was actually pleased by his concern. "And it only takes fifteen minutes or less to get home at this hour."

"I'll follow in my car—make sure you arrive home safely."

"Now just stop it. Thomas, you're becoming impossible. I can take myself home. In fact, I'm going to do that right now."

"Before Kelly gets home?"

"Absolutely. I just remembered she is not a child. Nor are we. Despite appearances to the contrary this evening."

"You're going to leave me to wait alone?" asked Thomas, his voice incredulous at the possibility.

"I suggest you go to sleep," said Reese like a parent to a child.

"How can anyone sleep in this house with all the noise you two are making," said Kelly as she stood in the kitchen doorway. "What is it with you two? Do you want to wake Teej or just the dead?"

Thomas was looking over Kelly's shoulder to see if someone else was there.

"I sent him home," said Kelly. Seeing their surprised faces, she explained, "He's a great jogger and a good dancer but a total nerd. I was bored. But it was nice to get out again. Only I'm tired. So tired that it's awesome! I'm going to bed. Thanks for taking care of Teej."

After kissing each, she was gone, leaving them with expressions on their faces that Kelly would have called dumb.

"Well, it's been a lovely evening," said Reese. "The next time the occasion arises, do ask her to do what most girls do: sneak out of the house and meet the man in some crummy hotel on the other side of town."

"Regarding the money I owe you—the one-hundred-plus grand—what say I take you to dinner one night next week and we'll call it square."

"Sounds perfectly reasonable to me," said Reese as she wrapped her scarf about her neck. "Just which McDonalds did you have in mind? I only ask so I'll know how to dress."

He was aware only of his mother-in-law's hand covering his while her other clutched her rosary. Together they waited; she praying, he thinking. His was not the usual anxious wait of the expectant father. No comical and typical situation this. Without past experience in these matters, he nonetheless knew something was wrong. Marti's labor had been too sudden, too quick, and too terrifyingly painful. Although not a religious man, Matthew clutched Carolyn's hand as if through her, he, too, might be heard in her constant silent prayers.

"The doctor was standing before him. "Dr. Strohl?"

He looked up into the drawn and concerned face of his colleague.

"Your child, Dr. Strohl."

"My wife," Matthew interrupted.

"Your child . . ."

"My wife!" bellowed Matthew in demand.

"She is sleeping. She has lost a considerable amount of blood but she should be all right."

"*Should* be?" challenged Matthew, his voice again rising.

"Should be, Dr. Strohl," said Trebe calmly. "There is no reason to suspect otherwise but there are no guarantees. There is always the possibility of infection."

"Can I see her now?"

"Dr. Strohl, your son . . ."

He didn't want to hear it. Carolyn was holding his arm, steadying more than his body, his very being.

"He is alive but very weak. He's only four pounds, nine

ounces but his heart is good and we have every hope he will survive."

Caught between joy and grief, Matthew felt as though someone or something had ripped him down the middle. A son, alive but near death. Too near.

"Can I see him?"

Trebe examined Matthew's face, saw its cold composure, and then acted as he saw fit. He nodded, turned, and led the way as Matthew followed.

*   *   *

OLLSON OBSERVES

Dateline: Friday, March 26, 1982. Washington, D.C.

One hundred and twenty ex-combat troops and politicians broke ground today on the Mall for the six-million-dollar Vietnam Memorial. I watched as they stood with shovels in hand all along the five-hundred-foot length of the V in which this controversial monument will soon rise. I saw men whose faces looked familiar although I had never seen them before. Where once they seemed hostile, they now appeared friendly. They could have been a mirror of my soul.

There was a joint service color guard, and the American flag they held flapped in the wind. There were many "flaps" this day; in the wind, the air, and in the hearts of those who listened as the command came to "Put your blades to the earth. Break ground." There was a mighty cheer from the several hundred spectators as the Marine Corps Band played "God Bless America." Some didn't cheer. Like me, they wept.

Although I opposed the Vietnam War, I do not oppose the memorial. I see it as a memorial to the people, *all the people,* who suffered this war needlessly. It will stand as a monument to all those who fought for and against the war. It is a tribute to all those who wanted peace . . . honor . . . dignity, and, whether you were for or against the war, these were the things for which you were fighting. I see this monument as a celebration of that fight. Not of the war. Never that. But of people's fight, the American people's fight to agree or dissent.

I disagreed, particularly with the men who fought the war. I

3 8 1

now understand they did what they must. Whatever their reasons. And so, the Vietnam veteran has been wronged. He has been tried and judged and found guilty—without trial—for crimes he truly did not commit. Today, he is battle-scared. Even now, a decade after the war, he is confused, angry, rejected, and hostile. He is a force his country must reckon with or be made to reckon with. He has survived the war only to fight another more insidious. He is in effect the Unknown Soldier. Some turn from him because this country lost a war it should never have fought. What they fail to realize is: he, our soldier, did not lose it. His government did.

The Vietnam Memorial can never assuage all the hurts those in this nation suffered. It cannot erase the humiliation, the pain, the rejection, so many of its "veterans" experience to this day. But it is a beginning. It is first of its kind: a monument that celebrates not war but people. When "they" try to tell us otherwise, we should remember that.

*   *   *

It was near midnight but Kay made no move to leave the third-floor offices of the Bloor Street Church, where the bulk of her volunteer work as a member of the Toronto Disarmament Network took place. The weekly Tuesday meeting had ended an hour ago but still Kay sat reflecting on the past, her present, and the future she, and others like her, were fighting to ensure. There were many such nights. There always had been. Her day never ended with the last patient at the animal hospital.

Years ago, thought Kay, as she brushed wisps of hair in disarray from her face, it was he who was single-minded in his work as an exile. Then, people drifted in and out of his life with few, if any, reaching the central core of the man. She had upon occasion, but just upon occasion. Often now, Kay felt as if she had become the person JJ had been then. People, wonderful people, concerned people, drifted into her life but few reached its core. Until JJ. Still, it was her work that mattered. More? As much? She had no slide rule to judge. But her work fed her, energized and revitalized. Not her work with animals, which she enjoyed and which was necessary, but her work for the people. As much as within her veterinarian offices, she was about saving lives.

3 8 2

Kay had never thought of herself as a passionate person but rather as one who was methodical, a solid, stabilizing influence on others with her cool logic. But she was passionate on the issue of disarmament. Her hours away from her practice were spent trying to reach the Canadian public, to make them comprehend that the disarmament issue was not something solely between the United States and Russia and that they and all others *between* the major powers could be annihilated. By bombs. Nuclear bombs.

She had made a convert of JJ. Actually, she hadn't but David had. JJ had questioned her position that children are deeply affected by the threat of nuclear warfare. He discounted as propaganda those studies that "proved" children suffer from nuclear nightmares that breed ongoing anxiety. When she had suggested he speak with David, he had been hesitant, not wanting, he claimed, to stir untroubled waters. She reminded him that those same waters often run deep. And so JJ had asked and David's responses had surprised him. Within his son, there were thoughts beyond Sesame Street, awareness and fear that should not lurk within one so young. The talk had disturbed both father and son with David awaking in the middle of the night, shaking and sobbing but unable to define his fears.

They had seen new sides of one another that night. He had seen her ineffectualness with children—no matter how she tried—and she had seen the opposite in him. She had also seen that at least one person had at last and indeed penetrated his core. She had remonstrated herself, thinking and judging herself deficient. Children were not like animals. You couldn't just pet a frightened child as you would a dog. A child required something more that she had not yet learned how to give. And yet she loved children. They, through all of her efforts for disarmament, were her priority. Others might disbelieve such a statement, but she knew it to be true. So did JJ.

They were closer now than they had ever been, each understanding the place of the other in the relationship. She was not his whole life or he, hers. For which Kay felt relieved. Except at late hours like this when she was tired and felt the need of comfort that could only be supplied in the arms and the bed of a man she loved. She would be without that comfort until the following Monday when she would join JJ in New York in preparation for Ground Zero Week. As the event drew closer, so did her anxieties. She would be meeting his family. She would be staying at his home. She would be within a role she both wanted and yet feared.

As Kay took her personal things from the desk and slipped them in her briefcase, she admitted something she preferred to ignore: her love for JJ. It was different than it had once been. A decade ago it had hurt and she had felt helpless and adrift within it. Then she thought he should be the part of her life that was missing. She had no such feeling today. He augmented her life but he was not necessary to it. Whether that was good or bad or a bit of both she no longer knew.

*   *   *

It was a day to rejoice, to feel the pluses and not the minuses, thought Marti, as she walked, her arm linked through Matthew's, from the limousine and through the April rain and into the hospital. Once again, they were greeted by the press, undoubtedly alerted by the hospital's public-relations person. Marti's brief statement: "We are so happy to be finally bringing our son home" temporarily satisfied those who had chronicled the life of Nicholas Strohl in detail these past weeks. And still, thought Marti, they did not have the full story. And never would, she determined. Her son was entitled to his privacy.

Despite all, Nicholas had lived, amazing the doctors. At seven weeks of age, he was just shy of seven pounds. No matter of his struggle. She would not look back, only ahead. To the future; his and their own.

As they walked from the elevator to where they were to meet Dr. Morris, the pediatrician, Marti could feel the tension in Matthew's body. Instinctively Marti knew only time could give Matthew the reassurance he needed. To see the days come and go, taking the months with them but not Nicholas, that would ease his fear.

If only his practice hadn't been just renewing itself, Matthew would be less smothering, thought Marti. He was everywhere, not only smothering her with attention she did not need but smothering Lynne, who rebelled against the emotional restrictions such intense love placed upon her. He also questioned everything, whether she was doing too much, and if Tisa Bannington had the ability to care for his children. She had assured him the governess did. She was carefully assuring him now, insisting Dr. Morris be quite specific in his explanation so there would be no misunderstanding, no room for false doubts and needless anxieties.

"Your son's condition is serious but not grave. There is absolutely no reason why, with the right care, he should not become a relatively normal, healthy child."

Did you hear, Matthew? Marti wanted to scream. A normal, healthy child. But she could hear his response . . . with the right care. Well, damn it, they would give that. Easily. Totally. Lovingly. It was not difficult. Let no one make it difficult. Which is why no one but the family knew of Nicholas's problem. No one must be allowed to make it more difficult for him than it truly was.

"I want to see Nicholas frequently, once a month at first," said Morris. "Of course, should you notice any change in his condition . . ."

"Such as?" interrupted Matthew, although they had been told the symptoms many times over.

"The general state of the child's well-being. Keep a daily diary. Note the child's appetite, his sleeping patterns. Check his pulse. Does he appear sluggish? Note the number and the consistency of his stools. Check his tongue for thickness, the texture of his skin, the consistency of his hair, the . . ."

She more than knew but had become keenly aware of all the physical signs of a child born with but a partial thyroid gland. She had asked; they had told her. She had asked again and they had repeated what they had already said. Unsatisfied, she researched still more in the medical library. Her son had a potential life-threatening malfunction. Without medication, he could suffer seizures and mental retardation. With the grain or less of desiccated thyroid tablets, the dosage to be determined month by month, the malfunction could be controlled. It *would be* controlled. She had determined that.

"And if we see that Nicholas is doing well, we can always reduce the amount of medication he is taking. Or add to it if need be. By all means do not hesitate to call at the slightest hint that something may be wrong," added Morris as he signaled to one of the nurses near the station by the nursery who nodded and then disappeared.

As they waited, Marti looked at the people coming and going, most looking happy. No, not happy but ecstatic, she decided. Babies did that to people. Babies and children. They were magical. Which is why she had refused the Elavil when offered it at the hospital. She knew when she returned home, Lynne would be one of her two best antidepressants. The other would be her work. Which was again about children. The Physicians for Social Responsibility had asked that she address high-school and college audiences on the perils of nuclear warfare during Ground Zero Week and she had accepted. Despite Matthew's objections. Nicholas would be home but two weeks, he had argued. He would need her. Yes, he would, but so would all the other children who hopefully would one day guide the world from madness to some form of sanity. And Nicholas would be cared for. She would be there for a good part of the day as would be Tisa Bannington. As she knew Matthew would be, hovering about, a foreman, a supervisor, a man who eventually could do more harm than good if she didn't wedge herself between him and their son. She could not allow Matthew's insecurities, which she well understood, to be transferred to Nicholas. Or to her. They must not bind Nicholas to them.

The nurse arrived holding their baby in her arms. She turned to give him to Marti but found Matthew taking the child from her, cradling it ever so gently in his arms. They turned and walked silently down the hall, Marti's hand in Matthew's coat pocket as his arms made a secure nest for their son. People in the elevator stared but none spoke, waiting for later to comment on the man with child, with tears in his eyes.

At the doors of the hospital, Marti heard Matthew say softly, "How can anyone so little have such very big problems?"

She wheeled him about to face her. She could feel the anger not just in her words but in her face as she replied, "It isn't a big problem unless we choose to make it one. Our son is alive. He is well. He is thriving. Treat him that way. He is entitled to a full life with no restrictions, and to call him a *little* anything with big problems is to restrict him. I'll not have it. Nor will he. And if you think about it, nor will you. Now let's take our child home," she concluded as she sped past the waiting press and to the limousine where she stood, holding the door open for her husband and child.

*   *   *

April 29, 1982

And now you poison the children. With talk that stinks
of communistic garbage. Although God continually
punishes, you persist in your evil. I warn you. Keep out
of our schools, away from our children. Children . . .
all children . . . even yours . . . the innocent . . . must
be protected and I, and others like me, will protect
them.

*   *   *

"Do you think they'll be able to come?" asked Thomas.

"Who?" replied Reese as she leaned across the kitchen table to see whose invitation Thomas was now addressing. "Oh, yes, I do. In fact, Marti said on the phone this morning that if Nicholas continues to do well, they would not only come but stay for a long weekend before she resumes work on her series."

Reese could see Thomas was pleased. His family's attendance at Kelly's high-school graduation was more important to him than to Kelly. As Reese addressed invitations first to Karl and then Kristan, she wondered how Thomas would accept what was sure to be their absence. Karl would again plead exhaustion from his exhaustive medical school studies and Kristan . . . Kristan was better at sending gifts, as Reese had learned. Scarfs and scents, things she could use but not love. Which was ironic now that she had learned how to love without using.

"Thank God our children are healthy," she heard Thomas say as an afterthought to her news about Nicholas. She loved him for that. No matter what his children did, or didn't do, Thomas loved them. Perhaps not in the way they would have wanted but in his way. Reese wondered if Karl or Kristan would ever understand that. She was grateful she finally did. Suddenly, Reese felt the

3 8 7

urge to talk, particularly since what she had to say was basically about children.

"Thomas, the reason Marti called. . . . I had mentioned I might be coming to New York for the June twelfth march for disarmament. There is a group of teachers from the New England area who wish to make their presence, and our feelings, known. Marti wanted to know if I wanted to stay with them. I'd like to go, but one thing concerns me."

He was not looking at her but focusing on the invitations, although she knew it was she who had his attention. "Could this pose problems for you? In your work, that is. I know how close you are to finally establishing an organization independent of the DAV to care for the Eagle Nest memorial and I don't want to hurt your work in any way. I mean . . . there is the possibility the press might pick up my participation in the march and make something of it."

She could feel him thinking. She knew how opposed he was to those who championed disarmament, thinking them short-sighted and dangerous even if sincere. When he remained silent, she wondered if he was replaying their disagreements on the subject. That there had been disagreements and not arguments or battles had surprised and pleased her. Whether or not he had understood her position had not mattered as much as the fact that he had tried. That had impressed her. She had liked him for that. She had liked herself for having expressed how she felt. She regretted not having done so sooner. Like twenty-three years sooner.

"It could be embarrassing," he said finally. "It just might give certain people an excuse to cop out. I need corporate funding. It's a long shot, but it just might look to some that since the ex-wife of a veteran has misgivings, why shouldn't they."

She flinched when he said that, aware there was more truth than not in his words.

"I'm not saying that would happen, only that it is a possibility," he continued. "So if you're asking, I can only say I'd feel a lot better if you didn't take the chance . . . didn't march. But only for the sake of the memorial."

Although she had asked, Reese had not received the hoped-for answer and was angry. She had wanted to make her presence known as a protest against war, any kind of war. She had learned from her own life that it wasn't just neutron bombs that kill families. But now she could not, would not go. She had seen the dedication with which he had worked for Eagle Nest. She could not risk his losing what meant so much to him.

"I won't go," she said softly.

"I appreciate that," he said as he patted her hand.

There was an awkward silence as Reese tried to work through her anger. He had not stopped her; she had stopped herself. But why? she asked. Because he is the priority. The answer surprised her as much as the question she heard him asking.

"Will you come to Eagle Nest with me this summer? I want you to see it. I thought we might all go when Kelly graduates and you finish your school year."

Reese had known Thomas would ask this of her as he had once before. She was glad she had a steady excuse this time, glad she did not have to risk an honesty that might hurt their relationship. She did not wish to visit Eagle Nest, not just this summer but at any time. It was too much of the Vietnam War. Which was exactly its intent. But for too many years the war had interposed itself on her life, and Reese simply was not interested in furthering any monuments to it. Although she understood its importance to Thomas, Reese also understood how that importance had at one time negated her, the family, and their lives together. Or so she felt. She knew he wouldn't agree.

"Not this summer, Thomas," she said as she finished addressing an invitation to Margaret in Los Angeles where filming on her series for the fall season had already begun. "Perhaps in the fall, over a long weekend, like Columbus or Veterans Day. But this summer I have plans. I'm thinking," she added slowly, hesitantly, realizing she would now have to tell him all, "of twenty-eight days in South America. There is a charter flight, sponsored by the Teachers Association, that leaves July twelfth. I've sent my deposit. It may be my last chance for this sort of vacation for a very long time. . . . Now that I've heard from Boston University," she added.

"What have you heard from Boston University?" he asked when she didn't volunteer any further information.

"To my surprise—I mean, they do tend to accept only much younger people—I've been accepted in their doctoral program."

She didn't wait for his response but hurried on with an explanation she prepared, never thinking it might be unnecessary. "Thomas, I have ideas. Good ones. I want to create the special educational programs and administrate, not just teach them. I can be of much more service that way."

She was sweating, anxious, and annoyed with herself for caring about his approval. She expected he would plead responsibility—hers toward Kelly and Teej. She was certain he would pounce on any number of things that would prove her idea foolhardy. She wouldn't allow him. "I've already applied for scholarships. And there are loans I can obtain from the teachers' union. I can manage. I plan whenever possible to teach by day and attend classes in the late afternoon and early evening."

"You do not need charity," he said softly, although she could see he was angry. "Those who truly need should receive it. You have family, damn it, so unless you have a problem with accepting my help, I'm offering it."

She looked at him, stunned.

"Damned if we don't have more than just Kelly's graduation to celebrate," he said as he sealed the invitation to Vinnie and Este. "Well, Eagle Nest will wait. There's always next year and the year after that. By then, you'll have your degree and how many families can boast of a doctor who makes house calls?"

It was a weak joke, but its strong sentiment made her reach across the table to hug him. She felt the rigidity of his body, as if he was afraid of her touch. Then, he softened. At first she thought she imagined him speaking, the words had been so barely audible. "I think, to cut expenses, you should give up your apartment and move back home," he whispered into her hair so she couldn't read his face. "It's not a condition, of course," he added hastily, "just something for you to think about."

17

JJ LEANED OUT HIS OPEN WINDOW TO TEST THE DAY, a not unusual occurrence with Manhattan apartment dwellers. It was sunny and warm. Nonetheless he called to David to take his jacket. The weather might change, he replied to the question that was more a protest.

"Are we ready yet?" David yelled from his bedroom.

"We are, but your Aunt Marti hasn't arrived. Soon as she does, we go. Do you need to make a last trip to the john?"

"I've already gone four times," said David, entering the room, wearing his Mets baseball cap, a Luke Skywalker T-shirt, and jeans. "I wish we'd go already."

"Me, too," said JJ as he signaled for David to climb onto his lap so they could both watch for Marti's limousine from their perch on the window sill. David was excited; JJ nervous. It was David's first march in a parade and JJ's first speech in many years before what was expected to be thousands of people. Including his son. Young as David was, JJ felt glad he would be with him this day. The march was for and about him and others like him who were just beginning their lives.

"Will there be balloons and floods?" asked David.

"You mean floats. And no, there won't be. This is a parade of people, David. And we're marching with them to show the world that we all believe in the same thing: peace."

"No bombs," said David earnestly.

"Right. No bombs," repeated JJ, knowing the word itself conjured up great fear in his child. Again, it was the power of television. To alarm and yet educate. Or numb, if one saw the same scene over and over again to the point where it had no meaning. Little children watching mushroom clouds on the news and in sci-fi pictures. It hardly seemed right and yet, it also wasn't wrong.

"David, if you get tired, tell me and I'll hoist you on my shoulders and we'll march together that way. And the w-h-o-l-e world can see you. And you'll be able to see the whole world."

"Will I be able to see Mama in Nicarawa?"

"Nicaragua, David. And no, you won't be able to see that far, but almost."

"Daddy, what are you going to talk about?" asked David just as JJ spied Marti's limousine rounding the corner.

"You, me, us, and people like us. How we want to live, demand to live, and are entitled to live. That's why I'm glad you're marching with me," said JJ as he gave David a squeeze. "You're adding your voice to mine. Making your presence known is what it's called."

"No bombs!" said David again firmly.

"No bombs," repeated JJ solemnly. "But there's Aunt Marti. She's late again."

Not since she was a little girl had Marti felt a similar excitement. The day reminded her of those she had spent with her father on the boardwalk at Nantasket, the two intent on having fun on a fine summer's day, as were the crowds who gently jostled as they, too, drifted along. She had that feeling now as they walked slowly up First Avenue toward Dag Hammarskjold Park where she and JJ would join the other speakers and address the crowd.

They had left the limousine at 42nd Street, as walking was the only possible way to reach their destination. The crowds were huge but they surged forward with a gentleness that denied their immensity. Although she and JJ were recognized, they were not disturbed. People smiled, greeted them, and moved on. She was not the focus but only a part of the day. She felt foolish pushing an empty stroller, but Lynne had insisted that if her cousin could walk, so could she. Marti didn't doubt her four-year-old at all. Her daughter lived in the fast lane and when her feet tired, her mouth picked up the slack and compensated. Nothing was ever quiet around Lynne, who was delighted to be at the march, at last singled out for the preferential treatment that more often than not went to the unasked-for and unwanted baby brother. Matthew would definitely have the easier day, thought Marti as she grabbed Lynne just as her daughter was about to join the Asian-American Caucus on their march uptown with the other groups of demonstrators. All he had to contend with was a barbecue pit and dinner for the family. And Nicholas, of course, although the baby now required so little care.

Lynne fell, scrapped her knee, and was crying until JJ hoisted her onto his shoulders where she could see the crowd pock-marking First Avenue, many already wending their way toward Central Park where the major rally would take place later on the Great Lawn. Just a stone's throw from the house on 76th Street, thought Marti, envying Lynne's perch. They were now in the immediate area of the U.N. and the crowds had thickened to the extent that any kind of movement was slow and awkward. From the sound system feeding the marchers with encouraging words, she heard the voice of Coretta Scott King. Although dwarfed by the crowd, Marti felt an incredible sense of safety, of oneness. She imagined this was what Woodstock must have been like.

About her, people were beaming. On the side streets, she could barely discern the groups waiting to enter the march. She saw flags announcing ARTISTS FOR NUCLEAR DISARMAMENT, LAWYERS FOR NUCLEAR DISARMAMENT, PHYSICIANS FOR SOCIAL RESPONSIBILITY. She and JJ would be marching with one of those waiting groups as soon as they delivered their three-minutes-each speech from the speakers' platform.

"Hey, Ma. Ma!"

Marti turned toward the direction of the familiar voice and saw Mark pushing through the crowd. His face flushed, his hand clutching the ban-the-bomb balloon Kay had sent from Canada, he looked more the excited kid than the serious composer/conductor soon to be a Juilliard graduate. "I saw Lynne on Uncle J's shoulders from across the street," he explained. "I'm marching with the performing artists group. Grandma's with me. She wants to know what time is dinner."

"Tell her about three and, Mark, make sure she doesn't over-tire herself," Marti yelled as Mark disappeared back into the burgeoning crowd. Ordinarily, Marti would have felt threatened by such a mass, but not this day. She was invincible. They were all invincible. Happily, she would soon see them all, stretching out before her from the speakers' platform. People with people. People shaping history and, whether they realized it or not, shaping policies of governments and politics of the world. A man by the speakers' platform tapped her on the shoulder, pointed at the sign he was carrying: WAR IS INSANE AND SICK and asked her to sign it. She did. He shook her hand. She kissed him.

JJ was grumpy, annoyed at what he had just heard. There was a backup among the speakers. One had overstayed his welcome, seemingly carried away not just by the significance of the occasion but his own voice. The committee wanted to know if they would double up, forget their notes in favor of their hearts, as he was asked by one of the organizers. Speak as one and for but three minutes total rather than each. With a dramatic gesture, JJ shredded the speech he had prepared over the course of the week. Although disappointed, Marti did likewise. They were thanked profusely by the agitated member of the speakers committee. Yes, she would indeed keep an eye on the children while the two of them were on the platform. No problem, she assured them. And if they, themselves, looked down, the children could be seen exactly where they had left them. Not to worry.

"David," said JJ as he knelt before his son. "Your aunt and I are going up on the platform for a few minutes. You stay here with Lynne. Don't let her out of her stroller no matter how she cries. You're in charge. And don't be frightened. In just a few seconds, you'll hear our voices."

But David wasn't frightened and David wasn't listening. He was too excited by the crowds of smiling faces, the party spirit, and the entire aura of the day. Marti took David's hand and placed it on the stroller, telling both children to be good, hoping Lynne would realize from the tone of her voice the implied penalty if goodness was not observed.

"No bombs!" yelled David laughing.

"No bums!" echoed Lynne.

"Never to both!" said Marti emphatically as she hugged first Lynne and then David. The crowd roared. She knew from the way all eyes were now turned in her direction that she and JJ had just been introduced.

*   *   *

"1-2-3-4-we-don't-want-a-nuclear-war. 5-6-7-8-we-don't-want-to-radiate."

What you are listening to is the chant of some of the estimated three quarters of a million people who demonstrated in New York today at what organizers called "A March for Peace and Disarmament."

Good evening. This is Jessica Savitch for NBC News in Washington.

They came from all over the globe, thousands upon thousands of concerned citizens. They joined hands, sang songs. In pairs, in groups, in numbers of one, they carried signs of protest written in dozens of languages that made it clear to world leaders that they want no more nuclear arms buildup, no new nuclear weapons built, no stockpiling. They want peace. They want disarmament. And they want it now.

The march began early this morning at a rally in Dag Hammarskjold Park by the United Nations where tens of thousands came to hear such speakers as Coretta Scott King, Orson Wells, John Ollson, Jr., and actress-activist, Marti Tiernan. It was for the latter that tragedy once again struck; this time in the form of a kidnapping. As she spoke, Ms. Tiernan's youngest child, Nicholas Strohl, was snatched from his carriage outside the family home on the West Side of Manhattan when his father left him unattended to answer a telephone.

Tonight, in New York, Marti Tiernan issued a plea for her son's safety to his kidnappers, revealing that the four-month-old prematurely born child is in need of daily medication for an abnormal thyroid condition.

First reports have a woman—five-foot-three inches, about one hundred and thirty pounds, blond, Caucasian—leaving the scene of the kidnapping in a blue Mustang.

3 9 5

Ironically, at the time Nicholas Strohl was kidnapped, his mother and uncle were marching with the Parents of Children for Survival, one of the protesting anti-nuclear-armament groups.

* * *

On the way home from his country club, Bennett Cours was replaying the last hole of his golf game when his beeper rudely interrupted his birdie fantasy. It was the first time that day that reality forced its way into Cours's life. Waiting for a break in the early evening traffic, Cours shifted from the outside to the inside lane on the highway and then onto the shoulder of the road. Relaxed from his Saturday on the golf course and rather pleased with himself and life in general, Cours picked up the phone in his Mercedes and dialed his answering service.

"You rang, madam?" he asked of the familiar voice. Seconds later Cours was dialing again. This time it was the number of the patient who said it was an emergency without giving details.

"Coreen? It's Dr. Cours. . . . What's the problem?"

As he lit his pipe, his mind only somewhat more focused on his patient than on his golf game, Cours took in the information. He laughed. "It reminds me of when the missus and I went to Hawaii two summers back but our luggage flew the friendly skies to Seattle. It happens all the time these days. Tell your sister if she's lucky, she'll meet up with her baggage sometime before she reaches that great baggage claim in the sky.

"Yes, I know. Her doctor can't write a prescription from Houston. It's not recognized out of state. . . . How old is the baby? Four months. . . . Did he make the trip all right? . . . Good. No problem. Except . . . Coreen, Wilton's Drugstore is closed at this hour. . . . Yes, I have the number of an all-night pharmacy in Newark. Yes, I can phone it in, but, Coreen, from what you tell me, that baby can wait until Monday morning when Wilton's opens. . . . Yes, I understand. Your sister will feel safer if she has the prescription with her. Fine . . . I'll make it for thirty days and two refills. . . . It's on Market Street. . . . Right smack in the middle of beautiful downtown Newark. . . . By the time you get there, the prescription should be ready. A quarter grain of desiccated thyroid. . . . No problem, Coreen. . . . By the by, have your sister bring the baby in for a checkup in a couple weeks. These cases can be tricky. Sometimes the picture changes rather quickly. . . . What? Yes. I'll do it right now. . . . Yes, that's the pharmacy. I'll tell them you'll pick it up in twenty minutes to a half-hour. . . . Anytime, Coreen. Good-night."

*   *   *

In his twenty-six years with the FBI, Kevin Maney had investigated every conceivable federal crime. Most cases he attacked dispassionately. Not kidnapping. A father himself, Maney, through the eyes of a child, felt the emotional and often physical abuse a kidnapped child endured. *If* he endured. Although outwardly a nonemotional man, Maney reacted to kidnappings with a rage that his outward calm and methodical approach to the problem belied.

At the moment, as he sat with the parents of the kidnapped child in the living room of their home, Maney was marveling at Marti Tiernan's calm and methodical approach to the problem. Without breaking once, she had answered the often repetitious, often rude questions of the FBI, the New York Police, and the Missing Persons Bureau. Almost dispassionately, she had described in the most minute detail her missing child, understanding that the information would be instantly fed to the computer at the National Crime Information Center in Washington. That it was now prepared to tell any law-enforcement officer investigating the similarities between a found child and her own was the only motivation she had needed to perform a difficult task. With the same calm, she had given the same description to the media. And when she had faced the TV cameras, had made her plea to the kidnapper with the information about her child's condition and the medication needed to control it, she had been emotional but always in control. It amazed Maney that Marti Tiernan had yet to crack. He suspected when she did, he would be among the first to know it.

Normally in kidnappings, among the first suspects were the parents. But it had been obvious to Maney from the beginning that neither Marti Tiernan nor Matthew Strohl had engineered their own child's kidnapping. There was no marital dispute here to prompt such an action, although a case could be made for an

3 9 7

ideological rift. She had marched in an antinuclear-armament parade; he, a former military man, had not. Interesting but not a lead, Maney had decided within the first few minutes of his investigation.

Maney had spent considerable time reading through the dossier on Marti Tiernan as soon as it had arrived from FBI files. If what he had seen of the Tiernan woman that afternoon was any indication, the dossier told but partial truths. She was more than just a past member in "good standing" on the Nixon enemies list. Marti Ternan was on several people's enemies list, if her hate mail was any barometer. To certain segments of the population she was a hero, to others a villain. Her activities during the Vietnam War and afterward, as an activist, feminist, supporter of several political candidates who not only leaned but toppled to the left and beyond, made her a controversial figure. In the biographical data, she was portrayed as intelligent but overly emotional . . . quixotic . . . prone to sudden changes . . . unstable. The picture did not match the one Marti Tiernan was presenting this afternoon. Her questions about the investigation had been precise. She did not complicate matters with hysteria. She was waiting. The few witnesses to the crime were now helping the FBI artist prepare a composite sketch. Upon its completion, it would be released to all media. Without doubt, the kidnapping would be the lead story on the eleven o'clock news that evening. A special phone number had already been established for persons with any information to call. Tomorrow's newspapers would front page the baby's picture.

As he sat observing the family with whom he would be closely involved for however long, Maney knew something he did not impart to those assembled: that even with all the information disseminated, the baby could disappear and remain hidden. All they could do was wait. For a phone to ring. Or a letter to arrive. Ransom demands. If there was no phone call, no letter of ransom, then they were dealing with a madman. Or woman. Or "person" as he knew Marti Tiernan would prefer he say.

Marti stared at the composite sketch, her memory searching for recognition. The woman's eyes were shaded by sunglasses, frightening Marti as it was the eyes that always gave her assurance or . . . reasons to be afraid. The face itself said nothing. It was round . . . nondescript, and framed by short blond hair. A small nose . . . flat cheekbones . . . a stingy mouth. She looked like no one and everyone at the same time. Familiar and yet unknown.

The witnesses had been as thorough as their memories allowed. One man, who had been walking his dog, had noticed her sitting behind the wheel of her car with the windows rolled up when he stopped to collect his dog's debris with his newspaper. She had not seen him as her focus was on the house directly across the street; the house from which the baby had been taken.

A couple had seen her in front of the house. They had not thought it odd when they saw her take the child from the carriage to the car because they had no reason to think the child did not belong to her. The couple had been quite exact in their description. The woman was about five-foot-three, one hundred and thirty pounds. Chunky but not fat. Wearing a nondescript print skirt, white blouse, and blue tennis shoes.

One other important piece of information had been supplied by the man with the dog, verified by the couple. The car was old, a Chevy or a Ford, blue. But neither could remember the license number, claiming they had not seen it. Under hypnosis, the man with the dog had remembered the car bore a New Jersey plate.

Marti handed the sketch to Matthew. He, too, stared and searched as much for comprehension as recognition. She could read from the tightness of his mouth that he found neither.

*   *   *

Thomas had taken Teej to the Common where the child could toddle and fall about the grass without hurting himself. Saturday afternoons were their private time together. When they had returned to the house, Thomas had been surprised, pleasantly so, to see Reese waiting when she hadn't been expected. But when he searched her face he knew her impromptu visit was not a social one.

As Reese had thought, Thomas had not heard the news. He was not one to amuse himself with a transistor radio in the park, not when he had his newspaper or *U.S. News & World Report* to read. Thomas's response had been immediate. Within minutes he had showered, dressed, and packed an overnight bag for a quick flight to New York. She had done the same before arriving at the house, but he had been adamant that she remain. She had been equally adamant about going until he asked who besides Kelly would remain with Teej? Suddenly, she understood what he was thinking . . . feeling. Could their child be next? It was a ridiculous thought, yet it frightened her, as it obviously did him. Ridiculous or not, she would stay. She would take special care.

He had promised to call as soon as he arrived. She had been certain with what he was about to face he would not remember. But he had.

Vinnie wanted Este to accompany him but she refused to take the children "into that environment." They were not babies, Este argued. They were old enough to understand, to be frightened. They would remain in Miami with her. He should go immediately. Vinnie went.

Ali was brushing her hair, preparing for bed, when the announcement was broadcast on the TV news. The hairbrush dropped to the floor, she along with it, she was so momentarily stunned was she. For the next hour she tried to reach New York but not even the overseas operator could cut into the constantly busy telephone in Marti Tiernan's home. Ali tried JJ. There was no answer. She tried her grandmother. Again, no answer. She was crying when her own phone rang. It was her mother, assuring her that everything possible was being done and that there was no need for her to fly home. Or worry. The last made them both laugh, although neither felt much like laughing.

Margaret's pulse was quicker than it should have been. Her heart was racing and she felt flushed and somewhat light-headed. She reached for the pills the doctor had prescribed for her high blood pressure. She wondered just as the light-headedness reached its zenith if she was dying. She decided she couldn't. Not now when she was needed by her niece and her sister who had nothing more than her faith to rely and lean on—which, Margaret realized as she hurriedly packed to make the early-evening plane to New York, was more than most people had.

Jessamyn had just come in from the field in Nicaragua. She was tired, hot, and somewhat frightened by the threat of violence she perceived most everywhere. She was greeted in the lobby of her hotel by a flock of reporters. There had been garbled news— not unusual in Nicaragua—that maintained her son and niece had been kidnapped during the march for disarmament in New York. Jessamyn had spun about as if shot by one of the sniper's bullets she so feared. Then she collapsed.

*　　*　　*

The house was finally still, as most houses are at five in the morning. The bedroom was beginning to brighten with the dawn light creeping through the windows' northern exposure. Matthew stirred, moaned, and rolled over, his face turned toward hers. Tears were streaming from his eyes even in sleep. She wanted to touch and comfort him as she had done earlier. But that was then. Now she was blaming him when she knew she should not. And she didn't. Yet she did. Back and forth. Which was no more or less than what he was doing with his guilt.

Intellectually Marti knew Matthew was not at fault. Given the circumstance, she would have done the same. A ringing telephone. An extension nearby in the hallway. Leaving a baby sleeping in the shade of a tree in one's own front garden. It was done all the time. Still, another part of her wanted to scream: How could you? How could you leave our child out there alone? On his own? Another part responded: But wasn't that exactly what you had been begging him to do these past weeks—let up and let go, not be paranoid about the child . . . give him breathing space . . . room to grow. And Matthew had tried. He had also succeeded, she now thought bitterly.

4 0 1

She was angry that he was sleeping, no matter how fitfully, when she was not. She had refused any kind of pill, insisting she be clear of head in case the phone rang or. . . . Or anything. But he had needed to rest. He had looked so worn, ragged, and suddenly small. Yesterday evening, when Thomas had come through the door, Matthew had come apart, allowing only Thomas to support him. She had sat there dry eyed and composed—which was good, since Vinnie had been neither when he arrived. Nor had been Arline. She had been of more comfort to them than they to her. She had been spared Margaret's arrival as her aunt went directly to her own apartment, knowing that at midnight guests are seldom welcome. But she had called and her mother had brightened when she realized Margaret was just across the park. It was as if one of her prayers had been answered.

Through her thoughts and recollections Marti heard a cry. Lynne? No. It was David. Marti heard JJ talking to him and wondered if Mark was sleeping through the upset or whether he had been awakened by the crying child sharing his room. Marti gently left the bed so as not to wake Matthew, deciding it wise to look in on Lynne. Her daughter did not understand what had happened, only that something was wrong. The strangers in her house frightened her, as did the frequent tears of the grown-ups about her. Particularly her father's. She had clung to Marti and would not sleep until Marti had lain down next to her.

David had been worse. Had JJ not accompanied her home from the park, had David not been witness to the upset, had he not been old enough to understand a child had been stolen, he might have been spared. But the child was terrified, and not even his father's proximity could reassure him. She had begged JJ to take David home, but JJ refused to leave her. She understood. She also understood that to be alone in his own house with David would have been far more difficult than remaining within the bosom of the family where they could all take comfort and find some measure of safety.

And so they were all bedded down in the house. In different rooms but under similar circumstances. They were waiting for the new day when the investigation would proceed, when the kidnapper might call and Nicholas would be found.

Oh, please, God, let that be, thought Marti as she entered Lynne's room. Lynne was uncovered, having kicked the light summer blanket to the floor. After she retrieved it, Marti folded it about her little girl, resisting the urge to pick her up, hold her, feel her warmth and bathe in it as if it alone could take away the cold that periodically made her tremble. She would not do it. She would not indulge herself. Nor would she use her daughter in that way.

Feeling bereft, Marti went downstairs to the kitchen, searching for something in the refrigerator or the kitchen cabinets that might fill her emptiness. There was nothing that interested her. Except the row upon row of baby food.

*   *   *

Frank Ridderman opened for business at nine even though on summer Sundays clients seldom arrived at his used-car lot until ten. Thus, Ridderman was surprised to find the woman waiting for him, particularly since this was not a holiday weekend and he had not advertised any specials. She was selling a '71 Chevy and Ridderman made pleasantries as he sized it up and mentally priced it down.

"You're up early," he bantered as he wondered how little he could offer without ruining the bargaining.

"We're moving out West today," said the woman as she shifted her baby from one arm to the other.

"Good thing you didn't try to drive it in this old heap," said Ridderman as he marveled at the near perfect condition of the eleven-year-old model. "Well, I can't offer you much. Three-fifty, tops."

He expected an argument. No one sells a car on the first offer. She didn't say a word but nodded her assent. "Just want to sell it," she said almost as an explanation. "No need for it in California."

Had Ridderman not been focused on his patsy and his good fortune, he might have thought the statement odd, since California was one place a person would need a car. But Ridderman was not about to look his gift horse in her mouth. He ushered the woman into his office and wrote out the forms. She had everything necessary for the sale with her. After he had removed her license

4 0 3

plates and handed them to her, Ridderman said, "How are you getting home, missus?"

The woman smiled: "My husband . . . he's a cabbie . . . be by for me in a few minutes."

And in a few minutes a cabbie pulled up at the lot. With his mind on profit and yet another early-bird customer, Ridderman didn't think it strange that the woman sat in the back of the taxi with her child rather than up front with her husband as most women would. So occupied was he that he also didn't think it strange when the driver put his flag down on the meter. In fact, it made no impression at all.

*　*　*

Tyne Philips had called JJ in the late morning to say that he should bring David to meet Jessamyn at Kennedy when her flight from Nicaragua landed at seven that evening. JJ refused, caring not for the tone of the woman's voice or the request.

"Jessamyn needs to see David," said Philips insistently. "She's been through a tremendous shock."

"David's shock concerns me more," said JJ, "and I'm not subjecting him to any further upsets. Airports and press can be traumatic for a child. He's suffered enough since yesterday. Tell Jessamyn I'll bring him to her apartment at eight-thirty. She should be home by then."

From her work as an agent, Tyne Philips had learned from tones of people's voices when they can be pushed no farther. Thus, she did not press the point with JJ, for which he was grateful. He had had enough to contend with this day. The morning newspapers had been spread about the house when he had awakened, tired from dreams he could not recall. When he had found his way to the kitchen, he also found Matthew buried in a depression JJ knew to be highly contagious. He didn't know what to say to the man who was his brother-in-law but with whom he had never established a particular rapport. But he was a father and so JJ knew how he felt. As he passed the kitchen table, en route to the counter offering fresh coffee brewed in an automatic machine, he gripped Matthew's shoulder with his hand. He was surprised when Matthew reached up with his own to touch his.

The story was, as expected, front page on every newspaper. Again, he ached for Marti. The picture of Nicholas brought back his feelings of helplessness and outrage. The sketch of the woman seemed more detailed than the one he had seen the night before and JJ wondered if it really was or whether he imagined it. By ten, the house was like a terminal with people coming and going. The FBI had installed "traps" on Marti's phone in the event the kidnapper called. The devices would permit tracing the call *if* the caller could be kept on the line long enough. The telephone rang every few minutes, but the caller was never the kidnapper but instead members of the family, friends, and the press. The latter collected outside the front door, waiting for any break in the story. With all the commotion, it was not your typical summer Sunday at home.

Tense and unable to just sit and wait for a call that didn't come from a person they didn't know, JJ had accompanied the FBI men on their rounds of restaurants and shops on Columbus Avenue. Each was asked to display the composite sketch. Most complied. None had seen anything unusual the day before, however. By the afternoon, a circular had been prepared and was being distributed to the local hospitals. Nicholas's picture and description was on the left side of the page, the composite sketch and description on the other. Nicholas's medical history comprised the bulk of the copy. Tomorrow those same circulars would be distributed in those parts of New Jersey that had yielded threatening letters to Marti in the past. Not that there was a definite link, but no possibility could be ignored.

When the evening had finally arrived, it brought with it a quiet that was not particularly welcome. All but one FBI agent had left. He would remain in the house indefinitely as a bodyguard and to monitor the telephone and the mail. Vinnie and Thomas had shared a taxi to LaGuardia, each bound for home, knowing there was nothing to do but wait and that Marti preferred to do that without them. What Matthew preferred no one knew, since he wandered about the house hardly speaking and when he did try to speak he broke down. JJ's heart repeatedly went out to the man. Throughout the day he kept thinking . . . suppose it had been David and Lynne who had been kidnapped. And it could have been. Hadn't he and Marti left them just as Matthew had left

Nicholas for minutes at most, thinking it perfectly safe? He mentioned this to Marti, seeking something from her in exchange for his own admission of guilt, of even possible negligence. She had looked at him oddly as though the thought was new to her. Afterward, she clung to Matthew, never leaving his side, often her hand in his, letting him know they were in this together. From the first.

And now he was standing outside his ex-wife's front door, David in hand, wondering what Jessamyn would say if she knew the situation could have been exactly as she had first heard. The door was flung open immediately after he rang. Jessamyn stood there looking as he had never seen her before: disheveled and uncontrolled. His heart sank as David flung himself into his mother's outstretched arms. He was sobbing as was Jessamyn who was on her knees clutching David to her. JJ wondered who this woman was. Certainly no one he had ever known. And then Tyne Philips took the boy from her, literally disengaging the two from each other, suggesting David might be hungry for the fettucine Alfredo she had prepared. Magic words. Sunday was pasta night, a familiar and loved happening. David brightened. Stability and permanence had returned to his life. JJ watched silently as Tyne Philips helped Jessamyn to her feet. Not a word was exchanged between the two, but within the gesture JJ saw a relationship that surprised him—and yet it didn't. As if it had been yesterday, he remembered Jessamyn saying that he was the only man who had ever excited her. Now, that statement and so much else about Jessamyn made sense to him.

She was facing him now, and he was unprepared as she moved into his arms. Her head rested under his chin and her voice was barely audible as she said, "JJ, no matter what happens between us or to us, promise me we will never let anything happen to David." She was crying again, softly this time, more softly than he had ever suspected possible . . . for her. "I promise, Jess," he answered.

"Jessie, it's time you, too, ate and went to sleep."

Tyne Philips, her apron splattered with butter and cream sauce, was standing but feet away, a concerned look on her face. She reached out for Jessamyn who took her hand as though she were too uncertain, unsteady, to find her own way about her own home. Almost as an afterthought, Jessamyn turned and stunned him again by asking, "Would you like to stay for dinner?" She didn't wait for his reply but instead asked another question. He heard it as he was leaving. It was . . . "Where's David?"

*　　*　　*

"My word, Coreen, but aren't you the early one this morning?"

"Well, they say the early bird catches the worm."

"From the looks of this withdrawal slip, it's more than the worm this early bird wants. You're going to break the bank, Coreen. My first customer of the week and you're closing out your account. My dear, was it something I said?"

"Just stop, Fern, and hand over my money. Lord! I'm only going on vacation and don't want to be caught short."

"Where are you going?"

"With my sister . . . to Hawaii."

"Well, aren't you the one! So how would you like the money, Coreen . . . a bank check or traveler's checks?"

"Cash."

"But traveler's checks are so much safer."

"Yes, well . . . after I pay for the plane tickets I'll do just that."

"Well, I hope so. It just isn't safe these days for a woman to walk around with several thousand dollars in her handbag. Big or small bills?"

"Fifties and hundreds. But do hurry, Fern. I have a plane to catch."

"You lucky girl. Have fun!"

"Aloha."

*　　*　　*

The phone rang; Marti jumped. It had been a week of ringing and jumping. Even in her sleep.

"Marti? It's Thomas."

She sighed, both in disappointment and relief. "There's no news," she said automatically, her voice listless. "Nothing. Not a word."

"Marti . . . I received a letter."

4 0 7

Why was he telling her this?

"This morning . . . as I was leaving for the airport. Marti . . . it's from her . . . the kidnapper."

Her heart stopped and then it began racing. She motioned to the nearby FBI agent who had lost interest in the call when he realized it was friend not foe. "What does it say, Thomas?" Marti asked hoarsely. "What does the letter say?" she all but screamed.

The agent grabbed the phone from her hand, identifying himself to the speaker. He listened to Thomas for a moment and then interrupted. "Can you bring that letter on the next shuttle flight to New York?" Satisfied with whatever response he had heard, the agent hung up the phone.

"What did the letter say?" asked Marti.

The agent wasn't listening. He was dialing a number.

"What did it say?" she screamed.

"Maney? A lead. A letter . . . to the brother . . . Thomas Ollson. Yes, the one in Boston. He's bringing it in. . . . About an hour and a half. Yes, I told him we'd meet him at the airport."

They stood there in the Eastern Airlines shuttle terminal at LaGuardia: Maney, two of his men, Thomas, Marti, and Matthew. The letter was spread atop an unused counter to be read again and again by each concerned.

> Dear Thomas Ollson:
> It is God's will. I have acted for Him. A tooth for a tooth, an eye for an eye. Justice. You, of all people, will understand. You who have also been an innocent at the mercy of the guilty. Make her stop! Tell her to call away the FBI. No more of her interferences. This is Judgment Day. All our lives are at stake. *All* our lives.

The postmark was West Orange, New Jersey, the area from which most of Marti's hate mail had arrived. Even to the untrained eye, the handwriting seemed similar to that of other letters Marti had received—as did the letter's tone. Maney was barking instructions. He wanted the letter on the next plane to Washington. He wanted to see if there were any fingerprints on the letter that would match any in the FBI computer bank. He then wanted the experts in the Behavior Science Division to review it. He wanted a profile, an analysis of the letter writer, and, if it matched the others, they would have one certain lead to follow: that the suspect and the letter writer were one and the same, a middle-class white woman.

Marti's fingernails bored into Matthew's palm. A lead. A bona-fide lead. Their child could be, *would* be, found. Once they traced the fingerprints, they would have her and their baby.

"Nicholas is safe, Marti," said Matthew. "Safe," he repeated to himself.

Maney looked at Matthew quizzically. "How can you be certain, Doctor?"

"Her letters. They're all about God. No God-fearing woman would hurt a child," said Matthew vehemently.

"Dr. Strohl, I hope you are right," said Maney, "but let me remind you of the millions of atrocities that have been committed in the name of God. From the Holy Wars and the Crusades to some of the worst murders known to man. By all means, Dr. Strohl, have hope. But also, for God's sake and your own, be realistic."

*   *   *

Hope became a transient thing in their lives, coming and going at will, its, not theirs. Hope about the letter leading to the kidnapper and Nicholas vanished when the fingerprints matched none in the computer-bank files. The letter writer had no known criminal record and could therefore not be identified. The profile analysis from the Behavior Science Division gave them precious little more than that they already knew. Their person was white, female, middle-class, and of strong religious persuasions. Possibly schizophrenic. Nothing more. A dead end. Except . . .

Maney was dangling another shred of the elusive quality known as hope.

"The letters are all from within the same twenty- to thirty-mile radius in New Jersey. Most are postmarked either Friday or Monday. I plan to send agents to the various post offices in the areas, distribute the composite picture, and ask if anyone has seen the woman. We will also set up hidden cameras to photograph people coming through to post letters on these days. We might get lucky. Someone we photograph might just match our composite picture."

"That is insane," said Marti harshly. "What makes you think this woman uses a post office rather than a letter box as most of us do."

Maney looked at Marti patiently. "I don't think anything, Miss Tiernan, but I try everything."

"But it's like looking for a needle that only may have fallen into a haystack."

"Yes," said Maney, his voice calm, "I know. Have you anything different to suggest?"

*　　*　　*

The weather was perfect, a startling sunny day of brilliant blue skies that formed the perfect backdrop for the outdoor celebration. Thomas focused his concentration on the occasion. Each time his mind wandered off to New York, to Marti, he brought it back to his own reality. He was not to be denied. Nor was Kelly. It was her triumph and perhaps to some extent even his. As he watched one student after another receive her diploma, Thomas squeezed Reese's hand. He felt her respond to the pressure, her hand warm in his. He looked at her and saw the tears but did not want to know their origin. Not this day.

Thomas placed his arm about Reese protectively, as if he could shield her from the outside world that constantly intruded these days. Next to him, his mother squirmed. Even as her eyes remained fixed on the platform where the graduates ascended and descended, her rosary turned in her restless fingers. Her faith was sustaining most but not all of the time. Thomas wished he could find the words to convey to his mother how much he appreciated her being there when he knew where her heart remained. Vinnie sat by her side, a surrogate father of sorts, proudly awaiting the moment when his little girl would take center stage.

They called her name and as Kelly stood and then walked toward the lectern where the diploma was to be bestowed upon her, Thomas began applauding. Suddenly it was yesterday, the

4 1 0

day she was born, the baby of his babies, his last and, for reasons he had never fully understood, his favorite. For many reasons, tears stung his eyes as Kelly received her diploma. After she shook hands with the principal, she turned toward the audience and with a triumphant smile, raised both hands above her head, clenched her fists like an athlete who had won her race, and shook them in the sign of victory. The audience laughed. Thomas responded by rising, Reese with him, and raising Teej above his head so that the child could see his mother, the mother her child, and the world could see them all: rejoicing as though they had nothing else on their minds and not a care in the world.

* * *

"I want to know what you are doing, day by day, minute by minute, to find my child," she yelled, her voice shrill, filling the corridor outside the FBI "command post."

"Marti, please," coaxed Matthew.

"Don't 'Marti, please' me. I do not wish to be placated or placating," she yelled, twisting out of Matthew's grasp. "It will be three weeks tomorrow—three weeks since my baby was kidnapped, and I see nothing. Nothing but a bunch of pictures of people in post offices. Three weeks and all I have to show for an FBI investigation is a goddamn photo gallery of strangers. No results. No leads. Nothing."

"Miss Tiernan, I know how you feel," said Kevin Maney patiently, knowing this moment was destined from the first.

"You know how I feel?" echoed Marti, her voice again shrill, causing passers-by to stare. "You've got to be kidding!"

"Marti!" cautioned Matthew, his voice now tight from mounting tension.

"You have no idea how I feel," spat out Marti, undeterred. "unless you've have had a child of your own kidnapped. Have you, Mr. Maney? I asked . . . have you?" Marti demanded.

Maney sighed. "No, Miss Tiernan, I haven't."

"Then you don't know how I feel, and pray you never do." Marti was trembling, thinking of the fear each time the telephone rang, hoping it was *her* or news and then hoping it wasn't, since the news could be bad. "No, you can't know the horror of not knowing and the horror of what your imagination thinks it knows. Sometimes, Mr. Maney, I even think that knowing my baby is dead would be easier than living with the fear, the uncertainty, an imagination that thinks such terrible things. It's so awful. So awful," Marti repeated, shuddering, the color and energy drained from her face and body.

Matthew put his arm about Marti. He followed Maney as he led them into an unused office near the FBI's "command post" on the twenty-sixth floor of the Federal Building where they had come, at Marti's insistence, for some answers that simply were not available. "They are trying, Marti," Matthew said softly.

"They should be trying harder," Marti replied bitterly.

"We're doing everything we can," said Maney.

"It's not enough," snapped Marti, refusing to give an inch.

Maney was trying to keep his calm in the face of mounting pressure caused by the mounting publicity on the case. He could handle Marti Tiernan. Past experience helped him understand how a parent's fear and frustration eventually got the better of him and how that frustration had to be released. It was the sense of impotence that killed, the knowledge that it was not you but someone else who was in control of your life. From what Kevin Maney could assess this is what finally had reached Marti Tiernan.

"Miss Tiernan," said Maney as he took a seat opposite Marti, noting how in three weeks she had aged, her face lined and her skin taut as if it might snap and she with it. "We just have to wait." Maney held up a hand as Marti started to protest. "I know that's hard, but finding someone who doesn't want to be found, who has never been arrested, has no record, and to date has made no mistakes, is very difficult. In cases like these we can do little but wait. It's not like the shows you see about us on TV, Miss Tiernan. Mainly, we are reactive. We capitalize on the error the person makes. In other words: We seldom find people on our own. Somebody has to tell us, give us a clue, which is why we have established the special phone lines, box numbers. It's why we encourage you to talk to the press. Keep the story out there in the front of people's minds. It's all we can do."

Marti's face was buried in her hands. In past weeks, she had done little else but talk to the press, showing what precious few pictures she had of Nicholas. And it was ironic, since for years, even as she made herself available to the press, she had fought to keep her children out of it. She had earned her fame; they had not. They might not choose to and they should be allowed their choices. Anonymity was an inalienable right, which many preferred to fame or notoriety. Now their lives were open for public inspection. They had to be, so that someone with a lead could walk right in.

The phone startled them. Even as Maney answered it, a sixth sense told Marti the conversation would be about the case. Maney was staring at the ceiling, avoiding her face, as he listened to the caller on the other end of the line. His pencil moved quickly across the notepaper. "Repeat it," he barked, checking what he had just written against the words the caller was speaking. "Okay, let's get on it. Have the letter taken directly to Washington for analysis."

"Okay, Miss Tiernan," said Maney as he hung up the phone. "Your brother, Thomas, has received another letter from our friend. Unfortunately, it slipped through the mails without a postmark. But it's a ransom note of sorts—only she's not offering to give up anything, although she's demanding you do."

As Marti sat quietly, Maney began reading his notes: " 'Tell your sister if she dares to begin work next week on her TV series, dares to poison minds again with her sickness, she will suffer the consequences. We know what she and her warped and evil thinking have done to people like us. We must now stop her from doing it to others. No more must suffer for her sins. I know I can rely on you to give her this message. The lives of children, *all our children*, depend on it. It is God's will.' "

"What do you think?" asked Matthew.

"About what?" asked Maney.

"Is she serious? Will she harm Nicholas if Marti continues with the show."

"It's hard to say," said Maney.

"It's blackmail," said Marti, "and I'm not paying it." The color had returned to her face. "Give her an inch and she'll take a foot—then a leg. No. The show must go on, as they say."

"But Marti, we don't know who we're dealing with here," pleaded Matthew. "She could kill Nicholas."

"Matthew, listen to me. She could kill Nicholas either way. Don't you see? If I give her this now, what more will she ask later? What's to prevent her from next saying she wants Lynne—that the only way to save Nicholas is to give up our daughter? Would you pay that price then? I wouldn't. Not then, not now."

The voice was firm, in control again, and Maney once more marveled at the strength of the woman. He could feel Matthew's question coming toward him before it was spoken. The only way to intercept it was to dodge it. "I want to get on that letter, so if you folks will excuse me," Maney said as he turned toward his notes on the desk. "I don't know whether you are doing the right thing or not, Miss Tiernan," said Maney, "but I can appreciate your decision." Silently, Maney also applauded it, as he did the skill with which he had finally answered Matthew Strohl's question without entering into a debate that no one could win.

*   *   *

He would not leave New York. Not without David, which Jessamyn now insisted he do. And so Kay was forced to leave her work, abandon her responsibilities, forced by the feeling that he needed her and that she needed to fulfill his need. She had not left without resentment. There were times she felt as if she was losing her identity, submerging her needs and her life in exchange for that bit of him that was hers from Friday night when she arrived in New York until Monday morning when she left.

She understood his distractions. Although Nicholas was not his child, Kay understood how JJ felt that he could have been. She even understood Jessamyn refusing to let David travel. At that moment, for David to be out of sight was for Jessamyn to be out of mind. The woman called each day of the weekend, something she had never done before. She needed the contact with her child. Kay noted that JJ never seemed to mind the interruptions. It sometimes seemed to Kay that JJ needed the contact as much as Jessamyn did. Even greater was David's need. He rushed to the telephone and often asked before going to sleep to speak with his mother again. The child needed frequent reassurance that not only was his father there but that his mother was too. Or was it that he needed to know he was there . . . still. Or just that his

4 1 4

world—that little immediate world of a six-year-old—was steady, firm, not to be snatched away and he along with it.

She hated the feeling with which they lived. She felt afraid the moment her plane landed at Kennedy. She could smell the potential threat of violence in the New York air. It was the worst kind of pollution, and Kay felt it hung over not just New York but all of the United States. Despite its problems, no such cloud clouded Canada.

The clouds had been thick over Marti and Matthew's last evening. Kay had dreaded going and was certain the visit would be tense and upsetting. It had been exactly that. It reminded her of a *shiva* she had attended for a friend's mother who had died suddenly. Only here, no one had died, although Kay could see the spirits of several were in danger of doing so. She had not known what to say. Her discomfort had passed only when she realized there were more pressing matters on their minds than any impression she might make with the "right words"—if there were any, and if only she had them. What had impressed and even soothed her was the care Marti and Matthew took with each other. It was wordless but their actions—hands that reached for each other as they sat side by side on the sofa—were loud and very clear in their statement. They were together in the experience and not pulled apart as other couples might have been.

Like she and JJ almost were. She had previously never thought of him as being high-strung or tightly wound. But now he was always on edge, snappish, a fuse that seemed to be cut shorter with the days that passed since the time she last saw him. Monday mornings were the worst. It was the end of their weekend together and he resented it, although he would never say so. Like today. She knew he did not want her to leave. Like David, he wanted his world to remain constant. It had taken Kay several weeks to realize JJ feared she, too, might disappear and not return.

"I wish you'd take the week and come to Toronto with me," she said softly to the form behind the morning newspaper.

"I can't. I'm needed here," JJ replied as he put down the *New York Times*.

It wasn't true. He wasn't needed in New York, but that was what he needed to believe. His nightly phone calls to David could have been made from Toronto, but his daily visits to Marti—his physical support—could not. Proximity reduced his feelings of helplessness, although it did nothing for his rage. Except intensify it. His only outlet for his frustration and anger had been his column. He had written articles that had surprised her and disturbed him. They were Reaganesque, an intellectual appeal for law and order that played on people's fears. He called for stricter penalties for crimes and stunned her with his suggestion of capital punishment as a possible solution to problems that plagued the general population, "the prey who could only pray," as he had written.

He had suffered that column and others, which his new detractors called "brown shirt," "fascistic" in feeling. He was still suffering these columns, as much from the overwhelmingly positive response to them as his own negative feelings to both the response and the "passions" within him that he didn't understand. But Kay did. For the first time in his life, JJ's other cheek wouldn't turn. He had changed. Saving the world for its people, for its children, suddenly wasn't as important as punishing those who punished it, particularly the one who had invaded his own.

"I'll see you Friday evening then," said Kay as she collected her luggage.

"I'll call later," he said as he rose to see her to the street.

She wanted to ask him not to. She hated those "check-in" calls. He had nothing to say, or, if he did, he preferred not to. He would ask about her flight and then wait for her to fill in the blank spaces in their conversation.

If only she could reach him. If only she could dig into his private space and weed out whatever was so disturbing to him.

He kissed her and for a moment she could feel him tremble. "It's a month this Saturday," he whispered. He didn't need to explain. Kay knew exactly which anniversary he was marking.

*　　*　　*

"It's a month tomorrow," sighed Gladys Kressner. "It's just awful," she said as she watched the images on the TV screen. "I feel for those poor people."

"What's a month tomorrow that's so awful, and who are you feeling sorry for now?" asked Dan Kressner as he put down the *Star Ledger* to look at the TV screen.

"Marti Tiernan. It's been a month since her baby was kidnapped. A four-month-old baby. Imagine the heartache."

Dan Kressner looked at his wife. It always surprised him to hear how she bled for other people's misfortunes. Not him. Hearing them daily made him psychologically deaf to their tugs. There was much disease and dying that surrounded a pharmacist's life. Particularly in downtown Newark.

"A month, eh? I didn't know," said Kressner, which made his wife roll her eyes in disbelief. Her husband never read anything that had to do with movie stars, an outgrowth of his belief that they were all *meshuga.*

"The worst part is the baby. Hopefully he's getting his medication. Without it, he could die."

"So? Medication isn't hard to get. Any drugstore carries medication."

"You of all people should talk," said Gladys. "So who would you give medication to without a prescription? Whoever took that child—look at that composite, that woman—if she took the baby she needs a prescription from a doctor so that a fine gentleman like you can give her thyroid tablets. Suppose she's afraid to see a doctor for fear of getting caught? Suppose she doesn't have a television or read the newspapers? What then? The baby could be sick, dying by now."

But Dan Kressner wasn't listening to the speculations of his wife. Something else was competing for his attention. A woman . . . an average-looking woman . . . carrying a baby . . . in his store about eight, or was it later, on a Saturday night. No, it was about eight because the Yankee game had just started when she came in. She had bought out the store. Pampers, baby oil, baby powder, pacifier, bottles. He remembered thinking it strange that a woman with such a small infant would be doing so much shopping on a Saturday night. Suddenly Dan Kressner remembered something else. The baby was wrapped not in a blanket but a woman's shawl. Why did that disturb him? What was it saying other than she couldn't afford a blanket. That she didn't have one, perhaps? Or had she just forgotten to take one with her? Unlikely.

She had blond hair. Washed-out blond hair. Like her complexion. How long ago? A month? Nah. Stop playing "Magnum,

P.I." Just a coincidence. Except didn't the newscaster just say the suspect's car had carried a Jersey license plate. He would check tomorrow when he went in for his usual four-to-midnight weekend shift. It could wait. It wasn't as if the woman had wandered in off the street without a prescription begging for thyroid tablets. No, this woman had a prescription which meant she had a doctor, which also meant she had a baby. Schmuck, of course she had a baby. The question is: Whose?

Dan Kressner hoisted himself up from his very soft, very comfortable easy chair. "Gladys, maybe you want to take a ride? There's something I have to check at the store."

"Are you crazy? Sit down. Your night off and you're schlepping to the store? I won't have it. Sit. I'll turn off the ten o'clock news; we'll watch 'Falcon Crest.' "

"I don't think so, Glady. We better go or I won't be able to sleep tonight."

*   *   *

Coreen Carouthers could not sleep the entire night. She was more frightened than usual, more frightened than she had been the day she had taken a taxi to Newark and a train from there into New York where another train had taken her from Grand Central to New Haven. She had always liked the sound of the city's name, which is why she had selected it. A new haven. It was right, fitting. It sounded biblical and ordained for just her needs. And her baby's.

As she lay in bed listening to the birds drown out the beating of her heart, Coreen smiled as she remembered how no one had paid the slightest mind to her that day. Particularly in New York. In Grand Central, there were many women with suitcases, many women with babies, and many women with both. She was part of the crowd. Just one of many. That wasn't true of New Haven. The town seemed empty and she was relieved when she found a furnished studio near the railway station within the first hour of her arrival. It was small, cheap, and filthy. The landlord hadn't looked to it any more than he had looked to her after he had accepted his one-month-in-advance. It was he who had told her of the doctor who saw patients on Saturdays. Mainly the elderly and the poor.

4 1 8

At half his normal fee. A good-doer. Lucky for her he had just returned from a month's vacation.

But now the story was everywhere. They were hounding her on TV, radio, and in the newspapers. *She* had done it. *She*, Marti Tiernan, was again responsible for making her life difficult. But the prescription had to be written and then filled. And only by a doctor in Connecticut since that is where she now was. Even if she could bribe a pharmacist, he couldn't give the baby an examination, which the papers said he needed. Of course that could be another of *her* lies. But she couldn't take the chance. She had not saved a baby to lose him to her own neglect.

She would risk it. As she lay in bed covered by a thin sheet, Coreen Carouthers looked again at the card her landlord had given her. Dr. Louis Mennzigert. She would put her hair up. Wear a hat. If she took precautions, there was little chance he would recognize her from the flimsy composite sketch. Her story was good. She rehearsed it again, even though she had been over it dozens of times during her sleepless night. She had just moved here from Newark and had forgotten to get her baby's prescription renewed. There was no reason for the doctor to question this or doubt her. No reason. God would see to that. It was His will that she be here, saving His child. That made sense. It had to as it was the only explanation Coreen could offer herself as to why she had taken the child. She hadn't planned to. She was simply spending a day like so many others—watching Marti Tiernan, as she had over the years at Altman's, Bellevue, the supermarkets in Chelsea, at the Ed Sullivan Theater. But suddenly that day, one month ago, she knew why she was watching. It was clear to her. Or it had been then. It wasn't always clear now. But it was God's will. Of that Coreen Carouthers was certain. In fact, as she wearily raised herself from the lumpy fold-out sofa-bed, it was the only thing of which Coreen was certain.

*   *   *

They had just finished lunch when the phone rang. Marti rushed to answer it as Matthew had just put Lynne down for a nap and she did not want the telephone to wake her. Lynne was not a charming child without her rest, little as she required.

4 1 9

The voice was brusque. "Miss Tiernan? Maney. We have a lead."

Marti's hands gripped the telephone, steadying it as though it was the instrument and not she that was trembling.

"A pharmacist in Newark phoned this morning. He filled a prescription the night of the kidnapping for a woman that matches our suspect. We have already spoken with the doctor who phoned in the prescription. It was for a patient he has treated for many years. A Coreen Carouthers. She explained the thyroid pills were for her sister's baby. We're on the way to her house now."

"I want to go," said Marti.

"I'm afraid not, Miss Tiernan. We're minutes away now and there's no time. Besides, we don't know what to expect, and it's best left to those trained for the situation."

"I want to go!" screamed Marti, her voice carrying up the stairs to where Matthew was standing.

"What is it?" he asked as he hurriedly descended the steps.

"I'll phone the minute we know something," said Maney.

The line went dead and with it, the feeling throughout Marti's body. Again she was helpless, out of control, as she had been from the beginning. "They think they've found her," she said in a whisper to Matthew.

"With Nicholas?"

Marti shrugged. "We'll be among the first to know. But not the first. Funny, isn't it? He's only our child."

*　　*　　*

Only during the summer did Reese do her marketing on Saturday afternoons. Then, the usual Cambridge crowd was but half, with most on holiday from the universities, and others at the beaches about the Boston area. At four, the stores were empty. She could not only leisurely fill her shopping cart but her mind with inconsequentials. The present could be obliterated as she poked about for weekly specials and read the labels on cans, searching for carcinogenics. The market also had music, sometimes with a gentle beat, other times not. It was preferable to her apartment where it was too quiet, too peaceful, too all the things that had once been so appealing to her. Those days seemed as far away as the plans she had so recently made and then broken.

South America would always be there. She couldn't say that about Nicholas Strohl.

Since the kidnapping, Reese needed distractions. Quiet was disquieting. It allowed her to think of possibilities that, when voiced by Marti, she had called ridiculous. No one would hurt a baby. No one. Please God, no one. Reese ached for Marti. Estranged as she was from Karl and Kristan, she at least knew where and how they were. She had never realized just how lucky that made her. Nor had she realized until Marti's loss just how deeply she cared and would always care for her children. It had nothing to do with "liking." They were her children, and that produced a bond that nothing could change. Not time. Not distance. Not all the misunderstandings that had created both.

Reese's system felt the shock as soon as she left the air-conditioned comfort of the store for the parking lot. The late afternoon sun scorched the pavement. She could feel the heat rising from the concrete through her sandals. When she opened the car door, she felt the hot, stale air leave its confines slowly as if it, too, was too warm to make any quick moves. She thrust the key into the ignition, started the car, and, the instant she felt the motor was warm, turned on the air conditioner. When cool air began to blow across her feet and her face, Reese began the drive toward her apartment. Uncomfortable with the silence, she turned on the car radio.

When FBI agents entered the garden apartment in West Orange, New Jersey, they found it empty. Based on the uncollected mail, authorities established that Coreen Carouthers disappeared sometime during or shortly after the weekend of the kidnapping. Evidence was found to establish that Nicholas Strohl had been in the apartment with her.

Reese's head snapped back as if she had just been struck head-on by the car she had just narrowly missed. Behind her eyes there was suddenly a pounding and she found herself unable to focus. The car screeched to a halt in a no-parking zone.

During the day, a profile of Coreen Carouthers has emerged and with it, the activities that make her a prime suspect in the kidnapping case. On the evening of June twelfth, the woman, a resident of West Orange these past fifteen years, called her doctor and obtained a prescription for thyroid tablets, she said were for her sister's child. Later that night, the prescription was filled by an all-night pharmacy in Newark. That Monday morning, Coreen Carouthers withdrew her savings from her local bank. According to FBI estimates, she then phoned the Acme Supermarket where she worked as a checker to inform them an illness in the family necessitated her being away for an indefinite period of time.

She was calmer now. She could hear herself think above the hundreds of questions going through her mind. Although no U-turns were permitted, Reese made one. There was only one place to go, to be, and it wasn't her apartment on East Concord.

Neighbors in the garden apartment complex where Coreen Carouthers had lived since being widowed fourteen years ago, described her as a quiet woman, a loner who kept to herself, although she was friendly to those she met on the street. They expressed shock at her disappearance and disbelief that she could be responsible in any way for the kidnapping of Nicholas Strohl. As one nearby neighbor stated: "She is a God-fearing woman. Sundays weren't Sundays unless Coreen was sitting in the third pew on the aisle in church."

The Carouthers car, a 1971 two-door blue Chevrolet had not been found and it is thought the suspect, whose husband, Sergeant Clifford Carouthers, was killed in Vietnam fourteen years ago, had used it to leave the New Jersey area, possibly with the kidnapped child, for parts unknown. FBI agents refused to comment on whether or not they thought that Nicholas Strohl was still alive.

She wanted Thomas. Not later but instantly. Reese pushed her foot down on the accelerator as far as reason would allow. She wondered if Thomas had heard and, if he had, whether there was something further he as a family member knew that the newscasters did not. From the moment she rushed into the house, she read the answers on his face. Like her, Thomas knew something. Like her, he knew much too little.

They all knew something more after the weekend. On Sunday, a teenage boy was arrested for speeding near Livingston, New Jersey. His car proved to be legally his but the former property of Coreen Carouthers. When questioned by the police, the used-car dealer had identified her, as had the cab driver who had taken her from the dealer's lot to downtown Newark. He had no idea where she had gone from there. Nor did the FBI until the unexpected, yet expected, occurred.

18

Louis MENNZIGERT WAS NERVOUS. HIS WAITING room was filled with patients. They would continue to wait just as he was waiting. He stared at his telephone, willing it to ring. The man called Maney lit a cigarette. Mennzigert wanted to ask that he put it out, insist, even as they waited anxiously, that his no-smoking ordinance be observed even now. Instead, Mennzigert focused on the telephone. Call, damn it, call! he thought as the clock moved to ten past ten.

His own fault. His own damn fault. Too quick. Too willing to help. She had been so persuasive, so sweet in her pleading for a prescription before the tests returned so that she would be spared another trip. And he had complied. Like a fool. Worse, like a medical quack. Still, in his defense, the baby appeared to be in perfect physical condition, not at all in need of an adjustment in his dosage.

Ten-fifteen. Now it was he who wanted a cigarette. It would have been his first since Sunday, the only day he allowed himself certain "luxuries." Like last Sunday. Typical. His one morning of the week when he allowed himself to play in bed with the newspapers and the TV. It was all there in both media to assault him. A kidnapped baby . . . a thyroid condition . . . the doctor who had prescribed in New Jersey . . . the photograph of the woman who had called herself Cora Carson but who was actually Coreen

Carouthers. No matter that she had come to him disguised. It was she.

He had instantly called the FBI, and they had arrived by the early afternoon. She was not at the address she had given. Obviously Coreen Carouthers read the same newspaper he did. Her room was exactly as she had rented it. Except it was clean. Too clean. Without a sign of life, particularly a baby's. On Monday, they had located the pharmacist who had filled her prescription. He could tell them nothing more than what they already knew.

And so they all sat, waiting for a phone call from Coreen Carouthers. She had asked that he verify the dosage of thyroid and that had meant blood tests. He had told the woman to call Tuesday morning after ten as that was when the results should be back from the lab.

The phone rang. He stared at it. As previously arranged, he would only answer if his nurse buzzed him. The noise burst through the tension in the office. Mennzigert knew from the moment he answered, the FBI's traps would do their work, provided he could do his: keep the woman on the phone long enough for the call to be traced.

"Mrs. Carson? Good morning. A very nice day, isn't it? How's the baby doing?" asked Mennzigert cheerily. "The tests? Er . . . let me see here a moment . . . I just got into the office, so I need a moment to collect myself. . . . Yes, here they are. Let me just go over them a second. . . . Actually, now that I have them in front of me, maybe it would be best if you could come in sometime this morning to discuss them. . . . Yes, I have the results. But it's not that simple, Mrs. Carouthers. No! Don't hang up! Mrs. Carson?"

Kevin Maney took the blood-test results from Mennzigert's hands. "You did fine, Doctor," he said reassuringly, although Maney knew the doctor's efforts had fallen short of being fine enough. "We'll release these results to the press. Our Mrs. Carouthers will get the message. She obviously does and rather quickly."

The phone rang. The nurse buzzed again. Maney picked up the receiver and listened. "Nothing more than what we already guessed," he said to the man in Mennzigert's office when he had concluded the brief conversation. "She disconnected before we could connect with her."

"What's your guess?" asked one of Maney's aides.

"Well, she's come from Jersey to Connecticut. My hunch says we should keep an eye on Boston. Since she's already made contact with Thomas Ollson twice, she just might again. I think our Mrs. C. feels a kinship with him."

"Why's that?" asked the aide.

"Again, it's just a hunch, but I'd say Vietnam is the key here. Her husband died in it, Thomas Ollson nearly died for it, and Marti Tiernan was against it. It's not much to go on, but it's a thread. For all we know, Mrs. Carouthers may not only have lost her husband in the Vietnam War but her mind."

*　　*　　*

Reese could see he did not want to leave, torn as he felt between his priorities. She understood. The completion of his work for Eagle Nest was near at hand. This particular fund-raising tour and lobby, of sorts, in Washington, could cement the future of the memorial. It was real, as concrete as the foundation of the memorial itself. No longer a pipe dream or a false hope. That could not be said of the reason he wanted to remain in Boston. *She* might call. The FBI was certain she would, as were the consulting psychiatrists who felt she needed an outlet for her aggressive feelings. Some even suggested Coreen Carouthers viewed Thomas as her accomplice. It was all theory, all nebulous, and yet . . . If she did make contact, he might be able to accomplish something as real but even more rewarding as the saving and perpetuation of the monument: the saving of a child's life.

To offset her feelings of helplessness, to do something to ease the despair she heard creeping into Marti's voice whenever they spoke, Reese offered to stay. She could speak to Coreen Carouthers, attempt to keep her on the line long enough for the trap. Or, if the woman insisted or agreed, she could forward the call to Thomas so that some rational contact could be made with her. But Reese had worried. Suppose the woman came to the house. Although the FBI thought it unlikely, Thomas sent Kelly and Teej to Vinnie's for the remainder of the summer. And so Reese would be alone, except for the FBI agent who would quietly but competently fill space in the house just as his counterpart did in Marti's.

Thomas had picked up his suitcases as soon as he spied the taxi rounding the corner. One sound of the car's horn and he had opened the door. He was never late, never guilty of keeping anyone waiting. But instead of walking briskly as was his way to the car, he signaled the driver that he would be a moment and closed the door. "Take good care," he said softly. "If you need me, call."

He was out the door when she began to tremble, suddenly face to face with the full responsibility she had taken upon herself. "I need you!" she called to the man who had now slammed the taxi's door firmly behind him. "I need you," she repeated softly as she glanced at the telephone and felt the emptiness of the house despite the presence of the FBI agent watching the morning news in the den.

*   *   *

They were laughing, softly at first and then raucously as the full meaning of the words became apparent. Marti heard the laughter but she did not feel it. No longer did it energize her when a dress rehearsal or taping went well. Her lethargy seemed permanent, as did the situation. Day after day, they waited. With nothing else to do, the TV show was what those concerned about her proclaimed it to be: a blessing. It occupied her time and her mind. Or so they thought. They were right about the time, but her mind, even now as they taped the dress rehearsal, was never fully on her work. There was always a part focused on what wouldn't come into focus: Coreen Carouthers.

The audience again laughed as she spoke her line. She wondered what she had just said to make them laugh. She heard herself speaking again and wondered what she was saying. Others, onstage and off, heard it; she did not. She was preoccupied, wondering—always wondering—what more she could do. There must be something they had overlooked. Suddenly, Arline's suggestion no longer seemed ridiculous. Why not a psychic to locate her baby?

The audience laughed again, and Marti thought bitterly, Isn't it nice that someone has something to laugh about.

Matthew was waiting in her dressing room. He would not argue. Whether she or the FBI liked it, he was hiring a private investigator. He was not satisfied with the results to date. Maney had said the FBI was "reactive." In psychological terms that meant they were passive-aggressive. Not good enough. He wanted more aggression and less passivity to find his son. He wanted to act. Now!

The dress rehearsal over, Arline was reading her notes to Marti as they entered the dressing room, each momentarily un- aware of Matthew's presence. Arline's line changes were easy enough to incorporate before the final taping in ninety minutes, but Marti was resisting. "Frankly, Arline, I think if we could, we should cancel the goddamn taping. What we have on tape from the dress is good enough. Quit while you're ahead, I say."

"Ahead of who?" asked Arline. "I'm not competing with any- one but myself, and I think the writing can be sharper and the show better."

"Oh, Christ, Arline. It's only a show. Classified as a 'sitcom.' A goddamn situation comedy. Let's not make it into more than what it is."

"I'll come back later," said Arline as she rose from the chair by Marti's dressing table. "*With* the changes. Try to learn them before the taping, but don't sweat it if your memory fails. They'll be on the teleprompter." At the door, Arline turned and said evenly, "You have every right to be a pain in the ass. I understand that, and God knows I feel for you. But having the right doesn't make it right and I want you to know I object to how you are acting, particularly toward me. I don't deserve it. Nor does anyone else on the crew." And she was gone.

"She's right," said Matthew.

"Look!" said Marti, whirling to face Matthew, "I don't need to be told she's right, particularly by you."

"What's that supposed to mean? What does 'particularly by you' have to do with anything?" asked Matthew, his voice rising. "Say it, Marti. Get it out. I don't have the right 'cause I was the one who was negligent?"

"Well, damn it, weren't you?" screamed Marti. "Weren't you?"

"What about you?" Matthew said as he stood with his face inches away from Marti. "What about your negligence? Yes, yours! You and your goddamn march. Your fucking causes. They were more important—always were—than your children. Did you ever think if maybe you hadn't gone, had been at home with your child, this might not have happened?"

Even if Matthew had used his hand, he could not have slapped her harder. Marti's face reddened. "Yes, I have!" she screamed. "And it kills me. It kills me every single second of the day."

She was sobbing, wanting to stop but, now that she had finally started, hoping she never would. Somewhere within she could feel the weighted knot that lived these many weeks between her throat and stomach begin to loosen. She suddenly became aware of Matthew holding her, rocking her as if she were a child and he the mother. His tears were warm against her face. She clutched him to her. Together, they released the emotions of despair and frustration.

"I don't blame you. I truly don't," said Matthew. "But I have to blame someone. I can't live with it alone."

"I know," she said consolingly. "We have no one to beat up on other than ourselves and each other. Oh, God, Matthew, it hurts so much. I can't remember his face any longer. I sometimes think if he was in this studio, I wouldn't know him. I've almost forgotten his smell."

He was silent, her words stripping him of the need to explain what she obviously already knew of his own feeling. His own child was barely real to him anymore. "Marti, we have to do something," he said finally. He talked about the private investigator; she of the psychic. They agreed to try both. Something would turn up, they assured each other. Particularly now as the fifteenth of the month approached. She would surface again for another prescription. She would, they assured each other while each thought . . . And suppose she doesn't. No. Their minds rejected such a possibility. She would not let their child die. Not this woman. Not her. No.

*　　*　　*

Maney was not pleased. He did not appreciate having a private investigator involving himself in FBI business. It was an unnecessary and possibly even harmful interference. Marti was unconcerned with Maney's reactions. She wanted her baby found and if the firm of Laurence Miller & Associates could find him, with or without the FBI's assistance, that was all that mattered. Maney understood Marti's motivation. He just didn't think it wise.

The psychic was one Maney had worked with several times before with mixed results. The results were very mixed this time. The woman kept visualizing the Great Wall of China. But Coreen Carouthers didn't have a passport. Still, Gretl Jaffe persisted. The Great Wall of China she saw, and it was by the Great Wall of China that she stood,

*　　*　　*

She had sat at the rear of the bus, hoping to go unobserved in the early Friday morning rush-hour traffic. The heat was oppressive and it threatened to overwhelm her. As the bus moved slowly up First Avenue and closer to its destination, her nausea increased. She could not do it. She could not risk it. The baby sleeping in her lap insisted she do.

It was difficult to rise when the bus pulled up before the main entrance at 28th Street. Her knees buckled and the baby nearly slipped from her trembling hands. And then she was off the bus, on her own with the scores of others streaming into the mammoth building. Once more, she hesitated. Once again, as the day before, she turned to go back. But she couldn't. She had already delayed the visit longer than she should have.

The unintentional pressure of her fingers on the baby's back caused him to cry. No one paid attention, concerned as they were with their own aches and pains. Quickly, before she could panic still further, she hurried down the concrete ramp, past the parking garage, and into the hospital. She was afraid to ask directions, afraid to call any attention to herself. At the information desk, she waited until someone else asked for the emergency room. She listened carefully to the instructions and followed the arrows, constantly watching over her shoulder for that moment when she would be pounced upon and seized. She would fight. She had come prepared.

She was standing in the room before she saw the police officers. She turned, trying to back out, but bumped into a bleeding man held by yet another policeman. She jumped back, afraid of the man, the blood, and the police. She could feel a scream begin in her throat, a scream she had to squelch. She looked again at the police officers. Most were standing about as if waiting. For her? Others were with patients—people from and of the streets. Any moment they would turn their attention to her. Not even the brown-hair wig she had purchased could hide her. She must run. No, she must sit. For just a second. Collect herself. The baby had to have his medication. By cutting the quarter grain in halves, she had already delayed the trip to Bellevue by a week. But she was worried. Always worried. Was the reduced dosage harming the child? Perhaps she should leave him here. Just leave him as one would an old newspaper and run. Or ask someone to hold him while she made a telephone call. But she couldn't. He was her child; she, his savior.

She took a deep breath, swallowed back the bile in her mouth, and approached the nurse on duty, keeping an eye all the time on the police who seemed not to notice her. But she knew better. She was pleased she had thought to dress Nicholas in pink this day. He was now a girl and not the boy the police were looking for. If the doctor asked, she would explain the child was wearing his sister's hand-me-downs. There would be no questions. They understood poor at emergency rooms.

She spoke and the nurse listened. She heard the words but she didn't believe them. The wrong room, the woman in white had said. Down the hall was the pediatric emergency room. Not true. A trap. They were waiting for her there. She would leave. But the medication, she reminded herself. Leave Nicholas and run. But suppose the police followed. Wouldn't they find that suspicious? Her bladder ached and after furtively looking over her shoulder and beyond, she ducked into the ladies' room. In the stall, she wiped her forehead with toilet paper, finding it impossible to stem the flow of perspiration that seemed to erupt at her hairline. She rocked the baby in her arms. Sweet baby. Good baby. Seconds later, she stood at the entrance marked PEDIATRICS EMERGENCY, scrutinizing the room for safety. It was small, smaller than the other room, but crowded, which is what she had expected on a Friday morning before the weekend. She had planned it just that way. To get lost in a crowd. No police. Just people and pink babies blending into the pink walls and chairs the colors of a rainbow. It was too good to be true. Too good. Quickly, she walked to the nurse on duty. The woman barely looked at her as she began filling out the necessary forms.

Her name. She blanked. Under what name had she rented the apartment? She hesitated; the nurse looked at her inquiringly. Or was it strangely. Martha, she blurted out. Martha Pearson. She blanked on the address and explained how she had just moved to New York. The nurse waited, uninterested until Martha Pearson gave her the numbers of a tenement building she had noticed en route to the hospital. The baby's problem: again, the nurse waited as the woman, Martha Pearson, hesitated. This was the moment she had feared. Thyroid, she finally said, her words tripping out quickly. The baby has only a partial thyroid. Needs medication. The doctor back home unable to prescribe.

The nurse didn't ask where "back home" was or the name of the doctor. She was too busy filling in the form, solving the hospital procedures rather than looking to fill in a puzzle. Without speaking, she took the baby's temperature, pulse, and heartbeat. Not an emergency. She would have to wait until the emergencies were seen. No one could say how long that would be.

She sat, awkwardly, aware that sweat was dripping down the inside of her thighs. She tried counting spots on the ceiling, humming past songs that she and her husband used to dance to Saturday nights. The Moonglows and the Penguins. "Earth Angel." And Aretha. Whip it to me. Just a little respect. She couldn't stand the remembering. It was more painful than the wait. But not as frightening. She was certain the nurse was calling the police. She should run, hide, take Nicholas away. Or leave Nicholas. But where? She started to cry. Then she stopped, focusing her attention on the sign on the wall.

> **Please be patient. The most seriously ill**
> **will be seen first. All other patients will**
> **be seen in order of their arrival.**

She closed her eyes, again letting her mind drift, remembering those days when she used to wait outside this very same hospital to keep tabs on Marti Tiernan. Now, Lord only knows who was keeping tabs on her. The walls have ears and the windows have eyes, she thought as she made circular motions with her hand on Nicholas's stomach, a gesture that always seemed to soothe him. She should take him and run. Now. Out of New York. A terrible city. But in New Haven that day, when she had thought it through, she instantly knew New York would be the last place they would look for her. Under their noses. In *her* own backyard. And it had been so easy. It was a train ride into Grand Central, another train ride downtown. She was one of the many. She could lose herself among the lost. And she had. In a furnished efficiency in a rundown tenement where no questions were asked by the superintendant in exchange for her extending the same courtesy. It was a little bit like visiting hell. Although she never met them, she knew who, and what, her neighbors were.

Her attention focused on the Raggedy Ann picture on the wall and the words sketched upon it.

> *Keep mealtimes pleasant. Serve nutritious food*
> *to help form good eating habits.*

Insulting. Of course her baby was served nutritious foods. And she didn't have to leave the apartment to buy them. She had the Lacey girl next door for that. The child had knocked on her door one night, terrifying her. But not that terrified. Clifford had taught her to shoot, and she seldom felt frightened with the gun in her hand. The child's baby was sick. She was frightened. Poor thing. She was no more than sixteen, seventeen, tops, herself.

Somehow, her baby had stopped crying the minute she had placed her down next to Nicholas. Since then, the girl often left the baby with her for an hour or two while she did the grocery shopping for both. Always at night. Always dressed in clothes far too mature and suggestive for one so young. With too much makeup. And heels that tipped her precariously from one direction to another.

"Martha Pearson?"

She heard the name called and then called again before she realized that for this day, the name was hers. She looked to see if anyone was watching as she slowly rose from her chair and proceeded to where the clerk was sitting. More questions. Instructions. Was this her billing address? Where was she employed? The questions came too quickly for her to give quick answers. She stumbled over herself but the clerk, accustomed to non-English-speaking peoples butchering the replies to her questions, paid no mind.

A babysitter, Martha Pearson finally said. But her husband is employed by the phone company. They have money to pay, she explained hurriedly. But the clerk wasn't interested. She had all she needed to complete her form. Take a seat. It will be a few more minutes.

She looked at the seat. She didn't know if she had another few minutes to spare. Something, a voice she had come to trust, was telling her to leave. Now.

Marcia Mendez was exhausted. It was only a little past ten and she had already seen more patients that morning than she could remember. The night before, having been on call, she had gotten no more than three hours sleep. She had done little better throughout the week. Marcia Mendez was running on empty, yearning for the time, but hours away, when she would be relieved, and she had thirty-six whole hours of rest before she returned to her life as a resident physician.

Marcia Mendez was a good doctor who one day after considerable experience would be an excellent one. Although medical school with its texts was behind her, the readings were not. Intent on a career in pediatric medicine, Marcia Mendez read constantly to stay abreast of the latest advances in her field. With her resident's schedule being what it was, she had no time for newspapers or magazines. Her interest in television, which she felt completely negated the presence of Hispanics in America, was minimal. Had Marcia Mendez been less devoted to medicine, she might have read the material that had arrived the previous weeks from both the FBI and the New York police. She might then have approached Martha Pearson's baby with considerable more than medical curiosity.

She never noticed the pink baby clothes on the boy. She never observed the mother's trembling or the sweat that drenched the front of her dress despite the fact it was comfortably air conditioned throughout the building. These minor things were lost as Marcia Mendez checked the child's tongue and skin texture. The baby's eyes were clear. His weight was good. No skin discolorations. No sores or bruises. An excellently cared-for child. Seemingly in excellent health. But of course blood tests must be taken to be sure.

Yes, take the blood tests but give me the prescription, said Martha Pearson.

But the dosage might need altering, protested Mendez.

I can return for a new prescription, countered Martha Pearson.

No. Best you wait for the results.

I cannot wait, the woman screamed, becoming almost irrational.

I will not prescribe until I have the results of the blood tests, said Marcia Mendez firmly, closing the issue with the sound of her voice. You can either wait or return in an hour or two.

Her heart was racing as fast as her mind. If she waited, the police would certainly appear. The doctor had recognized her. She would be calling the FBI now. But if she left, Nicholas could die. Unless she would find it easier at St. Vincent's Hospital. She screamed as a policeman entered the room. When people looked, they thought she was screaming at the woman who followed him carrying a bloody child to the nurse at the desk who was already on her feet, asking questions as she checked the baby's vital signs.

Coreen Carouthers was lost. The room was closing in on her

faster than her fears. She clutched Nicholas to her and began half walking, half running. But it was too late. The strong odor that surrounded her told her it wasn't just Nicholas who had soiled himself.

*　　*　　*

Lunch in her dressing room, her mother pretending to watch "All My Children" on the portable color television while really watching her, was now an everyday occurrence. The hour break in the rehearsals was among the most difficult times of Marti's day, as she could either rest or think. The former was impossible, the latter equally impossible but in a different way. Which is why she welcomed her mother's presence. It didn't matter that she was now the bigger of the two, the physically stronger; her mother still was safety, strength, a shelter in one horrible, lingering storm.

Time was not making things easier as people promised but more difficult. The more time that passed, the more frantic she felt. If she knew her child was dead, the pain might ease with time. If she knew Nicholas was alive and well, time then, too, might make it easier for her to accept her loss. But she knew nothing, and, as time went on, and on, she knew less.

They had been so certain Coreen Carouthers would surface around the fifteenth of August when another prescription was needed for Nicholas. But she hadn't, or, if she had, neither the doctor nor the pharmacist she had seen had noticed, despite the amount of literature each had received. Besides the leaflets the FBI had distributed, Marti had placed ads in medical journals and pharmaceutical house organs. Each had a picture of the baby, of the kidnapper, and a description of the illness and the medication needed to control it. Each had a number to call if there was reason to suspect anything or anyone.

There had been no calls. There had been nothing. The private investigator had spoken with ticket agents and conductors throughout the New Haven line. No one saw or remembered Coreen Carouthers. The psychic, after holding an article of clothing belonging to the Carouthers woman, visualized apple juice. Mott's apple juice. It led nowhere. Except to a despair and a depression that, had Marti been married to a less strong person, would have

4　3　6

ended the relationship. She clung to Matthew. They clung to each other. In all ways except one. She could not function sexually. She had dried up, was bereft of the juices that normally overflowed into all aspects of her life. Matthew did not pressure her. Nor did he move away from her, difficult as it was for him to be with her through those nights when she pressed against him for warmth that had nothing to do with season or temperature.

She worried about Lynne. The child was to have started nursery school in the fall, but Marti didn't feel Lynne was ready. Nor was she. Not for the separation. She knew Lynne was only receiving a small part of her and even that part was tainted. Just as she couldn't be there totally for Matthew, Marti was unable to be all she felt she should for her daughter. No longer did Marti encourage Tisa Bannington to bring Lynne to the set at lunchtime. Instead of the child's presence bringing solace, it created anxiety. Lynne was paying the price for the kidnapper's action, an innocent victim—but victim nonetheless.

Her food was once again getting cold as it sat untouched on her tray. The look of the creamed chicken made her ill. It was not food she needed but hope. She teaspooned the protein mix into the apple juice and drank the eight ounces in one long swallow, thinking of her call to Thomas that morning. He had agreed with JJ. She should take to the talk shows again, speak of her opposition to what she called Reagan's role in Central America, renewed defense spending, and those who thought the Right to Life was telling others how to live their own. If that didn't flush out Coreen Carouthers what would? And they needed to provoke her; needed another letter, some sign, some word, some postmark, some *thing* to go on. Do it, Thomas had urged, but not without checking with Maney first. Suppose the experts felt it was best at this point not to antagonize the woman.

At this point. Nearing Labor Day. And they were still dealing with an unknown X factor. Suppose her appearing on talk shows not only flushed out the woman but caused her to do something rash. Who could predict? They were not dealing with a sane person. Marti shivered as she thought this, fully cognizant of what the criminally insane were capable of doing.

She was surprised to see Matthew standing in the doorway.

Normally, the lunch hour was when he was at his busiest, his clients mainly professional people who stole away from busy business environments between noon and two. Marti did not need words. There was something reflected in his face that said there was something he knew that she should and it was not good. As she remained frozen, fearing what she was able to read in his much too controlled demeanor, her mother turned off the television and rose, placing herself between them. "What is it, Matthew," she asked calmly.

He hesitated. Marti stared at him, both demanding and defying him to speak. "Marti, they're not sure it's Nicholas. There are tests, blood tests, they can run to make sure . . ."

She heard. She understood. She felt the floor beneath her begin to sag. She felt her mother's arm, her husband's hand . . . his voice.

"The baby has been dead about a week. A man jogging found it in a plastic bag along the East River Drive."

She heard no more. Seconds that seemed like hours passed. Matthew, his voice tired, strained, insisted, "They don't need us to identify the body. An autopsy will determine if it is Nicholas."

"I want to go to him," said Marti, her voice flat but harsh.

"Marti!" her mother cautioned.

"I want to go to him," she repeated loudly.

"Marti, it may not be Nicholas," her mother insisted.

"But it's a baby. A baby," Marti repeated, "and he shouldn't be all alone in this world. He needs us. He needs someone now to be there with him."

It didn't matter if anyone else understood what she was saying. *She* understood. Matthew's hand, cold but there, under her arm, supporting, said he also understood. Silently, they left the dressing room followed by Carolyn, who was praying that her daughter be spared. No mother should ever know the heartache of burying her own child. Of all of life's hardships, of crosses to bear, that was in Carolyn's mind the worst.

19

SHE SHOULD HAVE FELT STRANGE, TENSE, THOUGHT Kay, to be seated in Jessamyn Giroux's living room. As she gazed about at the studied elegance, Kay realized nothing in her rather wide experience had prepared her for this encounter with her lover's ex-wife. Only this was not an encounter but a meeting, not of just the minds but to Kay's surprise the hearts. There was common ground in this room and she was standing upon it. That she was being treated as a person whose opinion was valued also was surprising. Yet Jessamyn repeatedly turned to her, as the seemingly sole objective person in the room, for guidance.

The immediate concern was David, and it was not a false concern, no ploy of an angry former wife trying to reduce the visiting privileges of an ex-husband. There was a problem and never was it more evident than during this past weekend when David was subjected, as they all were, although none directly, to a dead baby found in a plastic bag on the East River Drive. There was no way they could shield him any more than they could shield themselves. The news was everywhere, and if they as adults could make little sense of the horror of the senseless killing of an infant, what could they expect of David.

Jessamyn's public façade of cool, clear thinking was not evident in the privacy of her own home. She was frantic. The problem with David could not be denied. The child was constantly wakeful, on guard, defensive. When he did sleep, it was fitfully. Often he awakened with fears he could not express with words, only with tears. He clung to the adults in his life, afraid to venture out and explore his world as he once had. Each time the approaching school year was mentioned, the boy became nauseated. Often he vomited, which the pediatrician claimed was a sign of his extreme anxiety.

Kay had never thought of children as being anxious, but since the kidnapping she had seen David close off an exploring mind. She had mentioned to JJ that she thought David would be best off with her . . . with them . . . in Canada, away from the publicity surrounding the tragedy. It was an opinion Jessamyn didn't share.

"He needs to see a psychologist," said Kay, surprised she had voiced what she was thinking. The words had tumbled out just as they had tumbled into Jessamyn's apartment, unprepared for the invitation that was relayed by the doorman when they had returned David from their Labor Day weekend. As soon as she spoke, Kay expected the backlash. What parent wants to hear that his child needs help?

"Yes, you may be right," sighed Jessamyn as she looked to JJ for his reaction. He did not respond, numbed as he still was from the horror of the past seventy-two hours that continued to keep him fragmented. "He has been subjected to so much," continued Jessamyn, her voice beginning to waver. "If he doesn't have help working it out now, he could be working it out the rest of his life." JJ nodded his agreement, unable to put into words what he was feeling about his son. "Your brother-in-law is a psychiatrist. Surely he must know someone in the child-psychology field who can help us. If not, I have access to Benjamin Spock. He might offer some substantial suggestion."

Kay marveled at Jessamyn's ability to utter words like "substantial suggestion" when it was evident she was struggling to contain emotions that threatened to consume her. Her newscaster training, thought Kay, but not unkindly. Her ability to think on her feet and speak no matter what the event.

"I doubt if Matthew can focus on anything but his own problem at the moment," said JJ, finally breaking his silence. "Talk to Spock or whoever else you think necessary."

4 4 0

"Then you have no objection?" asked Kay.

"None. Just get him the best," said JJ wearily.

Kay wanted to plead with Jessamyn to also get the best for JJ. Someone wise and compassionate who could help him, someone who could relieve his anguish. She couldn't, although she had tried. She had stopped trying when she could sense his resentment at her intrusion into areas of his being to which he was reluctant to travel.

Suddenly they were at the front door and once again Kay was surprised, this time by the almost affectionate parting between JJ and Jessamyn. For a second she was jealous, feeling outside the circle until she realized she was and that she should be, since she was not David's parent.

They were silent as they walked from Sutton Place toward First Avenue. She hooked her arm through his to make him aware she was there if he needed her. There for him totally and without the resentment she had felt only till recently. She had a life apart from him. A good life. She enjoyed it. She needn't feel guilty about it. It sustained her, which allowed her to sustain him. Not once had she been dragged in and under by his ongoing depression. She had continued with those things that made her happy, the big and little involvements that made up her life. They had not suffered because of him, and that gave her the perspective, the insight, she needed. Suddenly she understood that they were a couple—in her mind they had always been that—but that didn't mean they were fused into one as she had feared. Had they been, she would have been of even less use to him than she was.

They were on Madison Avenue when she checked the clock on the Newsweek Building. If they did not take a taxi back to his apartment immediately, she would miss the last plane that evening to Toronto. She had surgery the following morning. She would remove a cancer from a living thing that mattered to her as a living thing. She wished she could do the same for JJ, rid him of that which was killing as it grew in his mind each day.

Kay took the initiative and flagged down a taxi. JJ sat in the back seat passive and silent. She wondered if just this once she could persuade him to return to Canada with her. He had closed his eyes and was resting, which allowed her to do the same. Unfortunately her mind couldn't rest but retraced the weekend. She had arrived at JJ's just as Arline had called to say Marti and Matthew were with the FBI trying to identify, if they could, a baby's body. Without thinking, they had taken David to wait for their return at their home. When Marti returned with Matthew, she could not speak, could barely walk, and Matthew had been no better. Their grief was overwhelming. It flooded the house, terrified her. So she could now imagine the effect it had on David and Lynne. It did not seem to matter that the baby was not Nicholas. It didn't make the crime any less horrible or even less involving. They mourned as if the child had been their own.

She had observed JJ emotionally isolating himself even as he held Marti, loving her in that special way between brother and sister. Throughout the afternoon, his only other contact was with David, his hand constantly touching the boy as if to reassure himself of his son's presence. And just when the house seemed to be calmed, the tragedy and their aborted participation in it was featured on the early evening news. Not that they were watching, but David had been, in Lynne's room, and they had heard him screaming.

As JJ paid the cab driver, Kay wanted to scream herself, scream "It's your turn" at the man who refused to let it out. In the apartment, she looked at her waiting luggage and felt conflicted and then angry with him for causing the conflict. If she remained with him an animal would remain in pain. If she left, what of his pain?

"I could kill," he said matter-of-factly.

The statement was made without the punctuation of emotion, but Kay knew in that one sentence JJ had told her of all that was twisting him into his knotted state.

"Me, the man who couldn't carry a gun in the war, couldn't conceive of harming another living person, could kill. Yes, I really could," JJ added, as if trying to convince himself as well as his listener. "I could pick up a gun and fire it into this woman gladly. I could pull the switch to execute her. I could do this and more," he said, his face contorted with a hate of which she had not thought him capable. "I would kill some fucked-up, crazy woman, and that I would and could is killing me," he said, his voice now filled with the anguish she had seen in his eyes these many weeks.

"Because she's hurt you," said Kay as she took his hands in her own. "And she's hurt Marti and David, the people you love most. Don't you see?"

"No. I see nothing. Except a fraud. I'm a murderer like everyone else."

"Yes," said Kay calmly. "Like everyone else who has been hurt, backed into a corner, seen a loved one suffer. Like all people who know right from wrong but who feel so horribly wronged that they want to hurt back, you can kill."

"What does that say of me? What am I?" he cried.

"Human, damn it. Human like the rest of us. JJ, listen. This woman and the war are not equatable. At least not in my mind. You believed the war was wrong. You believed taking innocent lives was wrong. You still believe that. But what you've discovered is what many have known: that each war is different, particularly the war that attacks you personally. It's human nature to fight back. People protect their loved ones. The principle of an-eye-for-an-eye is as old as turning the other cheek. Each person decides what he can or cannot do. JJ, I'm not God. Nor are you. But you're acting like Him. You are judging yourself, and you have decided against yourself and passed sentence. And you're wrong, JJ. Your guilt is what saves you. It's what distinguishes you from those you hate. War . . . killing . . . is abhorrent to you. You could never kill that woman."

"But I could, Kay. For what she has done to David, to Marti, to all of us, I could."

"Perhaps, and I wouldn't love you for it but in spite of it. Now you must do the same. You must welcome yourself to the human race and forgive yourself for your very human frailities."

As she finished her sentence, Kay began taking his clothes out of the closet and from the bureau drawers, packing them into a large suitcase she had taken from the upper reaches of the closet.

"What are you doing?" he asked wearily.

"Packing. You're coming with me," she said, her voice determined.

"But I'm needed here," he protested.

She stopped in her hurried sorting of socks and underwear to look him in the eye as she spoke. "No, you're not, JJ. You really are not. You're needed with me. Either you see that now or you

4 4 3

may never see it at all, and then you really would be guilty of killing something alive and truly rather wonderful."

*   *   *

Eleanor Heckessee took the good with the bad. The good was an annual vacation that began no matter what the day of the week on the fifteenth of August and ended the Tuesday after Labor Day. The bad was the day she returned to her part-time job in her husband Leo's pharmacy on 14th Street and found two, sometimes three weeks of filing of prescriptions to be done. It was a gruesome job, particularly since she assisted at the front of the store when Leo was too busy filling prescriptions to wait on customers.

Eleanor Heckessee enjoyed the four hours, three times a week, she spent in her husband's store. The job meant activity, contact with people, which she needed now that the children were married and had lives of their own. Of course some of the contact like some of the people was not so desirous. The customers were often animals and the store a zoo. Now 14th Street was no longer prime real estate, not like it was when Leo opened the pharmacy forty-four years ago. Gone was Luchow's and Klein's and Orbachs. Gone was the elegance and, with it, English as the most often heard language. Only one good thing could be said about this *new* 14th Street, thought Eleanor. The more shabby and sordid it had become, the greater the street people's need for medication. The Heckessees had become rich as the street grew poor.

Eleanor Heckessee thumbed through the prescriptions to be filed and was pleased to see that for the most part the relief druggist had kept them in their numbered order. Most just needed to be filed once she had ascertained each had a legible name and address typed across its top. Leo was a stickler for that kind of detail. Never once had a prescription been lost through misfiling. Which meant never once had one of their repeat customers been denied. Often as she filed, Eleanor Heckessee read through the prescriptions. Time passed more quickly as she tried to imagine the person, his or her life, and the disease he was fighting with medication she and Leo supplied. After fourteen years on the job, Eleanor knew as much about drugs as her husband, and a lot more about people, due to her fantasizing.

4 4 4

The prescription she held in her hand required no work on her imagination's part. The story was all there, although it might belong to someone other than the person whose name was written across the Bellevue prescription pad. But Eleanor Heckessee had been reading about this particular story for months. Now, to her great excitement and delight, she was living it. Whether or not she would become an actual part of it was a matter for the authorities, and Eleanor did not waste a minute dialing the number on the circular she had received from the FBI months ago.

* * *

Kevin Maney was never one to show emotion before those his government paid him to assist or protect, but his hand automatically reached for the telephone to call Marti Tiernan as soon as the call from the Heckessee woman led to the doctor at Bellevue and, from all information and descriptions garnered, to the woman who most definitely was Coreen Carouthers, now alias Martha Pearson. It had given Maney unexpressed pleasure to tell Marti Tiernan that her baby was undoubtedly still alive and when last seen by doctors at Bellevue was doing quite well. He had heard the sharp intake of breath, the heavy breathing, the fight for emotional control, and then the question: What now?

He hated his answer as soon as he spoke it. "We wait." Before she could challenge, he revealed his strategy. "This time we say nothing to the press. We keep it blind. Tell no one other than Dr. Strohl. The druggist and his wife, those involved at Bellevue, have promised their cooperation in secrecy. Our Mrs. Carouthers, now Pearson, has two refills coming on her prescription. Which means about the twenty-first of the month, she should be contacting Heckessee's pharmacy. We'll have a man at the store at all times. He and the Heckessees know exactly what to do from the moment she enters. Now, as we said, we just sit tight and wait."

"The address?"

"A false one," replied Maney. "But she's in New York and she thinks she's safe. We doubt if she would travel again. According to the doctor who saw her at Bellevue, our suspect is a very nervous woman, extremely high strung and irritable. Dr. Mendez was not certain the woman would return for her prescription after the examination, she was that impatient to be gone."

"And if she doesn't call?" asked Marti, afraid to believe it would now be as simple as Maney obviously thought it could be.

Maney could hear the fear in Marti Tiernan's voice. Again he did the unusual rather than the usual for him. He stated as fact what was pure speculation: "She will, Miss Tiernan." And as Kevin Maney hung up, thinking of Marti Tiernan's face the day she went to the morgue to identify the dead baby, he thought to himself, she better.

*   *   *

As the plane broke through the soft pillowy clouds and began its descent into Boston's Logan Airport, Thomas stretched languorously. He was anxious to see Teej and Kelly who had returned at Kelly's insistence, but he yearned to see Reese. Yet he resented the 727 jet leaving the protective seclusion of the clouds, fearful that as the plane descended so would his spirits. And he was high, as high as the plane had been, higher perhaps. And content. On the ground, below the clouds, there was another reality: his family's lives were being controlled by one woman withholding one baby.

The landing was smooth. He was home. Safe and sound, sounder than he had felt in years, except for the persistent tiredness that caused familiar and thus not-to-be-concerned-about pains. His work, his life, had not been in vain. The fact that there would be a national salute to the Vietnam veterans, culminating in the dedication of the memorial in Washington the week of November eleventh, was proof of that. He would attend. It didn't matter that the Washington memorial to the Vietnam veteran offended him, less so now that they were correcting its failings by adding an American flag and a sculpture of two white soldiers and one black. The memorial was his. It saluted him and others like him. It was recognition of a job well done. He would march that week with the others and be damn proud to be side by side with the men who side by side had fought for their country.

But the real cause for celebration, the one he wanted most to

4 4 6

share with Reese, was his accomplishment at Eagle Nest. His job was done. Incredible as it still seemed even to him, five acres of land surrounding the monument had been deeded to the DAV. And not just land but five gorgeous acres of lush greenery which made the setting that much more stunning. Like a bird soaring in flight, the Eagle Nest monument now stood, secure on land that was its own. Almost a million dollars had been allocated to perpetuate the memorial, and more would be coming through donations he would continue to seek. But the burden was not his alone. There was now, due largely to his efforts, a seven-member board of directors, the DAV Vietnam Veterans Memorial, Inc., to oversee Eagle Nest. The memorial, *their* memorial, would be rededicated, along with a newly created visitors' center, on the Memorial Day weekend next year. He would be there for that too. Perhaps then, finally, at last, Reese would see his memorial.

Reese . . . Thinking of her made him wonder if perhaps he should stop by her apartment before returning home. In some way, although it was not yet clear in Thomas's mind, he knew his victory was also hers.

✻　　✻　　✻

She knew he would be surprised, as she hadn't planned to meet him. Too much of their lives had taken place at airports. But the news was so wonderful and he would be so gratified. As she had been. Gratified and relieved.

Reese saw him as he emerged with the other travelers. He still is a gorgeous man, thought Reese as she moved toward him, no longer feeling competitive with those who wished to lay some sort of claim on him if only for a second. The surprise and then delight on his face when he saw her made her giggle. His hug was crushing, all encompassing and all inclusive.

"I have great news," he said as he held her now at arm's length.

"Me, too," she replied. She didn't wait for him to ask but plunged ahead: "Marti just called. Coreen Carouthers surfaced. A prescription was filled last month. Nicholas was examined. He is not only alive but well. In New York," she added.

He stared at her, almost afraid to believe what he was hearing.

She hugged him reassuringly and suddenly found herself swooped up into his arms, her feet off the ground as he swirled her about. "Reese, listen. It's done. The board is established, the land is ours, the monument is there and it is now assured that it always will be."

She didn't know what to say, so pleased was she. She started to laugh and then cry. Again he hugged her and this time their embrace, held longer than most at airports, drew attention. She ignored it as she focused on his obvious arousal and then her own. He kissed her and even as he did, she was giggling. They began to run and the moment wasn't lost on her: two children, almost skipping through an airport and then trying to find their car in a crowded parking lot. They were going home. Only they didn't get there.

Just past the airport, Thomas pointed to a motel. Her reply was to nod her head in agreement. She laughed as she realized this was without doubt the most spontaneous and sexiest thing they had ever done. And then suddenly they were in their room and all other memories of meetings at other airports vanished. There was only that day and that moment.

He removed her clothes, one article at a time. There was no hurry, no other duty to perform. He had all the time in the world to spare and to give. Reese took it gladly.

*   *   *

The call came shortly after two that Monday afternoon. At first, it seemed no different from many others. Leo Heckessee asked for the prescription number, the caller gave it and then he asked that the caller hold on while he checked to make sure that the medication was not only in stock but that the prescription was renewable. It was then he saw the name underlined in red, asterisked, at the top of the original prescription. His hand began to tremble as he lifted it from the file cabinet. He motioned to the FBI agent who looked at the prescription and immediately went to another telephone in the back of the pharmacy. As Leo Heckessee informed his caller that her prescription would be ready in an hour, the agent dialed Kevin Maney's phone number. He was not there, a voice informed. He was at Marti Tiernan's office, at her request, to meet with her and the private investigator she had hired.

It had been a useless meeting.

* * *

Carla Lacey loved Mondays as it was her day to be a lady of leisure rather than of the evening. The day was even more special now that she had the nice Pearson woman to take care of Lara. Funny woman. Never went out. Never seemed to do much of anything except tend to her baby and watch television on the set Carla had scored for her on the street one night. Living sixteen-inch color for fifty dollars. Not bad. Occasionally, Carla wondered about the Pearson woman's "money thing," but she never asked as she paid the dollar-fifty-per-hour babysitting fee Pearson charged. Paid it gladly. Five hours, six days a week. Without Pearson, she was with Lara and, sweet as her own little girl was, she couldn't add one dime to the rent.

It was an ask-me-no-questions relationship, typical of the kind Carla Lacey had known ever since she had become part of "the life" in New York some years ago. You don't get too close 'cause you don't want nobody messing in your business, thought Carla as she took her time climbing the steps of the BMT subway. Was shopping not the order of the day, she would never have worn heels. As she gazed about 14th Street, Carla felt a flush of excitement. She loved shopping at May's department store. Not that the clothes were well made but if a girl knew style, was "color-coordinated," she could do some fancy stepping in the ensembles she would select. Looking good for little money was a Carla Lacey specialty.

Carla checked the clock at the top of the Consolidated Edison Building just off in the distance. Should she shop first and then pick up the prescription for Mrs. Pearson or hit the druggist first and then the stores? Always save the best for last she decided as she headed toward Heckessee's Pharmacy.

Kevin Maney had tried to anticipate everything. His instructions to the Heckessees had been precise. Act naturally. When the

Pearson/Carouthers woman came in, say and do nothing. They would do it all. If she had the baby with her, he, or his man in the store, would make the arrest, hopefully without incident. If, by any chance, she left the baby outside in a carriage, his men stationed as passers-by in the street would take the baby as they were taking her.

At no time, given the woman's reclusive history, did Maney think that someone other than Carouthers would pick up her own prescription. Thus, he dismissed Carla Lacey the moment she walked through the door, although he noticed the shape of her calf in her stiletto heels. He was taken by surprise when Heckessee began yelling when she left: "That was her. That was her." Maney wanted to argue but acted instead, stopping his fellow agent from bursting out the door after Carla Lacey and arresting her. It had taken a shoulder block that had thrown the agent across the narrow store and into one of the displays to do this. The agent looked surprised and confused. Maney didn't. He knew now exactly what to do.

Follow her. If Carouthers was across the street waiting in Union Square, they could arrest her there. If she was but the baby wasn't, they would have her lead them to it by not making their presence known. And if Coreen Carouthers was nowhere about, they would tail this woman until she led them to her.

And so they waited and watched as Carla Lacey shopped May's for two hours. As they did, in a nearby government-issued car, Marti and Matthew, with two other agents, waited, following Maney's progress or lack of same through junior dresses and petite sportswear. And just when they thought they could bear the wait no longer, Maney announced he was following Carla Lacey out of the store . . . to the BMT subway . . . the downtown track. . . .

The car proceeded down Broadway, its occupants not knowing where they were destined but following the suspect's trail through Maney's instructions. Marti was trembling, her system under siege from the events that were happening faster than she could assimilate. One minute she was sitting in her office, the next, by her insistence, she was closing in on the woman who had occupied her thoughts for more than three months. Her urge for vengeance, to strike down the woman, was as great as her need to be reunited with Nicholas. That she wanted retribution disgusted

Marti; but she wanted it nonetheless. Looking at Matthew, Marti wondered what he wanted. She couldn't guess. He was sitting but inches away, yet he was miles from her.

Carla Lacey, struggling with her bulky boxes of purchases, stumbled up the steps from the subway and stood on the corner of Canal Street and Broadway. When she turned east, she was unaware that two men, one on either side of the street, were walking close behind her. One of the men had what he, himself, would have described as a "shit-eating grin" on his face. He was thinking of the psychic who had visualized the Great Wall of China and a very specific brand of apple juice. They were now on Mott Street, on the very fringe of Chinatown. The young girl was entering a tenement and inside, or behind the "wall" separating it from the ghetto, was Coreen Carouthers. Quickly, Maney signaled his aide. Together they rushed the entrance door, breaking through just as Carla Lacey reached the second-floor landing. Frightened by the noise, she dropped her bundles and fought the clutter in her handbag for the key to her door. But the men were quicker on foot than she was with her hand. She screamed as they came upon her. She saw their badges, heard the words "the FBI," even as their shoulders took to the door, their revolvers drawn.

A woman down the hall opened her door, calling "Carla?" as she did. There were no further words as she recognized one of the men recognizing her. She slammed the door and bolted it as his shoulder heaved to it. He was about to rush the door again when he heard Coreen Carouthers yell: "I have a gun!" But he didn't believe her. He heaved his weight against the door another time. Carla Lacey screamed as the noise of the bullet tore through the building. The man crumpled to the floor. Carla Lacey screamed again as Kevin Maney pulled her back, down the stairs into the street. She was fighting against him, trying desperately to force her way free from his grasp and back into the building. He didn't understand until she screamed into his face: "She has my baby!"

By the time he had arrived, access was impossible, even for him. The Emergency Services of the New York City Police Department had cordoned off the area for two blocks in either direction. Even as he fought with officials who thought he might be just another reporter, JJ could see the SWAT team on the roof of the Mott Street building. TV camera crews were everywhere. When he was recognized by one and asked for comment, that gained him access through the police lines and to the car in which he now sat with Marti and Matthew. Once again, they were waiting. Nine hours had passed since the FBI agent had been killed. Despite repeated attempts, there had been no communication with the occupant of apartment 2B. Coreen Carouthers did not have a telephone and if she heard the bullhorn from the street—which she had to—she was not responding. She was not ready or willing to talk, explained Maney, whose face revealed to JJ that this was not a good sign. But JJ knew that, knew that normally those who held others hostage had a price. They would use their temporary power to obtain what they wanted—whether that be a message to the world or some monetary gain. What frightened JJ was the possibility that Coreen Carouthers wanted nothing more than to keep Marti's baby. At all costs. At the thought, JJ's arm slipped about Marti's shoulders. She did not acknowledge it but continued to sit silently, her hand resting in Matthew's.

They had sought other means of access to her apartment. There were none. At the moment, Maney had men stationed in the apartment next to and above her, on the roof and in the back of the building. There was no escape possible for Coreen Carouthers. Except one, if she thought of it. Out the front door with a baby in both arms. They could not risk shooting if she used the babies or a baby as a shield. But Maney didn't think it likely that Coreen Carouthers would move. Trapped animals seldom did.

Again the agent negotiating on the bullhorn called up to Coreen Carouthers, urging her to come down with the children, giving his assurance that she would be well treated.

There was no response.

He was urging her to place just one child, just one, outside the door. In exchange, they would send up whatever she needed. But as Carla Lacey explained: Coreen Carouthers didn't need anything since she had done the weekly shopping for her that same morning.

The negotiator ceased talking, preparing to wait another quarter-hour before resuming his pleas and bargaining. He was surprised, as they all were, when a woman's voice cut through the night. "I want Thomas Ollson. Send me Thomas Ollson."

Maney rushed to the agent negotiating. "Yes, give her Ollson, but only in exchange for the children."

The message was relayed via the bullhorn. It was refused. Maney thought quickly: "Tell her she can have Ollson if she'll give us the Tiernan child."

Again the message was relayed. It, too, was refused.

"Offer her Ollson for the Lacey kid," barked Maney, frustrated, knowing this was an offer Coreen Carouthers could not refuse.

She didn't.

The weight was of responsibility and not the audio transmitter which fit neatly into the vest pocket of his jacket. From the moment he entered Coreen Carouthers's apartment, the hidden wireless would carry their every word on a special frequency into the parked car where Maney, Marti, and Matthew would wait. In another car, JJ, Reese, and other agents would be tuned in to the live broadcast. To Thomas, it felt as if more than a decade had slipped back in time and he was once again performing a mission.

Maney was issuing last-minute instructions, most no different from those Thomas had already heard from the agent over the past hour. Do not argue with the woman. Do not let her know about the transmitter since it might trigger feelings of betrayal. Do not fight for the gun. Offer possibilities, not promises, to make her leave the apartment peaceably. Reason, cajole, use all your fund-raising skills to make her give. Remember! She is dangerous. She is armed and she has killed once.

"By accident," Thomas interjected. "She did not intentionally kill the man."

Maney looked at Thomas curiously. "One of my men is dead—shot to death. To me, that's not an accident," he replied.

4 5 3

They were standing in the middle of a luncheonette the FBI had commandeered during the night. Marti and Matthew were sitting in a booth, the strain of the sleepless night showing on their faces. JJ was pounding on the video game machine, Reese was sitting at the counter, drinking yet another cup of black coffee, not at all surprised that of all the people in the room, the one with the most responsibility, Thomas, was visibly the least nervous. She knew he must be exhausted, but he looked sure, confident. A glance in the mirror facing her showed her own strain and fatigue.

She had been driving home from her second night of fall-term classes when she heard the news on the car radio. Instantly she had pulled over to an outdoor telephone. Kelly, and not the FBI agent still assigned to the house, had answered on the second ring. Thomas, she explained, had left for the airport immediately upon hearing the bulletin on "World News Tonight" but had called an hour ago to say the airport was socked in. As she sipped her coffee, cold and bitter, Reese remembered the low-hanging night clouds and the wetness of the evening. Her decision had been instantaneous. Twenty minutes later, she had found Thomas still waiting at the Eastern terminal. His face was drawn and his movements seemed constricted from tension. Within minutes they would know if the last flight of the night to New York was departing or, like the others, canceled.

She hadn't asked but told him she was going too. He mentioned Kelly but hadn't argued when she said Kelly was now old enough to take care of herself and Teej, too. The flight was canceled. Without hesitation, they had begun the five-hour drive to New York. When midway, they heard the news report that Coreen Carouthers wished to speak with Thomas Ollson but that the retired Vietnam war hero had yet to be located. Thomas had stopped the car and phoned the special number the FBI had given him months ago when they thought Coreen Carouthers might contact him then. Thus, he had been expected when he arrived at daybreak, and a course of action if not a plan had been designed.

Reese was frightened. There were FBI agents and police in the street, SWAT team members on the roof and in the building. Soon, Thomas would be among them and yet alone. She didn't like that.

She felt a hand on her shoulder. She was surprised by its

warmth and by its expression. It was the first time Reese could recall ever having had physical contact with JJ. She searched his face but saw nothing but the concern she read on all the others'.

Marti was watching Maney watching Thomas. Her mind wouldn't obey, no matter how many times she asked it to think like Coreen Carouthers. What did the woman want of Thomas? What bargain would she try to strike? What bargain might he offer to free Nicholas? Every part of Marti stretched toward the door, the street, to the building across the way that held the woman and her child. These past ten years, it had been she that Coreen Carouthers had stalked. She wanted me then but not now, thought Marti. If only the woman had offered a one-for-one, a Marti Tiernan for a Nicholas Strohl. She would gladly have gone. For Nicholas. For Matthew. For dear Matthew who sat and waited with the same patience she saw in her mother, but not assisted or guided by the same faith.

Suddenly Thomas walked toward her and Marti was aware that this, finally, was the moment. I'm frightened, her insides whispered. She slipped out of the booth to meet Thomas. The look in his eyes filled her with apprehension. He held her and, as she buried her face in his chest, he smoothed her hair with his hand, all the while whispering that she should not worry. And suddenly, she was back in time, a little girl once again counting on her older-by-minutes big brother to take charge. She hugged him and uttered one word: "Please!"

Thomas was at the door when he turned. Looking at Reese, he tilted his chin up. She understood and then did the same. For one more time, she was being his good little soldier.

The bullhorn broke through the early morning quiet. Coreen Carouthers now knew that Thomas Ollson was on the way up the flight of stairs to her apartment. If she wanted him to enter, she was instructed to immediately place Lara Lacey outside her front door. The Carouthers response was immediate. She would place Lara Lacey nowhere other than in Carla Lacey's hands, once she was assured Thomas Ollson was with the girl.

Carla Lacey was instantly produced. With Thomas holding her securely by the arm, they made their way to the second floor.

The door was partially open, and Coreen Carouthers was peering out. Assured there were no uninvited guests, she opened the door fully. Thomas saw the gun in one hand and the baby in the other. Gently, she eased the child into Carla Lacey's outstretched arms. The girl said nothing but ran down the steps, clutching her baby to her. As she did, Coreen Carouthers motioned for Thomas to enter. He no sooner had, and she had locked and bolted the door, than she flung herself against him. He was so stunned that it didn't occur to him until she released him from her embrace to have grabbed the gun.

"Thank God you've come," she whispered. "I was so afraid they wouldn't let you."

As he gazed into her face, Thomas thought he had never seen such wear and pain. "What are we going to do?" she asked, her voice near breaking.

He heard the "we," but he did not understand it. "I think *we* should go downstairs, put things right, give the baby back," said Thomas softly.

She bristled. "I'd rather die!"

Marti reacted as if every muscle in her body had spasmed. The woman would rather die than return her child. Did that mean that she would also rather the baby die than return him to her? Maney, listening in the front seat of the car, wondered the same thing.

"I asked you to make her stop but you didn't," said Coreen Carouthers bitterly, her anger now focused on Thomas. "She is even too strong for you."

"Mrs. Carouthers, help me to understand. What should I make my sister stop?" asked Thomas as he moved just an inch closer to the woman.

Coreen Carouthers withdrew in disgust. "Oh, my dear God. *You* should ask such a question. You, who she nearly killed like she killed the others. . . . Like she killed my husband."

"Mrs. Carouthers, Marti didn't kill your husband," said Thomas, his voice even, portraying no emotion.

"Oh, yes she did! She most surely did. She fought against the war, against her country."

"Mrs. Carouthers, why don't we discuss this later. Perhaps with Marti. She'd want to know how you feel."

"Oh, no, she wouldn't. Powerful people don't care about us little people. And she is powerful. Which is why people listened, why they turned toward her and away from you. From my husband. They left him to die. She's a murderer who will kill and kill again. We must get her out of our schools, away from our children," said Coreen Carouthers frantically.

"I'll save the baby," said Thomas. "Give him to me."

He reached for Nicholas, but Coreen Carouthers stepped back, holding the child up and away from his grasp. "She'll outsmart you, trick you, like she did the others. She'll hurt you again."

"Marti wouldn't hurt anyone, Mrs. Carouthers," said Thomas gently.

"She hurt my husband," snapped Coreen Carouthers. "She hurt me. She took his life and then mine. She's a traitor. A traitor!"

"No. Marti loves her country just as you do. That's why she fights in her own way for what she feels are its best interests."

"Her best is her worst!" screamed Coreen Carouthers.

"If you think so, say so. Tell people. But tell it the right way. This," said Thomas, pointing to the child in her arms, "is not the right way."

"It's my only way, God's way!" snarled Coreen Carouthers. "What access do I have to anything. When she talks, people listen. If I talked, who would give a damn? But they're listening now, aren't they? And why? Because sometimes, Major Ollson, the only thing left to people like me is action—and actions speak louder than words. You can bet your sister hears me now. Everybody hears me now. And I am saying for the world to hear: I want her stopped. Do you hear? Stopped!"

"I'll stop," cried Marti. "Oh, God, someone tell her if she'll just give me back our child I'll stop."

"Dr. Strohl, perhaps you and your wife should wait in the luncheonette," said Maney.

4 5 7

"I wait here!" snapped Marti, instantly composed by the threat of banishment. "And don't even suggest that I move."

He could feel his body wet with perspiration under the white cotton shirt and blue blazer. With the back of his hand, he wiped his brow. His body ached. The enemy, standing across from him, was considered dangerous but to him she looked weak, vulnerable, even pitiful. "Mrs. Carouthers," he began again. "You've been hurt. You suffered a terrible loss that no one can ever make up to you. And worse, no one has tried."

Over the car radio, through the static, each could hear the sounds of a woman sobbing.

"I wish there was something, anything, I could give you to replace what you've lost. But I can't. I don't think anyone can, Mrs. Carouthers. Some losses are irreplacable. Like your husband. Like relationships that die in another kind of battle. Like human spirit. It's a terrible thing, the effects of war," said Thomas as he stared at one of the effects. "With all I've seen and heard over the past few years, the cries, the whispers of boys and men who continue to fight long after the battle is over, I now wonder if war is ever justified."

She watched him rise and move toward her and the baby. "I'd like you and Nicholas to come with me now," he said softly.

"Don't touch him!" she screamed as she shrank back from his grasp. "We go nowhere. I will not be a prisoner of war. They will kill me."

Thomas moved toward the distraught woman. "We don't kill women or children," he said.

We did in Vietnam.

He stood as if struck, fighting for a leverage he suddenly didn't have. "Mrs. Carouthers, let me help you," he pleaded.

"God helps those who help themselves. I cannot lose this war."

"It's not a war, Mrs. Carouthers."

"You say that? You? So I'm all alone. Alone. Oh, God!"

The moan and the sobs that followed filled the interior of the car. Marti shivered, trying to shake free of the pity she did not want to feel for the woman.

"Mrs. Carouthers, I'm going to take Nicholas and go now," Marti heard Thomas say. "I want you to come with me. You have my promise I'll do everything I can to help you."

"It's over, all over," Coreen Carouthers mumbled. "I've lost the war."

"Not just you, Mrs. Carouthers. Everybody. You, me, Marti. All losers. No winners," Marti heard Thomas say wearily, his voice sounding as if it would break at any moment. "When we've hurt people like you as deeply as we have, there is no victory."

"There is nothing," said Coreen Carouthers, "nothing."

The voice was flat and it made all those in the car uneasy. It was devoid of feeling, almost dead. "Put down the child," they heard her say. "You cannot take him. I must be left something."

They heard his voice pleading: "Please put down the gun, Mrs. Carouthers."

"Nobody cares, you say. Not about me or you. So why should I?"

"Oh, my God, no!" cried Marti as she forced open the back door of the car. She was running toward the building, Matthew behind her, as Thomas said: "I care, Mrs. Carouthers. So don't."

"Nicholas!" screamed Marti.

"It's my baby!" screamed Coreen Carouthers.

"The gun, Mrs. Carouthers!" yelled Thomas. "Please. No."

Those in the car heard the scuffle, heard the baby crying and finally the gunshot. Marti, standing in the middle of the street, put her hands to her ears as if to shut out reality. Maney was running toward the building, two of his agents, guns drawn, following. They stopped as Thomas staggered out the door, Nicholas in his arms. From upstairs, another shot rang out. Thomas turned in its direction, grimaced, and moved on, his face contorted with pain. He walked slowly toward the woman running toward him. He gave her the baby. She clutched it to her breast and then screamed in horror as she watched her brother slump slowly to the ground.

20

REESE HAD PROMISED HERSELF THAT ON THIS DAY SHE would not cry. And so she marched past the White House, her chin and head leading into the bitter wind that pushed memories before and behind her. She was part of the celebrants, of the homecoming so long deserved and denied. They marched down Constitution Avenue toward a memorial as controversial as the war it commemorated. They sang, they chanted, they even danced as they welcomed themselves and one another home. With peace and honor. About her, also marching, each in his own way, were the disabled, hobbling along on canes, the blind, and the paraplegics, wheeling themselves or wheeled by a buddy or a member of the family.

She wished Thomas had been there. It was but one of many wishes she had about Thomas. He would so have gloried—and that was the word—in this moment. Rightfully so, as he had earned it.

She would not cry, Reese told herself. She *could* not, as this was Thomas's celebration and her tears would only be rain that fell on his parade.

Silently, Marti walked down the wide avenue with her arm linked through Reese's. Her eyes roamed the crowd. The men in battle fatigues or full-dress uniforms were of another era. They were men who refused to let the past die and the present begin. She watched as many, the so-called baby-killers, overcome by long-contained emotions, broke down and cried. That jarred her. As her eyes searched the avenue, she saw thousands of these men attending their own coming-out party. Thomas had cared about them. They had been a part of him because he had felt a part of them.

She marched, lost in a crowd of confused emotions. Suddenly she wanted to greet each one of the veterans and make her amends. They were not the enemy. Now she understood they never had been. They had been doing their duty as she had done hers. Each as he saw fit.

Thomas had a strong sense of duty. That as much as anything else distinguished him from others. It was what eventually restored Nicholas to her. And she never got to say thank you.

A bearded man wearing battle fatigues and a wide-brimmed hat with feathers studied her with resentment. Then he saw Reese. Then he looked and saw her again but Marti could feel it was in a different way. He took the carnation from the brim of his hat and raised it to her. She moved from Reese's side toward the man. Stopping before him, she searched his face for something or someone, and then she impulsively hugged him. She then took his offered flower to Reese who carried it in her gloved hand.

It was a picture he would later caption in his column, thought JJ as he watched Marti and the unknown veteran. He was moved by the significance of that moment and of the day itself. When David tripped, JJ caught the boy before he could fall, but when the child asked to be carried, JJ refused—which made Kay eye him curiously. Patiently JJ explained to his son that they were marching in honor of Thomas and the men whose names were inscribed on the memorial. They could be a bit discomforted, particularly since their discomfort was little in comparison to that of those who had fought the war. Each in his own way.

JJ was glad Thomas was not walking by his side. His brother would have been hurt, again, by a country that seemed constantly to hurt the people from whom they drew their strength. Thomas would not have known why this day, this moment in American history, was ignored by the president, the vice president, the secretary of state, by Richard Nixon and Henry Kissinger. Only General Westmoreland represented the establishment. One general and one entertainer . . . Wayne Newton. His brother and these men, thought JJ, deserved more and better.

Questions without answers. Perhaps that would always be true of this particular war. Yet, the crux of what this country was about, and for which one should always fight, was evidenced this day. At the front of the march were those who had fought or supported the war. At the rear, the dissenters, deserters, and those veterans who had fought the war and now fought against it philosophically also marched. Each allowed the other his space. That, too, JJ knew he would write about.

Flanked by Ali and Mark, who were holding Lynne's hands, Matthew marched, Nicholas clutched to his chest. The baby was bundled in wools but still his face was red from the winds that made the late November day particularly raw. But he and Marti had agreed: Nicholas must be there. For Thomas. Just as Thomas had been there for him.

Although he had determined not to think of Thomas, Matthew found him everywhere. And so the wound reopened on a day that was meant to heal. A celebration. How difficult it is, thought Matthew, to celebrate a war and its dead. One can only celebrate the living. As he looked into the sea of faces, the men marching en masse toward the monument, Matthew wondered how many were truly alive. He thought of his past work, work that had been largely motivated by Thomas's efforts to bring many of the Vietnam dead back into the world of the living, and again he felt the pain sear through him.

No matter what had been written on his death certificate or in the countless obituaries, Matthew felt Thomas had died in battle long after the war was over. The doctors called it a massive coronary. The newspapers called it an act of heroism. Which it was. But the taste was bitter. Perhaps it would have been less so had he died of wounds inflicted by a troubled person. But no. The troubled person had only inflicted those wounds on herself. Twice, when the first only partially did the job. As he did Thomas, Matthew viewed Coreen Carouthers as both a prisoner of war and just one of its many casualties. He marched for both this day.

It took a moment like this to make Kelly realize the person she had most loved and who had most loved her was dead. His will had long been probated and the children—or so the will said—had been left equal amounts. But the sister and brother who marched with her knew that wasn't so. She had received so much more. Because she had been open to him, he had given, and she had taken for her very own, a foundation. She stood on it daily. It supported not only her these past two months but her mother and child. She was strong. Like him.

As they neared the monument, Kelly hoisted Teej onto her shoulders, his legs straddling her neck. This is how his grandfather would want him to view the world and the world to view him. Suddenly tears splashed across her face, their sting made worse by the biting wind. Kelly felt Vinnie's arm slip about her waist. She smiled up at her uncle but her smile was not returned. Vinnie's face remained grim, his eyes perhaps focused on a time long ago when he, Marti, and Thomas were young.

Kristan's eyes were riveted on the monument but it was Denver she was seeing—Fox Street and an office on the second floor of a three-story, prefabricated concrete building. He had been there. For the first time in her adult life he *had been there*, as a man and not an image. Not as a father either. She remembered his enthusiasm, the pride he projected. She remembered her jealousy and then her anger that he had cared more for a project than for her. But she had understood. Even as she resented.

She remembered his words, spoken at the airport as they parted. "Do you have everything?" he had asked.

She recalled her unspoken response: "No, dad. I don't have you, not as a father. I never did and I doubt if I ever will."

It was very long ago and still it pained her. More now because it was fact and not feeling. And then, just as she reached the wall that loomed larger than life, just as her father had, Kristan remembered something more . . . his final words, spoken so quietly that she had heard without hearing: "If you need anything, call."

At the base of the wall, Kristan fell to her knees and began calling.

Karl watched Kristan as if from a great distance. As if she were once again on screen and he, in a balcony. Her grief seemed no more real to him than his own. Grieving for what? For whom? For something and someone that never was. A relationship. A father. But if it never was, why the hurt? Why the pain? How can you mourn what was never yours to lose? As he knelt to assist Kristan, Karl remembered a morning . . . in Boston . . . when a man, fully dressed, stood naked before him. The sight made him close his eyes, squeeze them shut. But that did not stop the pain.

Thomas's name would not be there, thought Carolyn as she and Margaret approached the huge black granite V wall that was the monument, but he would. She could feel his presence now. Without him, she could not have made the march, could not have moved past the persistent arthritic pains down Constitution Avenue. He was so much like his father in that respect: someone to lean on. Her firstborn. Dead, but not to her. He never could be that. Not while she was alive. As her eyes roamed the immensity of the wall of names, Carolyn wept. So many mothers and too many sons separated. Despite the difficulty, Carolyn knelt at the foot of the wall and prayed to God to give the same strength to others that He had given to her.

Marti stood near her mother, her sensibilities assaulted by the huge, black wall and the thousands upon thousands of names inscribed upon it. An honor roll of the dead. Overwhelmed, she stepped back, trying to distance herself from a sense of loss, and a grief so vast that she felt she might drown within it. But there was no refuge, no place to hide from the thousands upon thousands of names: the innocent victims of war.

Sobbing, Marti sought Matthew. His arm drew her to him and closed about her even as he held Nicholas. The three made a circle of one. As she felt her child's life throbbing against her, Marti felt the rage flush out the grief. There would be no more walls, she vowed. Not if she could help it. And she and others could. And would. Her life and her work would go on so that her child—all the children—could live.

JJ had read about it, seen pictures of it, but neither reading nor hearing had prepared him for the horror that rained down on him name after name. Men upon men. Like him. Some younger, some older. There, indelibly etched for generation after generation to see, was the truth of war. The dead upon dead for as far as the eye could see. It sickened him. The memorial was one black mark of granite, an accusation. And the guilty, thought JJ, slept within the shadow of the monument: the man-made machines, made of men, who made the war. All the power, money, and control.

Exactly when he had become separated from Kay, JJ did not know, but in that moment, at the wall, he knew the separation was in part permanent. He would never leave the United States, could never live in Canada. He was an American soldier after all. He needed to live on the battle lines. That was obvious to him this day. The war rages on for some men. He was one of those men. Some fights, the ones for dignity and peace, rage on forever.

Perhaps if Kay were willing, thought JJ as he walked to the woman holding his child, they could find the middle ground, meet halfway. If love and respect counted for anything, they would. At least he hoped they would.

Reese stood in the maelstrom of emotions, the cries and sobs of women and children, men, too, as their eyes and fingers climbed the wall searching for the name of the person they had loved and lost, cascading down about her. She was moved, pained, but for them and not for herself. She began to walk the length of the wall, her eyes searching for his name when she reached the O's. But she knew she would not find it any more than she would find him in this windswept place where a memorial rose like a black mark on its country's history. No, Thomas Ollson was not there—but Reese knew exactly when and where she would find him.

21

SHE HAD COME TO EAGLE NEST WITH KELLY AND Teej, and from the moment she saw the purple mountains majesty of the Sangre de Cristos valley, its beautiful spring flowers dotted among the sage and pinion pine, she began to grieve for what she had lost. As she stared at the memorial that slowly swooped up and into the sky like a white bird in flight, she understood why he had so much wanted to share this place with her. It was his gift, perhaps his ultimate expression of the one thing she had once thought he couldn't do: share. Reese stood rooted to the ground, sucking in the scent of prairie grass, relishing now the gift that was meant for her so many months ago. This was where Thomas Ollson had formally put down his arms and retired from active duty.

With her hand in Kelly's, Reese entered the chapel. At the foot of the stairs looking up to the gallery, she saw the pictures. As she moved closer, she saw they were row upon row after row of faces belonging to men who had died for their country in Vietnam. He had not died in Vietnam, but, as she had maintained to the board of directors, he had died from and because of it. And due in part to his efforts, this memorial now stood on solid ground, on a foundation made solid by his efforts.

They had all agreed when she had insisted he belonged there.

Reese stood before his picture, staring at the face she had seen more often than any other in her lifetime. Kelly was next to her, holding Teej in her arms so that he could see the picture of his grandfather. Reese looked from the picture on the wall to the child in her daughter's arms. Already her grandson was replicating his grandfather.

She began to cry, letting go of emotions she had long repressed. And as her whimpers became sobs, drawing people who formed a circle of concern about her, she became aware of Kelly cradling her, crooning words to ease the pain caused by recriminations and guilt, resentment and loss. And then Teej began to cry, frightened by the emotional outburst.

Her tears stopped abruptly. Within seconds, she was in control, reassuring the little boy who didn't understand why grandma was crying. As she steadied herself and those with her, Reese took a backward glance at Thomas. Then quickly, she led her family down the steps and out of the chapel. Shoulders back, head high, she was every inch of what he would have wanted but which she now chose to be: a good little soldier.

ACKNOWLEDGMENTS

For their time, personal experiences, and knowledge, we wish to thank:

Department of the Air Force, Headquarters Albert F. Simpson Historical Research Center, Maxwell Air Force Base, Ala.; Alanon House of Greater New York, New York City; Alcoholics Anonymous, central offices, New York City and Boston chapters; American Broadcasting Company, Television Network News, International Desk, New York City and Washington, D.C.; American Civil Liberties Union, New York City; American Friends Service Committee, New York City; American Heart Association, New York City chapter; American Indian Community House, New York City; American Indian Information Center, New York City; Ann Arbor, Michigan Chamber of Commerce; Lou Anzolut; Association on American Indian Affairs, New York City; *Aviation Week and Space Technology*, Editorial and Advertising Departments, New York City; Back Bay Boston Association, Boston; Bellevue Hospital, Child Life Program, New York City; Murray Berenson, M.D., Better Vision Institute, New York City; Virginia Blesso & Associates, Rancho Santa Fe; Boeing Corporation, Seattle; Lillian Bossinoff; Boston Latin School, Boston; Boston Chamber of Commerce, Community Development Division, Boston; Boston University, School of Special Education, Boston; Cambridge, Mass. Chamber of Commerce; Cambridge, Mass. Historical Commission; Canadian Consulate General, Library, New York City; Canadian Disarmament Information Service, Toronto; Jimmy Carter Office, Atlanta; Cedars-Sinai, Los Angeles; Century Plaza Hotel, Catering Department, Los Angeles; Citizen Soldier, New York City; Civil Aeronautics Board, Washington, D.C.; Coalition Against Registration and the Draft, national office and New York City chapter; Collegiate School, New York City; Jerry Condon; Tom D'Alessandro, attorney-at-law; Federal Aviation Association, Washington, D.C.; Federal Bureau of Investigation, New York City; Gen. Robert Feingersh, U.S. Army Ret.; Fernan and Associates, East Hampton, N.Y. John Finegan, manager, Air Canada, Boston; Flint, Michigan Chamber of Commerce; Gerald R. Ford Library, Ann Arbor, Mich.; Ford Models, Inc., New York City; Fort Benjamin Harrison, Indianapolis, Ind., Public Affairs Office; Jean Friedman; Charles M. Gibbons, principal, The Josiah Quincy Elementary School, Boston; Marcia Ann Gillespie; Mr. Hermann Goldschmidt; Gramercy Inn, Washington, D.C.; Henry Greenberg, M.D., cardiologist, director of the Coronary Care Unit, St. Luke's–Roosevelt Hospital Center, New York City; Greenpeace, Toronto; Mel Greer, M.D., professor and chairman, Department of Neurology, University of Florida, College of Medicine, Gainesville, Fla.; Stephen C. Grossman, attorney-at-law; Henry Harris, M.D., FAAP, private practice, Stamford, Conn., and instructor in pediatrics, Albert Einstein College of Medicine, New York City; Hilton Hotel, Office of the Manager, Indianapolis, Ind.; Edna J. Hunter, Ph.D., former acting director, POW Studies, and director, Research Center, U.S. International University, San Diego, Calif.; Sandra Jaffe; Dorothy Jonas; Mr. and Mrs. Michael Keller; Col. Fred Kiley, USAF, Office of the Secretary of Defense, POW History; Gretl Learned; Nick Lecakes; Legal Aid Society, New York City; Bethel Leslie; Los Angeles Chamber of Commerce; Marla Mandis; Marymount College, Communications Offices, Tarrytown and New York City; Massachusetts Certification Board, Boston; Massachusetts Eye and Ear Infirmary, Volunteers Department, Boston; Massachusetts Institute of Technology, Athletic Department, Cambridge; Massachusetts Vacation Center, New York City; Mayor of New York's Office for Film, Theatre and Broadcasting, New York City; McGuire Air Force

Base, Careers Division, Wrightstown, N.J.; Brenda McKinney; Kevin Meaney; *Ms.* magazine Library; National League of Families of Missing in Southeast Asia, Washington, D.C.; National Organization for Women, Alice Cohan, national office, Washington, D.C. and Teresa Bergen, Jennifer Brown, New York City chapter; New York Board of Education, Division of High School Tutoring Services, New York City; New York Board of Elections, New York City; New York Foundling Hospital, New York City; New-York Historical Society, New York City; New York Public Library, Mid-Manhattan and Lincoln Center, New York City; Larry Newman, Greater Boston Track Club, Cambridge, Mass.; Newton Country Day School of the Sacred Heart, Newton, Mass.; Niagara, Canada Visitor and Convention Bureau, Niagara, Canada; Omni Jet Trading Floor International, Rockville, Md.; Optical House, New York City; Barbara O'Sullivan; Dana Parsons, Physicians for Social Responsibility, New York chapter; Pollock-Bailey Pharmacy, Inc., New York City; Port Authority Police assigned to JFK International Airport, New York; Reeves Communications, Corporation, New York City; Kathy Robbins; Raoul Rosenberg; Cdr. and Mrs. Morris Rotchstein, USN, Ret.; St. James Academy, Del Mar, Cal.; San Diego Track Club; The Schools for Children, Inc., The Dearborn Elementary School, Cambridge, Mass.; Stu Schwartz; Shoreham Hotel, Washington, D.C.; Andy Skief, assistant athletic director, University of California at San Diego; Col. Norman Smedes, USAF, Ret.; Temple University, Philadelphia, Pa.; Torrey Pines High School, Del Mar, Calif.; Margo Thunderbird; University of California at Los Angeles, Medical Center; University of Michigan at Ann Arbor, Public Relations Department; University of Ontario Veterinarian College, Guelph, Ont., Can.; Ursuline Academy, Dedham, Mass.; U.S. Olympic Committee Headquarters; Veterans Administration, Readjustment Counseling Service, Outreach Center Program, Washington, D.C.; Veterans Administration Medical Center, Ann Arbor, Mich.; Vietnam Veterans Memorial Fund, Washington, D.C.: Jan Scruggs, Bob Dubek; Villanova University, Dr. Thomas D. Malewitz, premed advisor and associate professor of biology, Philadelphia, Pa.; War Resisters League, National Office, New York City; Dr. Victor Westphall, founder, Vietnam Veterans Peace and Brotherhood Chapel, Eagle Nest, N. Mex.; Dee Wolfe; Richard Wolke, D.V.M., Ph.D.; Women's Action Alliance, New York City.

We would like to extend a *special thank you* to the Disabled American Veterans, National Headquarters, Cleveland, Ohio, and especially to Robert H. Lenham, assistant national adjutant; Tom Keller, assistant national director of communications, and National Service Officers: William E. Comp, Baltimore, Md.; George Doring, New York City; Bruce Nitsche, Denver, Colo., and Vincent P. Reed, Dominic C. Spada, Boston.

. . . and Betty A. Prashker whose guidance and knowledge speeded the circuitous routes taken to *The Long Way Home.*

. . . also to David S. Surrey, who shared statistics and interviews from his book, *Choice of Conscience: Vietnam Era Military and Draft Resisters in Canada*, Bergen/Praeger, New York City, 1982.

. . . and to Jack Colhoun, whose experiences and articles lent a unique insight into the times of *The Long Way Home.*